Fantasy Fiction into Film

Fantasy Fiction into Film: Essays

Edited by LESLIE STRATYNER
and JAMES R. KELLER

McFarland & Company, Inc., Publishers
Jefferson, North Carolina, and London

3 1969 01879 8289

Library of Congress Cataloguing-in-Publication Data

Fantasy fiction into film : essays / edited by Leslie Stratyner and
James R. Keller.
    p.   cm.
Includes bibliographical references and index.

ISBN-13: 978-0-7864-3057-4
softcover : 50# alkaline paper ∞

    1. Fantasy films — History and criticism.   2. Fantasy fiction,
American — Film and video adaptations.   3. Fantasy fiction,
English — Film and video adaptations.   I. Stratyner, Leslie.
II. Keller, James R., 1960–
PN1995.9.F36F37   2007
794.43'615 — dc22   2007026172

British Library cataloguing data are available

On the cover: Gollum from *The Lord of the Rings: The Return of the
King,* 2003 (New Line Cinema/Photofest)

Manufactured in the United States of America

McFarland & Company, Inc., Publishers
  Box 611, Jefferson, North Carolina 28640
    www.mcfarlandpub.com

Contents

Introduction: Fantasy Fiction into Film

LESLIE STRATYNER AND JAMES R. KELLER

The general concern of this volume is the transformation of fiction into film, the adaptation of character and story from text to celluloid. Since text is not representational (and in most cases, films seemingly cannot help but be), we find fantasy fiction an especially provocative subject in this regard. No matter how loaded with action and description, novels are, in the end, symbols on a page, and thus there has always been and will always be a considerable imaginative distance between the page and the screen. As fantasy concerns itself with the fantastic (that is, elements of plot and character that are outside the realm of possibility), the imaginative distance between those symbols in a novel by a fantasy author and that novel's filmic counterpart is potentially far greater. The essays found in this volume chart that imaginative distance between text and film, from Tolkien to Jackson, Dahl to Burton, Jones to Miyazaki, and nearly everything in between.

The writer of fantasy and the fantasy filmmaker ultimately make demands on the reader and audience that the creators of more realistic fiction and film do not: they require that we abandon our conventions of realism. Abandoning these conventions would not have been difficult for an ancient or medieval audience, but many modern critics have some difficulty with it. Fantasy as a genre (whether in literature or film or art) has a history of being dismissed, and this is only now beginning to change. Though modernists and postmodernists have embraced texts containing non-linear narratives and linguistic experimentation, apparently many of them are not willing to embrace texts that contain paranormal rings, dragons, and elves. Magic is, of course, acceptable, but only if it is contained within a rational setting. Thus, magical *realism* is highly praised by the academic establishment. Magical fantasy is more often not.

Yet the oldest examples of both oral and written literature (and still some of the most popular) are rife with elements of the fantastic, in equally fantastic settings. From Gilgamesh to Gawain, the heroes of epic are more often found battling with extraordinary foes than human ones. It seems logical to assume that the examples that those cultures took pains to preserve were the most well-liked and most often requested and told. Cultur-ally, it seems that a hunger for fantasy is bred in the bone.

Fantasy films as well have been produced since the creation of the medium. Even in times of limited technology, during the era of the silent film, audiences flocked to movies like *The Lost World*, *She*, and *The Thief of Bagdad*. And should it be any wonder that these very films were themselves adaptations of existing texts? A brief foray into the history of fantasy film demonstrates that many (if not most) film fantasies have characteristically been such adaptations. This is not only true of more recent movies such as those in the Harry Potter series, *The Chronicles of Narnia*, and *The Lord of the Rings*, but movies like *The Wizard of Oz*, *Lost Horizon*, *Jason and the Arg-onauts*, and *Clash of the Titans*. (Not to mention, of course, Conan Doyle's *The Lost World*, Haggard's *She*, and the many authors of *One Thousand and One Nights*.) More recent offerings include films of Paolini's *Eragon*, and Pullman's *The Golden Compass* (the first volume of his highly praised *His Dark Materials* trilogy). The advent of advanced technological innovations such as CGI (computer generated imagery) seems to have accelerated Hol-lywood's thirst to adapt fantasy novels that already have a proven audience. As this trend continues, so will the need for analysis of the interaction between text and film, between the letter and image, between the author's vision and the vision of the auteur.

The Essays

In "Three Rings for Hollywood: Scripts for *The Lord of the Rings* by Zimmerman, Boorman, and Beagle," Janet Brennan Croft offers a history of efforts to adapt Tolkien's trilogy for the screen, demonstrating that Jack-son's recent success was preceded by several failed attempts to transform the text into cinematic images. Each of the scripts—Zimmerman (1957), Boorman (1970), and Beagle (1978)—reflect the era in which they were writ-ten, particularly through their portrayals of women. In each case, Croft evaluates the writers' success in capturing the essence of the novels and traces the influence that each script had in the evolution of Jackson's work.

Shadow boxing with the default criticism that any film version of a well known narrative is inferior merely because of its alterations, Gwendolyn A. Morgan in her chapter, "I Don't Think We're in Kansas Anymore: Peter Jackson's Film Interpretations of Tolkien's *Lord of the Rings*," argues that changes to the written text in a screen adaptation are not undesirable. The film text is not another edition of the original, but a distinctive art form that involves a unique set of priorities and requirements. Morgan discusses the alterations to Tolkien's text in its translation into film, noting Jackson's

undermining of the "anti-industrial thematic" and his secularization of the novels. The essayist's principle argument is that transformation of a written text into cinematic images necessitates "translation, recreation, and interpretation."

In "'Tree and flower, leaf and grass': The Grammar of Middle-earth in *The Lord of the Rings*," Robin Anne Reid offers a probing discussion of the imagery in Jackson's trilogy of films. Reid argues that the long held assertion of Tolkien scholars that Middle-earth is an active subject in the novel is also true of Jackson's films, and she demonstrates her thesis through the analysis of an abundance of cinematic images in which the tiny Fellowship of the Ring are swallowed up or engulfed by the imposing landscape of Middle-earth. Thus she reveals the value of understanding the cinematic as well as the textual or literary grammar.

Sharon D. McCoy, in a chapter entitled "'My brothers, I see in your eyes the same fear': The Transformation of Class Relations in Peter Jackson's *Lord of the Rings* Trilogy," focuses on the problems of class in Jackson's film version of Tolkien's classic. While Tolkien, in his novels, does not challenge the traditional class relations of Medieval society — "the master/servant dynamic" — Jackson modernizes the relationships between the characters, making his heroes more sympathetic by making them less willing to accept or assume power over others by making them "common men." Aragorn is perhaps the most compelling example. While Tolkien's Aragorn is fully aware of his rank and privilege, Jackson's struggles with his right and makes few or no demands upon his knights' loyalty at his coronation.

Two chapters address Andrew Adamson's adaptation of C.S. Lewis's first Narnia book. In "The Lion, the Witch, and the War Scenes: How *Narnia* Went from Allegory to Action Flick," Megan Stoner addresses the changes to C.S. Lewis's epic in its translation from text to cinema. Targeting a contemporary adolescent audience accustomed to lengthy action sequences rather than dialogue and narrative subtlety, Adamson has diminished the religious allegory of Lewis' books and replaced it with chase and battle scenes. Moreover, the moral certitude of Lewis's work is replaced by a more contemporary ambivalence. Aslan's divine origins are suppressed in the film narrative, and the Pevensie children question their destined role in the restoration of Narnia. Paul Tankard in "The Lion, the Witch, and the Multiplex" organizes his analysis of the cinematic adaptation into four categories: the children whose narrative development emphasizes contemporary family values or loyalties, a focus that is absent from Lewis's writing; Narnia itself, which is given an expansive epic scope in the film unlike the books, which repeatedly emphasize the limited size of the alternative world; the witch whose evil is less profound in the film, while her villainy is enhanced; and Aslan, who has a much smaller role in the film than in the book and whose religious significations are deemphasized.

Two essays attempt to elucidate the evolution of *Charlie and the Chocolate Factory* as represented in Tim Burton's recent cinematic version of the well-known narrative. Elizabeth Parsons's "Buckets of Money: Tim Burton's New *Charlie and the Chocolate Factory*" addresses the problems of socio-economic inequities, attributing the financial problems of Charlie's family to the growing modernization and globalization of big business. The ostensible message of the film is that family rather than money is the principal source of happiness. However, Parsons argues that this thesis is repeatedly undermined by the events of the film. Clearly the Buckets do desire relief from their poverty, relief that allows them to enjoy life, restoring health, happiness, and self-respect. Moreover, the film reinforces traditional class structure by suggesting that quiet acquiescence in and cooperation with the capitalist establishment will eventually lead to greater prosperity. Thus the film encourages its audience to patiently accept its social position because the most polite and unassuming child will eventually be lifted up.

June Pulliam's "Charlie's Evolving Moral Universe: Filmic Interpretations of Roald Dahl's *Charlie and the Chocolate Factory*" traces the progressive alterations of Dahl's narrative across the three distinct versions. Pulliam argues that the novel is a "straightforward morality tale," distinguishing "between good and bad children." However, the subsequent film versions constitute a more complex moral and ethical terrain than the novel. In the 1971 film version, Charlie proves his worthiness, refusing to practice deceit by selling Wonka's secrets to competitors. In Burton's (2005) version, Charlie's dilemma involves choosing to value his family over his economic and social advancement.

Donald Levin's "The Americanization of *Mary*: Contesting Cultural Narratives in Disney's *Mary Poppins*" contests the assertion that the Disney film reinforces the values of empire. Levin argues that the film repeatedly allies itself with the working classes in the depiction of Edwardian England, portraying the upper class as morally inferior in its indifference to the suffering of the poor. The essay focuses on the characterization of Bert the match seller, played by the American Dick Van Dyke, who urges the children to believe in the power of the imagination to transform reality. Van Dyke's nationality (represented by his accent) and the triumph of Mr. Banks at the conclusion of the film suggest the replacement of the British class system and the values of empire with the "new Americanized world order."

Matt Kimmich, in "Animating the Fantastic: Hayao Miyazaki's Adaptation of Diana Wynne Jones's *Howl's Moving Castle*," explores the choices made by the filmmaker Miyazaki in his screen adaptation of the novel *Howl's Moving Castle*, placing the film in the context of the director's other animated features and taking particular note of Miyazaki's use of spectacle, a quality shunned by Jones in her novels, and his omission of Jones's textual challenges to the conventions of children's literature and folklore. Kimmich attributes the changes in the story to the demands of the differing art forms and to the cultural differences in the respective artists.

Eric Sterling's "From Book to Film: The Implications of the Transformation of *The Polar Express*" examines Robert Zemeckis's cinematic version of the award winning children's story by Chris Van Allsburg. The film adaptation makes some crucial alterations to the text, such as adding an African American passenger to the train in order to give the narrative a multicultural appeal. In addition, the director makes a skeptic of the protagonist in order to emphasize the necessity of faith in pursuit of the fantastic, in the triumph of imagination over reality.

Sarah E. Maier's essay, "From *Peter Pan* to *Finding Neverland*: A Visual Biomythography of James M. Barrie," is a complex deconstruction of the margin between the real and the imaginary. Like several other films in this collection, particularly *Charlie and the Chocolate Factory*, *Finding Neverland* praises the power of the imagination to amend grim reality. Analyzing several interlocking frames within the narrative, Maier argues that the film mythologizes or fictionalizes while it simultaneously attempts to create an accurate biographical window on its subject.

Two chapters attempt to rehabilitate the morally ambiguous image of the witch. In her essay, "From Witch to *Wicked*: A Mutable and Transformational Sign," Jessica Zebrine Gray traces the evolution of the image of the witch through Western folklore, through L. Frank Baum's *Wizard of Oz* (novel and film), and finally through Gregory Maguire's novel *Wicked* as well as the successful musical of the same name. The traditional gender stereotypes of the early modern witch craze and the simplistic ethical dichotomy of good and wicked in Baum's narrative progressively give way to the moral ambiguity and complexity of Maguire's *Wicked*, in which the Witch of the West is reinvented and made more sympathetic through her suffering and mistreatment.

In a similarly recuperative gesture, Kathy Davis Patterson's "From Private Practice to Public Coven(ant): Alice Hoffman's *Practical Magic* and its Hollywood Transformation" discusses the conversion of the witch from an emblem of female corruption and potential malfeasance to a feminine principle inherent in all women and one that challenges the domination of patriarchy. However, Patterson argues that the film of *Practical Magic* does not manage to eradicate completely the negative stereotypes of women or witches. Moreover, the effort to normalize the witch through the observation of its universality undermines the usefulness of the tradition as a "transgressive tool of female empowerment."

Three Rings for Hollywood: Scripts for The Lord of the Rings by Zimmerman, Boorman, and Beagle

Janet Brennan Croft

Adapting *The Lord of the Rings* for film has been a tempting prospect for screenwriters since the book was first published. Tolkien's epic is a treasure-trove of dramatic and highly cinematic images. At first glance it seems made for the movies; it has exciting action and battle sequences, exotic locations and monsters, and even a few touching scenes of romance. But it also presents the scripting challenges of extraordinary length, unorthodox structure, a complex and many-stranded plot, and a confusing multitude of characters. There is much unavoidable exposition, and a certain subtlety of theme and philosophy difficult to translate to a medium that leaves less to the audience's imagination. Add to this a vocal fan base familiar with every nuance of the book and its background legendarium, and in many cases very unforgiving about any deviation from the original, and the task of adapting *The Lord of the Rings* becomes quite a test of the scriptwriter's skill.

Before Peter Jackson's recent blockbuster three-film series, released 2001–2003, there were a number of other efforts to develop a Hollywood movie based on *The Lord of the Rings*. The Tolkien collection at Marquette University in Milwaukee holds materials relating to three of these attempts: the 1957 Zimmerman treatment, which Tolkien read and annotated, the 1970 draft by John Boorman, and three revisions of the Chris Conkling-Peter Beagle script for the 1978 Ralph Bakshi film.

Tolkien called drama "naturally hostile to Fantasy" and felt that rewriting narrative fantasy for a performing medium was nearly impossible to do successfully ("On Fairy-stories" 49). Begging the question of whether any work of written fantasy can be filmed effectively, how well did each of these early scripts capture the essence of Tolkien's work? How do they compare to the efforts of Peter Jackson's scriptwriting team? What does each script say about its era?

Zimmerman

The earliest serious attempt to write a screenplay for *The Lord of the Rings* occurred in 1957, when Tolkien received a proposal for a motion picture from Forrest J. Ackerman, Morton Grady Zimmerman, and Al Brodax (Carpenter 226). The production notes indicate that the producers planned to use a mix of animation, miniature work, and live action, and to make a three hour film with two intermissions (Zimmerman, *Production Notes*). Tolkien told his publisher he was "quite prepared to play ball, if they are open to advice" (*Letters* 261). He thought the pictures he had been shown were "really astonishingly good," reminiscent of Arthur Rackham rather than Walt Disney (*Letters* 261), for whose works Tolkien had a "heartfelt loathing" (*Letters* 17). But Tolkien found the script itself "hasty, insensitive, and impertinent" (*Letters* 266), and this, in addition to the fact that the project would have brought in very little cash for the author, caused Tolkien to turn it down (Carpenter 226).

The script starts promisingly enough, but Tolkien soon complains of the addition of "incantations, blue lights, and some irrelevant magic" (*Letters* 271). When Gandalf hypnotizes and psychically frog-marches the eavesdropping Sam into Frodo's study, rather than hauling him bodily over the windowsill, it is a taste of things to come, and betrays a deep misunderstanding of Tolkien's conception of the proper use of power and the domination of other wills (Zimmerman, *Story Line* 3; Jensen). The company is assaulted at the Gates of Moria by wolves, which Gandalf dispatches with a few lightning bolts, and in Moria he magically opens a chasm to swallow up the attacking orcs. The Huorns are awakened by Gandalf's incantation, not by Treebeard and the other Ents. During Denethor's suicide scene, Gandalf casts a spell so the steward does not feel the flames as he dies, and levitates the body of Faramir from the pyre. In a final act of wizardry, he turns the ringwraiths to stone one by one at the Battle of the Black Gate while the assembled armies watch in silence.

Tolkien also criticized this script for making "eagles seem as common as buses" (Unwin). First Gandalf is carried from Hobbiton to Orthanc on the back of an Eagle named Radagast; then the whole Company is flown from Rivendell to the base of Caradhras. This script included the usually-dropped Tom Bombadil, Goldberry, and Old Man Willow, but they are unfortunate travesties of themselves, with Tom called an "old scamp" and Goldberry just a giggling glimpse of skin through a waterfall (Zimmerman, *Story Line* 6–8).

In his response to the script, Tolkien quoted C.S. Lewis's complaint about a film adaptation of *King Solomon's Mines*. In H. Rider Haggard's book, the climactic scene saw the heroes facing slow death trapped in the tomb of the mummified kings. But "[t]he maker of the film version, however, apparently thought this tame. He substituted a subterranean volcanic eruption, and then went one better by adding an earthquake" (Lewis 92). Similarly, Zimmerman often succumbs to this temptation to "up the ante," for example adding several armed attacks on Strider and the Hobbits as they flee from Weathertop to Rivendell, and sending the company over Rauros Falls in their flimsy rowboats.

But the most bizarre twist to this script occurred sometime between the earlier production notes and the treatment Tolkien read. In the production notes, Frodo's entry into Mordor and the scene at the Cracks of Doom follow the book fairly closely, but in the final script, Sam actually abandons Frodo to Shelob and carries the Ring to Mount Doom himself. He realizes Frodo is still alive, but his duty to Middle-earth triumphs—as Tolkien testily noted in the margin, "opposite of book" (Zimmerman, *Story Line* 50). At the Cracks of Doom, he is about to toss the Ring into the fire when he is attacked by a crazed Frodo, who in turn is attacked by Gollum — with no indication of where either of them has been hiding since Shelob's lair. The weakly written ending has Frodo awakening in Minas Tirith after Aragorn's wedding, and immediately sailing away with the Elves.

The whole script exhibits a certain brash carelessness about both the source material and the craft of scriptwriting. Annoying spelling errors are repeated throughout. The entire Treebeard sequence and the meeting with Faramir are both truncated to the point of unintelligibility. The intercutting of the separate story lines of *The Two Towers* and *The Return of the King* is disorienting, switching from Mount Doom to the Black Gate every few seconds at the climax. Tolkien is astute enough about film to note a particularly clumsy fade between scenes, where we go directly from one group of people in one tunnel (The Paths of the Dead) to another group in another tunnel (Shelob's Lair), which would be very confusing to an audience unfamiliar with the original (Tolkien, *Letter to Ackerman, Draft*). Zimmerman introduces the anachronism of signing the register and getting a numbered room key at the Prancing Pony, and calls lembas a food concentrate, both of which particularly irked Tolkien (*Letters* 272–74). He even gives the Balrog a speaking role and has Merry and Pippin tell Treebeard that attacking Isengard would be a "jolly" idea (Zimmerman, *Story Line* 30).

It is perhaps indicative of the group's attitude towards this adaptation that Ackerman jokingly called the project "Operation Ringslord" (Ackerman). Tolkien thought at first that the script could be rewritten in a way which would satisfy him, and his agent gave Ackerman a promise that the film rights would not be offered to anyone else for six months (Unwin). But Ackerman asked for a year, and Tolkien's publisher was unwilling to go beyond six months without some payment. The matter was referred to Tolkien's Hollywood agent, who forwarded the author's June 1958 criticisms to Ackerman and company, but there is no reply in the file, and there the materials at Marquette leave it.[1]

Boorman

In spite of his grave doubts about the suitability of *The Lord of the Rings* for the movies, Tolkien sold the film and merchandise rights to United Artists in 1969 for just over £104,000 (Harlow and Dobson 16). In 1970, the studio asked John Boorman, later known as the director of *Excalibur* and *The Emerald Forest*, to make *The Lord of the Rings*. With his collaborator Rospo Pallenberg, he condensed the work into a single two and a half hour script which he felt was "fresh and cinematic, yet carried the spirit of Tolkien" (Boorman 20). Boorman says he received a letter from Tolkien during the writing process, asking how he planned to make the film, and wrote back reassuring him that he planned a live action version. However, by the time Boorman had finished the script, the executive who had asked him to take on the project was gone, and the new management was unfamiliar with the book. Boorman said, "They were baffled by a script that, for most of them, was their first contact with Middle Earth [sic]," and rejected it (Boorman 21). He tried unsuccessfully to interest other studios in the script, including Disney, which is said to have been interested in the story in the years before Walt Disney's death (Lowson, Marshall and O'Brien 21–22) and at one time owned the rights (Bilowit 20). Boorman eventually used some of the special-effects techniques and locations developed for *The Lord of the Rings* in other films, most notably *Excalibur* in 1981.

But there is another side to the story. Ralph Bakshi, in a recent interview, talks about taking on the project several years later, and clearly exaggerates a bit for effect:

> And here comes the horror story, right? ... Boorman handed in this 700-page script ... [The studio executives said] "[H]e's changed a lot of the characters, and he's added characters. He's got some sneakers he's merchandising in the middle.... [W]e don't understand a word Boorman wrote. We never read the books" [Robinson 4].

Boorman's script was only 176 pages, and there were no sneakers, but it would not have helped if the studio executives had read the books, because the writer took off in his own direction quite early in his treatment.

To put it bluntly, Boorman's script has only the vaguest connection to Tolkien's *The Lord of the Rings*. Considering Tolkien's appalled reaction to the much lesser liberties taken by Zimmerman, it is unlikely he would have appreciated Boorman's script at all.[2] Characters, events, locations, themes are changed freely with no regard for the author's original intent. Situations are sexualized or plumbed for psychological kinks that simply do not exist in the book. (Tolkien would not have approved of Frodo's seduction by Galadriel, for example, and Aragorn's battlefield healing of Éowyn is so blatantly sexual it is not surprising Boorman marries them immediately.) Pipeweed seems equivalent to marijuana in its effects, and the hobbits' beloved mushrooms are hallucinogenic. Ideas that later worked brilliantly in *Excalibur* (Boorman's retelling of the King Arthur legend) are here as out of place as a dwarf in Lothlórien.[3]

Boorman was simply too full of his own creative spark to limit himself to what was in Tolkien's book. For example, when we first meet Aragorn, he is using the two shards of Narsil as a pair of swords. On the road to Moria, a vision of Arwen prompts him to give one to Boromir, and in a scene that would not have been out of place in a pre-Raphaelite painting of an Arthurian legend, all three ritually kiss the swords and each other. Boromir returns his half of the sword to Aragorn when he dies at Parth Galen, and on the battlefield outside Minas Tirith, the sword magically re-forges itself just before Aragorn is proclaimed king. It is a fascinating story with great symbolic possibilities, but it has little to do with Tolkien's narrative. In an even stranger sequence of events, Frodo, after the destruction of the Ringwraiths at the Fords of Bruinen, is carried into the sparkling palace of Rivendell, where in a vast amphitheater full of chanting elves, he is laid naked on a crystal table and covered with green leaves. A thirteen-year-old Arwen surgically removes the Morgul-blade fragment from his shoulder with a red-hot knife under the threatening axe of Gimli, while Gandalf dares Boromir to try to take the Ring (Boorman and Pallenberg 28–32). If the former seems unfamiliar, how much more so is this scene outside the Gates of Moria? Gandalf (who acts far more like the Merlin in Boorman's *Excalibur* than the Gandalf we know from the books) leads Gimli through a primitive rebirthing ritual, making him dig a hole and crawl into it, covering him with a cloak and violently beating and verbally abusing him, until he springs forth with recovered memories of his forgotten ancestral language and speaks the Dwarvish (not Elvish!) words needed to open the doors (Boorman and Pallenberg 59–60). One also has to pity the poor horses that would have been used in this movie. At one point Aragon has all four hobbits on his horse with him, and at another Éomer "leaps onto his father's horse and embraces him passionately" (Boorman and Pallenberg 122), and poor Shadowfax is reduced from a character to a symbol when he is last seen pulling a plow in the Pelennor fields.

To give Boorman his due, parts of the script have a compelling brilliance, though they are still unlike anything Tolkien wrote. The sober exposition of the Council of Elrond is recast as a fantastic medieval masque representing the history of the Rings. This highly stylized sequence combines elements of Kabuki theater, rock opera, and circus performance, and could almost be imagined as a later retelling of the legend by a tribe of decadent Dark Elves who had seen one too many Cirque du Soleil productions. It is strangely effective, and gets the necessary back-story across, but it is definitely not a straightforward adaptation of Tolkien's work.

And that is where the key problem lies. At this point, Tolkien was still alive, and as he insists in his introduction to the first authorized American paperback edition of *The Lord of the Rings*, a certain courtesy (at least) is due to living authors (Hammond 105). This is what he says in response to the changes in the Zimmerman script:

> I am not Rider Haggard. I am not comparing myself with that master of Romance, except in this: I am not dead, yet. When the film of *K.S. Mines* was made it had already passed, one might say, into the public property of the imagination. *The Lord of the Rings* ... is still the vivid concern of a living person, and is nobody's toy to play with [Tolkien, *Letter to Ackerman and Others, Draft*].

Boorman's abundant creativity, inspired by Tolkien's work, needed another outlet than the straitjacket of adapting a living author's writings. Eventually he found it in *Excalibur*, returning to the Merlin-centered project he had been working on before he was offered *The Lord of the Rings* (Boorman 20). Boorman's imaginative remaking of the story of King Arthur worked because the Matter of Britain is undeniably part of the "public property of the imagination." He could get away with combining the characters of Morgause, Nimue, and Morgan le Fay, for example, because other artists had taken similar liberties over the centuries. Arthurian tales also differ from *The Lord of the Rings* in that they can be traced to no single author; although they may be most frequently associated with Malory, he did not originate the tales, and others before and after him contributed to the body of the legend. Some might consider Tolkien's stories "public property of the imagination" now, close to fifty years after their initial publication, but at that time they were relatively fresh from his pen, and Tolkien could legitimately claim they were his alone to play with.[4]

Beagle

In 1976 the Saul Zaentz Company acquired the film and stage rights to *The Hobbit* and *The Lord of the Rings*, as well as licensing rights to names, characters, and places in Middle-earth (*Who We Are*). According to one account, Ralph Bakshi, the controversial writer and director of the adult cartoon *Fritz the Cat*, had just finished the post-apocalyptic animated film *Wizards* when he was called in to direct an already-scripted *The Lord of the Rings* for Saul Zaentz's Fantasy Films (Lowson, Marshall and O'Brien 36). But elsewhere, Bakshi says he had been "chasing the rights for fifteen years," and originally tried to get his boss at Terrytoons to take on the project shortly after the book was published in the late fifties (Zito 59). Bakshi says he initially approached United Artists himself when he heard about the Boorman project and told them it ought to be animated instead of live action. He did not, however, want to use the Boorman script; his reaction was, "Why would you want to tamper with anything Tolkien did?" Bakshi says he persuaded MGM to buy out UA, paying Boorman for a script that would never be produced, then got Saul Zaentz and UA to buy back the rights when his MGM producer was fired (Robinson).

Bakshi felt pressure from Tolkien fanatics, summarizing the letters he received after the project was announced in the following way: "You better do it right, or you're *dead*" (Zito 59). His final product, the uneven 1978 *The Lord of the Rings*, was much reviled by many Tolkien fans, primarily for his use of rotoscoping, a clumsy animation technique involving drawing over film of live actors. However, there are also many viewers who praise Bakshi for staying true to the spirit of Tolkien's characters and the original dialogue, and after the liberties some feel Peter Jackson and crew took with their source material, it is instructive to take a fresh look at the script Bakshi used.

Chris Conkling, who had written a thesis on *The Lord of the Rings*, was Bakshi's initial choice for scriptwriter (Zito 60). According to Conkling, he wrote about seven drafts in cooperation with Bakshi, experimenting with different ways of structuring the story — as three separate films following the books closely, as a single three and a half hour film, and so on. The draft in the collection at Marquette is one of the later experiments, in which there would have been at least two films, the first telling the story from Merry and Pippin's point of view and the second following Frodo (Conkling, *e-mail*). Had Bakshi used this draft, it would have been a very different film indeed, and Conkling says that Bakshi felt it was "a much too drastic departure from Tolkien" (Conkling, *e-mail*). This draft is comparable to the Zimmerman script in its departures from the original and the somewhat lax attitude towards its source material necessitated by the drastic structural change of the frame conceit. It tells the bulk of a story as a flashback, with Merry doing voiceovers as the young hobbits try to persuade Treebeard to enter the fight for Middle-earth. This is the only script in the Marquette collection which visualizes Sauron as anything other than a flaming disembodied eye; in this version, he has green teeth and long worm-like fingers, but the truly disturbing thing about this script is the way the writer almost never uses Tolkien's exact words. To be fair, it is possible Conkling was working quickly and sketchily by memory for this experimental rough draft. Access to the other drafts Conkling wrote would help us to determine his working method,[5] but it is still disheartening to read Tolkien's dialogue simplified to a level of banality found only in the worst mass-market paperback fantasy. The following, for example, is one of Galadriel's speeches:

> "Sam, come here. You've wanted to see some elf magic long enough. I have some for you...."
>
> "The mirror confuses past and future, Sam, all this has not happened yet...."
>
> "I know he is looking for you, even as he has ever looked to know my mind. But, you see, we are protected here...."
>
> "You see, I have long wondered what I might do if I should ever get the ring" [Conkling, *script* 107–10].

Compare the above to Tolkien's original:

> "[T]his, if you will, is the magic of Galadriel. Did you not say that you wished to see Elf-magic? ..."
>
> "Remember that the Mirror shows many things, and not all have yet come to pass. Some never come to be, unless those that behold the visions turn aside from their path to prevent them...."
>
> "I say to you, Frodo, that even as I speak to you, I perceive the Dark Lord and know his mind, or all of his mind that concerns the Elves. And ever he gropes to see me and my thought. But still the door is closed!"
>
> "For many long years I had pondered what I might do, should the Great Ring come into my hands, and behold! it was brought within my grasp" [*LotR* 2.7.353–56].

Other characters fare no better: Saruman's attempt to persuade Théoden that he is more sinned against than sinning seems likelier to put the assembled troops to sleep than to seduce them to the dark side. It would have been less disturbing, and more easily dismissed as simply a rough draft, had this not also been Jackson's breezy and colloquial method of dealing with Tolkien's dialogue some twenty-five years later.

However, this draft does include several cinematically effective moments which make it through to the final shooting script. For example, Frodo's song in the Prancing Pony is intercut with Merry's encounter with the Black Riders, and the audience does not know Aragorn and the hobbits changed rooms until after the attack on the inn takes place — both effective ways of increasing tension in the Bree sequence without altering the story significantly. Later, when Sam is trying to persuade Frodo to take him to Mordor, they are shown paddling the boat in opposite directions as they argue, a subtle touch which shows how action not specified in the original can be used to strengthen a scene without undermining it.

According to a letter accompanying the Bakshi scripts in the Marquette files, well-known fantasy author Peter Beagle was called in to rewrite the script after Bakshi and Zaentz saw the first draft (Villalpando), although in a contemporary interview, Bakshi says Beagle was hired only to "polish" Conkling's work (Zito 60). Conkling states that Beagle was brought on board after he had written another draft going back to a "more straightforward and true to the source form of storytelling" (Conkling, *e-mail*). The first script Beagle produced eliminated the flashback frame and plunged straight into the long-expected party. Beagle obviously had a great love for and understanding of Tolkien's work, and he restored much of Tolkien's original dialogue, but the result was still overly long and had a few rough spots. The second Beagle draft adds some opening exposition, showing the history of the Ring, but prunes other areas, for example, dropping a scene showing Aragorn finding swords for the hobbits in a graveyard. By this draft Galadriel's gift-giving scene has disappeared, and Arwen been eliminated along with all interaction between Aragorn and Éowyn. Beagle also replaced Glorfindel with Legolas on road to Rivendell, following an earlier draft by Conkling (Conkling, *e-mail*), which eliminated a minor character without too much damage to the story (Jackson, of course, replaced Glorfindel with Arwen, which was a more drastic change).

This script is not without its problems. A minor quibble is that Saruman is renamed "Aruman," apparently to distinguish him from Sauron, but now and then he is called Saruman or Ruman, even in the finished movie. There are a few logical holes caused by what was left out, and at the end those familiar with the story might feel Beagle has written himself into a corner. For example, since there was no gift-giving, how will Sam defeat Shelob without Galadriel's phial? Since we see neither Faramir nor Arwen, what will be done with Éowyn? Did they plan to marry her to Aragorn as Boorman did?

There was one major change between the third Marquette draft and the final film. The draft cuts from Gollum's near-redemption scene ("Where were you?" "Sneaking") to the Battle of Helm's Deep, then finishes with a brief scene of Gollum leading Frodo and Sam towards Shelob's lair. However, the final film runs the two Gollum scenes together and ends with the battle instead. According to the Villalpando letter accompanying the scripts, test screenings convinced the studio that the film needed to end on a more traditionally dramatic note, with the victory at Helm's Deep (Villalpando).[6] In spite of, or perhaps because of, the fact that Bakshi was given a nearly unlimited budget at the start of the project (Eyman 34), the film was not enough of a commercial or critical success for Bakshi to get financial backing to complete the second part, proving that Peter Jackson was wise to get New Line to commit to all three films before he began work.

Comparisons

How do these scripts measure up to Tolkien's original words? Zimmerman and friends, as Tolkien found, saw only the action and magic on the surface of his work and did not show any appreciation for its depths. Boorman's script had almost too much depth, but it was Boorman's themes, not Tolkien's, that provided the complexity. The Conkling-Beagle script worked well within its limitations, but time (and perhaps technology) did not permit a truly faithful adaptation. Peter Jackson had more time and resources to work with, but he still left untouched many of Tolkien's deeper themes.

In many cases, the authors of these scripts came up with the same solutions to the problems posed by Tolkien's material, as if they were referring to a standard textbook on adaptation. Consider the opening exposition. The viewer is about to be plunged into a totally unfamiliar world, in which the back story is essential to his understanding of current events. In the original, the history of the rings of power is revealed piecemeal throughout the first two books, requiring the reader to be patient and tolerant of ambiguity. But in all three of the Marquette scripts, as well as in Jackson, the opening sequence includes establishing shots of Mordor and varying amounts of the history of the Rings before cutting to the Shire. The reader can easily move around in the book to confirm an earlier fact or check a new fact against earlier information, but the viewer does not have this luxury and has more need of an establishing narrative.

The scene where Bilbo hands the Ring over to Gandalf after the party is handled the same way in two of the scripts. The Bakshi film follows the book fairly closely, with Bilbo sealing the Ring in an envelope, and Gandalf catching the envelope as he drops it. Boorman, as expected, does his own thing and has Bilbo drop it in Gandalf's hat. But Zimmerman and Jackson both use the opportunity to do something more cinematically interesting — in these versions, Bilbo drops the Ring on the floor and Gandalf refuses to touch it, leaving it for Frodo to pick up. Not only is the Ring a more obvious and visible menace, this also allows the director to visually echo Bilbo picking up the Ring in Gollum's cave.

Another interesting place to compare the films is Saruman's oration to his troops before the Battle of Helm's Deep. There is no such oration in the book, and for good reason — Saruman's army (aside from the Dunlendings, a small component of his forces) was bred to his specifications and controlled by his will, so why would he waste time addressing what were basically machines programmed to do his bidding? According to Merry, Isengard was silent until the army issued forth with a blaze of trumpets. But both Beagle and Jackson add an address to the orcs, in Beagle's case culled from things Saruman said to Gandalf when he was imprisoned in Orthanc, but in Jackson's script almost entirely invented. Perhaps the writers felt it was necessary to balance our glimpses of the Rohirrim preparing for the siege with a look into their enemy's mind, in the same way Shakespeare contrasted Henry V's Crispin's Day speech with the Constable's address to the French lords, but it detracts from the mindless and faceless menace of the orcs to treat them as free-willed troops requiring the encouragement of a rousing pre-battle speech.

Perhaps most intriguing, and indicative of the eras in which these scripts were written, is the treatment of women in each of them. The whole Zimmerman script, written in the late fifties, vastly reduces the importance of women in *The Lord of the Rings*, cutting Galadriel's temptation, bringing Arwen onscreen only for her wedding, and dropping Éowyn's attraction to Aragorn. In this script, for example, Aragorn tells Éowyn to look after Faramir in the Houses of Healing, and this is basically all we see of her besides her fight with the Witch-king—no honor for her achievement, no internal conflict over her attraction to Aragorn, and no courtship by Faramir. Women are primarily gift-givers and care-takers, and like Rosie the Riveter who was expected to happily return to her former place after the war.

At the tail end of the 1960s Boorman's version is a sharp contrast. He strengthened and sexualized Galadriel's role, turned Éowyn into Aragorn's warrior-queen, and made Arwen an ethereal vision of eternal adolescence. Boorman reflected the era's fascination with youth, equality, sexual freedom, and drugs. The Conkling-Beagle script, a product of the mid-seventies, goes back to reducing the importance and power of the female characters; by the time we get to the shooting script, there is no Arwen, Éowyn never speaks during the scene at Edoras, and while Galadriel's temptation is fairly well done, there is no gift-giving scene. It seems to reflect a social ambivalence about powerful and successful women; the only "meaty" female scene is Galadriel's rejection of power. However, since the second half was never written, we do not know how Éowyn's story would have played out.

One strength of the Jackson films is that they retain Tolkien's powerful female roles, although some of the most crucial scenes only appear on the extended DVDs. Some viewers may feel he went too far in expanding these roles, particularly in his recreation of Arwen as a warrior princess, but Jackson simply reflects the recent movie and television trend to glorify the beautiful yet physically powerful heroine—what Victoria Gaydosik has referred to as the "new Psyche" paradigm. For each script, time constraints dictated that some characters and events had to be eliminated; the choices the writers made imply that some felt the female roles were the least essential to the plot, while others believed that Tolkien's strong female roles were central to the story, and expanding upon them would attract a wider audience.

What is the solution to the problem of writing the perfect adaptation of Tolkien? Would a twenty-hour miniseries be long enough to cover all the nuances of his work, or would readers still be disappointed? Readers may dream about the day when a filmmaker will be daring enough to stick to Tolkien's unusual structure, dialogue, and original story, yet creative enough to add the touches that make a great movie more than just a literal transcription from page to screen. But it may be impossible, and perhaps even undesirable. Tolkien may have been right in saying that a film can never capture all the nuances of a work of fiction. The film playing in the individual reader's mind, after all, is the one that reader really wants to see.

Notes

1. In the years between the Zimmerman and Boorman scripts, after the Beatles founded Apple Films in 1967, they considered doing a film of *The Lord of the Rings*, casting John Lennon as Gollum, Paul McCartney as Frodo, George Harrison as Gandalf, and Ringo Starr as Sam; however, they weren't able to purchase the film rights and the project fell through (Foster 82). Foster points out how similar the plot of the Beatles' film *Help!* is to the plot of *The Lord of the Rings* in this article. The rights were also supposedly owned by Stanley Kubrick at some time during this period (Bilowit 20; Zito 59).

2. Iain Lowson claims the screenplay "earned Tolkien's seal of approval" (Lowson, Marshall and O'Brien 25), but I suspect he is extrapolating from Boorman's statement that Tolkien approved his decision to make it live-action.

3. Although, oddly enough, one scene in Boorman's script bears a striking similarity to a scene Tolkien drafted and rejected for the Farmer Maggot sequence. In the script, the hobbits, Puck-like, taunt and tease a group of clumsy men in a field, with Frodo slipping on the Ring and vanishing when they come too close to catching him (Boorman and Pallenberg 13–14). Tolkien wrote a similar scene where Frodo puts on the Ring and plays childishly mean pranks on Farmer Maggot (Bratman 16–17; *Shadow* 292–93). And Tolkien did originally intend to have Aragorn marry Éowyn, Arwen being a late addition to the story.

4. In 1978, five years after Tolkien's death, Arthur Rankin Jr. and Jules Bass made an animated version of *The Hobbit*. One critic says, "Ultimately this production fails of greatness despite all of its genuinely good qualities because its producers never seem to have taken seriously the inner journey of Bilbo.... [A]t the most crucial point of the inner narrative of the story they sent [Bilbo] over Gollum's head and down the tunnel to freedom with a flippant 'Ta-ta!'" (Hardy 140, Croft).

5. In an e-mail, Conkling told me he planned to offer some of his other drafts to Marquette, which will be a boon to any future student of film adaptations of *The Lord of the Rings* (Conkling, e-mail).

6. Interestingly, the picture book tie-in which was released before the film reflects the order of the third draft (Tolkien, *Film Book*), although the "fotonovel" follows the movie (Conkling, Beagle and Tolkien).

Acknowledgments

I'd like to thank Matt Blessing and the staff at the Marquette University Library Special Collections for their assistance, the University of Oklahoma Libraries for a grant which permitted me to visit the collections, and Chris Conkling for seeking me out with a fascinating and helpful e-mail. A version of this paper was presented at the Southwest/Texas Popular Culture Association Annual Conference and the Mythopoeic Society Annual Conference in 2004.

Works Cited

Ackerman, Forrest J. Letter to Rayner Unwin. 1958. J.R.R. Tolkien Collection, Marquette University, Milwaukee.

Bilowit, William. "Producing *The Lord of the Rings*." *Millimeter* 6 (1978): 18–20, 142.

Boorman, John. *The Emerald Forest Diary*. New York: Farrer, Straus and Giroux, 1985.

_____, and Rospo Pallenberg. *J.R.R. Tolkien's the Lord of the Rings: Screenplay*. 1970. J.R.R. Tolkien Collection, Marquette University, Milwaukee.

Bratman, David. "Top Ten Rejected Plot Twists from *the Lord of the Rings*: A Textual Excursion into the 'History of the *Lord of the Rings*.'" *Mythlore* 22.4 (2000): 13–37.

Carpenter, Humphrey. *Tolkien : A Biography*. Boston: Houghton Mifflin, 1977.

Conkling, Chris. *The Lord of the Rings Part One: The Fellowship*. 1976. J.R.R. Tolkien Collection, Marquette University, Milwaukee.

_____. "Lord of the Rings Paper." E-mail to Janet Brennan Croft, October 15, 2004.

Conkling, Chris, Peter S. Beagle, and J. R. R. Tolkien. *The Lord of the Rings: A Fotonovel Publications Fotonovel*. Los Angeles: Fotonovel Productions, 1979.

Croft, Janet Brennan. "Rankin/Bass Productions." *The Tolkien Encyclopedia*. Edited by Michael Drout. New York: Routledge, 2006.

Eyman, Scott. "The Young Turk: Junk-Culture-Junkie Takes on a Hobbit." *Take One* 6 (1978): 34–36, 41.

Foster, Mike. "Ringo and Samwise: Paradigms?" *Concerning Hobbits and Other Matters: Tolkien Across the Disciplines*. Edited by Tim Schindler. St. Paul: University of St. Thomas, 2001.

Gaydosik, Victoria. "'Crimes against the Book'? The Transformation of Tolkien's Arwen from Page to Screen and the Abandonment of the Psyche Archetype." *Tolkien on Film: Essays on Peter Jackson's The Lord of the Rings*. Edited by Janet Brennan Croft. Altadena, CA: Mythopoeic Press, 2004.

Hammond, Wayne G. *J.R.R. Tolkien: A Descriptive Bibliography*. Winchester, England: St. Paul's Bibliographies, 1993.

Hardy, Gene. "More Than a Magic Ring." Review of *The Hobbit*, directed by Arthur Rankin Jr. and Jules Bass. *Children's Novels and the Movies*. Edited by Douglas Street. New York: Ungar, 1983.

Harlow, John, and Rachel Dobson. "*Lord of the Rings* Is Worth £3bn but Tolkien Sold the Film Rights to Ward Off the Taxman." *Sunday Times*, December 16, 2002: 16.

Jensen, Todd. "The Zimmerman Film Treatment of *The Lord of the Rings*." *Beyond Bree* (December 1995): 7–8.

Lewis, C. S. "On Stories." *On Stories and Other Essays on Literature*. San Diego: Harcourt, 1947 (1982).

Lowson, Iain, Keith Marshall, and Daniel O'Brien. *World of the Rings: The Unauthorized Guide to the World of J.R.R. Tolkien*. London: Reynolds & Hearn, 2002.

Robinson, Tasha. *Ralph Bakshi*. Interview. The Onion A.V. Club. *http://www.theavclub. com/avclub3644/avfeature_3644.html*. Accessed January 31, 2003.

Tolkien, J. R. R. *The Lord of the Rings*. 2nd ed. Boston: Houghton Mifflin, 1994.
_____. *The Film Book of J.R.R. Tolkien's* The Lord of the Rings. New York: Ballantine, 1978.
_____. *Letter to Forrest J. Ackerman and Others, Draft*. 1958. J.R.R. Tolkien Collection, Marquette University, Milwaukee.
_____. *Letter to Forrest J. Ackerman, Draft*. 1957? J.R.R. Tolkien Collection, Marquette University, Milwaukee.
_____. *The Letters of J.R.R. Tolkien: A Selection*. Edited by Christopher Tolkien. Boston: Houghton Mifflin, 2000.
_____. "On Fairy-stories." *The Tolkien Reader*. New York: Ballantine, 1966.
_____, and Christopher Tolkien. *The Return of the Shadow: The History of the Lord of the Rings, Part One*. The History of Middle-Earth, vol. 6. Boston: Houghton Mifflin, 1988.
Unwin, Rayner. *Letter to Forrest J. Ackerman*. 1957. J.R.R. Tolkien Collection, Marquette University, Milwaukee.
Villalpando, David. *Letter to Matt Blessing*. 2002. J.R.R. Tolkien Collection, Marquette University, Milwaukee.
Who We Are. 1998. Tolkien Enterprises. Available: *http://www.tolkien-ent.com/new/index.html*. January 30, 2003.
Zimmerman, Morton Grady. *The Lord of the Rings Story Line*. 1957. J.R.R. Tolkien Collection, Marquette University, Milwaukee.
_____. *Production Notes*. 1957. J.R.R. Tolkien Collection, Marquette University, Milwaukee.
Zito, Stephen. "Bakshi among the Hobbits." *American Film* 3 (1978): 58–63.

I Don't Think We're in Kansas Anymore: Peter Jackson's Film Interpretations *of Tolkien's* Lord of the Rings

Gwendolyn A. Morgan

With good reason, our colleagues in film studies are suspicious of those of us in literature using their medium as grist for our critical mill. Too often, we expect to see the coherence and richness of a written tale depicted in narrative form alone, ignoring the fact that film is a *visual* art which depends as much upon the specifics of scenery, camera angle, framing, and timing, along with the actual acting, as upon the dialogue of the story that it relates. Indeed, overwhelmed by its visual richness, we tend to ignore it or, at best, consider it ornamentation of some essential storyline. This is especially true in the case of movie versions of literary texts. We see them as illustrated *books* on tape and consider the added dimensions of cinema as merely a means of compression. Yet such a film may be a masterpiece in its own right while still doing justice to its source tale. It can recreate rather than mimic, revitalize rather than preserve. Peter Jackson's cinematic adaptation of J.R.R. Tolkien's *The Lord of the Rings* does just this. An astounding undertaking in film-making and technology, Jackson's trilogy stands as a monument of the art, even for those who have never heard of Tolkien, as well as a successful translation of Tolkien's key ideas in terms the modern audience can relate to them. It is, in short, both a fine retelling of the novels and a masterpiece operating solely within the universe of cinematography.

Jackson's films do indeed employ many forms of narrative compression, and their success in doing so is a major strength, for clearly, the need to get to the end of the tale within even the generous running times of his films dictates that he use other means to convey Tolkien's text. After all, who among the audience could *read* the 1500-page epic in the ten hours of Jackson's version? Fortunately, in Treebeard's initial appearance on screen, we apprehend in seconds what it takes Tolkien pages to convey. Likewise, the opening sequence of *Fellowship of the Rings*, with Galadriel's commentary overlaying the scene of a 3000-year-old battle, gives us in less than three minutes the histories of the Rings, Sauron's first defeat, Isildur, Gollum, and Bilbo. So too does cinematic flashback, such as Aragorn's recollection of Arwen during his conversation with Eowyn in *The Two Towers*, elegantly compress the storyline. Nonetheless, literary critics judging Jackson's films seem to expect Tolkien's work to be reproduced word for word. As David Salo (23) comments, "[m]uch of their critique does not concern itself with the film's acting, direction or plot but rather with the appearance of *authenticity* and what one can only call, for lack of a better term, *historicity*," an attitude leading to another major vilification of Jackson's version: that some innovations are "anachronistic" to Tolkien's world.

Tolkien set *The Lord of the Rings* in a pseudo-medieval world, which he suggests existed in the pre-history of the current age but at the same time mirrors certain historical periods and peoples of England. Literary critics expect that illusion of "historicity" to be preserved in the films. Peter Jackson, to their chagrin, in some instances introduces "anachronisms" into that world, most significantly in characterization. Arwen, for example, becomes a twenty-first century *Buffy the Vampire Slayer* figure from her original "presence in absence" of Tolkien's medieval courtly mistress, while Aragorn transforms from his heroic, larger-than-life king to the angst-ridden, sensitive, existential '90s male. Similarly, Saruman's creation of the Uruk Hai owes less to the description in Tolkien's texts than to the current fear and moral dilemma surrounding genetic engineering. Martha Driver ("Accuracy" 19) timidly pleads forgiveness for such anachronisms, asserting they "might disturb the teacher of history or literature who hopes for a more realistic or truer representation," on the grounds that we should not expect film to give us "documentation" rather than the "fantasy" it is cinema's job to provide. I would rescind the apology, arguing that they necessarily provide touchstones for a modern audience in order to effectively engage the films' audience, confirming contemporary expectations and desires while nonetheless evoking responses ultimately similar to those Tolkien desired from his originals.

Other anachronisms may be more jarring. For example, in *The Two Towers*, as the Uruk Hai runs to ignite Saruman's gunpowder bomb, who can fail to see the Olympic torch runner? What about college drinking bouts in the contest (only in the director's cut) between Gimli and Legolas in *Return of the King*? Or skateboarding in Legolas' run down the stairs on a shield at Helm's Deep, or down the Oliphant's trunk on Pelennor Fields? Perhaps less familiar to American and European audiences is the reference to the Australian–New Zealand fad of dwarf-tossing of the 1990s, mirrored in Gimli's assertion in Moria that "no-one tosses a dwarf" and his later instruction to Aragorn at Helm's Deep: "Toss me. But don't tell the elf." Such may seem merely trivial and comic, but touchstones are necessary for the audience's "willing suspension of disbelief" that total involvement in film requires. The enormous popularity of Legolas' skate-boarding scene, evoking applause and verbal outbursts in theaters, attests to the technique's effectiveness.

The third, and probably most common, criticism of filmic versions of literary texts is the omission of entire episodes, usually due to running time restrictions. What major features of Tolkien's epic has Jackson omitted completely, and does this adversely affect its "message"? Two major instances come to mind. First is the Tom Bombadil episode. Literary critics argue that Bombadil is essential to Tolkien's complex vision of good and evil because he is the *only* character completely unaffected by the Ring's power. Although, in turn, he has no power over the Ring, it cannot tempt or deceive him: he can see Frodo when he wears it; he considers it a bauble for play. It is for this very reason that, according to commentaries in the director's cut, Jackson leaves him out: the audience, he claims, would not have understood why Bombadil simply didn't carry the Ring to Mount Doom. Tolkien, however, explains this in *Fellowship* (347–8), when he describes Bombadil as the first of all earthly creatures, unconcerned with the affairs of other races, childlike, apt to forget or throw away the Ring if he were persuaded to take it. He is, in a sense, amoral, appreciating all things *of* the earth for what they are, be they hobbits in distress or the trees who attempt to destroy them. The Ring has no power over him because he has no real conception of good or evil. He thus symbolizes human innocence before the Fall. In contrast, the Ring is in its very creation evil and with a will of its own, completely outside of Bombadil's ken. Hence, he would see no reason to destroy it or desire it, ultimately allowing the Ring to weave its own fate. Nonetheless, the films *do* make clear that the Ring's continued existence following Isildur's refusal to destroy it — the continuation of evil in Middle-earth — is the fault of men, and it is their duty to overcome it. Thus, although Tolkien's grand Catholic underpinning to the tale is not fully realized in the films, the underlying moral issue is not lost.

The other primary quality embodied in Bombadil is Tolkien's exaltation of the pre-industrial "simple life." Jackson gives this ample representation in the Edenic Shire, with its uncomplicated routines and the simple pleasures enjoyed by its inhabitants. Nonetheless, his representation throws into relief for us the second major omission of the films. The entire tale of the destruction, scouring, and rebirth of the Shire is not even implied, indeed a great loss. Not only is Tolkien's fervent anti-industrialism thus down-played but an important aspect of his spiritual theme undercut. In Sam's elfin earth and seeds, used to rebuild the Shire, in the destruction of

Saruman there, not, as in the extended edition of *Return of the King*, at Isengard, in the rising of a new and better Shire from the ashes of the old, Tolkien gave us his vision from the Book of Revelation: "I saw a new heaven and a new earth, for the old had passed away." The great evil represented by the Ring having been destroyed, Middle-earth may rise anew, with the unification of races and the return of peace, prosperity, and rejuvenation of the natural world.

Indeed, this omission is part of Jackson's overall secularization of the epic. The film-goer never knows Gandalf is a Maia, an agent of divine beings who actively involve themselves in the salvation of Middle Earth, or that Sauron is a fallen Vala, the top echelon of such beings and clearly representative of Lucifer. Gone are the prayers to Elbereth, Lady of the Stars and Blessed Virgin in disguise: Arwen's prayer in *Fellowship* to save Frodo is directed to no-one. Similarly, when Gandalf comments at Aragorn's coronation, "Now come the days of the king: may they be blessed," the film-goer can only ask, "By whom?" Only readers of Tolkien know that divinities answer such prayers.

The sense of an afterlife, too, is much reduced. Claire Valente (41) notes that Jackson's sole hint of a heavenly existence occurs in Gandalf's speech to Pippin immediately before the battle at Minas Tirith, and that it remains vague and unconfirmed. I would disagree. For those in the audience seeking to perceive it, the ending of *The Return of the King* provides such confirmation when the ring-bearers, including Frodo and Bilbo, depart on the last ship for the Undying Lands. The cinematography here is telling. As the ship, sails billowing, pulls away from the dock and moves across and *up* the screen, the setting sun appears to set it ablaze with fire for a brief moment; at the next it is gone. Any reader of the Bible cannot but recall the description of Elijah's translation into heaven in a chariot of fire in 2 Kings 2:11. Like Elijah, neither Bilbo nor Frodo will suffer death before moving to paradise, accompanied, notably, by Gandalf, who returns home to Valinor for the second time in the epic. Moreover, Gandalf's description of his own death and resurrection in *The Two Towers* after defeating the Balrog retains much of Tolkien's assertion that Gandalf had returned to "heaven" in Valinor, only to be "sent back" to Middle-earth because his work was not yet done. Such clearly depends on a sense of merciful divine powers who are most definitely interested in the salvation of the world. Thus, perhaps Jackson's epic satisfies both audiences, secular and religious.

What all this demands is that we consider the creation of a film from a written text a process of translation, translating *art* as well as words, into the language of the cinema. Moreover, just as literary translation of texts from other times and places requires they be reworked to be comprehensible and appealing to a very different audience, so must film do the same.

Indeed, Jackson actually employs a technique similar to Tolkien's practice of recalling a pseudo-medieval world to inform his commentary on his own era by referencing the "medieval period" of cinematic tradition to comment on Tolkien. Because film *is* an art in its own right, it exists within a tradition completely other than and independent of that in which literature operates, and it is within this tradition that Jackson's films validate themselves by weaving a net of allusions to earlier milestones.

Making this case requires a brief digression into film theory, beginning with that of filmic language. The linguistic school views the visual aspect of cinema as a system of signification — of conveying meaning — at least as important as the verbal, at the most basic level involving manipulation of camera angles "to capture the subtleties and nuances of socially resonant streams of kinesic expressions" (Prince 113). At the next level, a director uses non-narrative cinematic techniques to establish a more general relationship between a signified and a signifier. The result is a connotative leitmotif, a

> visual or auditory theme — or an arrangement of visual or auditory themes — [which,] once it has been placed in its correct syntagmatic position within the discourse that constitutes the whole film, takes on a value greater than its own and is increased by the additional meaning it receives…. In short, the connotative meaning *extends over* the denotative meaning, but without *contradicting* or *ignoring* it [Metz 76].

In other words, film language operates simultaneously on the levels of the specific and the universal to convey its message, just as does human language, but encompasses music, lighting, camera manipulation, timing, and acting as part of its vocabulary.

I would like to extend this concept by combining it with aesthetic film criticism, which Louis Giannetti (506) defines as recognizing "a tradition of masterpieces and great filmmakers … to concentrate on a relative handful of important works of art that have endured the test of time — that is, movies that are still great despite our viewing them in a totally different context." A logical extension of this concept suggests that cinematic language operates not merely within a particular film but in the meta-textual world of cinema in general, that is, within the collective tradition of individual cinematic works. This allows us to see Jackson's *Lord of the Rings* as functioning in a mythic cycle of which it, but not Tolkien's novel, is a part, drawing greater meaning from the filmic canon which it references and extends.

Jackson owes his greatest specific debt to *The Wizard of Oz*, a natural focus of allusion for him in its undisputed position as the first great fantasy film. Plot similarities, including the power and importance of the Ring and the ruby slippers, the assistance of wizard and wizard, of good witch and good elf queen, and the shared quest motif make allusion all the easier. Most importantly, however, drawing parallels between the films emphasizes the dark differences between them: on one level, *Lord of the Rings* becomes the nightmare version of Dorothy's dream. Thus, its power as epic — as serious, even apocalyptic, quest — is enhanced by the more trivial concerns and comedy underlying *The Wizard of Oz*. Finally, allusion, of course, is in large part a form of mirroring, which in *The Lord of the Rings* is Jackson's most favored cinematic technique.

Jackson's meta-textual allusion begins early on. As soon as Frodo discovers what the Ring really is, he cannot of necessity give it up; Gandalf has declared him its keeper and will not accept it from him. So, too, in *The Wizard of Oz* with the ruby slippers Dorothy finds on her feet (via Glenda, the Good Witch of the North), which she cannot surrender to the Wicked Witch of the West. This plot correspondence is enhanced by a visual echo. Departing dramatically from Tolkien's description (*Fellowship* 60–1) of Bilbo sealing the Ring in an envelope and then placing it on the mantle to await Frodo, Jackson shows the departing Bilbo reluctantly dropping the Ring on the floor. When Gandalf then reaches for it, he recoils, experiencing what appears to be an electrical shock. Such mirrors almost exactly the Wicked Witch reaching for the ruby slippers, which repel her with equal and like force. Similarly, it can be no mistake that Jackson chose to have Frodo and Sam accidentally encounter Merry and Pippin in a cornfield, a place where Dorothy also meets her first quest companion, the Scarecrow, rather than include them in the quest from the beginning (Tolkien, *Fellowship* 99 ff.).

Jackson's most obvious allusion to *The Wizard of Oz* occurs at Bree, where the tired, rain-soaked hobbits knock at the town gate. A doorkeeper opens first an upper door in the wooden palisade, then, unable to see anyone, closes it and opens a lower door, just as does the warden at the gates of Oz. Moreover, both apologize for their initial rudeness by claiming "they're only doing their jobs" in questioning the visitors. However, the scene from *Oz* is the film's prime moment of hope, set in brilliant sunshine with the companions having come through great dangers to reach the wizard they hope will grant their wishes. *Fellowship*'s corresponding scene occurs in the dark of a midnight rain storm and the fear of pursuit. Thereafter, both groups of companions encounter ponies on the street before entering an establishment (a beauty parlor vs. a bar) to prepare for their meetings with wizards—both of whom won't (Oz) or can't (Gandalf) meet them. Both groups then despair. And, prior to reaching their destinations (in *Lord of the Rings* not only Bree but also Rivendell and Mordor), both groups have been lulled into dangerous trances by poppies, or Rings, or Marshes of the Dead, or wastelands, or whatnot.

Such correspondences pervade Jackson's films, too numerous for all to be explored here. Nonetheless, I offer these few as a starting point for consideration:

- The Wicked Witch's crystal ball clearly equates to Saruman's seeing stone, but Jackson adds verbal echoes to emphasize the parallel between the two antagonists. "So, my Pretty," begins the Wicked Witch, viewing Dorothy's party en route to Oz. "So Gandalf," begins Saruman, when he learns the good wizard intends to lead the Fellowship through Moria.
- The Witch on her bicycle or broomstick, her cape flying about her, could offer a model for Jackson's Black Riders—insubstantial and ghostly in Tolkien's text—in their flying capes, galloping in pursuit on black horses.
- The filmic Saruman employs flocks of birds as spies, recalling the flying monkeys who perform the same duties for the Wicked Witch.
- In Moria, Goblins swarm up the pillars of the great hall, threatening the Fellowship. In *Oz*, monkeys swarm up the Witch's castle walls.
- Jackson has Sam fall before the gates of Mordor, almost alerting the Orcs to Frodo's position. Scarecrow does the same before the Witch's castle.
- Jackson includes the relatively minor scene of Frodo and Sam donning orc uniforms to make their way through Mordor, recalling Dorothy's rescuers in stolen uniforms joining the witch's marching monkeys.

Nor is it only in the ominous scenes that Jackson references *The Wizard of Oz.* Consider the homecoming scenes. Dorothy awakens in bed to find the faces of her friends—whom her dream transmuted into her quest companions—swimming around her. So, too, does Frodo awake—once in Rivendell and later in Gondor. Likewise, the gypsy Dorothy encounters early on (the Wizard of her dream) easily could have shared a wardrobe with Bilbo as he entertains Gandalf at the beginning of *Fellowship*; that both meetings are set in idyllic green countryside over teapots also cannot have been coincidence. Thus, even the comic moments in *Lord of the Rings* achieve additional hilarity, which in turn emphasizes the melodramatic seriousness which overshadows them, from their association with the earlier film.

In summary, Jackson's allusion to *The Wizard of Oz* not only situates his epic within the mythic cycle of cinematic tradition and raises it to the same landmark stature, but more importantly it underscores the gulf between the visions the two endeavors propound. The light-hearted, individual quests of Dorothy, Scarecrow, Tin Man, and Lion throw into sharp relief the collective, apocalyptic nature of Frodo's quest. Such is further delineated when one considers the *differences* between the directly paralleled scenes. For example, the ruby slippers repel an evil character, while the One Ring wards off possession by Gandalf, arguably the most moral figure in *Lord of the Rings*. Moreover, the slippers' power is ultimately trivial, serving only to send Dorothy home, while the Ring represents an all but limitless potential for evil. At the gates of Bree and Oz, identical action is contradicted by the weather and time of day, again accenting the dire threat to the world which Jackson's Fellowship seeks to avert.

Jackson also employs an established cinematic mirroring technique to underscore parallels within *The Lord of the Rings* films themselves, both those drawn by Tolkien and others he has himself added. One example is his portrayal of the Ring's seductive power. When Frodo offers the Ring to Galadriel, she appears in negative sepia color, backlit, with her hair flying and eyes preternaturally bright, as she faces down her temptation. Frodo, in Mount Doom, fails to resist that same temptation, and we see him backlit by the fires below him, turning dark, hair flying, eyes preternaturally bright, as he asserts, "the Ring is mine." The echo emphasizes the gulf between the unearthly power to resist and the all-too-mortal failure to do so. These scenes find foreshadowing in Bilbo's initial refusal to surrender the Ring to Gandalf and in his near-attack on Frodo at Rivendell. In both instances, Jackson also uses dark lighting, luminous eyes, and a suggestion of wind. One might also observe the recurrent white radiance used to link characters. Frodo, recovering in his beds at Rivendell and Gondor, appears clothed in white and nestled within white sheets, all subjected to reflective light. So, too, with the resurrected Gandalf the White: he is almost pure light as he confronts Aragorn's group in Fangorn, disenchants Théoden, leads the charge at Helm's Deep, and rescues Faramir's riders from the Nazgul. Galadriel also glows, as do her husband, Celeborn, and Elrond in their initial appearances. All these characters have one thing in common: they all leave, along with Bilbo, on the last ship to Valinor at the epic's close.

Action scenes, too, echo each other. Sam reaches to save Frodo from the Cracks of Doom in *Return* with the same grip Frodo uses to pull him from the water at the end of *Fellowship*: their friendship and loyalty is mutually strong, equally necessary to the quest's success. Galadriel reaches to Frodo through a dream in his battle with Shelob, and Aragorn to him on Caradhras: the support system and unity of races is thereby made clear. Mirroring also informs moments of crisis. The fellowship's near escape in Moria as the bridge of Khazad Dum crumbles beneath their feet repeats itself as Sam and Frodo flee the Cracks of Doom, the mountain self-destructing around them. And Eowyn imposes herself between Théoden and the Witch King in the same manner Sam leaps between the fallen Frodo and Shelob.

A final cinematographic technique used to parallel situations I would raise here is montage, the rapid flashing back and forth between situations to indicate interdependence and parallel. Here, Jackson's outstanding example is the last stand before the gates of Mordor, simultaneous with Frodo's struggle within Mount Doom itself. Aragorn battles orcs, then a gigantic Troll, as Frodo fights temptation, then Gollum. Loss equals loss, hit equals hit, near-miss near-miss, and recovery after apparently certain death the same. Both Frodo and Aragorn struggle to save Middle-earth as they also struggle to save themselves, Frodo to remain Frodo and Aragorn to become king. All these examples of visual mirroring to evoke association stand as a primary artistic strategy in Jackson's trilogy, and its calculated use within them suggests, moreover, that his allusions to *The Wizard of Oz* are equally deliberate.

I would like to turn now from discussion of Jackson's *translation* and *re-creation* of Tolkien's fiction to his *interpretation* of it. In his justification for fantasy literature laid out in "On Faerie Stories," Tolkien speaks of recourse to the "secondary reality" of Faerie (fantasy) for what he terms "Recovery ... a regaining of a clear view" (146). This "view" is not, for Tolkien, an understanding of the way things are but of the way they *should* be, or, indeed, once were. It is a recovery of ideals and archetypes lost in the disillusionment of the post–World War II industrial era. In *Lord of the Rings*, these are represented in two ways. The first and simplest is the idealization of the simple life in concert with nature represented by the hobbits, which Jackson amply illustrates in his films and which requires no additional comment. The second is the recovery of medieval period types and philosophies which Tolkien saw as heroic. Such figure in his epic in two ways: as archetypal figures and patterns (especially of hero and king), and in the manifestation of what he terms elsewhere ("Monsters" 20) the "theory of Northern courage." The code for human behavior dictated thereby is, for Tolkien, the key to rehabilitating the modern Western world, most especially England, and is the second (that is, in addition to his Christian message) ideological underpinning of his epic. It is this aspect of the literary text upon which Jackson concentrates most in his interpretation, but how he does so requires a summary of Tolkien's conscious technique.

Medieval types abound in Tolkien's books. That of the ideal king, of course, embodies itself in Aragorn; the ideal hero, too, finds a home there, although other facets of it surface in characters such as Faramir, Théoden, and Frodo. The pattern of courtly love shapes the affair between Arwen and Aragorn, while paternal feudalism and ideal friendship manifest most obviously between Frodo and Sam. Moreover, in Tolkien these archetypal qualities serve as models for modern man — represented in *Lord of the Rings* by the hobbits — in regaining the epic aspirations and ideals of his medieval past. On one level, Tolkien's different peoples represent the various cultural strains in England's history: elves, with their exuberance, love of nature and song, exaltation of spirits in nature, and proud heroism, clearly recall Celtic culture, just as the dwarves' *fear* of the natural world, love of craftsmanship and stone halls, overindulgence in feasting and drinking, and pessimistic defiance of death recall that of the Anglo-Saxons. Men, with their literate culture and penchant for magnificent cities and monuments, as well as their chivalric behavior, are medieval Norman to the core. The hobbits, of course, with their elfish ears, short stature, and Common Tongue, are the blending of the three, and this—along with their complacency, fear of adventure or even experience of things beyond the borders of the Shire, and inability to imagine anything more satisfying than an excellent meal followed by a pipe of good tobacco—clearly identifies them as that diminished descendent of the great medieval cultures: modern man.

To recover the greatness of things past — within *The Lord of the Rings*, to save Middle-earth and their beloved Shire — the hobbits of the fellowship must overcome complacency and fear, and aspire to the heroism of the other races. Frodo and Sam, of course, do so in finally fulfilling their quest to carry the Ring to Mount Doom. This very experience later makes it impossible for Frodo to remain in the renewed Shire, for he has outgrown it and must journey on to the Undying Lands with others who understand his sacrifice. The quest has indeed, in Galadriel's words, "claimed his life," but on the other hand he has also proved her prediction that "even the smallest of us can change the course of the future." Even so, his and Bilbo's manuscript is, significantly, left for Sam to finish (*Return* 380), a suggestion that modern man may once again reach for the greatness of his past. Merry and Pippin, too, succeed in this to a lesser degree. Having played their part in the War of the Ring by bringing the Ents against Saruman and later to Gondor, they return home to organize the hobbit rebellion against the evil industrial regime imposed upon the Shire by Sharkey-Saruman. They later are remembered in the Red Book as the greatest captains of the war for the Shire (*Return* 365) and become "Lordly" (377), ultimately figuring as patriarchs of their tribes. Moreover, their growth in character is symbolized by their literal growth after imbibing Treebeard's magical Ent-draught. Although the Scouring of the Shire is omitted from Jackson's films, the changes in Merry and Pippin and their modeling themselves after the heroes around them manifest in other ways. Consider Merry's ride with the Rohirrim in *Return of the King*. Initially, Théoden rejects him on account of his small stature, but Eowin carries him with her anyway because his "heart is as big" as any man's, and he echoes her "To battle!" without hesitation. He has learned that heroism is about fighting for right, no matter what the cost or the hope of success. Pippin similarly fights at Gandalf's side, though the wizard has told him, "There never was much hope." Even their increase in height is retained, and their chivalric appearances as they return home on horseback also indicate their transformation. Most poignantly, as all four hobbit questers toast the success of the Fellowship at the Prancing Pony, they simultaneously mourn their resultant isolation from what they now understand as the small-mindedness of the Shire — all have outgrown the narrowness of normal hobbit life. Thus, despite the loss of the Scouring of the Shire, the cinematic version retains the formula of reaching for the heroic through the heroic past and the condemnation of the diminished present race.

Jackson's films more successfully preserve the theory of Northern courage. Tolkien's "Monsters and the Critics" explores the dark vision of *Beowulf,* with its cultural background of the ultimately doomed Norse gods and Ragnorak, the final battle for the world lost by humanity and their divine allies to immortal monsters who then issue in an era of darkness. The outcome of Ragnorak is foretold in Northern literature by the Norns, and the destruction of both humanity and the gods thus a foregone conclusion. Despite this, divine and human heroes alike meet the enemy with sublime heroism. It is this courage to face horror and determination to do what is right despite certain doom that lies at the heart of Northern courage. This is manifest in both the literary and filmic *Lord of the Rings* most obviously in the culture of the Rohirrim. Of course, that Rohan is modeled on an ideal Anglo-Saxon society gleaned from *Beowulf* is a critical commonplace among Tolkien scholars; even its language is Old English. Thence they take their customs of the mead hall and the cup of peace, the sacred nature of the oath and of loyalty to one's lord and allies, of the commitment to a cause even when it means assured destruction. All this Jackson retains, and in both literary and film versions they are the race most to be emulated, especially when contrasted with the decadent Gondorians.

The Rohirrim evince Northern courage most completely in the two epic battle scenes of the films. At Helm's Deep, Théoden ponders aloud about his fitness as a leader, only to have his captain respond, "Your men, my lord, will follow you to whatever end." Here is the absolute loyalty of thanes to their king. Later, when his troops have been forced to retreat into the keep, Théoden's exchange with Aragorn, himself one of the Dunedain and therefore possessed of their greatness, further demonstrates Northern honor in the face of hopelessness.

ARAGORN: "Ride out. Ride out and meet them."
THÉODEN: "For death and glory!"
ARAGORN: "For Rohan."
THÉODEN: "Yes! The horn of Helm Hammerhand will sound in the Deep one last time.... Fell deeds await. Now for wrath, now for ruin, and the red dawn!"

Of course, the effort also provides the time needed for Gandalf and Eomir to arrive with reinforcements and the impetus which ultimately wins the battle. Such a fortuitous outcome would not, according to Tolkien, have been possible in the pagan vision of the Anglo-Saxons, but his epic anticipates Christian redemption, even in its patently pre-Christian setting, much in the way he sees it in *Beowulf.*

The Battle of Pelennor Fields again exhibits the Rohirrim's Northern courage. As Théoden's troops draw up before him in preparation for attack, they respond to his exhortation to "Ride now! Ride for ruin ... [for] Death!" as one, screaming "Death!" as they descend upon Mordor's armies. The significance of their battle cry can only be fully appreciated in the light of an earlier exchange at the mustering of the Rohirrim, when a captain observes that "too few have come. We cannot defeat the armies of Mordor." "No," responds Théoden, "we cannot; but we will meet them nonetheless." Even at the moment of his death, Théoden remains the Anglo-Saxon hero and king, responding to Eowyn's desperate assertion that "I am going to save you" with "You already did." The possibility of failure and ultimate destruction only hardens the resolve of these Northern heroes: it is what they expected all along.

While Jackson has preserved Tolkien's "recovery" of medieval heroic archetypes and his Northern theory of courage in good measure, his films are still severely criticized for obvious departures from his source text in individual characterization. Such, Valente (35) observes, "highlight divergences between the book and the film, particularly the elimination of pre-modern 'sensibilities': the toning down of majesty, the appearance of angst, the elimination of higher powers, and the downplaying of ambivalence about victory." Again, I would argue, this is a necessary result of re-interpreting Tolkien's epic for an audience fifty years removed from its original readers: Jackson has simply made the medieval archetypes more accessible to contemporary viewers.

The most obvious result of Jackson's re-characterization is the conversion of Tolkien's *H*eroes into *h*eroes, which, while on the one hand losing Tolkien's medieval sense of epic, does emphasize his message that diminished modern man can aspire to greatness and "change the course of the future." True, the Aragorn of the screen first appears as a "mere ranger." Angst-ridden, he mourns his past at the shards of Narsil and his mother's tomb. He tries to avoid his destiny as king repeatedly and even appears reluctant as he takes a deep breath at his coronation. Unsure of his worth, he rejects Arwen and doubts himself. By no means is this Tolkien's hero, who never once shies at taking the paths of the dead, and is hailed openly in Rivendell as Isildur's heir and one of the Dunedain. As early as Bree, Tolkien's Aragorn appears kingly and bears the broken Narsil, anticipating its re-forging. Except for the brief scene on Weathertop and a passing hint in the director's cut at Eowyn's bedside, Jackson omits all suggestion of Aragorn's ancestral, semi-divine healing powers, a right of kingship and of blood. Thus, Tolkien's decisive, epic figure becomes almost as unlikely and reluctant a hero as Frodo. Similarly, Faramir agonizes over his father's mistreatment of him and nearly succumbs to the Ring's temptation; Théoden and Treebeard initially decline involvement in the battles at Gondor and Isengard, respectively; and Frodo briefly rejects Sam's word for Gollum's. All these moments of weakness and self-doubt are absent from the original tale.

These changes in characterization serve to suggest modern self-doubt and angst, perhaps even to intimate that true heroism is no longer possible and thus to support Valente's contention (38) that "Jackson's work ... lacks. .a sense of *majesty*." On the other hand, I would submit that this is merely Jackson making that heroism accessible to his viewers, for, as Driver and Ray (4) note, to reach "a contemporary audience, film must reinvent the Middle Ages and create in the medieval hero a hodgepodge of traits derived from a mixed understanding of what is medieval and traits that we value in the heroes of postmillennial Western culture." It is in the contrasts to the heroic that the possibility of the heroic stands out best. For example, if Théoden had not asked why Rohan should go to Gondor's aid when Gondor had not come in his time of need, would his decision to answer the call be nearly as dramatic, or as heroic? "Gondor calls for aid," gasps Aragorn. During the following silence, the camera pans the unsure faces awaiting his response. Théoden's sudden "And Rohan will answer!" then puts all doubt in his heroism to rest, more so because he has, in the modern mind, good reason not to. Just so, the Ents' initial refusal to help only highlights their sense of righteous indignation and duty when they reconsider after seeing Saruman's destruction of the forests. It may be, as Treebeard observes, that they "go to our doom ... the last March of the Ents," but their courage stands out the clearer for the initial observation that it is not, after all, the Ents' war.

Indeed, other changes so often criticized as unfaithful to Tolkien ultimately remain true to his vision. Valente (38) observes that, "though Jackson alters the narrative to have Frodo (briefly) trust Smeagol over Sam — who undercuts Tolkien's portrayal of perfect friendship — the characterization of Smeagol/Gollum and the insistence on mercy is a highlight of the film." That insistence on mercy is, in fact, Tolkien's own. I would also disagree that the scene "undercuts" the portrayal of friendship. As with our reluctant heroes, Sam's return to Frodo *after* being unfairly accused highlights the depth of his affection and loyalty, while it simultaneously emphasizes Frodo's desperation and his growing possession by the Ring. So, too, with Arwen's active participation, for the courtly mistress's steadfastness and devotion while the hero completes his quest are difficult to depict in *absence* on the screen. To understand the love of a woman who gives up immortality for her lover, to perceive her unwavering belief in his mission to restore the land, one must see her. Moreover, that Jackson's Arwen appears as a warrior princess is not so far removed from her original, given the power of Tolkien's elfin females: after all, she *is* Galadriel's granddaughter.

What, then, would Tolkien think of Jackson's film adaptation? Certainly, he would have appreciated the grand-scale battle scenes, the courtliness of Aragorn and Arwen's love (despite Arwen's transformation), the Anglo-Saxon courage in the face of certain doom at Helm's Deep, Minas Tirith, and before the walls of Mordor. Would he have accepted that as fair exchange for the secularization of his tale, so that only those seeking the spiritual nature of it would find it? For the introduction of doubt and angst into the heroic? For the reduction of the medieval grandeur, majesty, and heroism he so painstakingly evinced? Of course, we cannot answer. Perhaps he would consider more important the preservation of his belief that "even the smallest of us" can — and should — make a difference, in an age where the heroic is generally believed to be dead. In Jackson's denying absolute heroism in his late 20th-century heroes, he has ironically allowed us to feel we might just have a chance to become so ourselves. He has preserved Tolkien's desire and formula for regaining greatness, beauty, heroism, if not his complete recipe, and he has done it in the language of his own art. In the end, to love both Tolkien's saga and Jackson's films diminishes neither, as long as one recognizes the difference.

Works Cited

Chatman, Seymour. "What Novels Can Do That Films Can't (and Vice Versa)" *Film Theory and Criticism*. Edited by Leo Braudy and Marshall Cohen. New York: Oxford University Press, 1999.

Driver, Martha W. "What's Accuracy Got to Do with It?" *The Medieval Hero on Film*. Edited by Martha W. Driver and Sid Ray. Jefferson, NC: McFarland, 2004.

_____, and Sid Ray. "Hollywood Knights." *The Medieval Hero on Film*. Edited by Martha W. Driver and Sid Ray. Jefferson, N.C.: McFarland, 2004.

Giannetti, Louis. *Understanding Movies*. 10th ed. Upper Saddle River, NJ: Prentice-Hall, 2005.

Harty, Kevin J. *The Reel Middle Ages*. Jefferson, N.C.: McFarland, 1999.

Metz, Christian. "Some Points in the Semiotics of the Cinema." *Film Theory and Criticism*. Edited by Leo Braudy and Marshall Cohen. New York: Oxford University Press, 1999.

Prince, Stephen. "The Discourse of Pictures: Iconicity and Film Studies." *Film Theory and Criticism*. Edited by Leo Braudy and Marshall Cohen. New York: Oxford University Press, 1999.

Silby, Brian. *The Lord of the Rings: The Making of the Movie Trilogy*. New York: Houghton Mifflin, 2002.

Tolkien, J.R.R. *The Lord of the Rings*. 1954–55. Reprinted, New York: Ballantine, 1965.

_____. "The Monsters and the Critics." *The Monsters and the Critics and Other Essays*. London: HarperCollins, 1997.

_____. "On Faerie Stories." *The Monsters and the Critics and Other Essays*. London: HarperCollins, 1997.

Valente, Claire. "Translating Tolkien's Epic: Peter Jackson's *Lord of the Rings*." *The Intercollegiate Review* 40:1 (Fall-Winter 2004): 35–43.

"'Tree and flower, leaf and grass': The Grammar of Middle-earth in The Lord of the Rings"

ROBIN ANNE REID

In a letter to Miss Beare, dated October 14, 1958, J.R.R. Tolkien writes, "I do not know the details of clothing. I visualize with great clarity and detail scenery and 'natural' objects, but not artifacts" (280). While the author's stated intention cannot be the final or sole authority on the meaning of a work of literature, additional evidence for the extent to which Tolkien visualized Middle-earth exists in the superb collection of his paintings by Hammond & Scull. From an analytical point of view, the importance of the natural world, of Middle-earth, in Tolkien's legendarium cannot be doubted. Given how the implied author of *The Lord of the Rings* devoted a great amount of text to loving and specific descriptions of the world (arguably much more than on descriptions of characters or most of the man-made settings), few would argue against the claim that Middle-earth is not a setting serving only as the backdrop to events but a character with symbolic and thematic importance in the novel.

The construction of Middle-earth in Peter Jackson's live-action film is perhaps the least-criticized aspect of his film. I use the term "criticized" in both its popular and academic meaning: critics and scholars who dislike other elements of the film often start their evaluations by admitting that the beauty of New Zealand–Middle-earth is perhaps the film's most successful aspect. However, little or no analytical work exists analyzing how that beauty was constructed on the screen. The unstated assumption seems to be that Jackson was sufficiently lucky or smart to choose to film in a naturally beautiful setting, rather than acknowledging the extent to which Jackson the director chose to construct a Middle-earth that, I would argue, resonates with Tolkien's.

A close reading of Jackson's cinematography as it regards Middle-earth provides ample evidence that the cinematic narrator does an excellent job of conveying in the film much of what Tolkien's implied author does in the novel, allowing for differences in media. The term cinematic narrator is drawn from Seymour Chatman, who argues that it is possible to adapt Wayne Booth's narrative theory to film. In *The Rhetoric of Fiction*, Booth argues that it is not only possible but necessary in literary criticism to distinguish between the historical or real author of a text and the implied author which is a constructed persona, a limited and perhaps idealized aspect of the real author. The cinematic narrator, according to Chatman, is equivalent to Booth's implied author, a construct differing from the real director. Chatman argues for a constructed cinematic agency that synthesizes all creative, production, and cinematic decisions reflected in the auditory and visual as well as narrative components of a film. This agency, which he calls the cinematic narrator, bears the same relationship to the actual people making the film as Booth's implied author does to the historical author. In evaluating the quality and meaning of the cinematic narrator's style of filming Middle-earth, I would argue that (apart from two exceptions which I will discuss below) the aesthetics of this element of the film version of *The Lord of the Rings* both mirror and equal the implied narrator's stylistic choices in the book.

In order to make this argument, my methodology is interdisciplinary, drawn from both film studies and linguistics. Since a large number of films are adapted from some other narrative work, film scholarship has developed a large body of theories and methods of analyzing adaptations of novels and other narratives into films. Karen Kline presents four paradigms that differ in the degree of importance to which each assigns the novel in relation to the film. The translation paradigm is most familiar to readers of both critical reviews and academic scholarship. Logically, for many, the first question asked of a film adaptation is how good a job the film does of translating the book. Film scholars have long argued that using only the translation paradigm and privileging literary elements over film elements tends to result in the same argument — that films are not as good as books — being made over and over again, with varying details. Most scholarship done on Jackson's film so far has fallen clearly into the translation paradigm and answers the question of how faithful Jackson's film is to Tolkien's 1200 page book with a resounding "not very." The scholarship, produced primarily by literature scholars, tends to focus on the elements of character and plot, as well as overall themes. A few essays by scholars in other disciplines (linguistics, film, religious studies) and by creative writers present more positive evaluations of the film because the authors consider different questions and analyze different elements.[1]

The translation paradigm is a valid approach to a film adaptation, but I share the sense of film scholars that it may be limited. One set of limits involves analyzing only the literary elements of the film (character and plot and theme) while ignoring cinematic elements (such as cinematography, music, light design, sound effects). Even if the translation paradigm is chosen as the primary focus, I believe that critical ground must exist between the two extremes of the evaluative argument which states that the films must either be seen as a "worthy rendition of J.R.R. Tolkien's novel into a different medium, or a travesty divorced from their claimed source" (Bratman 27).

In this paper, I first analyze Tolkien's work, his style, which has been overlooked or disparaged by a number of literary critics. Second, I compare Tolkien's style of writing to Jackson's style of cinematography. The question of Tolkien's style has not been considered as a major focus for comparative analysis in scholarship on Jackson's film. This lack may seem natural given the extent to which textual and visual media differ in modes of narrative production and reception. However, I argue that an analysis of Tolkien's style in selected passages can be usefully compared to Jackson's style in the equivalent scenes from *The Lord of the Rings*. The necessity of choosing equivalent scenes means I could not consider some book scenes and characters, notably the Old Forest, Tom Bombadil, and the barrows. Most of the film's scenes I chose are directly equivalent to the book scenes, and the film scene often has the same title as the book chapter.

There are only two, perhaps three, exceptions to this rule: in the case of *The Return of the King*, where the book has fewer passages focusing on the description of the natural world, I have taken some liberty with choices to highlight what I found was a shift in the patterns of agency and verbal processes in the novel, choosing scenes from the third film that can be argued are translations, showing similar themes through different narrative means.

The work I do with Tolkien falls under the broad category of stylistics; however, that term can refer to different methods in different areas of literary, linguistic, and composition scholarship. My method draws upon linguistic methodology created by M.A.K. Halliday and theorized by Roger Fowler in *Linguistic Criticism*. Fowler argues that the problem with much discussion of style by literary methods is the lack of a consistent methodology; that problem can be solved by drawing upon linguistic methodology.

One of the earliest essays on Tolkien's style, the essay by Burton Raffel that appeared in the first U.S. anthology on Tolkien's work, is an example of the problems of stylistic analysis unaccompanied by a consistent methodology. Raffel argues Tolkien's work cannot be considered literature (a claim many today would contest) primarily because of his style. Raffel's main point concerning Tolkien's prose style bears consideration for its lack of specificity and overabundance of subjectivity: "Tolkien's prose is brilliantly adequate, straightforward, just starched enough to have body, resilient enough to catch the echoes of speech, not a supercharged instrument, nor one with great range, but very competent" (220). The essay is even more dismissive of Tolkien's poetry. Raffel fails to provide criteria he believes define literature; instead, he lists perhaps a half dozen canonical works. Since Tolkien's style is not the same as the style in these works (although arguably their styles are not similar to each other's since the list includes *The Iliad*, *Paradise Lost*, and *The Great Gatsby*), Raffel concludes that *The Lord of the Rings* is not literature. Raffel offers no systematic evaluation of Tolkien's writing choices: the essay reads as a series of complaints about the lack of specificity of some of Tolkien's descriptions and word choices. I spend time on Raffel's argument because a number of the essays most negative about the film focus on the extent to which Tolkien's grand or epic style is lost in what is called the banality of an action film whereas more positive essays about the film emphasize how the important story elements survive. In this context, it is useful to remember literary critics who find Tolkien's style to be second-rate at best do exist.

While Raffel's essay, published in 1968, may be considered dated, no thorough stylistic analysis has confirmed or replaced it. Michael Drout noted in 2004 that Tolkien's style has "seldom been analyzed in terms of specific aesthetic effects," and that this "neglect ... has had the unfortunate effect of ceding important ground to Tolkien's detractors, who, with simple unanalyzed quotations, point to some work or turn of phrase and, in essence, sniff that such is not the stuff of good literature" (137). Only recently have scholars begun to counter the early dismissal. Shippey's argument in *Author of the Century* addresses the common criticism that Tolkien's style is uneven, arguing that the "clash of styles" was not only intentional but an artistic achievement that only someone trained in philology and the history and development of English could create (39). Shippey provides a valuable counter-balance to contemporary critics' commentary on Tolkien's style but does not deal in depth with specific evidence or sustained analysis although his work sets up a valuable foundation for later.

Drout's essay, published in the 2004 *Tolkien Studies*, provides just what Fowler called for: close and in-depth analysis of specific stylistic choices, melding linguistic methodology as well as situating Tolkien's text in the context of canonical literary sources (in this case, Shakespeare) which allows for a discussion of comparative aesthetics. Drout chooses two passages so he can deal with them systematically and in detail. Focusing on Éowyn's fight against the Nazgûl and Denethor's self-chosen death, Drout uses Halliday's methods to describe the style and then explore the intertextual parallels with *King Lear*, concluding that "it becomes clear that Tolkien's deliberate stylistic construct is in fact remarkably rich and successful not only in his own terms but also in terms of the stylistic canons of Modernist Literature in which, supposedly, form follows function" (154–5).

I rely on Halliday's linguistic grammar as the basis for the methodology of this study although my comparison is with Jackson's cinematography rather than Shakespeare's language. Linguists approach language descriptively rather than prescriptively, viewing language as a set of systems, and do not value any style as inherently better or worse than any other. One of the assumptions, often unstated, of much literary scholarship such as Raffel's is that literary style is markedly different from and superior to other styles of writing as well as from everyday speech. I share with linguists the sense that this assumption is problematic and unproven since academics that use the structuralist and aesthetic approach rarely if ever provide evidence for the superiority of the literary style or even a definition of it which has been assumed to be self-evident. Linguistic methodology does not contradict the notion of a range of registers and styles of discourse; it simply refuses to set any aside any single one, such as literary style, as superior to any other upon a structural basis. Halliday's linguistic grammar provides both a systematic method and criteria by which style may be analyzed.

Halliday's text, which explains his grammatical system, offers the model of functional grammar which can be applied to texts, word by word, clause by clause, to generate an analysis of selected text based on quantification. Halliday's functional grammar is a conceptual framework that focuses on how language is used; it can be applied to any text (verbal or written) in modern English. Functional grammars are generative rather than structuralist (drawing on actual utterances and texts and grounded in rhetoric and ethnography); a functional grammar does not seek a universal structure underlying language nor does it attempt to prescribe the best usages of language, being descriptive rather than prescriptive. By developing a system of grammar that allows a reader to generate specific descriptions of how clauses in a selected text construct meaning to support an interpretation, Halliday's functional grammar can be used in a variety of disciplines, for a variety of purposes. While the grammar uses some traditional prescriptive grammar terms in a few areas, it mostly relies upon its own extensive terminology. Much of my analysis will be familiar to anyone who can identify the grammatical subject of a clause, but my discussion of verbal processes draws on Halliday's categories for processes (verbs). The three main categories are material (the physical world), mental (the world of consciousness), and relational (the world of abstract relations). He also identifies sub-categories that exist on the borders of the three main ones: behavioral (behaving), verbal (saying), and existential (existing). Finally, one group that exists between the material and existential processes is important for my analysis: the meteorological processes (Halliday 106–107, 144). A stylistic analysis of a large text such as *The Lord of the Rings* is rarely undertaken because of the amount of evidence generated by the method. But, as Treebeard would say, anything worth saying is worth "taking a long time to say" (454).

In this project, I am using Halliday's functional grammar to analyze two aspects of Tolkien's style in selected passages of *The Lord of the Rings*: agency and verbal processes. The evidence generated from my Hallidayan analysis of theme, subject and agent and verbal processes of selected passages from *The Lord of the Rings* is summarized in the appendices and the tables of this essay. My analysis supports the extent to which Tolkien's grammar constructs Middle-earth as having agency which is shown in a marked pattern in choices made for the themes and grammatical subjects of clauses. In Halliday's terminology, the theme of the clause consists of the words at the beginning of the clause, ending with the main verb or, when the theme is not the subject, with the grammatical subject. My analysis shows the extent to which the themes and grammatical subjects of clauses as well as verbal processes serve to foreground the agency of the natural world as equal to or greater than the agency of human subjects.

Since my focus is the construction of Middle-earth through style and cinematography, my selected passages describe parts of Middle-earth as do the equivalent scenes in the films.[2] I have focused primarily on locations without constructions built by humans or hobbits; the selected passages are mostly told from the point of view of the detached or objective narrator, focusing on describing parts of Middle-earth. The narrative voices in the novel are extremely complex, multi-layered, and deserve much more attention than I can give them in this limited space. For this project, most of my passages included an external focus on details and the ongoing use of "they" rather than a single point of view character reacting to or reflecting upon what he sees. In the last set of passages, Pippin is foregrounded in the first passage, Sam in the second, and to a great extent Aragorn (guided by Gandalf) in the third.

In modern English, agency is primarily constructed through the grammatical subjects of the clauses. In English, word order plays an important part in meaning, and the majority of clauses have a subject-verb-object (SVO) structure,[3] and the majority of clauses default to the subject of the clause as bearing agency or authority. The default assumption that subjects have agency means that the presumption of agency often carries over to non-human subjects, even objects in nature. Subjects of certain verbal processes related to weather are a separate category in Halliday's analysis because they are unique in English being material processes without a clear agent. In English, for example, we can say, "It is sunny," which has a process but no agent, or we can say, "The sun shines," which seems to indicate the sun as actor (logical subject) as well as the grammatical subject. The high percentage of clauses with meteorological and material processes in my selected passages supports a reading the animism of Middle-earth which constructs the natural world itself as having agency.

The unmarked or default pattern in the majority of English clauses is for the theme (the language that begins the clause) and the grammatical subject to consist of the same word or phrase. As Halliday notes, the majority of subjects-agents of clauses will be humans or related to us because our language focuses around ourselves and our activities. While the clauses in my selected passages do follow the default in terms of 84 percent of the clauses having themes which are also the grammatical subjects, the percentage of grammatical subjects (whether in the theme or following it) that relate to Middle-earth is marked. Of 169 total clauses, 105 (62 percent) have grammatical subjects that are related to Middle-earth. The grammatical subjects of the majority of clauses tend to be aspects of Middle-earth rather than the human, hobbit, man, Elf, or Dwarf characters. For the most part, nouns or pronouns referring to the Fellowship are grammatically submerged within Middle-earth, either through being a subject but not a theme, or through being placed in dependent clauses.

Summary of Grammatical Subjects[4]

Passages	Middle-earth	Characters	Marked
Summary	*Themes/Subjects/Agents*		
FotR	10	4	2
TTT	32	3	3
RotK	8	4	1
Summary	*Subjects (not Themes)*		
FotR	19	16	1
TTT	21	13	1
RotK	15	13	3
Totals	**105**	**53**	**11**

The effect on readers, though few would notice it consciously when caught up in the story, is that the characters are not as important as the world in these passages. Other parts of the clauses (deictics, which are indicators of space and time) and circumstances (time, location, etc.) are framed within a natural setting: compass directions, the time based on day and night, light and dark, and on the distance between locations based on the perspective of people walking through the world. Readers have often spoken of being transported to Middle-earth, a claim stigmatized by critics as escapism, but Tolkien's style clearly works to embed readers in the world.

Finally, the verbal processes of many of the clauses with Middle-earth subjects not only include a number of the meteorological processes, using various "to be" forms, but also a number of material processes. Of 169 verbal
processes, only 47 are material processes, relating to the Fellowship's actions.
Of the remaining verbal processes, 53 are existential (involving some form
of "to be" verb describing meteorological or natural processes, such as "The
sun was shining," "The day was drawing to a close," "The air was warm").
Another 50 are material processes in clauses with grammatical subjects
relating to Middle-earth: "the outflung arm of the mountains marched," "the
pent waters spread out," "day leaped," "the boles of the trees glowed," "flies
… buzzed and stung," "clouds of hungry midges danced and reeled." The
clear default for the grammar of Tolkien's passages relating to Middle-earth
makes clear the extent to which the natural world is given agency and
authority through the grammatical subjects and verbal processes of a majority of the clauses.

An examination of the equivalent scenes in the film shows what I am
calling a similar grammar in the cinematic narrator's cinematography. The
camera angles, movements, and focus parallel the grammar of Tolkien's
clauses. Shots ranging from a few seconds long to over a minute start with
close-up or medium shots focusing centrally on one or more characters'
faces or figures then zoom back into long shots where the figures of the Fellowship gradually become smaller and smaller, eventually disappearing
within the landscape. The cinematography creates the sensation of characters being submerged within Middle-earth. In a number of instances, the
members of the Fellowship are filmed moving from one side of the screen
to the other as they walk across the land (rather than the camera focusing
on moving characters and tracking them). The impression is that Middle-
earth is the focus of those shots as well. These patterns are most prevalent
in *The Fellowship of the Ring* (book and film) and *The Two Towers* (book
and film). I found a marked difference in *The Return of the King* (book)
which required different choices of scenes. My review of the third volume
revealed relatively little sustained description compared to the first two volumes, and what description does exist comes primarily in short one to two
sentence long passages. This shift in narrative perspective was marked
enough to become a part of my analysis and a reason for selecting two passages from book and film that are not clear equivalents: the lighting of the
beacons, which is moved into a detached cinematic narrative perspective in
the film in a scene lasting over a minute rather than being seen by Pippin
and Gandalf as they travel to Minas Tirith, and Gandalf and Aragorn's surveying of the lands of Gondor from Mount Mindolluin which is translated
in Scene 58 where the camera zooms back from a close-up on Frodo's face
at Minas Tirith and dissolves into a view of the map of Middle-earth. I

argue that my stylistic analysis, detailed below, of the scene with Aragorn and Gandalf reveals a shift in the novel's focus to the Age of Man as wizard and king survey the lands from a high mountain. Agency in this passage rests with the characters who are observing the land. The marked contrast in that last volume can be seen only in contrast to earlier passages in which the narrative perspective and sense of agency is different.

In *The Fellowship of the Ring*, passages set in the Wilderness outside Bree, outside Moria and Lothlórien, and on the Great River, contain a total of 52 clauses. Of those 52 clauses, 29 have grammatical subjects which are parts of Middle-earth; only 20 have subjects relating to one or more members of the Fellowship. Two of the subjects cannot clearly be identified as either the characters or Middle-earth: "sight" and "their path." I do not read "path" in this clause as a literal path, but as the direction or way the Elves led the Fellowship through Lothlórien. These two subjects combine character and land, in one case, the Misty Mountains "receded endlessly as far as sight could reach," and in another "their paths now went into thickets." In both cases, the nouns reference the Fellowship's sight and path (direction) but in such a way that Middle-earth still seems to be the central focus. They are seeing the mountains; they are making their way through thickets.

The cinematography of the equivalent scenes in the film conveys a similar sense of the characters being submerged within the landscape. The 44 second shot in Scene 13 begins with a high angle, long shot of the country-side outside Bree, on a sunny day. A tree is just off-center. The small figure of Strider appears, the Hobbits following him, and they move across the screen. A quick cut shows a close-up of the Nazgûl riding along a road, a clearly marked road, unlike the trackless Wild into which Strider leads the hobbits. After a cut to a medium shot of Aragorn with hobbits behind him, and two close-ups of Aragorn's feet, walking, and one close-up of Frodo, the camera zooms back, keeping the group roughly in the middle of the shot, but growing smaller and smaller, with the focus moving to show the plan, woods, mountains, and sky. In the seven second clip from Scene 27, the camera moves from an eye level, extreme close-up shot of Gandalf's face as he looks at Moria, to a low-angle and long shot at a very steep angle up the mountain. A broken bridge soars overhead, foreshadowing the breaking of the Bridge of Khazad-dûm. Another eye-level shot puts Gimli's face in the center of the screen as he looks at Moria, and then there is a cut to the Fellowship (entering screen left) walking along the narrow beach between the pool and the Wall of Moria. After a close-up on Frodo's feet, showing him slipping into water, there is a cut to a medium shot as the Fellowship walks in front of the wall, across the water. The wall, the light, and the water are all gray and shadowy, and the Fellowship blends into the background like shadows walking.

Leaving Moria, in the 12 seconds in Scene 30, there are strong differences in the effect of the cinematography and lighting despite commonalities in setting. The light is a definite contrast to the darkness of the night they entered Moria; the sunlight, white rocks, and snow are almost blinding after the darkness of the Mines. The long shot, high angle, is looking down at the rock walls, and Gates, as the Fellowship flees after Gandalf's fall. The camera tracks them as they run onto open ground, from a long shot. After shots of members of the Fellowship grieving, the Company begins to move to the next stage of their journey. The camera moves from Aragorn running to a shot from behind him, eye-level, with his head nearly in the center but looking out over a long view of water, woods, and hills which will lead to Lothlórien. In the later, six second shot, a long shot at eye level, the Fellowship is shown running across grass into the woods, with Legolas at the center of the screen (the camera following his movement, keeping him in the center of the shot in the same way that Gimli was centered in the shot outside Moria). Entering the woods, the long shot of the Fellowship in the center then tilts up to focus on trees and sky above them.

In scene 35, in two scenes (the first 69 seconds long, the second 15), the journey down Anduin is shown, starting with an extremely high angle shot (an aerial shot from a helicopter, as many in this sequence are). Most of the journey on the River is shown through such shots, showing through a variety of landscapes, although there are brief cuts between the aerial shots from above and eye level shots of what they are seeing on the River. The second scene begins with an eye level shot of the Argonath, then the camera pans left to show an extreme long shot of the water, and the three peaks of Rauros. The camera travels over the Fellowship, shooting from behind then crossing over to shoot them from in front. The last shot of the scene is the waterfall.

The grammar and the cinematography of *The Two Towers* are similar to *The Fellowship of the Ring,* with the exception of the scenes in Ithilien. The selected passages have 72 clauses; 53 of those clauses have grammatical subjects relating to Middle-earth, and only 16 relating to the characters. Four marked subjects are different in reference, from a reference to a day, to empty subjects ('nothing," "no sight," "there") which do not clearly refer to either characters or Middle-earth.

The structure of the book and film do not correlate since Jackson chose to intercut the narratives from Books III and IV. However, the effect of characters submerged within Middle-earth continues in the scenes shot in Rohan, Fangorn, and the Dead Marshes. Several shots from two scenes (4 and 7) show the pursuit of the orcs across Emyn Muil and into Rohan. Three shots—65 seconds, 5 seconds, and 6 seconds—in scene 4, and a 22 second shot in scene 7 show strikingly similar patterns. All rely heavily upon aerial shots, the camera moving around and over the running figures, with the main focus primarily on the land, the hills, the river, mountains, and then to the plains. Few shots center on the characters, either full-face or full-body; they are small, with the camera pulling back, or stand with their backs to the camera so the audience shares their view of the land that lies ahead. Similar movements occur in the 12 second shot in Scene 11 where Merry and Pippin enter Fangorn forest — the woods are dark, and there's a medium shot, eye level of the two hobbits running into the woods, behind trees, through mist. When they finally sit, the camera cuts to a zoom, pulling back, leaving the hobbits center screen but small amidst the trees of Fangorn. The opening of this scene is much darker (and Treebeard much more threatening) than in the novel, but this shot and others do show the overwhelming weight which I would argue is part of Tolkien's construction of the forest.

Not all of Tolkien's description shows beauty; the Dead Marshes, even more than Fangorn, are a threatening place, nearly drained of life because of the malign influence of Mordor. Frodo and Sam follow Gollum into the Dead Marshes in Scene 12. The 77 second sequence opens with Frodo and Sam standing, Gollum crouching, and the full-figure shot of Gollum is from the two hobbits' point of view The next shot cuts to a long shot of the marshes, featuring pools, dead trees, grasses, and a cloudy sky. The cut to an aerial shot of the marshes alone, no hobbits visible, involves a slow movement of the camera across "miles and miles" to show the mountains on the border of Mordor. Then a cut to a medium shot of the hobbits traveling, through pools and flames, small and lost in the deadly landscape.

I would argue that the cinematography in all the scenes up to this point mirrors the style of the novel. The exception is the construction of Ithilien. I evaluate the entrance of Frodo, Sam and Gollum into Ithilien as the least effective of my selected passages in conveying the sense of the land. Ithilien is important because it is the outpost of Gondor most recently lost to Mordor, one still resisting, both in the presence of the Rangers and in the "dryad loveliness" that has not yet been corrupted to the sickly growth of the marshes or the brambles of the Morgai. All of the grammatical subjects in the description of Ithilien are either Ithilien itself or the plants which grow there; the lushness of the prose mirrors the beauty and life of the land. The hobbits perceive both beauty and danger in Ithilien, taking cover in a thicket, before they are discovered the Rangers. The film is perfunctory in its construction of Ithilien compared to earlier scenes. The opening shots in "Of Herbs and Stewed Rabbit" are a brief introductory 3 seconds, then a longer sequence as Frodo and Sam watch the battle (1.53), but there are no shots that focus primarily on the land of Ithilien. All the shots have a figure as the central focus (either faces or bodies or groups), so the land becomes simply the backdrop.

Finding sustained descriptions of Middle-earth in *The Return of the King* is difficult and the equivalent scenes are harder to pair. The passages I chose are Pippin and Gandalf riding into Gondor (excluding their dialogue), Frodo and Sam in the Morgai, and Aragorn and Gandalf on Mount Mindolluin. The most detailed descriptions of the land occur in Book VI, as Frodo and Sam struggle to cross the wastes of Mordor. In those sections, book and film were again equivalent. The implied author's focus shifts markedly in *The Return of the King*, Book V, and the passage that is markedly different in pattern than the earlier ones is the journey by Gandalf and Aragorn up Mount Mindolluin to discover the sapling of the White Tree. When they stand and look out over Gondor, the majority of the clauses construct the characters as the grammatical subjects and as the actors surveying the land, as a king, or a mapmaker, would.

The selected passages from *The Return of the King* contain 44 clauses. Of those 44, 23 of the clauses have grammatical subjects that are part of Middle-earth, and 17 have subjects that are members of the Fellowship. The four marked subjects are time ("the night"), a reference to "the dark journey" and "their sight" and the deictic, "and beyond that." The equivalent of the first scene in Book V of *The Return of the King* requires consideration of two scenes from the film: Scene 9 (81 seconds) follows Gandalf and Pippin as they ride Shadowfax to Gondor. The shots all tend to start with long and high angle shots of different parts of the countryside (hilly country, deep woods, crossing a river, then across a plain climbing a hill from which they can see Minas Tirith). The camera zooms in and out, from long shots to close ups on feet and legs (primarily Shadowfax' hooves), as they ride across the screen, the changing land showing the length of their journey behind and around them. The final shot is of Shadowfax climbing a hill, the camera moving behind the two riders to show the Tower of Ecthelion appearing over the crest of the hill, then cutting to a front shot of Gandalf and Pippin at the top of the hill (foreshadowing the entrance of the Riders of Rohan) against a backdrop of mountains, in full daylight. The cinematography in this scene creates a much more detailed sense of the land of Gondor than is the case in the book, with Pippin's point of view being foregrounded.

Scene 14, "The Lighting of the Beacons," is 98 seconds long, one of the longest of my selected shots, with minimal human presence (just the men lighting the first beacon). This scene, although equivalent in content to the book scene (the beacons are lit to summon Rohan), is dramatically different. Rather than Pippin seeing the lights from afar, fearing dragons, and being reassured by Gandalf, the audience watches as beacon after beacon is lit, the camera moving across the countryside. Scene 14 starts with Gandalf naming the first beacon (Amon Din), then moves into a lengthy sequence where aerial shots from the air, moving around and over individual mountains, and across a number of ranges, focus entirely on the lighting of beacons, moving across the countryside between Minas Tirith and Rohan. The lighting changes from daylight, to night, to sunrise, as the message for aid moves across Middle-earth. The stunning shots of high mountains, with snow, above clouds and valleys, is a tour de force, ending with a scene in which Aragorn seated off to the right, small against a building, is eating (as the guards were in Minas Tirith), and the beacon is still the central focus. Here, I would argue, the film exceeds the impact of the novel because of the cinematic narrator's ability to move away from a single character's point of view to dramatize the event. The focus of the scene shifts to the mountains of Middle-earth.

Two scenes from the film, one from *The Two Towers*, show Frodo and Sam's approach to Mordor through the Morgai. Scene 52 is the last shot of *The Two Towers*, and is 13 seconds long, consisting of a high angle shot of Frodo and Sam following Gollum through woods. The tree looks dry and dead. The camera moves up, losing focus on hobbits and pans over the dead forest. Then, starting from the foot of the mountain range, it moves up the stony, rocky, barren heights, to the top, ending with a shot of Mordor, the fiery mountain, Barad-Dûr, and a Nazgûl flying. In Scene 47 of *The Return of the King* titled "The Land of Shadow," a 68 second scene shows Frodo and Sam moving across the utterly dead land of Mordor. The scene opens with an eye level shot in which the audience's view of the hobbits is obscured by huge rocks and vents of steam. They cannot be fully seen as they move from left to right. No growing thing can be seen in this barren land. That shot dissolves into a low angle shot from ground level as they continue to trudge across screen, moving slowly, more wearily than before. A cut to a shot from behind them, the camera on boom moving up for high angle shot that moves away from the hobbits entirely to focus on what they see direction: Orodruin and Barad-Dûr, with lightning and fires.

In the passage in Book V which describes Aragorn and Gandalf on Mount Mindolluin, the construction of agency shifts abruptly. Only one of the themes in this passage is a grammatical subject. The majority of themes are conjunctions which act to show a relationship between clauses; the clauses are punctuated primarily as simple sentences, with relationships shown by conjunctions (fourteen of the seventeen clauses have themes which are a conjunction or a subordinating word). Only six grammatical subjects refer to Middle-earth; the others are all Gandalf, Aragorn, or the kings. Agency is overwhelmingly given to the characters rather than to Middle-earth. The sense of observers surveying, or mapping, the world was so clear after my analysis that I decided this scene can be seen as equivalent to the 78 second Scene 58. That shot starts with a close up of Frodo's face, pulls back, then dissolves into an aerial shot of Minas Tirith then dissolves into the map, tracking back across the map to show Frodo's and the Fellowship's journey in reverse: Minas Tirith, Rohan, Helm's Deep, Edoras, Fangorn, Isengard, Lothlórien, Moria, Rivendell, Weathertop, Bree, and to the Shire, dissolving to a medium shot of the hobbits, on ponies, returning to the Shire. The content is different, the book scene focusing on Aragorn's view of his kingdom, the film scene on the ending of the Fellowship and the return to the Shire, but in both cases the subordination of Middle-earth to the characters is conveyed. A possible interpretation of the shift in style of the book which is reflected, to some extent, in the film could be that with the beginning of the Fourth Age, the Age of Man, and the leaving of elves from Middle-earth, a shift to the human and Christian perspective of the land occurs. With the passing of the elves from Middle-earth, the animism of the land also passes.

This analysis is but the beginning of work that could be done, both with the novel's grammar and with the film's cinematography. Because of the amount of evidence generated both by a stylistic analysis and an analysis of the cinematography, moving frame by frame through a shot or scene, my project can cover only a few passages in book and film. These passages serve to support the ways in which the implied author and cinematic narrator constructed Middle-earth as agent within two very different texts. I would hope my argument serves to suggest the important of considering more than the literary elements of film (character, plot, theme) in an analysis; ignoring the cinematic elements (camera angles, movements, and sound) that have no parallel in the written text means that scholars are ignoring some of the constitutive elements of the medium. Such an approach means that always, inevitably, the film will be judged as inferior to the book. I do not take the opposite approach (arguing for the superiority of the film); instead, I would argue that in this case, the aesthetics of book and film are equal.

Appendix: LOTR Transcription
Themes; Subjects; Theme/Subjects

I.11 "A Knife in the Dark" (177, 178)

The sun was shining, clear but not too hot. **The woods in the valley** were still leafy and full of color, and seemed peaceful and wholesome. **Strider** guided them confidently among the many crossing paths, **although left to themselves** *they* would soon have been at a loss. *He* was taking a wandering course with many turns and doublings, to put off any pursuit. **Whether because of Strider's skill or for some other reason,** *they* saw no sign and heard no sound of any other living thing all that day: neither two-footed, except birds; nor four-footed, except one fox and a few squirrels. **The next day** *they* began to steer a steady course eastwards; **and still** *all* was quiet and peaceful. **On the third day out from Bree** *they* came out of the Chet-wood. *The land* had been falling steadily, **ever since** *they* turned aside from the Road, **and** *they* now entered a wide flat expanse of country, much more difficult to man-age. *They* were far beyond the borders of the Breeland, out in the pathless wilder-ness, and drawing near to the Midgewater Marshes.

II.4 "A Journey in the Dark" (294)

The day was drawing to its end, **and** *cold stars* were glinting in the sky high above the sunset, **when** *the Company*, with all the speed they could, climbed up the slopes and reached the side of the lake. **In breadth** *it* looked to be no more than two or three furlongs at the widest point. **How far it stretched way southward** *they* could not see in the failing light; **but** *its northern end* was no more than half a mile from where they stood, **and between the stony ridges that enclosed the valley and the water's edge** *there* was a rim of open ground. *They* hurried forward, **for** they had still a mile or two to go **before** *they* could reach the point on the far shore **that** *Gan-dalf* was making for; **and then** *he* still had to find the doors.

II.6 "Lothlórien" (325)

To the east *the outflung arm of the mountains* marched to a sudden end, **and** *far lands* could be descried beyond them, wide and vague. **To the south** *the Misty Mountains* receded endlessly **as far as** *sight* could reach. **Less than a mile away, and a little below them, for** *they* still stood high up on the west side of the dale, ***there*** lay a mere. *It* was long and oval, shaped like a great spear-head thrust deep into the northern glen; **but** *its southern end* was beyond the shadows under the sunlit sky. **Yet** *its* waters were dark; a deep blue like clear evening sky seen from a lamp-lit room. *Its face* was still and unruffled. **About** *it* lay a smooth sward, shelving down on all sides to its bare unbroken rim.

II.7 "The Mirror of Galadriel" (344)

The sun was sinking behind the mountains, **and** *the shadows* were deepening in the woods, **when** *they* went on again. *Their paths* now went into thickets **where** *the dusk* had already gathered. **Night** came beneath the trees as they walked, **and** *the Elves* uncovered their silver lamps.

II.9 "The Great River" (384)

The sun, already long fallen from the noon, was shining in a windy sky. **The pent waters** spread out into a long oval lake, pale Nen Hithoel, fenced by steep grey hills whose sides were clad with trees, **but** *their heads* were bare, cold-gleaming in the sunlight. **At the far southern end** rose *three peaks*. **The midmost** stood some-what forward from the others and sundered from them, an island in the waters, **about which** *the flowing River* flung pale shimmering arms. **Distant but deep** *there* came upon the wind a roaring sound like the roll of thunder heard far away.

3.11 "The Riders of Rohan" (412, 414)

Turning back *they* saw across the River the far hills kindled. **Day** leaped into the sky.

The red rim of the sun rose over the shoulders of the dark land. **Before them in the West** *the world* lay still, formless and grey; **but even as** *they* looked, **the shad-ows of night** melted, **the colours of the waking earth** returned: **green** flowed over the wide meads of Rohan; **the white mists** shimmered in the water-vales; **and far off to the left, thirty leagues or more, blue and purple** stood *the White Mountains*, rising into peaks of jet, tipped with glimmering snows, flushed with the rose of morning. **At the bottom** *they* came with a strange suddenness on the grass of Rohan. *It* swelled like a green sea up to the very foot of the Emyn Muil. *The falling stream* vanished into a deep growth of cresses and water-plants, **and** *they* could hear it tinkling away in green tunnels, down long gentle slopes toward the fens of Entwash Vale far away. *They* seemed to have left winter clinging to the hills behind. Here *the air* was softer and warmer, and faintly scented, **as if** *spring* was already stirring **and** *the sap* was flowing again in herb and leaf. *The sun* climbed to the noon and then rode slowly down the sky. *Light clouds* came up out of the sea in the distant South and were blown away upon the breeze. *The sun* sank.

Shadows rose behind and reached out long arms from the East. **Still** *the hunters* held on.

One day now had passed **since** Boromir fell, **and** the Orcs were yet ahead. No longer could any *sight* of them be seen in the level plains.

3.IV "Treebeard" (451)

They [Pippin and Merry] found it was further than they thought. *The ground* was rising steeply still, **and** *it* [the ground] was becoming increasingly stony. *The light* grew broader **as** *they* went on, **and soon** *they* saw that there was a rock-wall before them; the side of a hill, or the abrupt end of some long root thrust out by the distant mountains. *No trees* grew on it, **and** *the sun* was falling full on its stony face. *The twigs of the trees at its foot* were stretched out stiff and still, **as if** [*they* (the twigs) were] reaching out to the warmth. **Where** *all* had looked so shabby and grey before, **the wood** now gleamed with rich browns, and with the smooth black-greys of bark like polished leather. *The boles of the trees* glowed with a soft green like young grass: early spring or a fleeting vision of it was about them. **In the face of the stony wall** *there* was something like a stair: [*it* was] natural perhaps, and made by the weathering and splitting of the rock, **for** *it* was rough and uneven. **High up, almost level with the tops of forest-trees,** *there* was a shelf under a cliff. *Nothing* grew there but a few grasses and weeds at its edge, and one old stump of a tree with only two bent branches left; *it* looked almost like the figure of some gnarled old man, standing there, blinking in the morning-light.

4.II "The Passage of the Marshes" (612)

It was dreary and wearisome. *Cold clammy winter still* held sway in this forsaken country. *The only green* was the scum of living weed on the dark greasy surfaces of the sullen waters. *Dead grasses and rotting weeds* loomed up in the mists like ragged shadows of long-forgotten summers. As **the day** wore on *the light* increased a little, **and** *the mists* lifted, growing thinner and more transparent. **Far above the rot and vapors of the world** *the Sun* was riding high and golden now in a serene country with floors of dazzling foam, **but only a passing ghost of her** could *they* see below, bleared, pale, giving no color and no warmth. But even at this faint reminder of her presence *Gollum* scowled and flinched. *He* halted their journey, **and** *they* rested, squatting like little hunted animals, in the borders of a great brown reed-thicket. *There* was a deep silence, only scraped on its surfaces by the faint quiver of empty seed-plumes and broken grass-blades trembling in small air-movements **that** *they* could not feel.

4.IV "Of Herbs and Stewed Rabbit" (636)

South and west *it* looked towards the warm lower vales of Anduin, [*it* was] shielded from the east by the *Ephel D?ath* and yet not under the mountain-shadow, [*it* was] protected from the north by the *Emyn Muil*, [*it* was] open to the southern airs and the moist winds from the Sea far away. **Many great trees** grew there, planted long ago, falling into untended age amid a riot of careless descendents; **and groves and thickets** *there* were of tamarisk and pungent terebinth, of olive and of bay, **and** *there* were junipers and myrtles and thymes that grew in bushes, or with their woody creeping stems mantled in deep tapestries the hidden stones; *[there* were] sages of many kinds putting forth blue flowers or red, or pale green; and marjorams and new-sprouting parsleys, and many herbs of forms and scents beyond the garden-lore of Sam. **The grots and rocky walls** were already starred with saxifrages and stonecrops. **Primeroles and anemones** were awake in the filbert-brakes; **and** *asphodel and many lily-flowers* nodded their half-opened heads in the grass; deep green grass beside the pools, where falling streams halted in cool hollows on their journey down to Anduin.

5.I "Minas Tirith" 731

A light kindled in the sky, a blaze of yellow fire behind dark barriers. **Pippin** cowered back, afraid for a moment, wondering into what dreadful country Gandalf was bearing him. **He** rubbed his eyes, **and then** *he* saw that *it* was the moon rising above the eastern shadows, now almost at the full. **So** *the night* was not yet old **and for hours** *the dark journey* would go on. **He** stirred and spoke. [Passage of dialogue deleted since my analysis focuses on narrative prose. Pippin and Gandalf discuss where they are, and Pippin is afraid when he sees the fires of the beacons. Gandalf explains what they are, and names them: *Amon Dîn, and flame on Eilenach; Nardol, Erelas, Min Rimmon, Calenhad, and the Halifirien*]

6.II "The Land of Shadow" (900, 901)

The river-bed was now some way below the path. **They** scrambled down to it, and began to cross it. **To their surprise** *they* came upon dark pools fed by threads of water trickling down from some source higher up the valley. **Upon the outer marges under the westward mountains** *Mordor* was a dying land, **but** *it* was not dead. **And here** *things* still grew, harsh, twisted, bitter, struggling for life. **In the glens of the Morgai on the other side of the valley** *low scrubby trees* lurked and clung, **coarse grey grass-tussocks** fought with the stones, **and** *withered mosses* crawled on them; **and everywhere** *great writhing, tangled brambles* sprawled. **Some** had long stabbing thorns, **some** hooked barbs that rent like knives. **The sullen shriveled leaves of a past year** hung on them, grating and rattling in the sad airs, **but** *their maggot-ridden buds* were only just opening. **Flies, dun or grey or black, marked like orcs with a red eye-shaped blotch**, buzzed and stung; **and above the briar-thickets** *clouds of hungry midges* danced and reeled. **The land** seemed full of creaking and cracking and sly noises, **but** *there* was no sound of voice or of foot.

6.V "The Steward and the King" (949)

But *Gandalf* took Aragorn out from the City by night, **and** *he* brought him to the southern feet of Mount Mindolluin; **and there** *they* found a path made in ages past **that** *few* now dared to tread. **For** *it* led up on to the mountain to a high hallow **where only** *the kings* had been wont to go. **And** *they* went up by steep ways, **until** *they* came to a high field below the snows that clad the lofty peaks, **and** *it* looked down over the precipice that stood behind the City. **And standing there** *they* surveyed the lands, **for** *the morning* was come; **and** *they* saw the towers of the City far below them like white pencils touched by the sunlight, **and** *all the Vale of Anduin* was like a garden, **and** *the Mountains of Shadow* were veiled in a golden mist. **Upon the one side** *their sight* reached to the grey Emyn Muil, **and** *the glint of Rauros* was like a star twinkling far off; **and upon the other side** *they* saw the River like a ribbon laid down to Pelargir, **and beyond that** was a light on the hem of the sky that spoke of the Sea.

Notes

1. Scholars who have argued that the film, as a whole, is a weak or failed adaptation of the book tend to focus on specifically literary elements (notably plot structure and characterization). The most critical essays are by David Bratman, Jane Chance, Kayla McKinney Wiggins, and Daniel Timmons. Janet Brennan Croft does consider style and dialogue to a certain extent, but only as part of a larger discussion. More positive evaluations of the adaptation include Tom Shippey's comparison of narrative modes where he at least acknowledges that films are not made solely for readers of the original books. More positive evaluations come from scholars who focus primarily on theme, such as Jeffrey Mallinson's exploration of the religious theme in the first film, or emphasize how directorial changes may appeal more to contemporary viewers, especially with regard to female characters, such as Cathy Akers-Jordan, Victoria Gaydosik, and Maureen Thum. Diana Paxson considers Tolkien's own history of changes in his work as well as the film adaptation to argue for how changes in modes of storytelling occur over time. The majority of these essays appeared in Janet Brennan's collection which contains only one essay by a film scholar, J.E. Smyth, who analyzes how Jackson's film fits within the ideology of imperialism in film and does not mention the book at all.

2. The scenes are: *The Fellowship of the Ring*, scene 13 "The Nazgúl" (0:57:5–49), Scene 27 "Moria" (1:43:4–11), Scene 30 The Bridge of Khazad-Dûm (2:9:38–50 & 2:11:2–17), Scene 35 "The Great River" (2:25:44–26:13 & 2:28–13–28); *The Two Towers* Scene 4 "The Three Hunters" (0:12:47–13:12, 0:13:52–57, & 0:14:18–24), Scene 7 "On the Trail of the Uruk-hai" (0:20:20–42), Scene 11 "Treebeard" (0:30:48–60), Scene 12 "The Passages of the Marshes" (0:34:46–35:23), Scene 23 "Of Herbs and Stewed Rabbit" (1:16:4–7, 1:17:57–19:10). Scene 52 "Gollum's Plan" (3:51:5–18); *The Return of the King* Scene 9 "Minas Tirith" (0:31:37–32:11), Scene 14 "The Lighting of the Beacons" (0:48:1–49:08), Scene 47 "The Land of Shadow" (2:26:52–27:21), and Scene 58 "Homeward Bound (2:57:52–58:30). NOTE: Scene 52 which is in the film *The Two Towers* is actually equivalent to the scene of Frodo and Sam in the Morgai in *The Return of the King* because Jackson correlated chronology rather than plot events in the films.

3. In Halliday's chapter "Subject, Actor, Theme," he illustrates the different ways a speaker of English can construct a clause involving three different levels or types of subjects: *The duke gave my aunt this teapot*; *My aunt was given this teapot by the duke*; *This teapot my aunt was given by the duke* (32–33). Halliday provides a method to analyze the different grammatical construction of these three clauses which use different word order and focus to convey the same information. For the purposes of this paper, I am focusing primarily on grammatical subjects, rather than psychological subject or logical subject. The additional level of analysis does not change my conclusion that the agency of Middle-earth is the central focus in Tolkien's work.

4. Appendix A contains the transcribed text with theme-subjects, subjects, and themes marked.

Works Cited

Akers-Jordan, Cathy. "Fairy Princess or Tragic Heroine? The Metamorphosis of Arwen Undómiel in Peter Jackson's *The Lord of the Rings* Films." In Janet Brennan Croft.

Tolkien on Film: Essays on Peter Jackson's The Lord of the Rings. Altadena, CA: Mythopoeic Press, 2004.

Booth, Wayne C. *The Rhetoric of Fiction*. 2nd ed. Chicago: University of Chicago Press, 1983.

Bratman, David. "Summa Jacksonica: A Reply to Defenses of Peter Jackson's *The Lord of the Rings* Films, After St. Thomas Aquinas." In Janet Brennan Croft. *Tolkien on Film: Essays on Peter Jackson's* The Lord of the Rings. Altadena, CA: Mythopoeic Press, 2004.

Chance, Jane. "Tolkien's Women (and Men): The Films and the Book." In Janet Brennan Croft. *Tolkien on Film: Essays on Peter Jackson's The Lord of the Rings*. Altadena, CA: Mythopoeic Press, 2004.

_____. "Is there a text in this hobbit? Peter Jackson's *Fellowship of the Ring*." *Literature Film Quarterly* 30.2 (2002): 79–85.

Chatman, Seymour. *Coming to Terms: The Rhetoric of Narrative in Fiction and Film*. Ithaca, NY: Cornell University Press, 1990.

Croft, Janet Brennan. "Mithril Coats and Tin Ears: 'Anticipation' and 'Flattening' in Peter Jackson's *The Lord of the Rings* Trilogy." In Janet Brennan Croft. *Tolkien on Film: Essays on Peter Jackson's The Lord of the Rings*. Altadena, CA: Mythopoeic Press, 2004.

_____. *Tolkien on Film: Essays on Peter Jackson's The Lord of the Rings*. Altadena, CA: Mythopoeic Press, 2004.

Drout, Michael D.C. "Tolkien's Prose Style and its Literary and Rhetorical Effect." *Tolkien Studies* 1 (2004): 137–162.

Fowler, Roger. *Linguistic Criticism*. Oxford: Oxford University Press, 1996.

Gaydosik, Victoria. "'Crimes Against the Book'? The Transformation of Tolkien's Arwen from Page to Screen and the Abandonment of the Psyche Archetype." In Janet Brennan Croft. *Tolkien on Film: Essays on Peter Jackson's The Lord of the Rings*. Altadena, CA: Mythopoeic Press, 2004.

Halliday, M.A.K. *An Introduction to Functional Grammar*. 2nd edition. Oxford: Oxford University Press, 1994.

Hammond, Wayne G. and Christina Scull. *J.R.R. Tolkien: Artist and Illustrator*. Boston: Houghton Mifflin, 1995

Kline, Karen E. "The Accidental Tourist on Page and on Screen: Interrogating Normative Theories about Film Adaptation." *Literature Film Quarterly* 24.1 (1996): 70–83.

The Lord of the Rings. Theatrical and Extended Editions. Directed by Peter Jackson. New Line. 2001, 2002, 2003, 2004.

Mallinson, Jeffrey. "A Portion too Strong?: Challenges in Translating the Religious Significance of Tolkien's *The Lord of the Rings* to Film." *Journal of Religion and Popular Culture* 1 (Spring 2002).

Paxson, Diana. "Re-vision: *The Lord of the* Rings in Print and on Screen." In Janet Brennan Croft. *Tolkien on Film: Essays on Peter Jackson's* The Lord of the Rings. Altadena, CA: Mythopoeic Press, 2004.

Raffel, Burton. "*The Lord of the Rings* as Literature." In *Tolkien and the Critics: Essays on J.R.R. Tolkien's The Lord of the Rings*. Edited by Neil D. Isaacs and Rose A. Zimbardo. South Bend, IN: University of Notre Dame Press: 1968. 218–246.

Shippey, Tom. "Another Road to Middle-earth: Jackson's Movie Trilogy." In *Understanding The Lord of the Rings*. Edited by Rose A. Zimbardo and Neil D. Isaacs. Boson: Houghton Mifflin, 2004.

Smyth, J.R. "The Three Ages of Imperial Cinema from the Death of Gordon to *The Return of the King*." In Janet Brennan Croft. *Tolkien on Film: Essays on Peter Jackson's* The Lord of the Rings. Altadena, CA: Mythopoeic Press, 2004.

Thum, Maureen. "The 'SubSubcreation' of Galadriel, Arwen, and Éowyn: Women of Power in Tolkien's and Jackson's *The Lord of the Rings*." Croft 231–256

Timmons, Daniel. "Frodo on Film: Peter Jackson's Problematic Portrayal." In Janet Brennan Croft. *Tolkien on Film: Essays on Peter Jackson's The Lord of the Rings*. Altadena, CA: Mythopoeic Press, 2004.

Tolkien, J.R.R. *The Lord of the Rings.* Boston: Houghton Mifflin, 1994.
_____. *J.R.R. Tolkien: Author of the Century.* Boston: Houghton Mifflin, 2002.
Wiggins, Kayla McKinney. "The Art of the Story-Teller and the Person of the Hero." In
    Janet Brennan Croft. *Tolkien on Film: Essays on Peter Jackson's The Lord of the Rings.*
    Altadena, CA: Mythopoeic Press, 2004.

"My brothers, I see in your eyes the same fear": The Transformation of Class Relations in Peter Jackson's Lord of the Rings *Trilogy*

SHARON D. MCCOY

Galadriel sonorously intones that "the world is changed" in the opening of Peter Jackson's *The Fellowship of the Ring*. This sense of a new beginning is not unfamiliar to readers of Tolkien's novel, and yet Jackson's vision fundamentally changes the nature of that transformation in an attempt to bring the story to a modern film audience — an audience largely unfamiliar with a society in which masters and servants are an integral part of life. Jackson's revision of the social structure of Tolkien's world might at first be as disconcerting to lovers of the novel as his decision to give pointy ears to almost childlike Hobbits and pale ethereal Elves. Yet the films' transformation of the novel's class relationships invites closer examination, for in the end, Jackson's revision offers a new understanding of what it might mean to be a hero in the beginning of the 21st century. Tolkien's Middle-earth is a world of kingship, kinship and class-based societies, a "modern work" firmly based in a "medieval tradition" (Flieger 40), wherein the fundamental hierarchical structures are accepted and endorsed as an important part of a common past. And while Hooker demonstrates that such hierarchical relationships are not so far in the distant past as we might like to think and bases his own analysis of the novel on the relationship of the British officer class to its "soldier-servant[s]" in World War I (125), many readers and viewers today are not familiar with such relationships. Though there is some mobility in the class structure by the novel's end, as seen in Sam's elevation from servant to "Master Samwise" (a diminutive title for a child, heir to the master of the house, TT, IV, x, 337) to master of Bag End and mayor of Hobbiton, the narrative never openly questions the structure of the system and its essential rightness.

Abuses are exposed and dealt with in the novel while the underlying social systems remain not only unchanged but validated, "harmony" restored as members from high and low strata acknowledge their interdependence with and responsibilities toward one another. Each individual is both a separate "entity and a part" of something larger than himself (Zimbardo 68). Characters function and excel within the stratum into which they are born, accepting their position in society and striving to be the best within that level: while it is at first a "shock," Frodo learns to enjoy being "*the* Mr. Baggins of Bag End (FR, I, ii, 52), and Sam has no desire to be anything but Mr. Frodo's servant, at least until he has to choose between his master and his own family; Aragorn is content to be simply a Ranger of the North until circumstance, action and prophecy combine to compel him to claim his birthright, which he then does without fundamental doubt or hesitation. Social unrest and betrayal occur when a character wishes to challenge his place in the existing structure, to take more or less power than is rightfully his: Boromir wishes to be king, while Denethor denies the claim of Isildur's heir; Saruman desires dominion and underestimates Sauron's power over his mind, while Theoden, listening to the twisted whisperings of Wormtongue, has forgotten what kingship means. Tolkien's hero myth venerates the contribution of even the smallest member of society, challenging only the abuses of the system while leaving intact the essential master-servant dynamic at the heart of kingship and social class.

Jackson's vision, in contrast, critiques this central relationship, virtually demonizing characters that believe or take part in the master-servant relationship. As Hooker argues, understanding this sort of class relationship is one of the "key difficulties" of the text for a modern audience (131), and Jackson's revisions of the story attempt to erase that difficulty. Jackson's mortal characters are reluctant to take power because they do not want dominion over others, because they do not see themselves as fundamentally different from others—at least, not others who are white. As Sue Kim points out in her trenchant article on race in these movies, darker peoples are relegated to the roles of Sauron's or Saruman's slaves or servants (876–877). While in Tolkien's text, there is some sense of the possibility of understanding across national, ethnic and racial boundaries—as when Sam wonders about the home life of a dead Southron (TT, IV, iv, 269) or when the new King Elessar pardons the "Easterlings" and "[sends] them away free," makes "peace with the peoples of Harad" and releases the "slaves of Mordor," giving them land (RK, VI, v, 247)—in Jackson's modern revision, such gestures are notable mostly in their absence. Dark or foreign-looking characters are on the other side of a deep divide, and their position as servants or slaves puts them largely out of the reckoning of Jackson's "good" characters, except as members of a system of which these characters want no part.

Jackson's main characters do not accept the role of either master or servant, nor do they accept the essential rightness of social class or status. They are what Lynnette Porter classes as "everyperson" heroes, heroes "from the ranks of 'people' like us" (viii), and while Porter focuses on the "unsung heroes," such as women and other supporting characters, this description applies even to the apparently noble or obviously heroic characters in the films: they are all intended to be "people like us." We see these changes early in the films, and Jackson's revision of Tolkien's class dynamics remains consistent and coherent throughout. Frodo does not see himself as "master," and Sam, rather ambiguously, becomes Frodo's friend and employee, rather than his servant (servants, in fact, are markedly absent). We first see Sam at the birthday party, where he and Frodo are laughing together as friends, and apparently, as equals. Frodo is privy to Sam's romantic longings from the beginning and enters into them with playful abandon, laughingly pushing Sam into Rosie's arms (*The Fellowship of the Ring,* sc. 4). We discover that Sam works for Frodo only in their third appearance on screen together, when Gandalf catches Sam eavesdropping at the window, and this scene further illuminates how different Peter Jackson's social vision is from Tolkien's (sc. 8).[1]

As in the text version, Gandalf hears a noise outside as he is telling Frodo of the Ring, its history and its threat. Gandalf pulls Sam in through the window, and Sam pleads that he was merely doing his job, "cutting the grass" under the window; in the film, we see here for the first time that Sam is apparently Frodo's gardener. In contrast to Tolkien's version, wherein Sam appeals to "Mr. Frodo" as the master of the house, "Don't let him hurt me, sir! Don't let him turn me into anything unnatural!" (FR, I, ii, 73), in Jackson's film, Sam pleads directly with Gandalf on his own behalf. This is something the Sam of the book would not do, for he sees Frodo as his protector and ultimate authority figure, even in the face of a wizard whom he believes has the power to turn them both into something "unnatural." In the text, he appeals to Frodo, not Gandalf, as arbiter of his fate. Yet in the film, the master-servant relationship is firmly set aside. In appealing directly to Gandalf on his own behalf, Sam becomes, not a member of a lower class who will "do for Mr. Frodo" (FR, I, iii, 78), but an equal, not just to Frodo, but also, in a way, to Gandalf; in his plea, Sam acknowledges Gandalf's greater powers, but not his innate superiority. In the films, Sam is not a servant; Frodo is his friend and employer, but he is friend first.

The Sam Gamgee of Tolkien's text would never presume to call his master simply "Frodo." He unfailingly refers to him as "Master" or "Mr. Frodo." Nor are his appellations for Frodo simply public displays, but rather, they are reflections of Sam's feelings for Frodo in the deepest recesses of his heart. Even all alone in Mordor, when he thinks Frodo is dead, to Sam, he is "Mr. Frodo" and "master, my dear," and the young hobbit worries about putting himself "forward" (TT, III, x, 341–342), clearly possessing what Hooker calls a sense of "selfsubordination" (129). Jackson's Sam has no such concept of status. He calls his friend-employer "Frodo" and "Mr. Frodo" interchangeably, flattening the distinction between the two. As Frodo and Sam leave on their journey together, we see that Frodo is clearly the leader, but in the film it is solely because of his character — not his status. In both text and film, Frodo is worldlier than Sam. Though he has not traveled far, he is determined and apparently unafraid of traveling new ground; like Bilbo, adventure holds no inherent terror for him. Sam finds courage along the way, but in the film, making that first step into the unknown is perhaps his hardest. Jackson uses this scene to illuminate his characters and the nature of their friendship, while in the book, this scene is downplayed as Sam copes in silence with whatever fear he feels at this point, trusting his master and allowing himself to express only wonder as he looks for the first time "across lands he had never seen to a new horizon" (FR, I, iii, 82). In the text, Sam's courage to face the unknown comes partly from his sense of his place, from his acceptance of his status as a servant possessing unwavering loyalty to and love for his deserving master, and from his sense of the obligations inherent in that relationship.

In contrast, Jackson portrays Sam as comfortable expressing his fear to his friend, and Frodo responds kindly. When Sam stops in a field and says, "This is it…. If I take one more step, it'll be the farthest away from home that I've ever been," Frodo goes back and says reassuringly, "Come on, Sam." He waits as Sam makes the decision himself to cross that invisible line, and this small moment is crucial (*The Fellowship of the Ring*, sc. 8). Heroism, in Jackson's vision, comes from the individual; making the decision to face one's fear is a solitary process. Sam's determination must come only from within, from himself alone; a sense of duty no longer provides a moral foundation as in the text, and commitment becomes solely a matter of individual choice and integrity. Summoning his courage, Sam faces his fear and takes the step on his own. Only then does Frodo touch his arm, and they continue together, side by side, Sam's heavier pack the only indication of his employee status — or perhaps his way of pulling his own weight in the friendship. Frodo is not leading him; they are as brothers in this quest (sc. 8).

This notion of brotherhood develops throughout the films, making a striking contrast to the text. The films flatten differences between major characters, between leaders and their followers, while the text celebrates fellowship, obligation and friendship *across* those acknowledged lines of difference. Verlyn Flieger argues that in the text, Frodo is the "common man" type of hero, "who has the immediate, poignant appeal of someone with whom the reader can identify," in contrast with Aragorn, who is a "traditional epic/romantic hero, larger than life," someone we admire, but with whom we "do not identify" (41). I will discuss Aragorn presently, but Flieger's analysis of Frodo is crucial in understanding what Jackson's revision attempts to accomplish. Focusing on Tolkien's realism in the portrayal of Frodo, Flieger characterizes the novel's Frodo as "utterly ordinary," a character who "doubts, feels fear, falters, makes mistakes" (41). Flieger never addresses Sam in her discussion of Frodo, never addresses the fact that her "common man" is also a master, and yet this is not the contradiction it might seem, for she places Tolkien's characters firmly in a medieval tradition, and medieval society was highly stratified; being what she characterizes as "utterly ordinary" and a "common" hero would not contradict Frodo's role as master to Sam in the text. Jackson, by removing Frodo from the master class, removes the character from his medieval roots and plants him firmly in the present in an effort to make Frodo even more accessible to the viewer. And while Jackson's choice of casting for and portrayal of Frodo disturbs some viewers—Chance, for example, views Jackson's characterization of Frodo as "infantilization" (81)—Frodo's transformation from a hobbit of fifty to "the appearance of a robust and energetic hobbit just out of his tweens" has precedent in the book (FR, I, ii, 52). Jackson collapses Gandalf's long absence, removing the period of time wherein Frodo moves from "coming of age" and grows into comfort with his role as master and "*the* Mr. Baggins," partly because, in the director's vision, this distance from Sam and the others is not desirable. Removing this sense of Frodo as a master is an effort to bring the modern viewer significantly closer to him, and Frodo's journey becomes a coming-of-age story that perhaps increases its appeal for a younger audience which has little context for understanding a positive master-servant relationship.

Not only are viewers able, if they so choose, to identify with Frodo as a common man, but in the film, Frodo also sees himself in this way. We understand this in relation to Sam and the other hobbits, but it becomes particularly clear in his relations with Gollum, wherein Frodo comes to identify himself with the wretched creature. No such identification exists in the novel. In the text, while Frodo gains a deep understanding of and pity for Gollum's plight, their stations in life are fundamentally different. Frodo is a master, Gollum his servant or the servant of the Precious. While he pities Gollum and knows that the Ring could do terrible things to him personally, Frodo does not fear becoming Gollum — at first because he cannot picture Gollum as a Hobbit-like creature, but later because Gollum is simply not of his class. Though Sméagol claims that his grandmother was a very important person, when he takes the Ring, he takes it to hide, steal and "sneak." He is not a master, nor does he have the strength to attempt to *use* the Ring for mastery. Frodo, on other hand, however kind to his subordinates and however deferent to those he feels are higher than himself, is nonetheless a master, *the* master of Bag End and a hobbit to whom his cousins look up. He is rich and potentially powerful in his own land, though he prefers to be left alone. In Mordor, he accepts his role as master of the Precious and master of Gollum (TT, IV, i, 221–222).

But as the Frodo of the films is not master to Sam, neither is he ever really master to Gollum. Though Gollum in the film swears to "serve the Master of the Precious" and consistently calls Frodo "master," Frodo of the film has no concept of mastery. He reacts thoughtfully to Gollum's words, telling him only that "the Ring is treacherous; it will hold you to your word" (*The Two Towers*, sc. 2). This is a distinct contrast to the text — there, when Gollum offers to "swear on the Precious," Frodo reacts with anger, saying in a "stern voice" that "startles" Sam, "On the Precious! How dare you?" Frodo appears to grow tall, "a mighty lord who hid his brightness in a grey cloud, and at his feet" Gollum appears but "a little whining dog," yet the "two were in some way akin and not alien." Frodo acknowledges some kinship with Gollum, yet he accepts his role as "master of the Precious" and master of both Gollum and Sam. He tells Gollum, "Down! down!" and then accepts Gollum's promise by giving Sam an order, "Take the rope off, Sam!" (TT, IV, i, 224–225). In the film, it is Sam who angrily interrupts Gollum's promises, shouting, "I don't believe you! Get down! Sit down!" while pulling forcefully on the rope around Gollum's neck. Frodo tries to contain his friend's anger, then kneels next to Gollum, getting down on his level. He removes the rope himself, telling him, "You will lead us to the Black Gate." Though Gollum calls him "Master," Frodo accepts no mastery here (*The Two Towers*, sc. 2).

The Frodo of the film lacks a master's sense of distance between himself and others, and as they continue, he finds himself identifying with Gollum much more than his counterpart in the books. He sees, ever more clearly, that he could become Gollum. When Sam casually expresses deep hostility toward Gollum, whom he sees only as a threat and a dangerous scoundrel, Frodo responds angrily and almost violently, telling Sam, "You've no idea what it did to him, what it's still doing to him" (*The Two Towers*, sc. 21). Sam, worried about Frodo and concerned that Frodo's sympathy with Gollum will prove his friend's downfall, tells Frodo that he cannot "save" Gollum and that he himself must fight the ring. Frodo yells, "I know what I have to do, Sam! The ring was entrusted to me. It's my task. Mine. My own." Sam's horrified response reveals that he misses the point entirely. When he asks, "Can't you hear yourself? Don't you know who you sound like?" Sam cannot see that he has nailed Frodo's problem exactly: Frodo knows precisely who he sounds like. He has to believe he can save Sméagol, has to "believe he can come back," because therein lies Frodo's only hope for himself; if Sméagol cannot recover, neither can Frodo (sc. 21). Frodo's concern for Bilbo seems strangely absent in this cinematic version, but there is something emotionally powerful in Frodo's recognition that he could become Gollum. In the third film, *The Return of the King*, Frodo will tell Gollum, "I have to destroy it, for both our sakes" (sc. 29). He and Gollum are also brothers.

In the movies, Sam not only worries about Gollum's treachery, but is also concerned about and jealous of the relationship between Gollum and Frodo, as Tom Shippey argues (243). There is no distance of the master-servant here, and Sam fights the growing identification he sees between the two, as Frodo cannot do. Gollum sees the feelings of both hobbits and manipulates them deliberately, creating what Shippey calls a "triangle" (243). As they climb the stairs of Cirith Ungol, Gollum tells Frodo that he understands the heavy burden Frodo bears, tells him that he understands in a way that Sam cannot. When Gollum tells Frodo that the desire for the Ring is growing in Sam, that "the fat one will take it from you" (*The Return of the King*, sc. 17), Frodo has no reason beyond friendship not to believe. Sam here is not as he is portrayed in the text: he is not a beloved servant who has been trusted with the most intimate details of Frodo's life, but a companion who—weak, as all individuals are weak—might fall to the power of the Ring. Sméagol killed his friend to possess the Ring; what might Sam do? Further, though it is not explicitly stated, Frodo knows that through the power of the Ring, he grows more like Gollum with every passing hour. What might Frodo himself do to his friend? And so, when Gollum plays a ludicrous trick, to cast suspicion on Sam as greedy, Frodo seems to fall for it. Seeing his friend's growing violence and his lack of control when Sam brutally attacks Gollum, Frodo simply cannot risk having him along anymore. "You cannot help me anymore," he tells his friend, apologetic but firm, unable to contain his suspicions or his fear: "I'm sorry, Sam.... Go home" (*The Return of the King*, sc. 19). And yet, his gentleness in this apology seems to indicate that he worries as much for Sam as about the possibility of his betrayal. Without the ties of duty, interdependence and obligation that exist in the society of the novel, what prevents betrayal in Jackson's vision? Only the integrity of the individual, unsupported and subject to change, its quality unknown even to the person who possesses it until put to the sharpest test. And so, Frodo sends his friend away, and Sam, hurt by Frodo's words and horrified by the violence of his own actions against Gollum, turns back—allowing his friend to go on alone with the villain he knows will betray him. No sense of duty binds him to Frodo's side.

In Jackson's vision, Sam's decision to return to help Frodo must be a conscious, individual choice. Sam descends the stairs of Cirith Ungol only to find the *lembas* that Gollum has thrown over the precipice. Wordlessly, in anger or despair, Sam crumbles the Elf food and throws it away before bolting back up the mountain (which would be unthinkable waste to the Sam of the books, ever the thrifty servant),[2] having decided again to help his friend. Whether finding the *lembas* rekindled his anger at Gollum and his awareness of the creature's treachery, or whether Sam had some doubts about his own exhausted motivations is not clear; what is clear is that Sam alone makes the decision to return to his friend (*The Return of the King*, sc. 29). And later, when he takes the Ring from what he believes is Frodo's lifeless body, the Sam of both movie and text is bowing to a larger sense of duty, a sense of the importance of the quest itself, but the Sam of the film has no sense that he is stepping out of his place. When he discovers that his friend is alive, he decides freely to rescue him, drawing his sword and killing the three orcs in his path, crying, "That's for Frodo, and that's for the Shire and that's for my old Gaffer," or for friendship, country and father (sc. 45). When Sam finds his friend at the top of the tower, the first thing Frodo does—even before he tells Sam that the Ring is gone—is to apologize. Sam is moved, his friendship restored to its importance.

When Frodo asks for the ring, Sam gives it to him, hesitating for a moment, his individual struggle clear on his face. But against Sam's integrity and his friendship, the Ring has no final power. While Sam fights the power of the Ring in the brief moment during which he makes his decision, once he decides, he gives it to Frodo without doubt or ambivalence. We believe in this scene because of its similarity to an earlier one, in which Bilbo deliberately drops the Ring to the floor before he leaves (*The Fellowship of the Ring*, sc. 5). Like the old hobbit, Sam makes a choice, free and clear, to give up the Ring, Bilbo for the friendship of Gandalf, Sam for the friendship of Frodo, tempered by a new understanding of the Ring's damaging powers. When Frodo tells him, "The ring is my burden. It will destroy you, Sam," the hobbit truly understands for the first time that Frodo knows the ring is destroying him, too (*The Return of the King*, sc. 45). Frodo keeps the Ring because its power compels him, but he also does not want to share the burden with his friend: he does not want Sam, too, to be destroyed. Frodo has little hope, and Gollum's betrayal confirms his worst fears about the Ring and his own chances.

In Jackson's cinematic revision of the text, then, the Ring has a heightened power to test the mettle of an individual. No sense of duty or place helps a mortal individual in his struggles with the Ring; each must face the challenge on his own, and this is no less true of Aragorn than it is of Frodo or Sam. Like them, the Aragorn of Jackson's vision is changed, less comfortable with mastery, with being a leader. Jackson's character comes into his inheritance less easily, filled with doubt and fears that he will fail in the face of the Ring, as did his forefather before him. His "Strider" is less a "traditional disguised hero" (Flieger 43), and more a reluctant hero, uncertain of his birthright. Jackson's character of Strider is intended to be more attractive and less careworn than Tolkien's. While he does keep his face hidden in the inn's common room and he roughly pushes Frodo up the stairs, from the moment the character reveals his face and tells Frodo that he is "not nearly frightened enough" (*The Fellowship of the Ring,* sc. 12), Aragorn and Strider are one. His hair and clothes are dirty, but he is far from the novel's Strider, who says, "I look foul and feel fair" (FR, I, x, 184). In the text, Strider is far more frightening. When Sam expresses distrust of him, Strider towers over the hobbits and declares, "If I was after the Ring, I could have it — now!" After scaring them, he seems to shrink and says that "fortunately" for them, he is truly himself, "I am Aragorn, son of Arathorn, and if by life or death I can save you, I will" (FR, I, x, 183). In the text, Aragorn means this utterly. The Ring is not his, and he does not desire its power; he has seen what it has done in history and that path is not his destiny. Even at the council, when it is revealed that Aragorn is Isildur's heir and Frodo realizes that the ring "belongs" to him, Aragorn answers, "It does not belong to either of us" (FR, II, ii, 260). Unlike Gandalf, who says, "Do not tempt me!" (FR I, ii, 70–71) and Galadriel, who admits her desire for it, but "passes the test" (FR, II, vii, 381), Aragorn of the text betrays no desire for the Ring. Galadriel and Gandalf are wielders of Rings of Power themselves (FR, II, vii, 380 and RK, VI, ix, 310), and the temptation to try to use the One Ring for good is within their purview, but Aragorn's duty is to help right the wrong committed by his ancestor if he can. That sense of duty and his place in the grand scheme of things prevents him from succumbing to the pull of the ring. Aragorn, like Faramir later, has no desire for power above his station, and this sense of honor is part of their essential heroism in the novel.

The cinematic Aragorn, in contrast, is closer to the film's Frodo as he identifies with Gollum's fate. Aragorn sees that like his forefather Isildur, he himself might fall to the desire for the power of the Ring. In Jackson's vision, Aragorn possesses no certainty of station and duty, no certainty in regard to his own integrity in the face of the Ring.[3] In his first scenes in the film, meeting the hobbits at the inn, Strider seems to avoid the subject of the Ring, to avoid temptation and testing. Aside from saying "that is no trinket you carry" (*The Fellowship of the Ring,* sc. 12), in the inn, the Aragorn of the film refers to the Ring only when discussing the corruption and danger of the Nazgûl, whom he tells them are "drawn to the power of the One; they will never stop hunting you" (sc. 13). His moment of truth will come later, at the breaking of the Fellowship, but the source of his fear is clear. Galadriel's words from the opening scene of *The Fellowship of the Ring,* stating that men "above all value power" and that the "hearts of men are easily corrupted" re-echo in Aragorn's words as he tells the hobbits of the origin of the Ringwraiths, the fate of the nine Kings of men who "one by one [fell] into darkness. Now they are slaves of his will" (sc. 13). Aragorn fears the pull of power that leads to enslavement, fears the power that comes with being a King of men.

Jackson sees unquestioning fealty as, at best, misplaced trust, as part of an old world that should be allowed to slip away. To hammer home his point, Jackson shifts the scene to Saruman, who has already imprisoned Gandalf after the gray wizard has discovered that his trust in his leader was horribly misplaced. Saruman is using the black Stone of Orthanc to talk to his true master. Unlike the Saruman of the texts, who desires to overthrow the Dark Lord and take his place, "a potential saviour gone wrong" (R. Smith 6), the Saruman of the movies is a willing slave of an evil master: "The power of Isengard is at your command, Sauron, Lord of the Earth." Sauron directs him to "Build me an army worthy of Mordor" (*The Two Towers*, sc. 14), and Saruman does, literally pulling his dark army out of the mud (Kim 877). Tolkien's Saruman, in contrast, builds his war machinery and breeds his especially powerful, less vulnerable Uruk-Hai in order to challenge the power of Sauron and to conquer the free peoples of Middle-earth: Uglúk and his Isengarders, as they are called, do not serve Sauron and have nothing but contempt for the Dark Lord's orc-servants. Rather, the Uruk-hai of the novel are "the servants of Saruman the Wise, the White Hand: the hand that gives [them] man's-flesh to eat" (TT, III, iii, 49). In Jackson's revision of the text, however, Saruman seeks only to serve the Dark Lord, content with the diminished power of a servant. In Jackson's Saruman, the master-servant relationship becomes demonized, literally, for later, we will discover that Saruman wages Sauron's war against Rohan via the possession of its king (*The Two Towers*, sc. 16).[4] But Saruman is content with his choice, believing that to serve Sauron offers his only hope. Saruman tortures Gandalf, telling him that he must "embrace the power of the Ring or embrace [his] own destruction" (*The Fellowship of the Ring*, sc. 18). Gandalf's eyes have been opened, though, to Saruman's true status, and he knows that unquestioning fealty to Sauron means utter surrender and the enslavement of one's will. He answers Saruman, "There is only one Lord of the Ring. Only one who can bend it to his will, and he does not share power." Gandalf leaps off the tower, escaping to the back of the eagle he has summoned. Saruman, completely enslaved to Sauron's will, intones, "So you have chosen death" (sc. 18). And yet, even death, the film argues, is a better choice than submission to the will of a master.

Magic is shown in the films as another form of mastery, a danger even to wizards and definitively not the province of men, and the use of the palantir represents another of Jackson's fundamental revisions. In the text, the

Seeing Stones of Gondor belong to men. Their magic is wielded by the descendants of the Numenor, and Tolkein's Aragorn openly claims the Orthanc stone, the palantir, as part of his inheritance; "to the surprise" of their companions, Gandalf bows as he presents the stone to Aragorn, acknowledging his right and his superior claim (TT, III, xi, 199–200). Aragorn later uses the Stone to show himself to Sauron and challenge his power, wrenching the Stone from his control, an "encounter" even "Gandalf feared," as Gimli reminds us. Aragorn replies simply and sternly, "You forget to whom you speak.... I am the lawful master of the stone" (RK, V, ii, 53). Magic gives its wielders a certain kind of mastery, and the films do not allow mortals its use. In the film, Aragorn is as adversely affected by touching the palantir as Pippin, writhing under its power and unable to hold it (*The Return of the King*, sc. 6). Magic belongs to human-like, but distinctly non-human folk: wizards, elves and evil-doers. While in the books, Aragorn has "immortal ancestry," being of mixed blood, the descendant of the distant "union of Elves and Men" (Flieger 44), in the films, there is no such mixing. Men, in the films, are of "pure" and mortal blood. While in the text, Aragorn boldly claims his kingship, his power and his mastery, the Aragorn of the films is a man, and only a man, who comes reluctantly into his heritage, claiming no mastery of magic or of men.

In the films, Aragorn grows into his leadership gradually, reluctantly. When Elrond openly and scornfully doubts the strength of men, Gandalf says to him, with hope, "There is one who could unite them. One who could claim the throne of Gondor" (*The Fellowship of the Ring*, sc. 20). Shippey argues that "Jackson's version insists that the source of weakness is disunity" and Aragorn's role is the "focus of union," the character who will bring all people together against the evil they fight (246). And yet, Aragorn of the films has to consciously choose this role as unifier, a role he has previously rejected. Elrond tells Gandalf that Aragorn "turned from that path a long time ago. He has chosen exile" (*The Fellowship of the Ring*, sc. 20). The film never fully explains Aragorn's situation, how precisely he has "chosen exile," and "turned" from the path of kingship, but his doubts about his fitness to rule are explicit:

ARWEN: You are Isildur's heir, not Isildur himself. You are not bound to his fate.

ARAGORN: The same blood flows in my veins. The same weakness.
ARWEN: Your time will come. You will face the same evil, and you will defeat it. The Shadow does not hold sway yet. Not over you ... not over me" [*The Fellowship of the Ring*, sc. 21].

Arwen believes in him, in a way that Aragorn cannot believe in himself. As many have pointed out, Arwen takes on a more central role in the films, but for all her active involvement in getting Frodo safely to Rivendell and her influence on later events, Arwen is essentially still the woman-behind-the-man, serving as his inspiration, his sounding board and his helpmeet. In spite of Arwen's faith, it is only as Aragorn earns the trust and the commitment of followers that he gains the right to be king — especially in his own eyes. Tolkien's Aragorn likewise earns trust and commitment of his followers, but in the text, Aragorn is the man he is partly because he is destined to fulfill the prophecy. In the text, Aragorn is, as Flieger argues, an "epic/romantic hero, larger than life" (41); he knows that he is the heir of kings and knows that if he and the quest succeed, he will be king of Gondor and Arnor. It is his birthright. In the films, Aragorn takes on the characteristics of the "realist" hero that Flieger argues the text reserves for Frodo; he "doubts, feels fear, falters, makes mistakes" (41). In short, Aragorn becomes a man with whom the viewer can identify, and we enter into his struggles in the same way we do Frodo's.

In the council, we learn that the trouble lies in the division between peoples, a division Gandalf believes Aragorn possesses the power to heal. Yet Aragorn does not see himself in this role at this point in the films. Elrond tells them all, "You will unite or you will fall. Each race is bound to this fate, this one doom" (*The Fellowship of the Ring*, sc. 23). Their disunity is articulated as Frodo brings forth the Ring and Boromir expresses openly the secret desire of all — "Why not wield this thing?" Aragorn speaks up and tells Boromir that they cannot use the Ring, tells them all that "the One Ring answers to Sauron alone; it has no other master," and in doing so, he is expressing his understanding of their common danger, not imposing the judgment of a king or leader. Boromir responds with contempt, both when he thinks the speaker a "mere Ranger" and when he learns that this is Aragorn, whom he knows to be Isildur's heir. Legolas would defend Aragorn's right to the throne and attempt to force Boromir to acknowledge his allegiance to the rightful king of Gondor, but Aragorn stops him. Aragorn feels no such right and does not answer when Boromir sneers, "Gondor has no king. Gondor needs no king" (sc. 23). Further, Aragorn kneels to Frodo when the hobbit agrees to take the Ring, saying, "You have my sword." Aragorn is the only member of the fellowship to kneel to Frodo, and the moment is a telling one. In kneeling, he reverses the role of king and knight; far from claiming his kingship, as Legolas wants him to, Aragorn offers his sword and his service. In kneeling, too, Aragorn literally and figuratively gets down on Frodo's level, being normally about twice his height. With his action, he puts himself and Frodo on the same footing — they are common men, brothers. In contrast, Boromir calls Frodo "Little One," and stands looking down at him, saying, "If this is indeed the will of the Council, Gondor will see it done" (sc. 23). While Aragorn is offering his service to the quest in honor of the hobbit's courage, inspiring both dwarf and elf to offer their service in spite of their racial and cultural differences, Boromir is haughtily declaring himself as "Gondor," in a manner reminiscent of kings.

Boromir serves his part in the Fellowship, though his actions on Caradhras and in Lorien offer some indication that he is a danger to Frodo. It is not until the company reaches the border between Mordor and Gondor, however, that Boromir and Aragorn each face the greatest crisis, with markedly different results. In a lovely cinematic moment, Frodo stands before the stone head of a dragon as Boromir succumbs to the monster within, to his desire to save his people — allowing the Ring to overcome him at last (*The Fellowship of the Ring,* sc. 36). In one of the movie's most extreme revisions from the texts, Aragorn meets Frodo immediately after he escapes from both Boromir and the Great Eye of Sauron (sc. 36). Frodo tells Aragorn that "It has taken Boromir." When Aragorn asks sharply about the Ring, Frodo sees only desire and corruption in his companion. He runs, shouting "Stay away!" Aragorn reminds Frodo that he offered him his service, that he has sworn to protect him, but Frodo asks, "Can you protect me from yourself?" — and further, "Would you destroy it?" Service and fealty do not have the same meanings in the world of the film as they do in the text. In the film, Aragorn approaches Frodo as the hobbit holds the Ring on his palm, hearing its whispers. He does not answer Frodo, but kneels once again and reaches for Frodo's hand, closing it around the Ring, saying, "I would have gone with you to the end, to the very fires of Mordor" (sc. 36). The tears in Frodo's eyes, which Chance argues are part of Frodo's "infantilization" in the film (81), are matched here by the tears in Aragorn's own and by the break in his voice. Here, at this moment, Aragorn can make the choice to let Frodo go. But would he be able to destroy it? Would he be able to protect Frodo from himself? Would he be able to resist the Ring as its power and his need grew? Would his oath hold him in the face of such pressure? Aragorn does not and cannot answer these questions. But here, in this one moment, Aragorn finds the strength within himself to let Frodo go, and he does, promising Frodo that he will care for the others. This moment marks Aragorn's recognition, not only of his own choice in the face of his fear of weakness, but of Frodo's right to decide for himself whom he can trust and whom he can risk.

When Aragorn's face suddenly changes and he draws his sword, doubt crosses Frodo's face, but Aragorn is reacting to the presence of enemies and he tells Frodo to run. Aragorn reveals himself to be an intrepid warrior, taking on a company of Uruk-hai by himself, in order to buy Frodo time. He hears the horn of Gondor, and, as in the books, goes to Boromir's aid. Boromir falls defending the hobbits, but not before he and Aragorn share a poignant moment, though one vastly different from that of the text. In the film, as Aragorn kills the Uruk-hai warrior who is about to finish off Boromir, the man of Gondor acknowledges his equal as a comrade-in-arms. As Aragorn tells him that he let Frodo go, Boromir, for the first time, acknowledges his superior: "Then you did what I could not. I tried to take the Ring" (*The Fellowship of the Ring*, sc. 39). But Aragorn does not accept Boromir's fealty based on this. He knows that he is not above temptation, not above Boromir. On another day, he, too, might fall. As Frodo sees his kinship with Gollum, Aragorn acknowledges his kinship with Boromir, saying, "The Ring is beyond *our* reach now." Boromir still sees Aragorn as superior, but hears the distinction Aragorn makes, as he responds, "Forgive me, I did not see. I have failed you." Aragorn tries to reassure him, but Boromir gives in to despair, and he slips back into his wonted habit of thought as he says "*my* city" will come "to ruin." Aragorn's response breaks through all of Boromir's defenses: "I do not know what strength is in my blood, but I swear to you that I will not let the White city fall, nor our people fail." Aragorn acknowledges his doubt in his birthright, his uncertainty of his fitness to be king, but he promises to save what Boromir loves and claims kinship with him. This kinship is what disarms Boromir completely, and he repeats the words, "Our people. *Our* people." With his dying breath, Boromir acknowledges Aragorn's merit and his worthiness to wear the crown: "I would have followed you, my brother. My captain. My king." (sc. 39). Throughout the next two movies, Aragorn gradually takes on more responsibility, becoming a leader of men, but it is here that he himself first believes in his own power to lead, in his right to be king. It is here that Aragorn first sees that being a king and a captain need not mean that he is putting himself above others, but that kingship can also mean kinship, brotherhood, and a freely offered fealty based both on his own merit and a mutual recognition of the weakness of men. In this scene, Aragorn finally finds a concept of kingliness that he can embrace.

As Aragorn and the others enter into the wars of Rohan, they see no brotherhood, only division: uncle against nephew and neighbor against neighbor. No faith in the old alliances exists, and Gondor and Rohan are divided. Aragorn's first attempts to build some sense of decency and unity are clumsy, as he acts the part of ally to Rohan as the future king of Gondor, stopping Theoden from soiling the steps of Edoras with Wormtongue's blood (*The Two Towers*, sc. 16). Yet his action has grave consequences, for Wormtongue leaves only to reveal Rohan's retreat plans to Saruman, advising him to ambush the king and the women and children as they are on their way to Helm's Deep (sc. 20). Further, Aragorn has much to learn of handling the pride of kings. When Theoden worries about the strength of his armies, Aragorn tries to convince him to send for Eomer, whom he assures the king is loyal to him. When Theoden says that Eomer would be of no help, and that he will not risk open war, Aragorn makes the error of telling him bluntly, "Open war is upon you, whether you would risk it or not" (*The Two Towers*, sc. 18). The king responds angrily, "When last I looked, Theoden, not Aragorn, was king of Rohan," and the king makes the decision to retreat to Helm's Deep, which almost spells disaster for his people (sc. 18). But Aragorn fights to correct his mistakes, almost losing his life defending the Rohirrim from the ambush (sc. 26). He returns, as from the dead, to bring word of Saruman's massive forces and to encourage Theoden to call for help, still not understanding fully the isolation and divisiveness he sees, so different is it from his own nascent concept of brotherhood. When Theoden tells him that none would come, that the "old alliances are dead," Aragorn insists on the integrity of his people, saying, "Gondor will answer." Theoden lets a hammerblow fall when he tells Aragorn that in the recent past, Gondor has not honored its alliance, leaving Rohan to lose her own battles: "No, my lord Aragorn, we are alone" (sc. 34). Yet Gondor is there, in the presence and body of Aragorn, and it is up to the future king to unite them all, to prove that they do not stand alone.

His opportunity comes through the frustration and anger of one of his companions. While watching the gathering of boys and old men in defense of Rohan, Legolas sneers aloud that he can see the fear "in their eyes." His words attract the attention of all within earshot, and when he says that they all will die, Aragorn shouts in response, "Then I shall die as one of them!" (*The Two Towers*, sc. 36). His commitment to serve these people, to honor his country's alliance even without hope, to be "as one of them" though he could escape and leave them to their fate, inspires the elf to follow him. For the first time, Legolas makes a conscious choice to follow his leader (sc. 38). Up to this point he has simply been loyal to Aragorn out of what Jackson sees as a sense of antiquated duty, because Aragorn is the beloved of Arwen Evenstar and is destined to be king. Yet here, for the first time, Legolas—as an individual—chooses to follow Aragorn. We begin to see that Gandalf's trust in Aragorn's ability to unite disparate peoples was not misplaced. Reinforcing that notion, on the eve of battle, an army of Elves arrives "to honor their allegiance" (sc. 38). Again, this is a revision of the text, for in Tolkien's version, while an army rides out of the North to join Aragorn, they come after the battle of Helm's Deep and are his own loyal kinsman, Rangers of the North; only the sons of Elrond ride with them (RK, V, ii, 47–48). In the film, Aragorn plays the role of unifier, bolstering the courage of the defenders and helping them hold their defenses until Gandalf arrives with Eomer's army. Without the efforts of Aragorn and Gandalf in uniting his armies and defending his people, Theoden's kingdom would have fallen, and Theoden acknowledges this when he says, "It was not Theoden of Rohan who led our people to victory" (*The Return of the King*, sc. 4).

Aragorn's role as the unifier continues as he brings the armies of the dead to Minas Tirith's defense and takes command of the forces of the West. As in the books, he arrives after the death of Denethor, coming as a captain of war, and it is in this role that Aragorn earns the right to the kingship of Gondor. As his armies face the hordes pouring from the Black Gates, Aragorn takes Legolas's damaging words in Helm's Deep and turns them into a statement of brotherhood, an acknowledgement of their common weakness as men, and an expression of their hope. While they do not know the future, or how they will react, they can choose, in this moment, to be what they will: "My brothers, I see in your eyes the same fear that would take the heart of me. The day may come when the courage of men fails and we forsake our friends and break all bonds of fellowship. But it is not this day. By all that you hold dear on this good earth, I bid you stand, Men of the West" (*The Return of the King*, sc. 48). Aragorn is a captain, but one who acknowledges no mastery, acknowledges no "bonds" but those of freely chosen fellowship. They fight together, not because he forces them to go to war, but to defend what they themselves "hold dear."

Further, Aragorn becomes king in the same spirit, betraying his doubt in himself only by a heavy sigh before turning to face his people after his coronation, declaring as he does so that "This day does not belong to one man, but to all. Let us together rebuild this world, that we may share the days of peace" (*The Return of the King*, sc. 57). A king by the will of his people, Aragorn sees them all as brothers united in a single purpose. And yet, seductive as his sense of the brotherhood of a king to his people is, as powerful and moving as this final battle scene and the coronation are, Jackson's modernization of the story begs the question: precisely who are his brothers and what defines the "all" to whom the day belongs? For whom are they rebuilding — not just their lands — but "the world"? While in the text, part of the new king's duty is pardoning and treating with his conquered enemies, no such concerns muddy Jackson's very white portrayal of the brotherhood of man. The lighting here emphasizes the actor's blue-green eyes and light skin, and the whiteness of the elves is blinding as Aragorn claims his bride. Men fought for Sauron, too, but men who look darker or foreign to Aragorn and his people, enemies who "embody abstract evil" that conveniently "disappears when defeated" (Kim 879). This cinematic sense of brotherhood is compelling and attractive, but it is a brotherhood defined clearly against a foreign Other.

Porter argues that "definitions of *hero* should reflect a culture's values" (3), and perhaps, in more ways than we are comfortable acknowledging, Jackson's definitions do that. It is easier, perhaps, to accept the brotherhood of allies, to accept the humanity of those from whom you feel no threat, and Jackson's hero does this. When he tells the four bowing hobbits, "My friends, you bow to no one," and bows to them himself, followed by his queen and all his people (*The Return of the King*, sc. 57), his words and actions have a markedly different effect than in the text. Aragorn has been on his knees to Frodo twice before in the films, but this time he kneels to all the hobbits, and his people kneel with him. In contrast, in the text, Aragorn bows to the Ringbearers alone, on the Fields of Cormallen, crying, "Praise them with great praise!" (RK, VI, iv, 232). In the text, Pippin and Merry remain "knights of the City and of the Mark" (RK, VI, iv, 233) and very proud of their service to their kings; there, Aragorn reminds Pippin that he remains in his king's service, subject to recall at the king's need and reminds them all that his realm extends also to the North, to their lands (RK, VI, vi, 260). In the film, Aragorn, strangely, but in keeping with his ideals of brotherhood, makes no distinction between the Ringbearers and the other hobbits and makes no claim of service on his knight, no claim of dominion. The Shire, too, is strangely untouched in the film's revision, which Smith and Matthews argue is "the ultimate proof of the success of Frodo's mission" (102). The Shire is insulated from all events and not subject to allegiance with men or to sustained threats from the outside world. The hobbits "return to their former lives wiser and more appreciative of simple virtues; they do not glorify power" (Porter 169).

But Frodo, like the hero of chivalric romance or the American Western, must lose the land he has given so much to save. He has become the outsider. This sacrifice is necessary in both Tolkien's vision and Jackson's, but in the books, we are left only with Sam as the future in which we see ourselves. In Sam, we find the hope that as ordinary people, we, too, may find courage and do great deeds. In the text, we do not identify readily with Aragorn: the line of Great Kings will end many ages before our own time. Tolkien's books have the flavor of older days, and there, history is as important as the present; it has a meaning all its own, and its significance resonates in our own world. Jackson's vision is rooted very much in the present, focused so that the broad expanse of history has significance only in how it relates to the present and the future. With Jackson's revisions, Aragorn becomes closer to many viewers' level, less of a high king, less distant: the right to rule becomes something that must be earned, and the man who earns it is one whom we can call "brother." While limiting its vision to people it defines as "like us," the film's concept of the brotherhood of man, great and small, attempts to emphasize the possibility that any one of us can be a hero—if we so choose, when our moment comes.

Notes

1. Smith and Matthews also note the transformation in Sam and Frodo's relationship from one of master-servant to that of friend (110), but their analysis does not focus on the importance of this change or its application to the rest of the narrative.

2. See also Hooker, 126–129, for a description of the procurement responsibilities of a soldier-servant.

3. Porter, too, argues that the film's Aragorn "often doubts himself and expresses modern angst over the difficulties" of being a leader, but she still sees him as a "traditional hero" (4).

4. Smith and Matthews argue that in the films "Theoden has become the embodiment of everything that can go wrong with having a hereditary system of government" (148), but they do not see that it is not Theoden himself who is at fault here, but the combined machinations of Wormtongue and the possession of Theoden by Saruman. Though Theoden is weakened and saddened by the diminution of his realm, he recovers more than Smith and Matthews give him credit for, in both the films and the text.

Works Cited

Chance, Jane. "Is There a Text in this Hobbit? Peter Jackson's Fellowship of the Ring." *Literature Film Quarterly* 30.2 (2002): 79–85.

Flieger, Verlyn. "Frodo and Aragorn: The Concept of the Hero." In Neil D. Isaacs and Rose A. Zimbardo. *Tolkien: New Critical Perspectives.* Lexington: University of Kentucky Press, 1981.

Hooker, Mark T. "Frodo's Batman." *Tolkien Studies* 1 (2004): 125–136.

Isaacs, Neil D., and Rose A. Zimbardo. *Tolkien: New Critical Perspectives.* Lexington: University of Kentucky Press, 1981.

Kim, Sue. "Beyond Black and White: Race and Postmodernism in *The Lord of the Rings* Films." *MFS Modern Fiction Studies* 50.4 (2004): 875–907.

The Lord of the Rings: The Fellowship of the Ring. Directed by Peter Jackson. DVD. New Line Home Entertainment. 2001.

The Lord of the Rings: The Return of the King. Directed by Peter Jackson. DVD. New Line Home Entertainment. 2003.

The Lord of the Rings: The Two Towers. Directed by Peter Jackson. DVD. New Line Home Entertainment. 2002.

Porter, Lynnette R. *Unsung Heroes of The Lord of the Rings: From the Page to the Screen.* Westport, CT: Praeger, 2005.

Shippey, Tom. "Another Road to Middle Earth: Jackson's Movie Trilogy." *Understanding The Lord of the Rings: The Best of Tolkien Criticism.* Edited by Rose A. Zimbardo and Neil D. Isaacs. Boston and New York: Houghton Mifflin, 2004, 233–254.

Smith, Jim, and J. Clive Matthews. *The Lord of the Rings: The Films, The Books, The Radio Series.* London: Virgin Books, 2004.

Smith, Ross. "Why the Film Version of *The Lord of the Rings* Betrays the Novel (Part 1)." *English Today* 83, 21.3 (July 2005): 3–7.

Tolkien, J. R. R. *The Lord of the Rings.* 1954–5. 2nd rev. ed., 1967. 3 parts. Boston: Houghton Mifflin, 2nd Edition, 1987.

Zimbardo, Rose A. "The Medieval-Renaissance Vision of *The Lord of the Rings*." In Neil D. Isaacs and Rose A. Zimbardo. *Tolkien: New Critical Perspectives.* Lexington: University of Kentucky Press, 1981.

The Lion, the Witch, and the War Scenes: How Narnia *Went from* Allegory to Action Flick

MEGAN STONER

Andrew Adamson's 2005 film *The Chronicles of Narnia: The Lion, the Witch, and the Wardrobe* reflects a continuation of the trend towards large action-oriented adaptations of fantasy fiction, as seen in films like the incredibly successful adaptations of the *Lord of the Rings* trilogy and the ongoing *Harry Potter* books. Unlike these two epic series, however, the Chronicles of Narnia are rather small books, both in size and in focus: none of the seven books are over three hundred pages in length, and *The Lion, the Witch, and the Wardrobe* is smaller even than the average at barely over two hundred pages, or about a quarter the size of J.K. Rowling's *Harry Potter and the Order of the Phoenix*. In addition, the cast of characters is fairly limited in *Narnia*: unlike the dozens of principal characters in the *Lord of the Rings* books or the *Harry Potter* books, *The Lion, the Witch and the Wardrobe* focuses primarily on the four Pevensie children. Not even Aslan, the god-figure of all seven books, receives as much attention.

The result of this is that in the filmmakers' attempt to transform Lewis' small, rather cozy allegory of divine grace and childhood innocence into a full-out action blockbuster, decked out in all the requisite action sequences and epic battles demanded by modern fantasy filmgoers, they have lost sight of Lewis' *Narnia* and its peculiarly intimate blend of naiveté and pathos. Rather than telling a fairly small story with more talking than action, and more exploration than combat, Adamson's adaptation instead invents long action scenes and set pieces that are nowhere to be found in the book, reshuffling plot points and adding cliffhangers at every corner. This results in a movie that frequently feels forced rather than charming, as if it is desperately trying to be its *Lord of the Rings* elder brother rather than its smaller-scale self.

More disappointing than this, however, is the film's distinct dilution of Lewis' pervasive and unquestioning sense of morality and allegorical emphasis in favor of more and grander action and modern sensibilities. This is easily seen in the film's treatment of the Pevensie children: gone are Lewis' distinct and ingrained moral codes (for example, in the book, even Lucy's older siblings have to admit that she never lies), replaced by a very modern sense of ambivalence. In the book, the Pevensie children really never question the prophecy that they, with Aslan's help, are meant to restore Narnia. It is accepted that this is the destiny pre-ordained for them by the divine Aslan, who is also present in their England, albeit under another name. This idea of pre-ordination and divine destiny is one that is prevalent throughout Lewis' *Narnia* books, reflective of his own deeply-held Christian faith.

In the movie, however, both Peter and Susan repeatedly question and quarrel over the idea of their prophesied role (and indeed, the idea of prophesy in general), creating a tension between the siblings that is not present in the book. For example, at one point in the film, after Peter, Susan, and Lucy have seen Edmund disappear into the White Witch's castle (a sequence not in the book), Susan screams hysterically at Peter: "This is all your fault! None of this would have happened if you had just listened to me in the first place!" The only line of dialogue similar to this that is present in the book is Susan's exclamation of, "Oh, how I wish we'd never come" (*LWW* 90), which is a far cry from the moody tension created in the film.

There is also a greater emphasis on Peter's reluctance to take up arms in the fight for Narnia. For example, in the book, he eagerly asks to see Aslan before they discover that Edmund is missing; indeed, it is because the children and the Beavers are so engaged in discussing Aslan and the prophecy of the thrones in Cair Paravel that they fail to notice his departure. In the film, it is only Edmund's disappearance that forces the three remaining Pevensies to go to Aslan rather than returning home. In addition, Peter repeatedly insists that he is not interested in becoming king of Narnia. This is most obvious in a scene just after the Witch's wolves attack the Beavers' dam: the invented character of the Fox brings up the battle against the Witch and Susan immediately retorts that they are "not planning on fighting any witch." The Fox turns to "King Peter" for support, but Peter replies only that the siblings "just want to get our brother back." Even when Aslan shows him the castle of Cair Paravel, the site of the four thrones on which the children are prophesied to sit, the film's Peter retains his self-doubt: "I'm not who you all think I am," he tells Aslan. He is still doubtful even after Aslan's disappearance from the camp at the Stone Table, although in the book he has been given clear instructions on what he is to do and Aslan makes it fairly clear that He may not be there (*LWW* 160). In the film, it is only his brother Edmund's belief in his ability to lead the army against the Witch that allows Peter to finally take up arms.

This uncertainty is hardly demonstrated in the book, where Peter accepts his sword and shield and their corollary responsibilities seemingly without a word: Lewis says he "was silent and solemn as he received these gifts, for he felt they were a very serious kind of present" (*LWW* 118). Lewis' use of the word serious here is key to understanding his idea of the children's conception of duty and responsibility in Narnia. In an academic essay of his own, Lewis makes reference to the "indisputably religious overtones" of the word serious and its traditional usage as a "nearly-theological" word ("Essays" 177). With the use of a word recognized by himself as religious by implication, Lewis is imparting to this passage a definite sense of a divine destiny which cannot be argued with. Father Christmas is acting in this passage as a messenger from the god-figure Aslan, providing the children with the religiously-imbued means to perform the task that Aslan and the prophecy have set for them. The film's neglect of this religious emphasis in favor of a more modern, individualist approach does much to change the tone of the children's relationship to one another and to others.

More importantly, however, this modernist sense of reluctance and ambivalence significantly changes the character of Aslan as well. In the book, he is a very obvious Christ-figure, a source of redemption both for the Pevensies and Narnia, a sacrificial lamb who offers himself in exchange for the sinner Edmund. In addition to all this, Mr. Beaver refers to him in the book as the "son of the great Emperor-beyond-the-Sea" (*LWW* 86), whose knowledge of his father's "Deeper Magic from before the Dawn of Time" is instrumental in his defeat of the White Witch. The prophesy Mr. Beaver quotes in this passage is clearly messianic in nature:

> Wrong will be right, when Aslan comes in sight,
>   At the sound of his roar, sorrows will be no more,
>   When he bares his teeth, winter meets its death,
>   And when he shakes his mane, we shall have
>   spring again [*LWW* 85].

Yet the film mentions very little of this: no mention at all is made of Aslan's lineage or real importance in Narnia's cosmology, and the "Deeper Magic," which the Witch does not know, does not exist. In the film's interpretation, it is not the Witch's failure to know of this "Deeper Magic," but merely her misinterpretation of the Deep Magic itself that results in her defeat. And although in the film Mr. Beaver does quote the other prophecy,

> When Adam's flesh and Adam's bone
>   Sits at Cair Paravel in throne,
>   The evil time will be over and done [*LWW* 87],

he fails to mention at all the one regarding Aslan's role in the end of the Witch's reign. Instead, the emphasis is subtly shifted to the roles of the chil-

dren, not Aslan, as the primary saviors of Narnia. For example, in the film
Mr. Beaver tells the children that "Aslan's return, Tumnus' arrest, the secret
police — they're all happening because of you!" He even goes so far as to
assure the children that they must be the prophesied saviors, because "Aslan's
already fitted out your army!" It is almost as if the children have brought
about Aslan's return and are the source of his power.

Nor is it only the children whose significance seems proportionately
greater than Aslan's. In the book Aslan wields a much greater authority over
the White Witch than is anywhere visible in the film. For example, in the
book Edmund asks if the White Witch "won't turn [Aslan] into stone too?"
(*LWW* 85). Mr. Beaver is shocked by the mere suggestion of this unthinkable notion, as his reply demonstrates:

> Lord love you, Son of Adam, what a simple thing to say! ... Turn him into stone?
> If she can stand on her two feet and look him in the face it'll be the most she can
> do and more than I expect of her. No, no. He'll put all to rights [*LWW* 85].

And indeed, at the confrontation between the Witch and Aslan in Chapter
Fourteen to decide Edmund's fate, her parting audacity is met with such a
ferocious show of authority by Aslan that she "after staring for a moment
with her lips wide apart, picked up her skirts and fairly ran for her life"
(*LWW* 158). In sharp contrast, the confrontation between the two in the
film is a far more balanced meeting: the Witch shows little sign of distress
at being in Aslan's divine presence, and their discussion is more one of
equals deciding upon a fair trade than that of a superior and his inferior.
Nor does her exit demonstrate any great anxiety: rather than fleeing in
ignominy from Aslan's wrath, she is carried in her litter from the camp, in
a manner that is stately, almost triumphant. This coolly collected demeanor
serves to make her a far more chilling figure of evil, certainly, but it also
greatly diminishes Aslan's stature as a figure of great significance and power.

Similarly diminishing Aslan's importance is the scene with Father
Christmas. In the book, Father Christmas directly relates the thawing of
Narnia to Aslan's return: "She has kept me out for a long time, but I have
got in at last. *Aslan is on the move. The Witch's magic is weakening*" (*LWW*
117, emphasis added). In the film, however, Father Christmas credits the
Pevensies with the advent of Christmas and the thaw: "Now you have arrived
... the hope that you have brought, Your Majesties, is finally starting to
weaken the Witch's power." Even his farewell to the children is slightly
different: rather than the book's "Long live the true King!" (*LWW* 119), the
film's Father Christmas leaves them with a mere "Long live Aslan!" Aslan is
no longer the omnipotent ruler of Narnia as much as he is another prop for
the Pevensie children in their journey towards what director Adamson calls
their "empowerment": "They are ultimately the thing that's going to save

[Narnia]" (Moore 135), Adamson says, making them the true heroes of the story.

This subtle shift in emphasis from Aslan to the Pevensie children clearly reflects the influence of modern moviegoing tastes: with modern children as the film's target demographic, a reinvention of the children as slightly more central and heroic than their book counterparts is understandable. However, this influence is not only demonstrated in this reinvention but in the very structure of the action. Lewis' book contains very little in the way of modern action sequences: Peter's first real battle, a duel with one of the Witch's wolves, happens in the space of one paragraph, and the climactic battle at the end in which the Witch herself is defeated takes less than three pages and is mostly told in retrospective. There are no significant chase scenes, and little actual fighting.

The movie is drastically different: no fewer than three chase scenes (all invented for the film) take place before the Pevensies even get to Aslan's camp, and the grand-scale battle at the end lasts nearly twenty minutes. Many of these scenes seem rather decorative, contrived more as a way to keep the audience "on the edge of their seats" than to actually enhance the narrative. In one scene, the Wolves attack the Beavers' dam while they are still at home with the Pevensies, chasing them through an elaborate network of tunnels before they are diverted by the invented character of the Fox, while in another the children are chased yet again by a sleigh that both they and the audience are led to believe is the Witch's but turns out to be Father Christmas.' This emphasis on close calls and attack-and-chase sequences, even when they become repetitive and do little to further the plot, reflects more of a concern with catering to action-flick standards than traditional fantasy storytelling.

The most obviously action-enhanced sequence is the melting river scene. Here, the children and their protectors, the Beavers, face a perilous crossing over shattering ice while having to fend off an attack by the White Witch's wolves. There is nothing similar to this anywhere present in Lewis' fiction, and the scene lasts for four minutes while providing almost nothing new to the narrative: although Peter and Susan do express doubt again about whether it is a good idea to be in Narnia, and Peter has another chance to question his leadership abilities, the audience has been exposed to this before, and will see it again before the end of the film. What this scene does reflect, however, is a pronounced interest in action and peril that Lewis' rambling, sometimes timid narrative does not, and what appears to be an intentional reinforcement of the difficulty the Pevensies face simply by their presence in prophecy-laden, danger-ridden Narnia. This difficulty is something left untreated by Lewis: his children seem to have very little difficulty accepting their mission as the defenders and future rulers of Narnia. Once again the intrusion of modernity is clearly visible.

One other noteworthy intrusion of modern sensibilities into the action scenes is the presence of both Lucy and Susan on the final battlefield, and their active participation in the fight. Lewis's books reflect a very conservative idea of gender roles, and he has his Father Christmas espouse very much the same ideas when he gives out the gifts, in Chapter Ten. He tells Susan she must use the bow and arrows he has just given her "only in great need … for I do not mean you to fight in the battle" (*LWW* 118). His words to Lucy are very similar: "[The] dagger is to defend yourself at great need. For you also are not to be in the battle … battles are ugly when women fight" (*LWW* 119). While perhaps more authentically medieval — Lewis' academic specialty — this sort of protection of the female would be unlikely to be successful with the modern adaptation's target audience, which would include many young girls looking for role models. Modern expectations do not include keeping females away from action and danger simply because they are female: they are far more likely to celebrate the girls' participation in and triumph over the peril than their isolation from it. Adamson's allowance of the girls onto the battlefield reflects this very modern sensibility, even though it is at odds with Lewis' own ideas and presentation.

Ultimately, although Adamson and the filmmakers claim to have set out to make "an adaptation that's true to an original book and true to an image and a memory that a lot of people share" (Moore 135), their Narnia reflects the obvious influence of modern ideas regarding the roles of children, gender, even moral codes. Lewis' admittedly tamer Narnia, less action-oriented than allegorically-guided, is one in which the children (and indeed, all Narnia's inhabitants) possess the innate certainty that a higher power than themselves is directing them and their actions, and it is this reliance on something other than their own judgment and feelings that allows them to carry on with their destinies and ultimately save Narnia. The film's Narnia bears little resemblance to this allegorical and highly Judeo-Christian-influenced universe, instead choosing to emphasize large-scale action sequences and moral uncertainty and self-doubt. While this allows for a more modern feel, and certainly provides more action-packed excitement for modern audiences, it sacrifices the very foundational elements of Lewis' *Narnia*: belief, salvation, and destiny. In the end, Adamson's *The Lion, the Witch, and the Wardrobe* is not a transcendent tale of the triumph of childhood belief so much as a chase-laden, battle-heavy epic, catered for action-craving moviegoers but that seems too much like its larger, longer predecessors: it is more action-flick than allegory, and is not better for it.

Works Cited

Caughey, Shanna. ed. *Revisiting Narnia: Fantasy, Myth and Religion in C.S. Lewis's Chronicles*. Dallas: Benbella Books, 2005.

The Chronicles of Narnia: The Lion, the Witch and the Wardrobe. Directed by Andrew Adamson. DVD. Walt Disney Video, 2005.

Lewis, C.S. *The Chronicles of Narnia: The Lion, the Witch and the Wardrobe*. New York: HarperCollins, 1994.

_____. "A Note on Jane Austen." Selected Literary Essays. Edited by Walter Hooper. Cambridge, England: Cambridge University Press, 1979. 175–186.

_____. The Collected Letters of C.S. Lewis. Edited by Walter Hooper. 2 vols. New York: HarperCollins, 2004.

_____. Letters of C.S. Lewis. Edited by W.H. Lewis. New York: Harcourt, 2003.

Moore, Perry. *The Chronicles of Narnia: The Lion, the Witch and the Wardrobe: The Official Illustrated Movie Companion*. New York: HarperCollins, 2005.

Schakel, Peter J. *Imagination and the Arts in C.S. Lewis: Journeying to Narnia and Other Worlds*. Columbia, MO: University of Missouri Press, 2002.

The Lion, the Witch
and the Multiplex

PAUL TANKARD

C. S. Lewis was not a movie buff. In letters he mentions having seen three movies: Noel Coward's *Cavalcade* (1933), *King Kong* (1933), and Disney's *Snow White and the Seven Dwarves* (1937) (*Collected Letters*, 114–15, 120, 242). In an important essay, "On Stories" (5 ff.), he discusses the 1937 film of one of his old favorite books, Rider Haggard's *King Solomon's Mines*; he has very little positive to say about it. When he was once asked who was his favorite movie star, he said King Kong.

Yet as early as 1954, Lewis was approached about the possibility of a film of the first of his children's novels, *The Lion, the Witch and the Wardrobe* (1950). This was to have been an animated version for television (Hooper, 438). Although this project did not proceed, there have been four film versions of the novel since his death, all but the latest made for television (*Lion*). Lewis's brother Warren mentions in his diaries seeing the first of these, in black and white, on television in 1967. It screened over a number of Sunday nights, and after the final episode Warren Lewis wrote that it was "admirable both as regards acting and production, not a jarring note in either from start to finish. How I wish J [Jack, i.e., C.S. Lewis] could have seen it!" (279–80).

The first to be made for cinema is the 2005 film directed by Andrew Adamson for Walden Media, with financial backing from Walt Disney Productions (*Chronicles*). *The Lion, the Witch and the Wardrobe*, as a classic of literary fantasy — and the first book in a series, with the tantalizing promise of six sequels — was an obvious candidate for a follow-up to the cinematic success of Peter Jackson's three films of Tolkien's *The Lord of the Rings*, and the films of J.K. Rowling's "Harry Potter" stories. The Lewis Estate, closely administered by Lewis's younger stepson, Douglas Gresham, knowing that cinematic treatment of the Narnia books was inevitable, had long been looking at scripts from various production companies. In the sale of the film rights, the estate had retained the right of veto, which enabled versions to be rejected which did not do sufficient justice to the story Lewis had written. The treatment proposed by Walden Media seemed to offer the sympathy of aims that the estate was looking for. In order to have a hands-on role in the production, Douglas Gresham was taken on as co-producer. The huge budget of the film seems to have repaid the investment, having within six months of its release become (according to the Pazsaz Entertainment Network) one of the twenty-one top-grossing films of all time.

There are many levels at which we can compare a film to the book upon which it is based. Between the naivety of seeing the two as virtual equivalents ("I haven't read the book, but I've seen the film"), and the high level of theoretical abstraction which insists that any meaningful sense of relationship between two different "texts" is coincidental and illusory, we can learn a great deal about a story and story-telling in general, and about the two media, by thoughtful comparison. It is explicitly as dramatic structures that I wish to look at the novel and the film, although I will comment occasionally on other issues. This is a treatment which suits Lewis, who was concerned with story as the neglected element in fiction and, in his opinion, the main vehicle of literary meaning.

Walden Media is not in origin a movie production company, but a developer of educational materials, now aiming (so its Web site says) to "make movies that are inherently educational." *The Chronicles of Narnia: The Lion, the Witch and the Wardrobe* represents its first effort at a major cinema-release movie. While not explicitly promoting Christian values per se, the company's owner, Philip Anschutz, is known (and demonized in the media) as a religious and political conservative. Walden's coming movie projects, such as *Charlotte's Web* and *The Dark is Rising*, emphasize stories with strong and traditional literary and moral values. I suspect a deliberate ambiguity in their stated aim to "produce faithful film adaptations of great literature."

"Faithfulness" to the novel is a troublesome notion to critics—how much it is desirable and how much it is possible. Putting aside the latter philosophical question, it is obvious that some productions strive for faithfulness of a kind that others do not attempt. Adaptations of, for instance, Shakespeare or Jane Austen always have half an eye to scholars as well as readers; some versions are self-conscious and artful exercises in adaptation theory and *auteur*-ship. But with *The Lion, the Witch and the Wardrobe*, which has not previously been adapted for the cinema, and in which a large audience feels a particular kind of ideological investment, the filmmakers have been careful not to take too innovative an approach. Peter Jackson courted the goodwill of Tolkien fans by setting up an elaborate Web site to keep them informed about his work-in-progress, and Walden likewise has been careful to cultivate Lewis's particular constituency.

So it is fair to ask how well the product reflects C.S. Lewis's intentions. The meaning or relevance of authors' intentions has given rise to many controversies in literary criticism in the twentieth century: Eliot's impersonal theory of poetry, Lewis and Tillyard's personal heresy, Wimsatt and Beardsley's intentional fallacy, and Barthes' death of the author. But the dispersed or layered authorship of any major film, and the more explicit process of decision-making, means that everything that the audience experiences in the finished product is more or less deliberate. In particular, where a process of adaptation is involved, none of the perceived differences between the two texts will be accidental. Furthermore, it is often possible to find accounts of the process of decision-making. Some of my comments below have been helped by having been in the audience at a public conversation about the film involving Don McAlpine (director of photography) and Tracey Reebey (make-up and hairstyle). I cannot observe every deviation of plot. I will examine the film under four topics which seem to me to take in the major thematic variations from the novel.

The Children

Despite the book's title, its main characters are the children. A major change from Lewis's story is the depiction of Edmund. From the opening of the film he is the focal character. Adamson, in his unpublished director's notes, said of Edmund, "He's not just a bad kid.... He's troubled, with real issues—easy to create a back story." His back story is that he is misunderstood, missing and anxious about his father, jealous of his older brother's authority, and smarting from being corrected. In the film, Edmund is the first character we see, by himself, looking out the window of his suburban home at night during an air-raid—fascinated by the danger, and flouting the wartime black-out regulations. As the bombs fall around or near the house, he is pulled away from the window, and the children are rounded up by their mother and rushed out to the backyard air-raid shelter. When Edmund runs back into the house, with fire and explosions all around, he is established for the audience as brave or foolhardy, certainly, but mainly as an independent agent.

We soon see that Edmund has run back into the house in order to rescue a photo of his father. This gives him clear (and commendable—family-oriented) motives for his behavior or attitudes. Rather than being merely disobedient, he is willful, and motivated by strong feelings. Edmund is certainly the most interesting character of the film. Peter (who rushes back into the house after him, to rescue or protect him) yells at him, "Why can't you think of anybody but yourself? You're so selfish!" This is manifestly untrue, as we have seen he is thinking of his father.

When they arrive at the large, old and unpredictable house, they are left to their own devices, as in the book. The film depicts more bickering and boredom and general ill-temper between the children than does the book; this was felt (rather disturbingly) to be more in keeping with the experience or expectations of contemporary children. In the book, they all finally find their way into Narnia when they are trying to avoid Mrs. Macready and a party of tourists. In the film, they are trying to avoid her after breaking a window when playing cricket. This is not consistent with the generally responsible attitudes that Lewis bestows upon the children. The filmmakers seem to believe that taking responsibility for one's actions, in the specific terms of owning up and apologizing for misbehavior, are conventions which their audience won't appreciate.

The film also plays up the resentment and rivalry between Edmund and Peter. After Edmund has been rescued from the Witch, and had his private talk with Aslan, the girls hug him; but he and Peter do not shake hands. Hand-shaking as a form of greeting and other social negotiations may now be rather old-fashioned, but it is still understood; earlier in the film Lucy shakes hands with Tumnus. It is rather the mechanisms of apology and forgiveness that the film-makers are uncomfortable with. Lewis is very firm on the subject; "Edmund shook hands with each of the others and said to each of them in turn, 'I'm sorry,' and everyone said, 'That's all right'" (13: 128). The filmmakers instead prolong the tension between the two boys. However, Peter does say, "Get some sleep ... and [with a smile, which is returned] try not to wander off."

Perhaps the more distinct personalities of the children and their pursuit of individual agendas are more like a contemporary family; in any case, it opens the door to particularly contemporary-sounding reminders about family values. When Peter and Susan tell Lucy's story to the Professor and ask him, "So we should believe her?" he tells them, "She's your sister; you're a family — try behaving like one." This sort of appeal to family loyalty, which ends the discussion, is stressed by the film-makers, and is apparently consistent with the corporate aims of Walden Media. When the Fox tells them that Aslan has prepared an army for them to lead, Peter replies, "We're not heroes," to which Susan adds, "We're from Finchley" — a London suburb, chosen, I imagine, for its domestic-sounding name (this is not in the book) — "We're not fighting any war." Peter adds, "We just want our brother back," reinforcing the family loyalty theme. This is not a theme in any writing of C.S. Lewis. In fact, in his dystopic adult novel *That Hideous Strength* (51, 52, 93, 117, 208, 209) it is the deputy director of the National Institute for Co-ordinated Experiments ("N.I.C.E.") who employs this rhetoric, with the repeated sinister assurance, "You will find us ... a very happy family."

It is not a mere failure in loyalty that leads to Edmund's betrayal of Lucy, then of the children to the White Witch. After Lucy's second visit to

Narnia, she and Edmund — who has followed her, and has met the White Witch — return to England and the Professor's house, and Lucy wakes up the others. Edmund says he's just been playing along with Lucy's Narnia game. The film provides a different explicit motivation for this lie and betrayal, which Lewis in the voice of the narrator — and using this voice for the first time in the story, as Peter Schakel points out (*Way* 124) — calls "one of the nastiest things in this story" and "the meanest and most spiteful thing he [Edmund] could think of" (5: 45). This is strong language; but the film suggests that Edmund decides to betray Lucy only in order to avoid having to say what he was doing while Lucy was visiting Tumnus. It is depicted as an at least understandable effort to side-step a question he'd rather not answer. Lewis also emphasizes the impulsiveness of the decision: while Lucy is talking to the others, Edmund "hadn't made up his mind what to do. When Peter suddenly asked him the question he decided all at once," but Lewis gives no motive for it, even in terms of self-preservation. But we are told that he is "annoyed with Lucy for being right." In other words, his lie is gratuitous; in fact, had he admitted to at least having been in Narnia — and neglected to mention the Witch — he could have more easily enticed the others through the wardrobe and into her clutches. Lewis five times uses the terms *spite* or *spiteful* to describe Edmund's early feelings or behavior (3: 29, 5: 44–5). These rather old-fashioned terms do not constitute a reason or motive of any kind, for spite simply means an ill-natured desire to hurt or annoy. Lewis did not think that spitefulness betokened "real issues," beyond the post-Edenic human condition.

Peter on the other hand could fairly be described as paternalistic in his treatment of his three younger siblings. "You think you're Dad, but you're not!" Edmund shouts at him, which confirms our impression of him as a bit of a mommy's boy. Much later, after the other children are re-united with Edmund, Peter considers their mission in some way accomplished, and talks of sending the others back to England, in fulfillment of his promise to his mother. This is not in the book, and we have no idea whether he thinks it could actually be done, or how. Edmund, who now has the broader vision and authority, objects, "I've seen what the Witch can do. We can't leave these people behind to suffer for it." When the girls arrive on the battlefield with Aslan, Peter again says that the others must return to England. Edmund ignores the direction to head for safety; he rushes into the fray saying, "Peter's not king yet!" Again, Edmund is depicted as independent and brave. Edmund fights the Witch, as in the book, though the film has him come to Peter's rescue. For him, family values are more important than obedience. Later, after the battle, when Edmund is healed by Lucy, the two boys are finally reconciled — not, it might be observed, by Peter's hand of forgiveness earlier, but by Edmund's brave and sacrificial intervention in the fighting. This is in some ways the climax of the film, and it's a different climax than that of the book. There is a group hug. Edmund is the first to emerge from the hug, and look towards Aslan. This suggests that he has gained insight or moral depth from his walk on the wild side, and that a little knowledge of evil functions help to make us wise. To believe so is an ancient temptation.

The Land of Narnia

Film-makers, no matter how "faithful" they aim to be, usually need to truncate any story that has already been told in a novel. But they also need to make additions, in terms of dialogue and incident. One of these for which there is no obvious need is the moment when Peter takes in the view of Narnia from the Stone Table to Cair Paravel, and says, "It's so far." Mrs. Beaver responds, "It's the world, dear. Did you expect it to be small?" The film-makers clearly intend to alter the sense we have throughout the books of Narnia being a small world. One of the strongest contrasts between Narnia and Tolkien's Middle-earth is the matter of scale, and it is a particularly important topic when we consider the depiction of Narnia in other media. The film-makers are trying to emulate Peter Jackson with his version of *The Lord of the Rings*— to give the story an epic aspect, rather than the fairy-tale aspect of the books. Adamson in an interview has said that on re-reading the book for the film he found it "much smaller than I remember it ... and I really wanted to make the movie as epic as that memory." This vision is represented in a great number of ways, such as the musical soundtrack, which is full-on symphonic, whereas Lewis wrote a poem (not in the books), called "Narnian Suite," which is written as two "marches," to be accompanied by strings, kettledrums and trumpets (*Collected Poems* 20–21).

Strictly, of course, epic is a kind of poem. It is a narrative of a high or serious subject, often concerning the fate of a nation or world, and focused on the doings of a divine or heroic figure. But we apply the term in a loose way to novels that seem to embody the spirit of epic in the scale and seriousness of their concerns, like *War and Peace*, *Moby Dick*, and *The Lord of the Rings*. The many (and still-increasing number of) literary fantasists who follow in Tolkien's wake have written multi-volume stories set in continent- or planet-sized worlds. In these terms, Lewis's Narniad is not an epic.

In the first book in particular, Narnia is a very small realm, the size of a state or province, not a nation. Mr. Beaver tells the children that Aslan is "the King of the Wood," as if "the Wood" were the whole world (8: 76). The battle with the forces of the White Witch happens in isolation from the neighboring lands and territories, Calormene, Archenland, Ettinmoors, Telmar, and of course the sea and the islands; we learn of these only later in the series, because Lewis thought of them only later. As the series developed, the world of Narnia and its surrounding countries expands from the wardrobe-sized land of the first book. But it remains a small world. It is consistent with this that the children never talk in terms of comparing or traveling between Narnia and Earth, but always Narnia and *England* (Lewis, "Outline" 420).

In the book, the journey of the children and the beavers to Aslan is rather uneventful. It takes up one chapter and the start of another (10 and 12), interrupted by a chapter of Edmund's adventures. Briefly, they search for Edmund outside, pack up, leave the Beavers' dam under moonlight, spend the night in a secret retreat, hear bells and meet Father Christmas the next morning, and after some more walking through the thaw, arrive at the encampment of Aslan's army at the Stone Table. Much more is made of this is in the film, which adds to the story at least seven moments of lethal danger which are not in the book: the children almost expose themselves to the Witch at her castle, the wolves break into the Beavers' house, the children (and beavers) climb a tree while the fox misdirects the wolves and is mauled by them, they are pursued across the ice, they are caught by the wolves at the frozen waterfall, they escape into the rapids from the thaw, and then Lucy disappears for an anxious moment in the torrent.

Presented in this way, the changes certainly seem over-many, yet they are no more than audiences have come to expect in a film of this kind. They are oddly reminiscent of what Lewis himself observed about the film of *King Solomon's Mines*, in which Haggard's ending, with "the heroes awaiting death entombed in a rock chamber and surrounded by the mummified kings," is replaced by "a subterranean volcanic eruption, and ... an earthquake" ("On Stories," 5). The imaginative atmosphere which, Lewis felt, "lays a hushing spell on the imagination," is replaced in the more literal medium of cinema by simple excitement — "a rapid flutter of the nerves" (6). This succession of dangers and fears added to the first Narnia story as Lewis conceived it are not exactly prosaic, but they are all this-worldly: of pursuit, wild animals, capture, natural disaster; what they drive out of the audience's imagination is the more profound but subtle fear (and pleasure) of simply being in and journeying through an alien, magical world, and of being on one's way to a meeting with a divine lion. A film that accurately represented such journeying would seem very slow-moving — too slow-moving for a movie audience. Readers relish immersion in narrative atmosphere; multiplex audiences are assumed to be in a hurry to get home.

What all worlds are contingent upon, of course, is the will of Aslan. Mr. Beaver at the end of the book, explaining Aslan's anticipated comings and goings, tells them, "Of course he has other countries to attend to" (17:

168). As A.N. Wilson has remarked (226) of the books, "[t]heir whole theme is the interpenetration of worlds." The suggestion that there could be "other worlds ... just round the corner," invites readers, as Peter Schakel says (*Way* 117), "to take a new look at the narrowness of modern materialistic certainty and recover a sense of the openness of Platonic and Christian possibility." This, he says, is "[t]he most important effect of the series as a whole ... to make room for the spiritual." Such "room" must be made — if the spiritual is to be real and accessible — in the midst of the ordinary; however, the ordinary is not cinematic — or at least, not multiplex cinematic.

The eponymous wardrobe is the emblem of the "interpenetration of worlds." It is significant that Narnia is entered not via some dramatic means, but through an item of domestic furniture. However, the film is less interested in Narnia as a representation of spiritual possibility, than as merely fantastic. When Lucy first runs into the wardrobe room, the 1940s song "Oh Johnny" on the soundtrack stops suddenly and the music becomes more ethereal. The wardrobe itself is draped, so we do not (leaving aside extratextual knowledge) know immediately that it's a wardrobe. It doesn't exactly glow or hum, but certainly gives the impression of being something ominous. It's in the tradition of another other-worldly cinematic artifact, the famous monolith in *2001: A Space Odyssey*. To Lucy, as we can tell from her expression of wonder, it must look both mysterious and attractive.

In the book, there is no such build-up; in fact, Lewis emphasizes the wardrobe's ordinariness: it is introduced in a sentence which seems to begin as an afterthought: "And shortly after that they looked into a room that was quite empty [no pause, no suspense] except for one big wardrobe" (1: 12). Lewis wants by this lack of fanfare to emphasize that things are *not* always what they seem. The small can be momentous, the undramatic can be wonderful, the ordinary can be marvelous.

The Witch and the Party Animals

When Edmund follows Lucy, on her second trip through the wardrobe, he meets the White Witch, played by Tilda Swinton. In the film, she is initially less frightening than her dwarf. The dwarf chases Edmund with his whip and captures him, leaps on him with a fierce snarl and goes to kill him, but the Witch stops him. In the book, the Witch is far more abrupt and imperious: her speech has lots of exclamation marks— she says "Ha!" twice. She calls Edmund "an idiot" (4: 36). She stands up, about to obliterate him, but re-considers. In the film, she does not have to ask what he is; she knows immediately he is not a "beardless dwarf"; as soon as she sees what they have captured, she addresses him as "Son of Adam." She very swiftly (and I think,

far too swiftly) decides her strategy; we do not see what the book emphasizes—her shock or dismay at finding a human child in her realm. In the
book, the Witch is far more frightening for being, much of the time, on the
verge of panic. Although in the film she is just as cajoling and manipula-
tive, she is very sarcastic and not so capricious or brittle.

Edmund cuddles up next to her in her sled rather than, as Lewis
describes, sitting at her feet (this is done in the BBC film too), which—
especially with her bare shoulders—tinges the encounter with more than a
little eroticism. She puts her arm around him, and talks softly. Lewis makes
it clear enough in the book that the White Witch is far removed from the
old and ugly kind of witch, with warts and long pointed nose and chin. She
is a witch in the tradition of Snow White's stepmother, "the fairest of them
all." Lewis says she is exceptionally tall and very beautiful; she has white (he
says "not merely pale") skin and a "very red mouth" (3: 33). The illustrator, Pauline Baynes, gives her long black hair. In *The Magician's Nephew*, we
learn that she is seven foot tall, and very beautiful—though her beauty is
of a kind that apparently has a particular appeal to young boys; Digory
thinks she is beautiful, Polly does not, or says she doesn't. This seems to
suggest that her glamour—from a more mature or informed perspective—
is too overt to be believable. Tilda Swinton's blonde dreadlocks connect with
no such tradition; she will look, to viewers in a few years' time, "very second millennium," as one of my students said. She is in this version less a
principle of evil or a fairy-tale archetype, than a plausible and merely contemporary human character.

Another addition to the film's version of the story is the introduction
of the character of the Fox. He appears as the Beavers and the children
emerge from the badger's tunnel, where they find the party of woodland animals, already turned to stone. In the book the children do not meet this
ensemble of animals at all; they are depicted much later, after Father Christmas has come and furnished them with the elements of their feast. Moving
this tableau forward adds (even) more drama to the journey of the children
and the beavers. But it does so at the expense of the important scene of the
Witch turning them to stone (11: 108), which emphasizes her character as a
tyrannous ruler. In the film she petrifies the Fox, who is brought before her
by the wolves, and (in an odd humorous touch) a passing butterfly. But this
is the punishment of a traitor or collaborator and is not equivalent to turning to stone a group of innocent partying animals, which is, in fact, the only
direct evidence we have of the White Witch's cruel and oppressive regime;
the rest of the time she is simply fighting an enemy.

A number of critics of the book have emphasized the importance of
the scene. Wesley Kort argues that in Narnia we see a country which is tyr-
annized by a witch whose "principal goal is to kill joy, to stop celebration."

He adds, "when the witch turns creatures into stone in the midst of their festive meal" we see that "[n]othing marks Jadis more than her antipathy toward celebrations" (153). Under her rule, there are no natural and seasonal cycles, no revels and no Christmas. The crime of her rule is the suppression of beauty, imagination and celebration; she uses sheer power to ensure that Narnians have no sources of joy that suggest the possibility of independence from her. In the film she is less evil, and more just a villain.

The omission does not only alter the depiction of evil, it alters the depiction of the celebratory aspect of everyday life. Eliane Tixier observes (152) that in Narnia, "joy is frequent and inspires various kinds of rejoicing, from play and games to dances and feasts." Narnian creatures experience "real joys and pleasures in their everyday lives," and Lewis depicts these privileged moments, equally with the moments of numinous awe, which if we recognize them are patches of eternity and forms of the presence of holiness. Of course, Lewis is also slyly critiquing joyless forms of Christianity, in which pleasure is regarded as suspect.

Talk of the Lion

Aslan is the least ordinary character in the story, and Lewis relies on mystery and anticipation to evoke the appropriate sense of awe. Yet, curiously, in the film, the Beavers do not mention that Aslan is a —*the*— Lion (and the children don't ask), nor do they make the important statement about his character, that "he isn't safe. But he's good" (7: 75; a distinction typical of C.S. Lewis). It is an important statement because it signifies that Aslan is beyond our usual categories. When the Fox gives them news of Aslan, the word "Lion" still is not mentioned, and the Fox tells them rather lamely, he's "like everything we've ever heard," which is, in the case of the children, not a lot. When the three children see Aslan for the first time, there is little in the way of awe or even surprise, which reinforces the sense that the film-makers expect the audience to already know he's a lion. In the book, the quality of Aslan's presence is conveyed by descriptions of the effect he has on people; but there is no filmic equivalent to remarks such as narratorial remarks as, "People who have not been in Narnia sometimes think that a thing cannot be good and terrible at the same time. If the children had ever thought so, they were cured of it now ... they couldn't look at him and went all trembly" (12: 119).

The film-makers may imagine that the audience will already know who Aslan is, either first- or second-hand from the books, or simply from the film's title and the publicity. Or the line may have been omitted in order to enhance suspense or the viewers' curiosity. But in his critical writings, Lewis again and again stresses the imaginative difference that story elements make to the mere excitement that may be generated by plot alone. In "On Stories" (8), he says, "*Jack the Giant-Killer* is not, in essence, simply the story of a clever hero surmounting danger. It is in essence the story of such a hero surmounting *danger from giants*" (Lewis's emphasis). He makes similar claims about the effects of pirates and Red Indians in stories, which he claims are "to the young reader almost as mythological as the giants." In *The Problem of Pain*, in explanation of the numinous element he believes to be part of "all developed religion," Lewis stresses that the feeling (of fear) we have on being told that there is a tiger in the next room, is different in quality to the "uncanny" fear we might have on learning there is a ghost in the next room (4–5). In the same way, we might distinguish the feeling of anticipation of meeting a king who is a great man, and of meeting a king who is a great lion.

The most sensitive part of the story for Lewis's Christian readership is Aslan's sacrifice and resurrection, and the film depicts this with straight-faced fidelity to the book. And — Christian agendas aside — why should it not? Stories of heroes dying and rising to life are not — as Lewis would have been the first to remark — unique to Christianity. What is, is the Christian claim that it actually happened, about which *The Lion, the Witch and the Wardrobe* says nothing. As readers, Christian and otherwise, have recognized for decades, it makes a great story. The only departure or elaboration is a matter of style. Here we come to what I believe to be the most significant divergence between the two texts. In the book, after his resurrection, Aslan has a great romp with Lucy and Susan — "It was such a romp as no one ever had except in Narnia" (15: 148). The film omits it completely. Also downplayed is the sequence which immediately follows this, when Susan and Lucy ride on Aslan's back, which the narrator says "was perhaps the most wonderful thing that happened to them in Narnia" (15: 149). The terms in which the narrator glosses both these events, the romp and the ride, emphasizes their significance.

The importance of these scenes to the story is emphasized by the fact they are depicted by Pauline Baynes on the front wrapper of the original hardback edition of the book, and in the rarely reproduced color frontispiece to that edition and (a different picture) on the cover of the first (Penguin) paperback edition. These two editions were published in Lewis's lifetime, and it is reasonable to believe that he was consulted about them. Baynes depicted Aslan and the two girls a fourth time, on the cover of the hardcover "deluxe 50th Anniversary edition" (2000), and Christian Birmingham depicted the same scene on the front cover of the 1998 abridgment (by Amanda Benjamin). As we have seen, Lewis deliberately de-emphasizes the battle in favor of depicting Aslan's resurrection as a warm, purring, roaring beast. His romp with Susan and Lucy indicates that he has at this point returned to "real" life; and that he's not an austere and remote figure, but warm and intimate. Lewis emphasizes the feel of his fur, the warmth of his breath. But in film, a short battle is a waste of the medium, and having set it up as a (visual) climax of the film, the filmmakers understandably do not want a sentimental and hard-to-interpret scene of two girls romping with a digital lion to detract from the climax of their "epic." We have not got to know Aslan as well in the film as the books, and the concentration seems to be not on the children's relationships with him, so much as on their relationships with each other.

Conclusion

No one can doubt the intention of Walden Media and the director to treat the film in a way that did not displease Lewis's large and articulate readership. It was possible that another treatment might have done anything: made the children American, set it during the Vietnam War, or omitted Aslan's death (as I've heard that one stage version did — no doubt without the *imprimatur* of the Lewis Estate). On the whole, those who value *The Lion, the Witch and the Wardrobe* for the resemblances between its story and that of the Gospels have very little to complain about. Likewise, non-Christians have no more cause to complain about the film than the book. There have always been readers who have not noticed the allegorical aspects of the story until or unless they have been pointed out to them, and it is hard not to imagine that the number of such readers — innocent of any knowledge of the Christian religion — is growing. Neither text is religious propaganda nor even religious allegory, properly understood. The reader or viewer is free to enjoy the story as such.

But much is lost here. There is a reluctance to depict evil as unprovoked or inexplicable: Edmund is given a number of motives for his betrayal, and the Witch is less an evil principle than a mere enemy. The film diminishes Aslan's authority, awesomeness and intimacy. The sense of wonder which Lewis takes trouble to convey is replaced by excitement. What is missing from the film is a certain atmosphere, the atmosphere of *faerie*. Apprehending faerie involves an exercise of imagination of a kind or to a degree which is not called forth by cinema. What I hope I have shown is that using substantially the same plot materials is not sufficient, with the change of medium, to present the same experience.

Works Cited

_____. Interview, "New Zealand, *Narnia* and Beyond." Http://www.ComingSoon.net. Accessed December 1, 2005.

Adamson, Andrew. Unpublished Director's notes for the film. "Chronicles of a Director." *The Chronicles of Narnia: The Lion, the Witch and the Wardrobe*, DVD, disk 2.

The Chronicles of Narnia: The Lion, the Witch and the Wardrobe. Directed by Andrew Adamson. Walt Disney Productions and Walden Media, 2005.

The Chronicles of Narnia: The Lion, the Witch and the Wardrobe. Directed by Andrew Adamson. Special two-DVD collector's edition. Buena Vista, 2006.

Hooper, Walter. *C.S. Lewis: A Companion and Guide*. London: HarperCollins, 1996.

Kort, Wesley A. *C.S. Lewis, Then and Now*. New York: Oxford University Press, 2001.

Lewis, C.S. *Collected Letters, v. 2: Books, Broadcasts and War, 1931–49*. Edited by Walter Hooper. London: HarperCollins, 2004.

_____. *Collected Poems of C.S. Lewis*. Edited by Walter Hooper. London: HarperCollins, 1994.

_____. *That Hideous Strength: A Modern Fairy-Tale for Grown-Ups*. 1945; New York: Scribner, 1996.

_____. *The Horse and His Boy*. 1954; London: Collins, 1998.

_____. *The Lion, the Witch and the Wardrobe*. Illustrated by Pauline Baynes. London: HarperCollins, 1998.

_____. *The Magician's Nephew*. Illus. Pauline Baynes. 1955; London: Collins, 1998.

_____. "On Stories" (1947). *Of Other Worlds: Essays and Stories*. Edited by Walter Hooper. London: Geoffrey Bles, 1966.

_____. "Outline of Narnian History, so far as it is known." 1979; reprinted in Walter Hooper, *C.S. Lewis: A Companion and Guide*. London: HarperCollins, 1996.

_____. *A Preface to 'Paradise Lost.'* London: Oxford University Press, 1942.

_____. *The Problem of Pain*. London: Centenary Press, 1940.

_____. *The Silver Chair*. Illustrated by Pauline Baynes. 1953; London: Collins, 1998

_____. *The Voyage of the 'Dawn Treader.'* Illustrated by Pauline Baynes. 1952; London: Collins, 1998.

Lewis, W.H. *Brothers and Friends: The Diaries of Major Warren Hamilton Lewis*. Edited by Clyde S. Kilby and Marjorie Lamp Mead. San Francisco: Harper and Row, 1982.

The Lion, the Witch and the Wardrobe. Dramatized by Alan Seymour. Produced by Paul Stone. Directed by Marilyn Fox. BBC Television, 1988. Live-action with life-size animatronic puppets, and some animation.

The Lion, the Witch and the Wardrobe. Directed by Bill Melendez. Produced by Steve Melendez. Children's Television Workshop, New York, and the Episcopal Radio-TV Foundation, Inc., 1976. Animated.

The Lion, the Witch and the Wardrobe. Adapted by Trevor Preston. Directed by Helen Standage. Prod. Pamela Lonsdale. ABC Television (UK), 1967. Live action.

McAlpine, Don, and Tracey Reebey. "*The Chronicles of Narnia*: From Book to Film," chaired by Robert and Linda Banks. "C.S. Lewis Today" Conference. Robert Menzies College, Sydney. May 6, 2006.

Pazsaz. "Worldwide Top Grossing Films," *Pazsaz Entertainment Network*. http://www.pazsaz.com/ wldfilms.html. Accessed May 17, 2006.

Schakel, Peter J. *Reading with the Heart: The Way into Narnia*. Grand Rapids, MI: Eerdmans, 1979.

_____. *The Way into Narnia: A Reader's Guide*. Grand Rapids, MI: Eerdmans, 2005.

Tixier, Elaine. "Imagination Baptized, or, 'Holiness' in the Chronicles of Narnia," *The Longing for a Form: Essays on the Fiction of C.S. Lewis*. Edited by Peter J. Schakel. Kent, OH: Kent State University Press, 1977. 136–58.

Walden Media. Http://www.waldenmedia.com. Accessed April 10, 2006.

Wilson, A.N. *C.S. Lewis: A Biography*. London: Collins, 1990.

Buckets of Money:
Tim Burton's New Charlie and the Chocolate Factory

Elizabeth Parsons

Tim Burton's 2005 film version of Roald Dahl's *Charlie and the Chocolate Factory* (1964) makes a specific and overt addition to the ideology of the narrative, one that recodifies the events so as to irrevocably change the story's import. In the final scene, the hitherto disembodied narrator asserts that family is more important than money. However, this message about the happiness that families produce is consistently undercut in the film, and in particular by a further range of intricately connected alterations that Burton makes to Dahl's story. Burton's changes point to the new political agendas that emerge in the *Charlie and the Chocolate Factory*'s translation across time and medium, most notably in the models of contemporary western world capitalism the film promotes.

The implications of these changes can also be exposed through comparison to the 1971 film *Willy Wonka and the Chocolate Factory*, for which Dahl wrote a portion of the screenplay. Despite Burton's message about family, it is money and the happiness it brings that is a central feature of all three versions. The hero, Charlie Bucket, is desperately poor, and his story embodies the classic rags to riches motif. In contemporary children's narratives, the life-changing transformations that shift characters across class boundaries are somewhat more complicated than in traditional tales like *Cinderella*. The political, economic and social agendas in Burton's revisioning of this archetype demonstrate the changes in class politics under capitalism over the forty years since the story of Charlie Bucket entered the popular imagination.

Those forty years have seen the emergence of what Ulrich Beck describes as "risk society," a world in which the responsibility for one's economic and social well-being is individualized, social inequality is elided, and the problems of class are "transformed into personal failure" (89). As a result, the problem of class tends to be attributed not to economic poverty, but to an impoverishment of civic values. Given this socio-cultural landscape, the complex position of the story's protagonist, Charlie, and his family's class location can be most clearly elucidated by Pierre Bourdieu's theories of capital. Bourdieu proposes that capital moves beyond any clear-cut economic definition in order to encompass what he calls social, cultural, and symbolic capital. By positioning Burton's remake of *Charlie and the Chocolate Factory* in terms of both economic and non-economic forms of capital and their implications for social mobility, participation, and cohesion, this analysis of the film responds to the interrelationship between class and citizenship under conditions of globalization. The following discussion, therefore, segues between interrogating the individual characters and the political contexts within which they are framed and constructed.

Burton is well known for his stylized sets and characters in films like *Edward Scissorhands,* and *Charlie and the Chocolate Factory* is similarly composed. In terms of class hierarchy, the characters exist within a tight symbolic framework in which factory workers and factory owners are visually opposed to each other. They are also embedded in the film's industrial setting as signaled by the factory's prominence in the title. In synopsis, the story shows a poor child's capitalist dreams come true when he becomes the owner-in-waiting of a highly profitable business, servicing a vast international market. Thus, in many respects, this prescient story centers around the most significant issues associated with globalization, neoliberalism, the plight of cheap foreign laborers, and post-Fordist factory processes. The winning of a chocolate factory that neatly closes the narrative foregrounds the rewards inherent in wealth and power as promoted by all three versions of the story.

To interpret the significance of this win, it is possible to apply Bourdieu's theory of the cultural field that describes the institutions, rituals, conventions, and categories that surround and construct the individual. The cultural field is linked to both class positions and social connections as a set of practical limitations around individuals, but, as Bourdieu says, this does not stop agents from gambling for capital in order to improve their place (Webb et al. 23). When Charlie tries to win the golden ticket, he engages in this gamble and upholds the mythology of the lucky break that produces the greatest moments of transformation across class boundaries. Burton's film, however, problematizes this class mobility by asking Charlie to abandon his family in order to take up his new entrepreneurial position in the factory. Wonka essentially asks Charlie to choose between his family and their abject poverty or the wealth and business success that winning the chocolate factory will produce. As a good citizen who is true to the film's moral agenda, Charlie chooses his family.

By comparison, in Dahl's ending none of the Bucket family will ever need to toil as part of the blue-collar lower class again. There is no question that the whole Bucket family will accompany Charlie to live a life of decadence in the factory while Charlie is inducted into the business. But Burton's version shifts this final success for the Buckets so that Charlie's father goes back to work in the toothpaste factory that had earlier made him redundant, and all the Buckets, including Charlie, stay living in the dilapidated family home which is ostensibly still on the socially marginalized outskirts of their town. I say "ostensibly" because there is a very brief final frame that suggests the rundown home has ended up in the factory. But it seems that this tiny gesture (and the wavering frame that precedes it) only indicates that Charlie Bucket's story occurred in the past and has now become a chapter of the Wonka fantasy world. The narrator of the story is an Oompa Loompa, suggesting that Charlie's tale is but one of the mythologies produced in the long-running Wonka empire.

Prior to that final frame, the narrative centers on the happiness that Mr. Bucket's new job, and the pay rise (the money) that accompanies it, brings. The decision to reinstate Charlie's father as a factory worker can, therefore, be read as undermining the overtly positioned moral message in the film. Mr. Bucket gets something of a promotion so that he is engaged in repairing the machines that had taken his job, and he's now paid enough to provide a home-style, but nonetheless quite lavish roast meal around the family dining table (although he is not paid enough to buy a comfortable home). Rather than Charlie and the Buckets being upgraded to the palatial factory, Willy Wonka has joined them as an honorary member of the family, and this maintenance of the Buckets' original class location makes everyone happy. Clearly, Mr. Bucket's new factory job suggests that the Buckets do need more money to make them happy, but they do not need so much money that they are lifted out of their class station.

Burton's closure essentially nullifies the upward mobility motif of the original story in ways that seem to be a direct contradiction of the American dream in which anyone can make it through free enterprise. Burton is not alone in this approach. His film's social rigidity is very similar to that celebrated in another recent children's blockbuster, *Shark Tale*. In the latter, Will Smith plays a lowly fish called Oscar who learns that the vast riches enjoyed by the elite society in the penthouses at the top of the reef are not his aspiration; he is much happier with the modest climb from worker in a whale wash to part owner of the business. Like the Buckets, Oscar is lower class; he is also racialized in that his characterization trades on Will Smith's African American accent and is augmented by a direct depiction of Oscar's social place in a simulated ghetto in the early scenes of the film. There is a bizarre contradiction in both these contemporary children's films: the characters learn that wealth is not important, but they learn that lesson within a profoundly capitalist class hierarchy, one that upholds the economic sta-

tus quo rather than challenging the injustices that uneven distribution of
wealth causes. Essentially, these stories suggest that the poor will be happy
if they accept their place and only aspire for a small hike up the economic
ladder rather than a full class shift. This conflicting logic works to maintain class politics under capitalism.

In line with John Stephens' argument that the manifestation of ideology in children's texts is often implicit rather than explicit, one might more
safely maintain that the values expressed in the *Charlie and the Chocolate
Factory* unintentionally reinscribe those beliefs necessary for the continued
dominance of capitalism and the class differences it encodes in the contemporary western world. However, the film cannot be easily divorced from its
cultural context; it is not only a vehicle for, but also a product of capitalist
motivations. The lucrative children's film industry is designed as more than
just saleable entertainment. The Nestlé corporation stood to make enormous
profits from the increased market share of chocolate sales through their
ownership of the Wonka brand name.

There is a frightening synchronicity of the childlike size of the Oompa-
Loompas with Nestlé's supposed commitment to ending child labor on West
African cocoa farms. According to the Campaign for Labor Rights collective (anti-sweatshop activists whose work is endorsed by Noam Chomsky),
little has been accomplished in preventing child labor, and the problem continues unabated. Further, in 2005 two union leaders trying to bring labor
conditions in line with international standards at the Nestlé factory in the
Philippines were murdered in suspicious circumstances. Nestlé's recent
move into a single line of fair trade coffee at the top end of their product
range has also sparked considerable outrage from many Fair Trade and anti-
sweatshop activists who claim that this minimal gesture is a public relations
stunt designed to deflect attention away from the company's abuses of poorly
paid workers. In light of these global economic contexts, this film's
glorification or idealization of factory work, can be seen as driven by broader
issues.

Throughout Burton's film, the class hierarchies forged by the processes
of free-market capitalism are made most patently apparent through the contrast between the lower class factory worker, Mr. Bucket, and the upper class
factory owner, Mr. Wonka. Burton populates his film with many factory
workers. In addition to reinstalling Mr. Bucket in the toothpaste factory, he
also makes Grandpa Joe one of Wonka's ex-workers. When Charlie chooses
his family over a life of success with Wonka, he also chooses the simple
pleasures of a worker's happiness rather than the riches offered by Wonka's
empowered position. As indicated above, Wonka comes to the party in the
end, but he is in control of the events. Charlie must simply be good and
hope for the best. In this logic, the Buckets are representatives of family hap-

piness, but their oppressed working lives belie the message. Rather, child audiences are more effectively positioned to recognize and appreciate the immense happiness Wonka enjoys. His work is entirely pleasurable, particularly as understood by the implied child audience for whom being a chocolatier is a job that involves the ultimate satisfaction of their oral desires.

In addition, his work is made particularly easy by his workforce of Oompa-Loompas. Wonka's carefree existence is emphasized when the children follow him in to the factory entrance hall at the beginning of their visit. Wonka grandly instructs the children to "drop [their] ... coats anywhere" and strolls away without concern. The implication is that there are people around who will pick up after him. Wonka's highly groomed appearance implies that his clothes are not left lying around in a crumpled heap. In one of the later scenes when Wonka undergoes a Freudian style analysis with one of his Oompa-Loompas, he reveals that he works only for his own pleasure: "I've always made whatever candy I felt like." Clearly this is a recipe for happiness. Neither of these events come from Dahl's novel, they are part of Burton's reshaping of the narrative to suit the contemporary conditions of capitalism in which the pleasures of wealth are more overtly celebrated than in England during the 1960s.

In contrast to the immaculately dressed Mr. Wonka, replete with age-old English class markers of a top hat and cane, Mr. Bucket's demeanor suggests a painful sense of oppression, his face scarred by the hard life he has led. Unlike the happy capitalist success story of Wonka, he has never enjoyed working in the toothpaste factory where "the hours were long, and the pay was terrible," sweatshop conditions. He clearly has no union protection because he is laid off without pay and has no recourse to industrial relations action. His job is mind-bogglingly tedious. He screws lids onto toothpaste tubes, an activity made still more monotonous when viewed in contrast to the chocolatier's globetrotting lifestyle. Burton's Wonka is shown in lush and exotic settings such as India and the jungles of Loompa Land where he finds his workforce. This exciting life is heightened by the enjoyment Mr. Wonka experiences while taking children on a tour of his factory.

Wonka's success in business is what makes this life-style possible, but the economic success of the individual is always entrenched in the broader capitalist economy in ways that Burton makes patently apparent. Where Dahl's Mr. Bucket lost his job when the toothpaste factory "went bust" (43), Burton's Bucket loses his job because Mr. Wonka's promotional activities have lead to higher toothpaste sales; children get more cavities while they desperately devour chocolate bars in the hope of finding a golden ticket. The increase in sales means the company can buy a more efficient machine. The interrelationship between these industries in a capitalist economy is thus made obvious in Burton's revisioning, and Wonka's success increases the economic success across the board, even for Mr. Bucket who will eventually get a better-paid job at the film's close. Further, in Burton's film Wonka's father is a dentist; thus all three men gain from Wonka's increased productivity. That these recipients of capitalist fortune are only men encodes a gender motif that will come to the fore as the argument progresses. But in terms of capitalist politics, this economic boom is a patent example of the film's wholesale promotion of a right-wing ideology, one that directly contradicts its overt message that successful entrepreneurialism like Wonka's, and the money it brings, does not make people happy.

Mr. Bucket's return to work in the Fordist production line at the end of the film offers no reason to expect that fixing the machines that screw the lids on the toothpaste tubes will improve the intellectual richness of his daily labor contribution. Certainly Mr. Bucket is depicted smiling about his increase in pay, but there is little question that he works only for the money to support his family, not for pleasure. That this wealth does indeed produce family happiness is encoded in the presence of all four grandparents at the dining table in the final scene. When the family was suffering under conditions of abject poverty, their despair seems to have kept them bedridden.

Food is crucial in this logic. Burton's narrative makes an implied comparison between Mr. Bucket, who is happy as long as his wages in the toothpaste factory can feed him roast rather than the grim cabbage soup that sustains his family early in the film, and the Oompa-Loompas who are happy to be paid in the cocoa beans rather than the green caterpillars they hated eating before they were recruited by Wonka. Clare Bradford has read the Oompa-Loompas' position using postcolonial theoretical perspectives, so I will not follow that line of argument here. As will have been apparent from the preceding comments, however, food is profoundly blurred with money in the film, and the intrinsic relationship between food and money reveals that the latter is not only a necessity for physical survival, but also a source of immense happiness and pleasure, particularly in its ability to provide adults and children alike with delicious comestibles such as chocolate and candy. In her 1980 research, Wendy Katz famously and contentiously claimed that "food may be, in fact, the sex of children's literature" (192).

In another of Burton's additions to the original narrative, Charlie is prepared to give up his desperately longed for golden ticket which he knows he can sell for a considerable amount of money. He altruistically says, "We need the money more than we need the chocolate." Charlie's gesture provides a platform for the speech that voices the film's moral agenda. Grandpa George says to Charlie: "There's plenty of money out there. They print more every day. But this ticket, there's only five of them in the world and that's all there's ever going to be. Only a dummy would give this up for something as common as money. And you're not a dummy are you Charlie?" But given their desperate situation — one in which the only food available is a cabbage soup even more watered down than when Mr. Bucket was working — the Buckets are likely to starve soon. The grim reality is glossed over by Grandpa George's description of money as common. To be common is a hallmark of lower class families, and it is in this conversation that the Buckets identify themselves with the genteel poor and lay claim to a measure of cultural capital. The highly class-located concept of manners, as it turns out, is the key to Charlie's success in the story.

Essentially Charlie's good manners are his cultural capital because they are, to use Harker's reading of Bourdieu, the symbolic goods "that present themselves as being rare and worthy of being sought after in a particular social formation" (22). Charlie wins his way out of a lifetime of poverty because he is the only child to tour the factory who displays good manners in accordance with the rigid British codes that shape the cultural field in the original story. Dahl's novel was very explicit about manners, the Oompa-Loompa songs describing the children's crimes: Augustus Gloop is punished for his greed, Violet Beauregarde is punished for her disgusting habit of chewing gum all day, Veruca Salt is punished for being spoiled and rudely demanding as a result, and Mike Teavee is punished for wasting time watching television, and in particular violent television. The opening pages of the first paperback edition make the logic explicit:

> *There are five children in this book:*
> AUGUSTUS GLOOP
> *A greedy boy*
> VERUCA SALT
> *A girl who is spoilt by her parents*
> VIOLET BEAUREGARDE
> *A girl who chews gum all day long*
> MIKE TEAVEE
> *A boy who does nothing but watch television*
> *and*
> CHARLIE BUCKET
> *The hero*

Charlie's manners make him rare and single him out for the ultimate prize. Despite being poor in economic capital by comparison to these other children, he has this cultural capital in abundance, and the upper-class Wonka rewards him accordingly. In the introduction to *Distinction: A Social Critique of the Judgment of Taste*, Bourdieu says: "the importance attached to manners can be understood once it is seen that it is these imponderables of practice which distinguish the different — and ranked — modes of culture acquisition ... and the classes of individuals which they characterize" (2).

The question of manners points directly to another important addition that Burton makes to Dahl's story, namely in the characterization of Violet Beauregarde. Burton does not seem to be particularly troubled by gum-chewing, the rudeness that offended Dahl's sensibilities in the 1960s. Instead, Burton reconfigures the narrative's cultural field by making Violet into an emblem for the crassness of competition. Violet's page on the film's official Web site describes her in the following terms:

> 10 year old Violet Beauregard can now add a golden ticket to her 263 trophies and medals. A born competitor, Violet excels in every sport she attempts—from karate to gum-chewing. She currently holds the record for the longest time chewing one piece of gum: three months and counting! Mrs. Beauregard, Violet's mother and manager, believes Violet is a look to win Wonka's special prize. As she puts it, she's a WINNER!"

Similarly, in the film Violet is depicted excelling at karate and is then interviewed in front of her trophy cases. Dahl's novel describes Violet with the focus on her constant chewing. There is a small reference (three short sentences in more than a page of text) to having beaten her friend in a chewing gum competition. However, her world record for gum-chewing trades more on the committed constancy of Violet's habit, than on her competitiveness, which is figured as but one facet of her consummate rudeness. For the most part, Dahl's descriptions center around the unladylike vulgarity of gum itself (37) and includes Violet sticking bits of gum on the lift (elevator) controls so that the next person gets the residue on his fingers (38). The 1971 film shows Violet chewing and also behaving in brash and rude ways. In that version, her class location as new-money is modeled by her Americanness (which the British typically consider crass) and especially by her father's position as a used-car salesman.

Burton's critique of Violet for her competitive behavior is a potential glitch in my reading of the film which asserts that it upholds capitalist values, as competition is a necessary functional feature of the system. But the messages are very inconsistent in this regard. Indeed the whole storyline in Burton's version becomes brimful with competition. Nowhere in Dahl's tale is it clear that the children who visit the factory are engaged in a competition to win a secret special prize. It is only after Charlie has inadvertently won this competition by his good manners that Dahl's Wonka discloses this agenda. Because the original Wonka wanted to find a good child who acted appropriately without knowing about the potential rewards, he did not announce the competition, a revelation that would have would have undermined his project.

Whereas Dahl's golden ticket promised only a lifetime supply of chocolate and a tour of the factory, Burton's includes an additional temptation: that one child will win a special prize. The children are thus vying against each other throughout the tour, and this takes the form of a particularly savage representation of the girls who deceitfully vow to "be friends. Yes, best friends," even though they are in competition. Interestingly both girls speak of their desire to win the competition, while the boys do not vocalize their hopes. Augustus Gloop is happy with the truckload of chocolate; Mike Teavee inquires, "What's the special prize and who gets it?" but it becomes clear that he thinks the whole place is rather less enthralling than watching television; and Charlie is too self-deprecating to think that he could win. But the idea of competition in itself is positively presented in that Charlie, the underdog that audiences are positioned to support, wins, and this is a part of his success and equally a part of the pleasure child viewers take in the narrative closure.

Thus it is not competition that is negatively portrayed; it is the girls, but principally Violet's competitiveness that is demonized, thus foregrounding the significance of gender in the film's ideology. Violet's gender is a particularly telling issue because Burton's film glorifies father figures and makes them important in finding happiness. There is no Mr. Wonka senior in Dahl's novel and Charlie's father in Dahl's novel is so irrelevant that he is excised from the 1971 film. In that earlier film, the inability of Charlie's single mother to provide adequately for the family invokes a range of related gender assumptions regarding women's political and economic capital; Charlie's success in winning the chocolate factory recuperates his mother's inadequacy. Empowered by patriarchal capitalism, he becomes the new family provider, bundling his grandparents into the elevator and rescuing them all.

Patriarchy is prominently celebrated in all versions of the story, but Burton's takes the representations to an extreme by inventing a father figure for Wonka. He has no need to devise an equivalent mother figure because the messages of the film are about empowering men. Burton's Wonka senior is the city's most successful (famous) dentist. Likewise, Willy Wonka is the world's most successful (famous) chocolatier, and as I have argued above, Mr. Bucket finds a level of success, rising up the capitalist ranks via his pay rise. So success in the competitive economic environment is essential for patriarchal capitalism, but as the representation of Violet (and to a lesser extent Veruca) in Burton's film indicates, this does not include girls.

That said, none of the other children who tour the factory find the happiness that Burton promotes, and they are all wealthier than Charlie in the first instance (although he eventually becomes the wealthiest of all). His poverty has made him a better person, and it is perhaps for this reason that Burton has him cling to his poor home environs at the end of the film. This logic justifies class difference and, in fact, glorifies poverty as much as does the concept of the noble savage or its contemporary equivalent, third world envy. In this aspect of the narrative, all three versions of the tale are in concordance.

There is license in all versions of *Charlie and the Chocolate Factory* to feel that the poor are happy because the love of family (which becomes like a special privilege that is adjunct to their poverty) sees them through tough times and that there is no way to resolve inequalities. Burton's film embodies the same message that patriarchy taught to Cinderella: if you passively accept your disenfranchised circumstances, are polite, and work hard and uncomplainingly, something wonderful will happen. In the real world, waiting for a lottery win is like waiting for the prince to come, and it invites apathy, implying that there is no need to change the class system or economic inequity because the deserving poor will get the happiness they deserve in the end. For wealthy viewers of Burton's film, this means they can happily enjoy the sweets of their economic status without the bitter aftertaste of guilt that they are not sharing nicely with the other boys and girls.

Works Cited

Beck, Ulrich. *Risk Society: Towards a New Modernity*. London: Sage, 1992.

Bourdieu, Pierre. *Distinction: A Social Critique of the Judgment of Taste*. Translated by Richard Nice. Cambridge, MA: Harvard University Press, 1984.

Bradford, Clare "The End of Empire? Colonial and Postcolonial Journeys in Children's Books." In Elizabeth Lennox Keyser and Julie Pfeiffer, eds. *Children's Literature*. Vol. 29. New Haven: Yale University Press, 2001.

Charlie and the Chocolate Factory. Directed by Tim Burton. Warner Bros. 2005.

Dalh, Roald. *Charlie and the Chocolate Factory*. Harmondsworth, England: Puffin, 1975.

Katz, Wendy. "Some uses of food in children's literature." *Children's Literature in Education* 11 (1980): 192–199.

Webb, Jen, Tony Schirato and Geoff Danaher. *Understanding Bourdieu*. Crows Nest, NSW: Allen and Unwin, 2002.

Willy Wonka and the Chocolate Factory. Directed by Mel Stuart. Warner Bros. 1971.

Charlie's Evolving Moral Universe: Filmic Interpretations of Roald Dahl's Charlie and the Chocolate Factory

JUNE PULLIAM

Roald Dahl's 1964 novel *Charlie and the Chocolate Factory* and the two film versions it has inspired nearly three and a half decades apart are testimony to the story's enduring popularity, first with children, and later with adults. Mel Stuart's 1971 musical version is a children's movie that remains extremely faithful to the original story, which is not surprising since Dahl wrote much of the screenplay[1] for Stuart's film. Tim Burton, a director known for his surreal versions of children's stories that also appeal to adults, released his own interpretation of *Charlie and the Chocolate Factory* in 2005. This version, while also faithful to the original, is clearly aware of its adult audience whose members derive enjoyment from the novel's surreal qualities and the deeper understanding of the enigmatic candy maker supplied by Burton's back story. Stuart's film emphasizes morality, even more than does Dahl's novel. Burton's film emphasizes this theme as well, but is also concerned with the seemingly magical effects of capital.

Dahl's story is a non-sectarian morality tale. The novel opens not with the first chapter, but with a cast of characters whose descriptions tell us exactly what we should think about each child protagonist. Augustus in particular is singled out for his moral turpitude — he is described as "a greedy boy" — whereas Charlie is simply described as the hero. In Chapter 1 we are introduced to the long-suffering Buckets, an impoverished bastion of family values who cheerfully care for both sets of aging parents while existing on the wages of one breadwinner, who is barely able to earn enough for half of everyone's needs.

Willy Wonka, the reclusive chocolate maker, is the god of this universe. In Chapter 4, it is revealed that while Wonka used to be a presence among the people of the nameless town that houses his factory, he has not been seen for over a decade after his supposedly loyal employees sold his secrets to rival chocolate makers. A dejected Wonka fired his workforce, closed his factory, and disappeared. Later, when the factory resumed production, Wonka was nowhere in evidence, and even more curious, workers were never observed going in and out of the building. Now Wonka's faithful consumers enjoy his sweets, so original and masterfully concocted as to be nearly magical creations, without knowing about the hands that made them. Wonka himself has gone from being a master craftsman, whose handiwork was in evidence in his candy, to a capitalist whose confections are fetishized objects, the product of unseen hands. His candies "come out through a special trap door in the wall, all packed and addressed, and they are picked up every day by Post Office trucks" (Dahl 18). All that anyone knows of the hidden hands that make the candy come from the "faint shadows that sometimes appear behind the windows" (Dahl 18), revealing impossibly tiny people.

Mel Stuart's 1971 film *Willy Wonka and the Chocolate Factory* is a relatively faithful interpretation of Dahl's novel, but implies a bit more strongly that Wonka might have supernatural powers. The film was called *Willy Wonka and the Chocolate Factory* rather than *Charlie and the Chocolate Factory* out of concern for the sensitivities of a racially diverse audience: "Charlie" at the time was African American slang for a white man. (Tregrown 189). For similar reasons, the Oompa Loompas were changed from African pygmies to creatures with orange faces, green hair, white eyebrows, and dwarf-like bodies. Stuart's interpretation of the Dahl's story as a musical builds upon the Oompa's own musicality.

Dahl conveys the Buckets' extreme poverty by describing both his hero's monotonous diet of cabbage soup and bread, and the coldness of his home in winter. Stuart's *Willy Wonka* mitigates Dahl's bleak picture of deprivation. The city where the Buckets live is a charming sunny village with red tiled roofs, a stark contrast to Dahl's wintry setting or the cold and snowy landscape of Burton's film. We first see Charlie on the day that he begins contributing to the meager family resources: he is to receive his first paycheck as a paperboy (Charlie is not employed in Dahl's novel). Charlie's humbleness is further underscored by Stuart's decision to cast the unknown Peter Ostrum in the role. His other performers had extensive Broadway resumes, and Jack Albertson, who plays Grandpa Joe, and Gene Wilder, who plays Wonka, were very well-known film actors when they were cast. The family home is not Dahl's Dickensian picture of poverty; instead it is the site of shabby cheerfulness. While the ancient maternal and paternal grandparents still sleep in the family's single bed in the common area, the room is warmly lit. And on this evening, Charlie brings home a loaf of bread, purchased with his first week's earnings, to contribute to the family's meager supper. Gone is much of the Buckets' appalling poverty described in the novel, where they come close to starving to death after Mr. Bucket loses his job. But Stuart's film does not improve the family's financial situation by much. In fact, Stuart underscores their poverty by removing Mr. Bucket out of the picture entirely and making Mrs. Bucket the primary breadwinner.

The opening scene of Tim Burton's *Charlie and the Chocolate Factory* is more in the spirit of Dahl's first chapter, immediately establishing the family as the film's moral center. The Bucket home is an expressionistic picture of cheerful poverty. The house itself is angular and lopsided. Charlie's upstairs bedroom is dark, and cold wind howls through a hole in the roof. When Mr. Bucket arrives home, his expectant wife asks if he has brought them anything to contribute to the evening meal of cabbage soup. When he replies in the negative, she cheerfully quips, "Oh well, nothing goes better with cabbage than cabbage." Still, Mr. Bucket does manage to come home with a present for his son—irregular caps from the toothpaste factory where he is employed. Charlie uses these to build a rough model of Wonka's factory, establishing the degree to which he idolizes the candy maker.

Unlike Stuart, Burton elected to cast many big name actors, even in bit parts. Johnny Depp, who plays Wonka, has also worked with Burton in other films. Christopher Lee, known for his roles in horror and fantasy films, has a cameo as Wonka's father. Burton's Charlie, Freddie Highmore, previously co-starred with Depp in *Finding Neverland*. The well-known British actors Helena Bonham Carter and Noah Taylor play Charlie's parents, and Irish character actor David Kelly plays Grandpa Joe. Deep Roy, who has a cult following, plays the entire Oompa workforce with the help of CGI technology. Though the cast is mainly European (Depp is one of the few Americans), their collective accents are a creole of American, English and Irish dialect, contributing to the "any town" feeling of the story.

Once Dahl's novel and Burton's film firmly establish the Buckets' warm and loving relationship, the family is tested by their first serious crisis on screen—Mr. Bucket's unemployment. In the original story, Mr. Bucket inexplicably loses his job and can only find odd jobs that pay considerably less than did his factory position. As a result, the family is now close to starving. Burton's version of Mr. Bucket's unemployment is more sophisticated, as he ties it to a complex chain of events that Wonka has inadvertently set in motion with his contest. The golden ticket frenzy has vastly increased candy consumption, resulting in an escalation in tooth decay, which in turn increases the demand for toothpaste. The toothpaste factory that employs Mr. Bucket now must generate more of its product faster if it is to benefit from the boon, and so lays him off in favor of a machine that can perform his job more efficiently. In this slightly more realistic context, the Oompas become more than exotics from parts unknown. Instead, their situation is similar to that of illegal aliens who can be exploited for much lower wages. Based on these facts, one can speculate whether Wonka is partly responsible for the Buckets' poverty. After all, in this version, Grandpa Joe was one of those factory employees laid off fifteen years previous to the film's present day. But just as important as the cause of Mr. Bucket's unemployment is the way it affects the entire family. In both versions, all take his joblessness with good humor, glad that they are at least together in the face of such grim prospects. Their cheerfulness in the face of adversity is particularly important in Burton's version, which shows that a loving relationship with one's family is more valuable than any material comfort.

The contest itself offers more than just a lifetime supply of chocolate and a tour of the factory. Instead, in all versions it is a test of the participants' moral character and provides yet another opportunity to demonstrate the Buckets' basic sense of decency. The odds of finding a golden ticket seem to be increased in direct proportion to the lack of moral character of the winners. On the surface, winning would seem to be determined by sheer luck. But the odds of finding a ticket are greatly improved if one can purchase large quantities of Wonka's products. This is certainly the case with the first two winners. The gluttonous and morbidly obese Augustus Gloop finds a ticket because his outsized appetite leads him to purchase many candy bars. Veruca Salt, the over-privileged daughter of a factory owner, wins because her father can afford to buy cases of chocolate bars and dedicate his employees to opening them until a ticket is found. Violet Beauregarde ferrets out a golden ticket by dent of her overly competitive nature, simply switching her attention from championship gum chewing to searching for a chocolate bar with the winning ticket. In Dahl's and Stuart's version, Mike Teevee seems to get a ticket through luck more than anything else. He does not demonstrate an inordinate love of anything other than television, particularly shows that are violent. Burton's version, however, explains Mike's success by changing him from a lover of television to an addict of violent video games. Mike's passion for virtual play has taught him one important skill — how to quickly crack each game's system in order to win. He turns this ability to finding his own golden ticket. Only Charlie seems to get his ticket through either sheer luck or divine intervention. Limited financial resources do not permit him to have more than one Wonka Bar a year, so when he stumbles upon the money in the street that will allow him to find a golden ticket, the course of events is so fortuitous that it seems to be the result of divine intervention. In fact, in Dahl's novel, the chapter where Charlie finds the ticket is entitled "The Miracle." Interestingly, Charlie finds the ticket at the one time in the story he does something completely for himself. When he first finds the money, Charlie resolves to just buy one chocolate bar and to give the remaining cash to his mother. But eating the first bar does not satisfy him. Hunger and a long pent-up desire for something sweet drives him to purchase a second chocolate bar, the one containing the golden ticket.

The contest itself does not highlight the foibles of the first four ticket winners exclusively; it reveals the Wonka Bar buying frenzy of the entire world. Even adults are driven to acts of gluttony and larceny. In the novel, "fully grown women were seen going into sweetshops and buying ten Wonka candy bars at a time" and a famous gangster robs a bank to finance his own mass purchase of Wonka Bars (23). A Russian woman manufactures a counterfeit ticket. A scientist invents a machine that can detect even the minutest amount of gold in an attempt to ferret out a ticket. And when Charlie finds his ticket in a stationery store, nearby adults attempt to take advantage of him and offer to purchase it for far less than it is worth. Both films likewise present this worldwide frenzy. Burton interprets this part of the novel thorough scenes in global capitols, showing Wonka Bars disappearing as quickly as they are put on the store shelves. Richard Seiter sees Stuart's version of this part of the story as a satire of "the mindless preoccupations of the general public" (196). Charlie's teacher dismisses class when he hears of the contest in order to permit everyone to start buying chocolate bars. A psychiatrist tells his client that it is a sign of insanity to believe one's dreams, but only moments later, demands to know the details when the patient reveals he dreamed an angel told him where to find a golden ticket. A woman whose husband has been kidnapped wants time to think over the ransom demands when she learns that his abductors want her case of Wonka Bars. When adults behave this way, it is not difficult to see the four naughty ticket holders as the norm rather than aberration.

But it is with the physical appearance of the characters that each filmmaker is able to use his greatest powers of interpretation. In the novel, characters are described by their actions rather than appearances, with the exception of the Oompas and Wonka himself. In fact, the pen and ink illustrations in Dahl's text are so rough that they do not fix any specific appearance in the reader's mind. So both Stuart and Burton were free to invent the look of these characters. Stuart's Augustus is downright thin by 21st century standards when first-world children are commonly obese. Burton's Augustus is a good hundred pounds heavier than Stuart's. Stuart's Veruca is more shrewish than she is in either the novel or Burton's film. The ill mannered daughter of upper middle class parents, Stuart's Veruca is heard before she is seen, alternately shouting at her harried father to make his employees work faster to find her ticket and whining about the injustice of not having what she desires immediately. Burton's Veruca comes from a patrician family, and while she also demands her father instantly gratify her smallest whim, she is a bit too well bred to throw the sort of tantrums characteristic of Stuart's Veruca. Also, the Salt family's upper class status in Burton's film implies that Veruca's outsized sense of entitlement does not derive solely from overly indulgent parenting, but also from a world that permits members of her class to behave badly with impunity.

Burton also changes Violet from the brash Montana daughter of a used car salesman to the over-scheduled child of an Atlanta southern belle who lives vicariously through her child. When reporters come to the house to interview Violet, Mrs. Beauregarde calls their attention to her lone trophy for baton twirling, a sad contrast to Violet's shelves and shelves of awards. Burton's Violet is also slim and athletic, whereas Stuart's Violet is plump. And Mike goes from being a passive television addict to a child whose precociousness with video games and propinquity for violence make it frightening to contemplate what sort of adult he will become. Finally, the Charlies of the two films differ greatly. Stuart's blond and pale Charlie has the soulful look of someone who would become a chronically depressed adult had he not won the contest, whereas Burton's dark-haired, bright-eyed Charlie has the perpetually alert appearance of someone whose good humor cannot be shaken by external circumstances.

Unknown to anyone, Wonka has an ulterior motive in holding the contest. While he may at times seem to possess magical powers, Wonka is, nevertheless, mortal and has no heirs, and so is eager to find someone to take over his candy-making empire. Thus the tour of the factory is more than an experience of a lifetime: it is a test in order to find someone worthy of carrying on Wonka's traditions and caring for his family of dependant Oompa-Loompas. The golden ticket itself reveals the fantastical nature of what is in store for the winners: Wonka's message on this document explains that receiving a lifetime supply of sweets is by no means the most exciting thing that will happen to them on February 1st, the day of the tour (changed to October 1st in Stuart's film). He is also preparing "mystic and marvelous surprises that will entrance, delight, intrigue, astonish and perplex [the ticket holders] beyond measure" (Dahl 50). The groundwork is being laid for more than just incredible material gain. Instead, the tour of his factory will be a unique experience where each participant will be judged by his/her moral character and rewarded accordingly.

The fantastical nature of the tour is echoed in Stuart's version. The lyrics of the song Charlie and his grandfather sing the night before the tour make it clear that the experience offers the possibility of transcendent happiness. In Burton's version, Charlie abruptly announces that he is not going on the tour, but will instead sell his ticket to the highest bidder since the family needs the money. Grandpa Joe then explains to his grandson the rarity of the opportunity he has been given. "There's plenty of money; they print more and more every day," says Grandpa Joe, "but there will only be five golden tickets in the whole world and only a dummy would sell that ticket for something as common as money."

The very nature of Wonka himself changes with each retelling. Dahl's and Stuart's Wonka have the most special ability of all: they are men who have never completely lost touch with the children in themselves, as they always take time to play and to indulge in things simply because they are pleasing. We know the least of all about Dahl's Wonka and must just accept at face value everything that is presented to us. Stuart's Wonka is a trickster god figure with an obvious sadistic streak. Just before the tour, Wonka requires that all guests sign a contract containing a suspicious amount of fine print, describing the secret and inflexible rules of the contest, rules which even Charlie unknowingly violates. It is clear that this Wonka possesses omniscience as well: he will later know without having seen that Charlie and his grandfather have broken the tour rules by helping themselves to fizzy lifting drinks.

But Wonka's sadistic nature is most in evidence when he encourages one of his employees to masquerade as a rival candy maker, Slugworth, who offers a secret boon to each child in exchange for the theft of Wonka's trade secrets. This thread presents Wonka as a deity who, similar to John Milton's god in *Paradise Lost*, cruelly sets up his creatures for failure. "Slugworth," Wonka's Satan, is also endowed with supernatural abilities. He can get close to all of the children entirely too easily, making his offer to Charlie before anyone in the media — not to mention his immediate family — knows that he has found a golden ticket.

Burton's Wonka is more human, represented as a whimsical, addle-pated genius with awkward people skills. Wonka would like to be seen as larger than life, and his first appearance in the real time of the film is similar to the moment in *The Wizard of Oz* when the identity of the magician controlling the city is found out. Guests are greeted not by the candy maker himself, but by a singing automaton show extolling his virtues. As the display catches fire and his guests become even more confused, Wonka slips among them trying, but failing to seem like part of the crowd: Wonka's difference is obvious from his psychedelic neo-Victorian clothing. But behind his façade of successful confectioner is a sad little boy who was never allowed to have a normal childhood. Wonka's father was an overly rigid and rejecting dentist who never permitted his son to be a child. Young Willy was forbidden sweets on the grounds that they would rot his teeth, which his father is currently molding with a particularly torturous set of braces that encircle his head and pull his lips into an unwilling smile. The braces are emblematic of Wonka Sr.'s over-controlling relationship with his son. Not surprisingly, Willy is disowned by his father when he announces that he would like to grow up to be a candy maker, and his relationship with his father causes him to see all family life as fundamentally stifling. The adult Wonka is subsequently uncomfortable with everyone, particularly children, and always wears gloves to avoid physical contact. When the film was first released in theaters, some people commented that Depp's performance seemed to be influenced by the public persona of Michael Jackson, who displays a similar discomfort at the prospect of human contact.

The Oompas are arguably the most controversial element of Dahl's story. They are Wonka's Greek chorus, providing scathing moral commentary about the fate of each naughty child, saying things their master is too polite to articulate. Yet the romanticization of Wonka's diminutive workforce is a particularly disturbing element of the story, one that has never satisfactorily been mitigated in subsequent versions. Lois Bouchard observes that the Oompas in Dahl's 1964 novel are African pygmies who were "incompetent in jungle living." They were practically starving to death when "Wonka (the Great White Father) saves [them] by taking them back home and giving them work" (112). Dahl revised his book in 1973, in part due to Eleanor Cameron's 1972 article in *The Horn Book*, which was highly critical of *Charlie and the Chocolate Factory*, particularly for its characterization of the Oompas. Dahl's publishers took Cameron's criticism to heart, and in 1973, "to accompany its new sequel, *Charlie and the Great Glass Elevator*, a revised edition of *Charlie and the Chocolate Factory* appeared. Here, the Oompa-Loompas had become dwarfish hippies with long 'golden-brown' hair and 'rosy-white' skin" (Treglown 203).

Still, through their various color changes, the Oompas continue to resemble slaves in that they are brought from far away, from an "uncivilized" land, to live a better life, working for a white man in a factory they never leave — receiving payment in cocoa beans. The Oompas of the 1973 revision retain elements popularly associated with savagery, such as their native costume of deerskins for the men, leaves for the women, and nudity for the children (Dahl 71). Wonka even smuggles them over to his home country in packing cases with breathing holes (Dahl 71), a method of transportation reminiscent of the Middle Passage. The Oompas are also the picture of racist popular culture representations of enslaved African Americans. They demonstrate their unequivocal happiness with their work by constantly singing, and they possess a preternatural intelligence in some matters, but are too childlike to survive without Wonka's benign paternalism.

Stuart's representation of the Oompas sidesteps some of the racist implications of Dahl's text. Here, with their green page boy hair cuts, orange faces, and rotund bodies, they resemble the Munchkins from *The Wizard of Oz*. Burton's Oompas, played by the Indian actor Deep Roy, are dark skinned, but are members of a tribe hidden deep in the Amazon Rain Forest rather than Africa. In Loompaland, they still wear the native costume originally described by Dahl, which suggests savagery, but of a different sort, one not associated with African American slavery, but with stereotypical representations of Native Americans. When attired in Western clothing, the brown-skinned Oompas resemble Latinos, making Wonka's smuggled-in workers who are not paid in regular wages resemble undocumented labor from across the border.

The Oompa songs are a significant presence in both films, and the Oompas perform them as musical numbers, but these songs are shorter than their original versions in the novel. Richard Seiter observes that the Oompas' lyrics in Stuart's film "are not as dark and threatening, and their content emphasizes the cause for this mindless, gluttonous, spoiled, gum chewing, TV-addicted generation [is] ... parents who neglect to set limits for their offspring" (195). The truncated lyrics of Burton's Oompa songs likewise fit this description. As for the performance of the musical numbers themselves, Burton's are by far the most elaborate. The Oompa songs in Stuart's version always follow the same chanting melody, and the Oompa dances make liberal use of jazz hands and finger pointing gestures. Burton's Oompa songs are performed as elaborate individual musical videos, and each typifies the sound of a particular era. The fourth song about Mike Teavee's fate is particularly ironic as it is a jeremiad against the evils of television, which is performed as a series of vignettes seen on television. As Mike's harried parents chase their shrunken son through the various television channels, the Oompas act out parodies of classic TV shows. To fully appreciate all of the visual and musical allusions, one would have to be conversant in the very medium the Oompas vilify.

The tour itself is where Wonka fully reveals his nature. His often scornful attitude towards his guests makes no sense from a purely capitalist point of view. It stands to reason that those most loyal to Wonka's products might get fat, as is the case with Augustus, or be inordinately found of gum chewing, as is Violet. And consumers such as Veruca and Mike are highly desirable to any capitalist. Mike is perpetually in a position to be sold something, for he watches all television indiscriminately; he is even glued to the commercials and the programs he thinks are not very good. Veruca is particularly adept at bullying her parents into purchasing things to meet her whimsical and boundless desires. Wonka's disgust for the fat Augustus in particular does not make sense from a capitalist point of view and would seem about as logical as R. J. Reynolds making fun of smokers. Yet Wonka prefers the humble Charlie, whose dime a year allowance cannot permit him to demonstrate his loyalty to Wonka's product through mass purchases. Instead, Charlie will win the contest because he does not behave as the ideal consumer. While Wonka demonstrates concern for the success of his business through the extraordinary measures he takes to protect trade secrets, he seems curiously uninterested in making money. His creation of everlasting gobstoppers for children with very little pocket money is the opposite of controlled obsolescence, and his efforts to create a chewing gum meal could eliminate hunger. Instead, he is more concerned with purity of character, which he tests during the tour.

Inside the factory, Wonka instructs the children about what they can and cannot do, and each is eliminated through willful disobedience. Both films faithfully represent these episodes. Burton's film even visually references Stuart's sets for the Chocolate Room and the Television Chocolate Room, recreating and improving the original scenes. Burton had at his disposal the technology to produce a more "realistic" version of Stuart's original conception of the Edenic Chocolate Room. The scene also shows everyone, barring Wonka, Charlie and Grandpa Joe, making absolute pigs of themselves when invited to partake of this eatable universe. Burton's Television Chocolate Room, where Mike gets his comeuppance, likewise references Stuart's stark white set, but his and Stuart's version of this scene show Mike's family learning nothing from his experience. In Dahl's novel, Mike's mother is the only one of the parents to learn a lesson from her child's transformation. Over her shrunken son's protests, Mrs. Teavee declares her intention to throw "the television set right out the window the moment" (Dahl 134) they get home. But she shows no such sign of learning this lesson in Stuart's version; she is only outraged. And in Burton's version, she is not even present to take the tour.

Burton made the greatest changes to Violet's and Veruca's elimination from the tour. Thirty-four years of film technology gave Burton the ability to show Violet actually turning into a blueberry. Stuart effects Violet's transformation by dressing her in blue clothing and using a blue filter before photographing the actress in closeup. And perhaps one reason he cast a slightly plump actress in this role was out of consideration that she could actually resemble a blueberry with the help of some simple costuming and makeup. Burton's Violet is shown in the act of turning blue and swelling to the monstrous proportions of a Macy's Thanksgiving Parade balloon. Technological limitations in 1971 dictated that Stuart radically change the story of Veruca's failure to complete the tour. In Dahl's novel, she is judged a "very bad nut" by the squirrels in the Nut Room and unceremoniously chucked down the garbage chute. But trained squirrels are not easy to come by, and so Stuart relocates events to the Egg Room where Veruka ends up on a machine that judges her to be a very bad egg before tossing her down the same garbage chute. Burton was able to return to Dahl's original story, using trained squirrels and increasing their numbers through the same CGI techniques that multiply Deep Roy.

Stuart's "Slugworth" plot thread necessitated adding a few scenes to the tour. First was an episode in the Inventing Room which gave each child the opportunity to obtain an everlasting gobstopper, the item that "Slugworth" urges each child to secure for him. After leaving the Inventing Room, the tour must pass through the part of the factory containing the fizzy lifting drinks so that Charlie and his grandfather also have the opportunity to displease Wonka by disobeying his secret rules. In Dahl's novel and Burton's film, the gobstopper and fizzy lifting drinks are not prominent Wonka products, but are only mentioned in passing.

The novel concludes with Charlie's winning the contest because he was the only child able to behave long enough to complete the tour. Richard Seiter observes that Charlie wins ultimately because he is "kind, quiet, obedient and *passive*" (193). But in Stuart's film, Charlie wins because of something he does. Charlie too is a flawed human being, and nearly loses the contest along with the other bratty children who have already been disqualified by failing to follow the rules. Only Charlie's honesty and refusal to profit from the tour melts Wonka's heart and causes him to reconsider the boy's qualities. After Mike has been omitted from the tour, Wonka abruptly dismisses Charlie and Grandpa Joe because he knows that they too "have disobeyed him by sampling the fizzy lifting drinks" (Seiter 194) without permission, thereby violating a rule in the unreadable contract they signed at the beginning of the tour. Grandpa Joe angrily prepares to leave with his grandson, advising him to contact "Slugworth" immediately and sell his gobstopper. It is here that Charlie shows his true character when he sadly leaves the gobstopper on Wonka's desk without comment and prepares to depart. Wonka, impressed by Charlie's actions, embraces the child and declares that he passed the test. Wonka's Slugworth ruse is revealed, and Charlie becomes his heir.

Burton's film similarly represents Charlie as morally superior, but demonstrates this quality when Charlie chooses his family over riches. In Burton's version, Wonka offers Charlie his empire on condition that he leave his family behind, since they will only hold him back and stifle his creativity. To Wonka's astonishment, Charlie rejects his offer, and the next day dawns with Charlie happy, though still poor. His father finds another job, the hole in the roof is fixed, and there is more food on the table. It is *Wonka* who is sad without Charlie and must seek him out. Charlie can accept Wonka's prize only after helping the candy maker understand the importance of family. Charlie facilitates a reunion between Wonka and his estranged father. The film ends with Wonka understanding the importance of family in Charlie's life. He permits the Buckets to live inside of his factory with his heir-in-training and participates in evening meals with Charlie's extended clan.

Dahl's novel is a fairly straightforward morality tale, a conduct book of sorts that clearly defines the differences between good and bad children. While both Stuart's and Burton's versions of the same story can similarly be read as such, and while both treat the same themes of loyalty, family, and obedience, Stuart's musical is framed in a quasi-religious context — as it is subtly implied that his Willy has supernatural powers and is running an experiment of sorts which pits predetermination against free will. Burton's version, however, strips Wonka of his magical powers. It deconstructs the larger-than-life candy maker and shows us that, for all of his preternatural skill with confections, he is all too human.

Notes

1. Director "Mel Stuart was unhappy with the progress of Dahl's script for Charlie and, without telling the author, brought in a young unknown named David Seltzer to rewrite it" (Treglown 189).

Works Cited

Bouchard, Lois Kalb. "A New Look at Old Favorites: Charlie and the Chocolate Factory." *The Black American in Books for Children: Readings in Racism*. Donnarae MacCann and Gloria Woodard, eds. Metuchen, NJ: Scarecrow Press, 1972.
Charlie and the Chocolate Factory. Directed by Tim Burton. 2005
Dahl, Roald. *Charlie and the Chocolate Factory*. New York: Penguin Puffin, 1998.
Seiter, Richard D. "The Bittersweet Journey from Charlie to Willie Wonka." In *Children's Novels and the Movies*. Edited by Douglas Street. New York: Frederick Ungar, 1983.
Treglown, Jeremy. *Roald Dahl: A Biography*. New York: Farrar, Straus and Giroux, 1994.
Willie Wonka and the Chocolate Factory. Directed by Mel Stuart. 1971.

The Americanization of Mary: Contesting Cultural Narratives in Disney's Mary Poppins

Donald Levin

Critical considerations of the films produced by the Disney studios tend to be rather harsh. They are exemplified by Henry Giroux in *Breaking in to the Movies*, who, like many others, decries the "Disneyfication" of America. While allowing that Disney's animated films may offer "opportunities for children to experience pleasure and to locate themselves in a world that resonates with their desires and interests" (107), Giroux asserts that Disney studio productions usually celebrate "deeply antidemocratic social relations" (122), and present a world where men rule, rigid social hierarchies are upheld, and racial and gender inequities are enforced through coded language and representations. He also suggests that films such as *Song of the South*, *The Jungle Book*, *Beauty and the Beast*, *Aladdin*, and *The Lion King* suggest "a yearning for a return to a more rigidly stratified society, one modeled after the British monarchy of the 18th and 19th centuries" (122).

This kind of critique is echoed by Lori J. Kenschaft in "Just a Spoonful of Sugar? Anxieties of Gender and Class in 'Mary Poppins.'" While noting how the film version of P. L. Travers's series of children's books may offer "implicit critiques of class, capitalism, and middle-class gender relations," she concludes that the motion picture restores, at its end, an order based not just on family and gender but also on class and empire, though there are, as she notes, "glimpses of other utopian visions" (240). As Kenschaft points out, other critical approaches to the film also argue that the film reinforces the social or familial status quo (Hibbin 1982, Donaldson 1981, and Campetier 1977, all quoted in Kenschaft). Even the Marxist critic Jon Simons notes how more recent critical attention underscores the film's role in helping the audience understand how to "get back to what really matters: family and home" (qtd. in Simon), and Simon himself argues that the film reasserts the status quo in that it "instructs its audience to find new roles for themselves in a form of capitalism," even as it pretends to subvert the harsh patriarchal order of 1910 England.

This chapter comes neither to bury Disney nor to praise him. Instead, it will suggest a way of understanding the wildly successful 1964 film production of *Mary Poppins* as an artifact of popular culture that does in fact offer an explicit critique of its representation of the rigid, authoritarian, patriarchal middle-class culture of the Edwardian England in which it is set. It accomplishes this not simply by reinforcing the importance of family values, which many critics suggest as the film's primary effect for both child and adult viewers, but by subverting the characteristics of the rigidly stratified society in two ways: through a sympathetic focus on the situations of the underclass and through its subversive subtext, which symbolically and thoroughly replaces cultural narratives associated with the British Empire as a world power with alternative narratives associated with America.

Neither of these subversive threads exists in the original book. As Kenschaft points out, the film version differs from the original book in a number of important ways. The setting of the book, 1930s England, is changed in the movie to 1910 London; three of the five children from the book disappear in the movie; the characters of Mrs. and Mr. Banks are changed in the film; and the connection between Mary Poppins and Bert the Match-Man, only hinted at in the book, is expanded into a larger relationship in the film, as is the character of Bert himself. Finally, the original book and the sequels are episodic while the film has an imposed narrative. Indeed, the entire narrative line of the Disney movie is fabricated. Mary Poppins, a fabulous nanny, appears literally out of the blue to care for two children, Jane and Michael, in 1910 England. They live with their distracted parents in a comfortable middle-class home where they are taken care of mostly by servants. Their father, Mr. Banks, goes off to work each morning to his position in a bank and in song and dialogue exalts the world of finance, the solidity of the British pound, the stability of the British Empire in "an age of men," and the well-run household in which he is the lord of his castle. He also shows how all of these institutions are interrelated. He runs his home on a rigid schedule, railing against "disorder, catastrophe, and disaster." His refrain advocates "tradition, discipline, and rules." He treats his family as his possessions (his wife as a ninny and the children as his "valuables" who need a firm and guiding hand). "Lordly is the life I lead," he crows in his first song.

The children's mother, Mrs. Banks, is a worker for women's suffrage, whose own first song, "Soldiers in Petticoats," talks about casting off the shackles of the patriarchy that her husband represents for the benefit of her daughter's daughters. She literally throws eggs at the establishment and visits her sisters in jail for their suffragist protests while the nannies and the servants manage the household and children. Commentators on Mrs. Banks describe her as "delightfully flibbertigibbet" (Knight 30) and talk about how her suffragist sympathies are secondary to what is taken to be her "real" role, fawning and subservient wife and inadequate mother; "Oh, George," she says when her husband takes charge of the search for a new nanny after the children drive away the old one, "you're always so forceful." It is more helpful, however, to place her more in the company of another underrated mother of British literature, Mrs. Bennett in *Pride and Prejudice,* who, despite being the butt of her husband's constant sarcasm, is one of the wiser heads of that book; both women show a keen understanding of how to function in the diminished circumstances of a patriarchal culture.

Interpretations of Mary Poppins' character are often similar to Sally Hibbin's: Mary is the upholder of the imperial status quo: the "practically perfect" governess who successfully prepares her charges for their places in their culture's ruling order. Yet at virtually every point in the film, Mary Poppins acts as a subversive agent. From her first appearance in the Banks household, for example, she subverts Mr. Banks' pretensions. She is assertive with him in their first interview and rejects the usual employment process by refusing to give references or be cowed by his pomposity in any way. Giving him a probationary period, she reduces him to stuttering consternation. She also subverts the laws of nature by sliding up the banister. When Mary and the two children jump into a painting by Bert the sidewalk artist, they encounter (in an alternative animated universe) two old British institutions, the fox hunt and the horse race, and Mary helps to undermine both. In the fox hunt (an enduring symbol of British aristocratic cruelty), Mary aids the fox's escape. The fox's voice is that of a "faith and begorrah" stage Irishman, suggesting that Mary Poppins' disruption of the hunt also dislocates British colonial force. Also Mary wins the horse race on her merry-go-round horse and becomes the toast of the horsy set.

In the original book, only Bert and Mary jump into the sidewalk painting on her day out, and their afternoon is much more placid as they enjoy lunch and a modest merry-go-round ride. The elaborations in the movie are revealing. As in the episode with the fox sequence, every representation of British imperial pretension is parodied and undermined. Mr. Banks, in whom the worlds of finance, patriarchy, the crown, and the home converge, is a pompous, bullying figure of fun that constantly gets his comeuppance from Mary Poppins and ultimately, thanks in large part to her efforts, from the elders of his bank. After Mary Poppins manipulates Mr. Banks into taking his children to see where he works, the patriarch is cashiered from his job because his children fail to invest their tuppence in his bank and, by extension, in the empire's business.

Other representatives of the British Establishment fair equally poorly in the film. Admiral Boom who lives next door is portrayed as a comically dotty military man who wants the world to run like his ships on the crisp schedule of his cannon; yet conversely, he is shown to have a cruel streak, which becomes clear when he fires his cannon on the chimney sweeps during their big musical number. Obviously, the British did not win or hold their Empire by being simply lovable figures of fun. The elders of the bank where Mr. Banks works, represented by the ancient Mr. Daws, the bank's founder, are a slapstick crew straight out of Dickens: materially grasping, avaricious, miserly, and ridiculous.

Although Nina Ponier argues that the film is concerned only with the middle class, representing the working classes as fit only for "leading the middle class back onto the right way," an examination of how the working classes are portrayed (vis-à-vis the middle classes) suggests instead that the film's sympathies are firmly with the Others of this culture: with chimney sweeps, women, servants, and the homeless. Just as the film makes us see that the representatives of Edwardian England's cherished values (as constructed by the movie's romanticized view of the era, of course) are mean, pompous, rigid, silly, or cruel, *Mary Poppins* the film inscribes the Others with uniformly positive values. Mary Poppins herself answers an ad that the children write for a nanny who is kind, sweet, and generous and who will love them as her own children. The heavy father Mr. Banks tears up their letter and throws it contemptuously into the fireplace, but the pieces magically recombine and escape up the chimney to make their way to Mary Poppins waiting on a cloud, a sequence of events suggesting that the natural world itself colludes against Mr. Banks. As previously noted, the nanny easily stands up to Mr. Banks' officiousness. She sings a lullaby to the children about the bird woman, a homeless woman who lives on the steps of St. Paul's Cathedral, begging tuppence for bags of food not for herself but to feed her birds; the bird woman is a saintly, Franciscan presence who barely survives in the harsh shadows of Britain's economic and spiritual heart (St. Paul's is across the street from the bank where Mr. Banks works).

In another of the large set pieces of the film, one that ranges over the rooftops of London, a balletic corps of chimney sweeps celebrate their lower socioeconomic community realm with an athletic production number (to the tune of "Knees Up, Mother Brown," that great British working class anthem), dancing ecstatically through the smoky byproducts of industrial capitalism. The number celebrates their joy and their kinship as part of the underclass, and structurally it immediately follows the key scene when Mr. Banks takes his children to his joyless, prison-like bank run by desiccated old men. We might endlessly deconstruct this production number: the chimney sweeps perpetuate a favorite capitalist narrative (the myth of the happy worker); the community they form is, except for Mary Poppins and little Jane Banks, entirely male; chimney sweeps of the historical moment were largely ill-treated and malnourished children, and so on. Yet the events of this scene appear in stark contrast to the materialistic, loveless male world of the numbers crunchers of the British Empire (another bundle of cultural stereotypes, to be sure). Fittingly, the musical number ends when Admiral Boom, calling the sweeps "cheeky devils," decides to "teach them a lesson" by launching some artillery in their direction and forcing them to scatter down the Banks' chimney and invade Mr. Banks's home, upsetting his carefully regimented castle.

Perhaps the character whom the film sets in clearest opposition to the Establishment values is not Mary Poppins at all but Bert. In the novels on which this movie is based, Bert has an extremely small part. Also known as the Match-Man, he is a sidewalk artist who sells matches when it rains to scrape out his meager living; he pops up only a handful of times in each of the books. The film of *Mary Poppins* expands this role enormously until Bert is arguably the movie's central character. He is represented in a particularly important way, which is the key to my argument about the subversive nature of the film.

Bert opens the film and assumes the narrator's role. In contrast to the novel, where he is described as having two professions, match seller and sidewalk artist, in the film he is shown to have multiple occupations and incarnations: he is a sidewalk artist, a singer, a dancer, a one-man band, a pantomime artist, and a comic poet. He will later show up as a chimney sweep and later as a kite seller. He, not Mary Poppins, is the human heart of the film; while Mary continues the role as the icily distant, vain and sniffing governess that she occupies in the book, Bert compels sympathy for Mr. Banks from young Michael, telling the boy that the elder Banks is "imprisoned" in his job at the bank and thus deserves understanding. He convinces Mr. Banks of the importance of paying attention to his children while they are young, which initiates Mr. Banks' rehabilitation as a parent. Bert is a man of words, images, movement, music, wisdom, charm, and joy. He challenges the rigid social stratification of the British caste system; challenges the narrow, limited world of employment possibilities; challenges the mean-spirited perspectives on life that the Establishment characters represent and foster. While Mr. Banks and his ilk create an oppressive institution that sucks the life out of all who enter, Bert creates the world of the imagination that Mary Poppins and the children jump happily into via one of his street paintings.

Bert sings one of the songs most identified with the movie, "Supercalifragilisticexpialidocious." As Mary Poppins explains, this word is a linguistic charm that makes good things happen. In its long string of bound morphemes that seem to make different kinds of sense depending on which parts of the word you look at (while ultimately refusing to make sense at all), it captures the poststructural play of signification that is directly contrary to Mr. Banks' rigidity and fear of disorder. That it makes good things happen suggests the value of poststructural linguistic play in the world that Bert and Mary Poppins represent. This value is emphasized when Mary Poppins and Bert visit Uncle Albert, whose laughter sets everyone free from gravity. (In the novel, only Mary Poppins and the children visit Uncle Albert.) The jokes Bert tells with Uncle Albert are linguistic jokes ("I met a man with a wooden leg named Smith." "What was the name of his other leg?"); for Bert, language is a form of efficacious play that has beneficial, even, as we shall see, magical results.

Thus the enlarged character of Bert in the film represents the life-enhancing consequences of living in a world of the imagination, which gives him the freedom to move easily through different circumstances, and the freedom to act with decency and politeness. Bert is, in summary, an enterprising, mobile young man who makes his own way through life with hard work and wit, recreating himself as the moment demands, playing numerous roles that help to open others up to an appreciation of the world of possibilities. These characteristics are not only opposed in *Mary Poppins* to the negative qualities the film identifies with Establishment characters (who are, as I've noted, deliberately represented as essentially British characteristics through associations with British types like Admiral Boom). They are also qualities that we might associate with the cultural mythology surrounding *Americans*. In his consciously myth-making "Letters from an American Farmer," for example, Crèvecoeur praises just those qualities: he respects Americans, Crèvecoeur says, "for [their] accuracy and wisdom ... for the decency of their manners; for their early love of letters ... for their industry, which to me who am but a farmer is the criterion of everything" (273). Another early man of American words, Benjamin Franklin, in his equally mythic *Autobiography*, shows these characteristics in action and inscribes them forever in the American imagination. Ben, like Bert and numberless other incarnations in both high and low art, succeeded through a combination of native wit, talent, resourceful courage, respect for the equality of all people, and daring.

Bert is also played by the American Dick Van Dyke, and his film role is burnished for the film's audiences by his fame as the beamish, all-American husband Rob Petrie in *The Dick Van Dyke Show*, which was in its heyday in 1964 (it ran from 1961 through 1966). Critics of his performance in *Mary Poppins* complained about Van Dyke's wavering accent, but it served to underscore for audiences that he was really an American pretending to be British, and represented values that as I suggest are constructed as American within the conceptual framework of the motion picture's audience.

The film version of *Mary Poppins* makes several deliberate and significant allusions to American colonists as it constructs American values in opposition to British values. When Mr. Banks takes his children to his bank, for example, he tries to force Michael to invest his tuppence in the bank, preventing the child from giving the money to the bird woman, which is what he really wants to do. Mr. Banks's employer, the ancient bank director Mr. Daws, explicitly tells Michael that his investment will support the British Empire and encourage a "sense of conquest": the old man tells the child that investing a mere tuppence in the bank will help to fund railways to Asia, dams across the Nile, and plantations of tea. The bankers' song explicitly links British colonial subjugation of people of color with the structure of finance capitalism — "how stand the banks of England, England stands." His rhetoric fails to persuade Michael (unlike Bert, Mr. Daws is no man of words, though they are played by the same actor, Van Dyke), and when Michael refuses to invest, quick as a wink Mr. Daws snaps the coins out of the boy's hand; tuppence is tuppence, after all.

At this point, Michael yells, "Give me back my money," and tries to wrestle the old man for his coins. A customer of the bank overhears the struggle and concludes that someone wants his money back so the bank must be in trouble, which starts a run on the bank. When Mr. Daws calls Mr. Banks back to work that evening to cashier him, he tells Mr. Banks there has been only one other run on the bank in its history, and that was when the bank financed the tea that turned up in the Boston Tea Party, a comment that specifically places Michael's act of resistance solidly within the framework of the American Revolution, and locates the bank (and, by extension, the conflated British social and political institutions) in binary opposition to the impulse for freedom. When Mr. Banks is humiliatingly (yet comically) stripped of the symbols of his membership in the old boys' club (his boutonnière is torn off, his bowler hat is punched through, and his umbrella is turned inside out), he undergoes a kind of personal transformation. Deprived of the features of the imperial uniform that has given order to his life, he shouts the magic word, "Supercalifragilisticexpialidocious," and tells the wooden leg joke that Bert had related earlier in the film (the same that Mr. Banks did not understand at the time). By virtue of the charm of that magic word, his respect for rules and order and discipline is at once replaced by an appreciation for the postmodern play of language and the imagination. He becomes a man of words, a man of the imagination: an American man. The magic word also transforms old Mr. Daws, who suddenly not only gets the wooden leg joke, but begins to levitate, as Uncle Albert did.

At the very end of the film, Mr. Banks shows up at home with his clothes askew and is now able to show affection for his children and his wife. He goes out to fly a kite (provided by Bert, who has transformed himself again, this time into a kite seller). A kite means play, certainly, and thus the opposite of Mr. Banks' grim, soulless workaday world. But for Americans a kite is also a signifier of and another reference to one of our cultural icons, Ben Franklin and his famous experiment. Mr. Banks has gotten Michael's tuppence back, coins that as we have seen are associated with freedom and revolution, and has bought string and paper to fix the kite that was broken in the opening scene of the movie. He has become a Franklin-like character.

When they go to the park to fly their kites, they see the rest of the bankers out, sailing their own kites. Old Mr. Daws died of laughter, they learn, and left an opening for a new partner, which Mr. Banks becomes. Though, as I have noted, some critics assert that this represents the reemergence of the world of finance capitalism and the validation of the old order, I suggest that Mr. Banks' transformation instead implies that the society will reform around him as the representative of the new, Americanized world order. The subversion of the old British Empire is complete; a second American revolution has been accomplished. Signifying the symbolic overthrow of the empire, Mrs. Banks gets her suffrage sash and makes a tail for the kite (an act that some commentators see as abandoning her political role in an accommodation to her gendered role as child care provider, but which I prefer to see as helping to write "finis" on the patriarchal oppression earlier in the film).

The reading of the film of *Mary Poppins* offered here asks for the film to be seen not as an occasion for interrogating visions of class and gender, activities that Giroux and others want us to undertake, but as the site of clashing cultural narratives. Resetting the film at the beginning of the twentieth century instead of the grimmer Depression era 1930s of the novel becomes not just an excuse for a picturesque mise-en-scene but a kind of going-back-to-the-beginning, back to when the American century began. The film does not reveal the "operations of power" of our own national imperialist power, as Kenschaft suggests, by reflecting and ratifying those operations of power in its British setting; rather it serves up a narrative of how the American century began by overthrowing the British who ran the world in the nineteenth century. Looked at from this perspective, the supernatural nanny Mary Poppins is not the upholder of the status quo, but the catalyst in its transformation. The virtues she espouses through her advice to the children — about the importance of hard work, cleanliness, and so on — are not simply virtues of the empire, which as we have seen tend more toward rigid adherence to tradition and rules, at least insofar as they are represented in the film. What Mary Poppins offers her charges are, rather, nothing more than repackaged saws from *Poor Richard's Almanack*. But Mary Poppins is a *British* nanny, after all, and so she has no place in the reconstitution of society that she helps to bring out; thus she must be expelled from the reformed society of the film; she catches a stiff breeze at the end and flies away on the same breezes that blow in the film's Americanized culture.

Finally, what this examination of the film version of *Mary Poppins* suggests is a way of interpreting the film as a cultural statement that symbolically subverts representations of the dominant values of one society and replaces them with representations of the values from another. The extraordinary and enduring popularity of *Mary Poppins* as a film (and, most recently, a theatrical event; a Broadway version opened in the fall of 2006) thus arises not from its technical characteristics (the special effects, the acting, music, and so on — all the characteristics that won Oscars) but from the ways in which it inscribes certain broad cultural narratives, that is, certain stories that we tell about ourselves. Viewed in this light, the film thus becomes both an example of what Josef Joffe calls American "soft power"— the ubiquitous global presence and influence of American cultural products, especially films— and, in its normalization of the ideology of American superiority that I have argued for here, a covert inscription of that power as well.

Works Cited

de Crèvecoeur, St. Jean. "What is an American?" 1782. *The American Tradition in Literature.* Edited by George Perkins and Barbara Perkins. 9th ed. Vol. 1. Boston: McGraw Hill, 1999.

Franklin, Benjamin. *The Autobiography of Benjamin Franklin.* New York: Simon & Schuster, 2004.

Giroux, Henry A. *Breaking in to the Movies.* New York: Blackwell, 2002.

Hibbin, Sally. "Reissue/Mary Poppins (1964)." *Films and Filming* 333 (June 1982): 34–35.

Joffe, Josef. "The Perils of Soft Power." *New York Times Magazine*, May 14, 2006.

Kenschaft, Lori. "Just a Spoonful of Sugar? Anxieties of Gender and Class in 'Mary Poppins." *Girls, Boys, Books, Toys: Gender in Children's Literature and Culture.* Edited by Beverly Lyon Clark and Margaret R. Higonnet. Baltimore: Johns Hopkins University Press, 1999.

Knight, Arthur. "It's Supercalifragilisticexpialidocious!" *Dance Magazine* 3 (October 1964): 30–32.

Ponier, Nina. "Class in Walt Disney's *Mary Poppins*." <http://angam.ang.univie.ac.at/class/ko/mary%20poppins-class/Mary%20Poppins_start.htm>. Accessed May 15, 2006.

Simon, John. "Spectre over London: Mary Poppins, Privatism and Finance Capital." *Scope* July 2000. University of Nottingham Institute of Film Studies, Nottingham, UK. <http://www.nottingham.ac.uk/film/scopearchive/articles/archive.htm>. Accessed May 15, 2006.

Animating the Fantastic:
Hayao Miyazaki's Adaptation
of Diana Wynne Jones's
Howl's Moving Castle

MATT KIMMICH

In representational terms, animation would seem to be ideally suited to adapting fantasy novels to film — more so perhaps than conventional live-action movies. Even though cinema screens are replete with CGI dinosaurs, giant apes, epic battles, and entire worlds created pixel for pixel in computers, at least mainstream cinema (provided it wishes to attract audiences) is for the most part a markedly realistic medium as far as its means of representation are concerned. More often than not this realism is skin deep only, the conventionalized appearance of reality, and thus already at a remove from what it purports to depict; nevertheless, audiences glutted on visual effects-saturated blockbusters have strict standards of what images they will accept as believable and real on screen.

Arguably, it is also because of this insistence on a narrowly (yet vaguely) defined realism that traditionally, fantasy has fared less well on cinema screens than its sister genre science fiction; the usually more technological, hard-edged spectacle of sci-fi[1] poses fewer (or at least different) technical problems to filmmakers than the by and large more organic worlds and creatures of fantasy. Potentially, animation can sidestep this issue in that it "may be viewed as a film-form which finally liberates text/screen debates from the preoccupation with issues about 'realism,'" as Paul Wells (200) writes. Animation is by definition less literal than live-action film; it is abstract and stylized in ways that lead audiences to look for believability in other elements than narrowly literal visual realism. By moving the means of representation towards the more abstract or iconic end of the spectrum (a point that Scott McCloud has notably discussed for the comic book medium [cf. McCloud 1994: ch. 2], yet one that remains valid for animation), filmmakers in this form are more free to take off on flights of fancy than live-action filmmakers–not only because of the audience's different

124

response to the formal means of representation, but also due to the considerable costs of visual effects work of the scale and quality required to create images of fantastic worlds and beings while melding them with live-action footage of actors and scenery in believable ways.

The Japanese director Hayao Miyazaki is no stranger to animated fantasy films. He has been writing, animating, and directing TV series and films since the 1970s and is internationally acclaimed as one of the pre-eminent filmmakers in the medium of animation. Miyazaki is one of the few Japanese film directors, whether of animation or not, who has achieved a certain renown in the United States,[2] and his 2003 feature *Spirited Away*[3] won that year's Academy Award for Best Animated Feature, just one of many awards his work has garnered. Produced and distributed by Disney, most of his films have been released on DVD and video in Europe and the United States in translations dubbed by celebrity actors.

While not all of Miyazaki's films can be described as outright fantasy, most of them contain fantastic elements. One fantastic motif that recurs in his film is metamorphosis: e.g. the eponymous hero of *Porco Rosso* (1992) is a pilot who for reasons left ambiguous has been turned into an anthropomorphic pig; similarly, the parents of child heroine Chihiro in *Spirited Away*, too, are transmogrified into pigs,[4] which is only the first metamorphosis in a story filled with fantastic shapeshifts and changes. The mythological world of medieval Japan depicted in *Princess Mononoke* (1997) as well features a number of metamorphoses central to the plot. The director's films also share other stylistic and formal features beyond their fantastic elements: Miyazaki's stories and aesthetics show considerable Western influences, from the literary precursors of Lewis Carroll, Jules Verne and L. Frank Baum (all writers of the fantastic in one form or another) to films such as *Casablanca* and the history and aesthetics of 19th and 20th century Europe.[5] Finally, many of his films have children or adolescent characters as their protagonists and are aimed, albeit by no means exclusively, at young audiences,[6] and as Osmond (28) writes, "his career has been shaped by western children's writers from the start."

In 2004, Miyazaki's latest film, *Howl's Moving Castle*, based on the children's novel by English author Diana Wynne Jones, was released in Japan and became one of the nation's biggest-grossing films. Like Miyazaki's previous movie, it was released in the United States in a dubbed version, starring actors such as Christian Bale, Jean Simmons, Lauren Bacall, and Billy Crystal. Like *Spirited Away*, the film was nominated for an Academy Award, which it lost, however, to the claymation adventures of *The Curse of the Were-Rabbit* (2005). Jones's novel features displays of magic and fantastic conveyances as well as an adolescent protagonist who is transmogrified; the film mixes the marvelous and the domestic in ways that Miyazaki has done previously in *Spirited Away* or *Kiki's Delivery Service* (1989). The novel could be considered well suited to the motifs and themes, temperament and tone of Miyazaki's films, at least in theory. Miyazaki's film could have been a fascinating cross-cultural hybrid, with Jones's witty humor and no-nonsense approach to the conventions of fairy tales, folk tales, and fantasy, enriching the Japanese author-director's blend of visual spectacle, protean shape-shifting, and contemplative stillness.

In practice, however, the film often comes across as an uneasy compromise between two plots and two imaginations that rarely interact in a productive way. Rather than adding to one another, the two points of origin of the animated *Howl*— Jones's novel and Miyazaki's aesthetic and thematic preoccupations— are imperfectly joined and detract from one another throughout much of the film. In the following, I wish to discuss which broad strategies the film follows in adapting Jones's work, what effects the creative decisions of Miyazaki and his team have on the film, and why the result is only partly successful, either as a fantasy adaptation or as a film in its own right.

Representing the Fantastic: From Jones's Page to Miyazaki's Screen

In order to characterize Miyazaki's translation from book to anime, we first need to examine the novel on which it is based. For the plot and style of *Howl's Moving Castle* (1986), Diana Wynne Jones clearly took her inspiration from fairy tales and folk tales, as the beginning of the novel already indicates:

> In the land of Ingary, where such things as seven-league boots and cloaks of invisibility really exist, it is quite a misfortune to be born the eldest of three. Everyone knows you are the one who will fail first, and worst, if the three of you set out to seek your fortunes [9].

Even though the title of the book may suggest otherwise, the main protagonist is the young woman Sophie Hatter, the "eldest of three" alluded to in the introductory paragraph. Sophie, who thinks that she is not destined to achieve anything and is thus content working in her stepmother's hat shop, is one day turned into an old crone by the Witch of the Waste and finds refuge in the titular castle, whose owner, the wizard Howl, is reputed to eat the hearts of young girls. In the castle, Sophie meets Howl's apprentice, Michael, and the fire demon Calcifer, and she enters into a deal with the latter: if she can find a way to break the demon's contract with Howl, Calcifer agrees to break the spell put on her. In order to be able to remain in the castle, Sophie takes on the job of Howl's housekeeper.

In the novel, the castle literally moves around Ingary, powered by Cal-cifer; it also has a magical portal that, controlled by a switch, opens onto four different locations, one of which is a world distinctly different from Ingary, a strange and frightening place to Sophie — our world, Howl's home and the place where his family lives. In addition, Sophie learns that, in spite of Howl's magical powers, he himself has been cursed by a Witch — a curse hinging on the first stanza of John Donne's "Song."[7] Hoping to escape the blight, Howl tries to "slither out" (in Sophie's words) of helping the king of Ingary find his court wizard, Suliman, and brother, Prince Justin, both rumored to have been captured or killed by the Witch. In the end, how-ever, Howl's antagonist catches up with him and is revealed to be under the control of her own evil fire demon which has been insinuating itself into Howl's world. With Sophie's help, Howl manages to vanquish the Witch of the Waste and her evil demon and rescue Suliman and the prince; as Cal-cifer is released from his contract, Sophie returns to her young form, and she and Howl realize that they have come to love one another.

As the synopsis may already indicate, *Howl's Moving Castle* is a novel that is loosely plotted and peopled by a plethora of characters, aspects which rarely survive adaptation into film. Because of the different needs of the two mediums (i.e. novel and cinema) as well as the different cultural back-grounds of the novelist and director,[8] changes to the narrative were inevitable. Not all elements of a novel can or will be retained in adaptation, as Brian McFarlane writes:

> [T]here is a distinction to be made between what may be *transferred* from one narrative medium to another and what necessarily requires *adaptation proper* [...] "adaptation" will refer to the processes by which other novelistic elements must find quite different equivalences in the film medium [13].

Due to these different equivalences, showing fidelity to the original text is a challenge as it is difficult to predict what will be accepted as equivalent by audiences. Moreover, Jones's novel contains a multitude of characters, plot strands, and events, arguably too numerous to be transferred into a film of roughly two hours without judicious cutting. This necessitates certain changes to the plot and its dramatis personae, as is common to film adap-tations. Imelda Whelehan writes that

> the impetus for most adaptations rests with the relationship between characters rather than the overarching themes of the novel in question, and that those char-acters, taken from their original context, may to some extent carve out a separate destiny [8].

In spite of these provisos, the caption on the movie's title screen ("From the novel by Diana Wynne Jones" rather than the more cautious "Inspired by") would suggest that the adaptation endeavors to remain close to Jones's novel.

Indeed, the first half-hour of the film, as well as a number of episodes set later in the narrative, are close (at times transferring minute details onto the screen) to the book. The changes appear to be minor at first: Sophie's family plays a much smaller role, and she is only given one sister on screen;[9] Michael has been turned from an adolescent, who courts one of Sophie's sisters in the book, into a boy of much younger age; and Calcifer's appearance in the film is more endearing than demonic, as Jones describes it. In fact, most differences initially seem to be first and foremost of an aesthetic nature; for instance, Miyazaki takes the titular moving castle, described as "tall and thin and heavy and ugly and very sinister indeed" (Jones 39) and makes it a character in its own right. The film starts not with Sophie and her family but with the castle, emerging from a bank of fog. It is no longer the tall, thin and sinister wizard's tower that Howl inhabits in the book; it has been transformed into a parodic reflection of the steam-and-magic Ingary that Miyazaki evokes, a place more historically specific in its aesthetics than Jones's own Ingary. The castle is a rotund collage of chimneys, roofs, steam pipes, and other odd appendages, borne along on mechanized bird legs that recall Baba Yaga's hut rather than the castle of Jones's novel which hovers above the landscape. For all its mechanical elements, it seems strangely organic and alive, which is emphasized by its resemblance to a grotesque face of sorts, complete with eyes, mouth, teeth, and tongue. Howl's castle in the film is a creation not of Jones's but Miyazaki's imagination (perhaps via the animations of *Monty Python* alumnus Terry Gilliam).[10]

This change, while not integral to the adaptive strategies of Miyazaki and his team, suggests the first fundamental difference between Jones's fiction and the film. Being a primarily visual medium, cinema tends towards the spectacular, and Miyazaki's films indeed make frequent use of spectacle. Jones's fantasies, however, shun the exotic and spectacular to a large extent. She makes familiar (to the point of ordinariness) that which is unfamiliar to the reader, often by means of focalization: the fairy-tale world of Ingary, for instance, is presented to the reader through the eyes of Sophie, whose reactions to the fantastic are different from ours, precisely because her world is by and large not fantastic to her. According to Farah Mendlesohn, this is a common feature of Jones's writing: she "refuses us the right to make exotic the worlds she creates." It is this feature that prompts Mendlesohn to assign *Howl's Moving Castle* to the subgenre of immersive fantasy, in which "a truly fantastic world must have moments of mundanity" (106). This mundanity is seen for instance in Sophie's function in the castle. Far from performing the stereotypically heroic deeds common to the protagonists of high fantasy, she cleans Howl's fairy-tale counterpart to a bachelor pad. The everyday actions of the characters are underlined by some of the ironic chapter headings, e.g. "Chapter Five. Which is far too full of washing" (Jones 64). Stylistically, Jones's liminal fantasy is a far cry from more heroic or exotic fantasies.

While the animated *Howl* contains visually spectacular elements, starting with the refashioned moving castle, it nevertheless attempts to capture the ordinariness of Jones's world. Even at their most fantastic, Miyazaki's films frequently juxtapose spectacle and domesticity.[11] Miyazaki depicts the domestic elements of life in the substitute family Sophie finds in the castle in at least as much detail as Jones does; for instance, Sophie cooks breakfast and does the washing, aided by Howl's apprentice and an enchanted scarecrow, the latter no longer a frightening character to Sophie, but instead a helpful sidekick. Jones's characters are also domesticated in Miyazaki's film, and, as a result, they are stripped of some of their ambiguity.

In terms of its depiction of an essentially fantastic world, then, Miyazaki interprets yet arguably does not fundamentally change the Ingary of the novel. The world his film depicts is more readily impressive, and it is more historically and geographically specific than Jones's folk tale world. His Ingary is a steam- and electricity-powered place inspired by the look and technology of late 19th or early 20th century Europe, recalling the earlier *Castle in the Sky* (1986) in its allusions to writer Jules Vernes and illustrator Albert Robida, but it remains familiar to its characters for the most part.

The Ingary that Miyazaki depicts may not share the details of the world in Jones's novel, but its function of appearing fantastic yet familiar and ordinary remains the same. However, the film's omission of the most unfamiliar and subversively fantastic element and its addition of a war subplot largely foreign to the book seem like an intrusion of elements from Miyazaki's earlier films. Here the adaptation deviates most strongly from its source, changing its motifs and themes considerably. These deviations from the source will be addressed below.

Strangers in a Strange Land: Metafiction and Frame-Breaking in Howl

Jones's use of the John Donne's "Song" foreshadows Sophie's entrance into a place that is unfamiliar and fantastic to her and, filtered through her perception, made strange to the reader, yet it is our own modern, unfantastic world and specifically present-day Wales, made strange thorough the unfamiliar depiction of cars, television, and videogames. Here *Howl* ruptures its fairy-tale framework most clearly, a frame-break that is omitted from the film. However, as my earlier quotation from the novel's introductory paragraph suggests, Jones destabilizes her fantasy world from the beginning by infusing it with metafictional elements. Not only does the narrative allude to the conventionality of its folkloristic, fairy-tale ontology, but the characters also seem aware of these conventions, such as when they predict that the oldest of three siblings will "fail first, and worst, if the three of ... set out to seek ... [their] fortunes." While the metafictional element in this example is subtle, it is, nevertheless, indicative of Jones's efforts to play with genre; as Teya Rosenberg writes, the author "seems ... to be rethinking the fairy tale" (5) in *Howl's Moving Castle*.

The ontological integrity of Jones's fantasy world is undermined most consistently through the repeated incursions of our world into the fairy tale, intrusions that affect a shift in genre. Mendlesohn writes: "*Howl's Moving Castle* is a fully immersed fantasy in which the world is thoroughly known to the protagonists as we experience them.... But partway through the tale, [it] contains within it a portal fantasy" (88). Portal fantasies are a common subgenre, which conventionally begins in a world familiar to the reader from which the protagonists travel to an unfamiliar, fantastic world. Classic examples of the subgenre include C.S. Lewis's *Chronicles of Narnia* and Lewis Carroll's *Alice* books. The conventional distinction of familiar-unfamiliar is upheld — even more so when the protagonists' adventures in a fantastic Otherworld are given a potential rational explanation at the end of the narrative (as is the case with *Alice's Adventures in Wonderland*), which suggests that the fantastic events of the story may have been a mere dream. Not so in Jones's novel, however. What is represented as familiar is the fantastic fairy-tale world of Ingary, whereas the Otherworld on the other side of the portal (the magic door leading out of Howl's castle) that ought to be familiar, being our own essentially unfantastic world, is defamiliarized, made strange (cf. Nikolajeva 26).

While all portal fantasy implies that the borders between our world and the world of fiction are permeable, traditional portal fantasy does not question the integrity of our reality; Narnia, Wonderland, or Oz remain strange and unfamiliar to the protagonists and the readers, thus reinforcing the hierarchy between reality and fiction. In *Howl,* Jones reverses the conventional relationship between the fantastic and the real. It is our reality that is entered by fictional, fantastic elements. Characters and objects pass both ways, from fantasy to reality and vice versa. Thus in contrast to conventional fairy tale, *Howl* generates questions that are "no longer moral but ontological," as Colin Manlove (187) writes.

Jones's narrative and stylistic strategies are reminiscent of those of magic realism; much of the magic in *Howl* is normalized or naturalized, while what ought to be familiar to us is defamiliarized, creating a sort of double-vision. The reader recognizes present-day Wales, while at the same time, it remains fantastical, arguably at least as much so as the more extreme displays of magic in Ingary. Even the most ordinary objects — e.g. items of clothing such as jeans — are made outlandish by representation:

Michael's jacket had become a waist-length padded thing. He lifted his foot, with a canvas shoe on it, and stared at the tight blue things encasing his legs. "I can hardly bend my knee," he said.

"You'll get used to it," said Howl [Jones 146].

The "fantastication" is stressed when Sophie perceives reality as magical: "There seemed to be people in the house. Loud voices were coming from behind the nearest door. When Howl opened that door, Sophie realized that the voices were magic colored pictures moving on the front of a big, square box" (Jones 146–7). Through the heroine's eyes, modern Wales is made as fantastic as Oz or Narnia.

Nikolajeva argues that *heterotopia* — i.e. the presence of "a multitude of discordant universes" — is a strategy that Jones frequently uses in her fiction, including *Howl*. The critic describes its effect: "[F]ocusing on a variety of frame-breaking elements, [it eliminates] clear-cut boundaries between fiction and reality" (25). While it would be a critical exaggeration to present Jones as a radical postmodernist, her variation on the portal fantasy can accurately be described as a postmodern feature in its destabilization of the ontological divide between fiction and reality; Nikolajeva writes that "heterotopia interrogates the conventional definitions of children's and juvenile fiction based on simplicity, stability, and optimism. By definition, heterotopic space is neither simple nor stable" (25). In *Howl's Moving Castle*, Jones does not ignore the conventions of children's literature or of fairy tale and fantasy; she destabilizes them, a strategy that is arguably more complex and interesting.

Clearly, this destabilization could not be transferred to the medium of film to exactly the same effect. In realistic visual representation, the modern Wales that is Howl's homeland would be quite readily recognizable as our world, its cars and TV sets familiar to our eyes. In animation more so than in live-action film, an element of stylization could suggest the alienated perspective, although this would be a different kind of defamiliarization; Jones makes our world strange by denying us the conventional linguistic signifiers, showing how in fiction, reality is constructed and made recognizable for us by means of language. It would be very difficult to transfer to cinematic images the effect the real-world passages in her book have on the reader in that they delay the recognition of what is represented. In his adaptation, Miyazaki not only forgoes this defamiliarization effect, he effectively omits the framebreaking strategies of metafiction; his fictional world does not include self-awareness or the reverse of the portal fantasy of Jones's novel. In his film, the castle's door still leads to different places in Ingary, but not to a fourth, otherworldly destination. The portal loses its function in that it becomes only a means of conveyance, without undermining the distinction between the fantastic world and reality.

The omission of Jones's portal fantasy as the most tangible symbol of the novel's destabilizing elements is linked to Miyazaki's most significant addition to *Howl's Moving Castle*, which I will discuss in the next section; it is also somewhat of a surprise, considering the director's previous film, *Spirited Away*. Possibly the decision was also due to present-day Wales hardly being more familiar to Japanese (or, for that matter, American) audiences than fantastic Ingary, but Miyazaki did not choose to change the cultural specifics while keeping the portal fantasy as part of the plot. *Spirited Away* provides an interesting comparison in that it is a portal fantasy, reminiscent of (and in Western reviews often compared to) *Alice's Adventures in Wonderland*. In *Spirited Away*, the young protagonist, Chihiro, and her parents, characters set in a recognizable present-day Japan, get lost on their way to their newly acquired home. Driving through the woods, they come upon an old tunnel, on the other side of which they find what the parents take to be an abandoned theme park. Instead it turns out to be a fantastic world inhabited by spirits and gods from Japanese folklore and mythology, and when Chihiro's parents are turned into pigs, she has to learn the strange rules of this strange land in order to save them. In the end, she manages and returns to the normal world with her parents; it is unclear whether any of them remember the fantastic world beyond the tunnel, but Chihiro returns an enchanted keepsake to her reality that she is given on the other side of the portal.

While Chihiro's journey is different in plot and tone from *Howl*, *Spirited Away* shows that the subgenre of portal fantasy is one which Miyazaki has previously employed, a fact which makes his changes to Jones's narrative stand out more. Arguably, the change that, together with the removal of the destabilizing, metafictional elements, moves his film furthest away from Jones's book is the introduction of a dominant war theme.

When Howl *Goes to War: Revisiting Miyazaki's Earlier Work*

In Jones's novel, Howl asks Sophie to blacken his name with the king, as he does not wish to be tasked with retrieving the king's brother, presumed to have been taken by the Witch of the Waste. In conversation with Sophie, the king remarks: "The fact is, my brother Justin is a brilliant general and, with High Norland and Strangia about to declare war on us, I can't do without him" (Jones 176). Apart from this sentence, there is little in the book that could foreshadow Miyazaki's decision to introduce war as an integral theme to his film adaptation; more than this, though, his main addition to *Howl* is reminiscent of his earlier work, primarily of *Princess Mononoke* and *Porco Rosso*.

Already in Jones's novel, Howl is frequently absent and his absences are taken as an indication of his womanizing ways. Sophie finds out that his rumoured habit of eating girls' hearts is in effect metaphorical, as the wizard is said to be in romantic pursuit of young, beautiful women — that is, until they fall in love with him, at which point he loses all interest. As a result, Sophie initially considers the wizard as emotionally cruel, superficial, cowardly, and immature, and the novel only reveals his inherent decency late in the plot. Although movie Howl is also often absent from the castle, it is for a very different reason, and he lacks the rakish qualities of Jones's character. While Sophie does not know what he does during his absences, the audience is shown that Howl, having transformed himself into a gigantic bird, fights against both sides in the horrific ongoing war. This constitutes a major change, not only to the character, but to the plot. In the film, the king — manipulated by his sorceress, Suliman (a partial composite of the book's Mrs. Pentstemmon and the wizard Suliman) — orders Howl to fight on his side instead of asking for his help in finding the prince. Madame Suliman's motives are not made very clear, but her actions suggest that she may be using the war to strip other wizards and witches of their power. We see her taking away the Witch of the Waste's magic powers, for instance, and she tries to do the same with Howl.

Whereas the Witch is the main antagonist in the novel, Miyazaki (whose films rarely have clear-cut, unambivalent villains, unlike most Disney features, for instance) evokes some sympathy for her by having Madame Suliman reveal the witch's true form, that of a grotesquely old and withered crone who makes old Sophie look positively spry. Sophie shows that witch pity adopting her into the substitute family of Howl's castle. Although she still presents some danger, she is far from the irredeemable, yet in the end unimportant, villain of Jones's book.

While the Witch of the Waste may gain an additional, more sympathetic dimension by means of pathos, Sophie becomes more stereotypical and particularly more stereotypically good in her translation to film. She loses much of the cantankerousness she has in the book, and her love for Howl is not only made apparent much earlier than in the novel, but even voiced explicitly by the character herself. Jones's narrative, as well as her Sophie, resists sentimentality until the very end. Due to the changed characters, the closest the film comes to a traditional, sustained antagonist is Madame Suliman, but one could see war as the real enemy.[12]

The reasons for the war in Miyazaki's film remain as vague as the parties involved, just as it never becomes clear who is fighting whom. In the film, there is only one brief reference to the king's brother having vanished,[13] and when the enchanted scarecrow is revealed to be that same prince, his reappearance brings a sudden end to the war. Since there is no build-up to this revelation, many critics have shared Andrew Osmond's assessment that, in the film, "the war is sidestepped by an outrageously arbitrary happy ending … *Howl's* climax … only makes sense as pure emotional allegory" (31). Howl's involvement in the war is contextualized when read against Miyazaki's *Princess Mononoke* and *Porco Rosso,* yet this comparison also highlights the earlier films' more complex themes, their representation of protagonists caught between warring factions, and the brutalizing effects of war, even if one endeavors to fight for peace.

In contrast to *Howl, Princess Mononoke* presents more clearly defined opposing sides. On the one side is Irontown, a human settlement that is slowly destroying the forest for its own gains, and, on the other, are the gods and creatures of the forest, determined to defend their home to the death. Although Miyazaki's agenda is clearly an ecological one, as the film laments the destruction of nature in the name of progress, power, and economic gains, he does not allow for a simplistic reading. The progressive Lady Eboshi, leader of Irontown, is by no means a simple villain. Her actions exploit the natural resources, and she does attempt to kill the enigmatic forest spirit, yet she is also attempting to create a safe haven for societal outcasts such as the prostitutes and lepers in her care. Similarly, the forest creatures are not anthropomorphized or even the cute animals of much American mainstream animation; they are feral and dangerous. Christine Hoff Kraemer writes, "Both sides [i.e. the humans and the forest creatures] have justifiable grievances; both sides care deeply for the protection of their own groups … Miyazaki avoids the clichéd Western trope of good vs. evil." By omitting any similar contextualization of the war and its opposing factions, Miyazaki's *Howl* would seem to reduce its critique to a simplistic message: war is bad. This simplicity is disappointing when compared to the complexity of his earlier treatment of the theme.

The protagonist of *Princess Mononoke*, Prince Ashitaka, enters the film's conflict from the outside. At the beginning of the movie, he is infected with the rage of a boar demon, rampaging against humans, itself a victim of the war over Irontown. The infection gives Ashitaka demonic strength. At the same time, the rage not only slowly kills him, it threatens to possess him and make him as monstrous as the giant boar he has killed. Struggling against the demon sickness, Ashitaka does not join either side of the conflict in his search for a cure; instead, he attempts to negotiate a peace between the humans and the forest creatures, risking his own life. In spite of the movie's ecological sensitivities, it is notably even-handed in its depiction of the conflicting factions. "[J]ust as Ashitaka refuses to take sides, so also does Miyazaki," Osmond writes (30).

The film's version of the wizard Howl could be read as another take on Ashitaka and his pacifist agenda. Where Ashitaka is infected by the dehumanizing demonic rage, he resists it, remaining himself. Howl's avian form, in which he crosses through the magical castle door, not to Wales but to the frontline of the war, also gives the wizard superhuman powers similarly to Ashitaka's demon sickness, yet as Howl gives in to his more bellicose and thus highly ambivalent anti-war rage, he risks losing his humanity. When he returns from one of his sorties against the warring armies, the transformation back to human form appears to cause him pain, and Calcifer comments, "Soon you won't be able to turn back into a human." Howl's bird shape also becomes not just animal-like but monstrous as his involvement in the war progresses, and in a later scene, even his private room in the castle changes into something more akin to a beast's lair.

Whereas Ashitaka resists the urge to fight fire with fire and, as a result, become complicit in the war, Miyazaki's Howl is doing precisely that. Osmond writes: "Howl's pure-hearted anti-war stance is presented as nihilism with no alternative as he fights forces from each side and becomes the worst terror of all" (31). While Howl's self-chosen position between the opposing forces and its visual representation recalls *Princess Mononoke,* Osmond suggests that it also harkens back to *Porco Rosso* and its protagonist, likewise a "hollow hero" in a hybrid man-beast shape, a "hero-avatar at a macho dead-end" (31). Osmond's argument is that both *Porco Rosso* and *Howl's Moving Castle* become "reflection[s] on the limits of masculinity, portrayed as both nobly idealist and incorrigibly childish, except when redeemed by love" (31). As a result of Miyazaki's radical changes to Howl's character and his insertion of the war plot, his adaptation is a very different creature from Jones's novel. In the last section, I will address how the changes interact with the elements taken from Jones's book and how the film adaptation is finally compromised by its double nature.

An Imperfect Join: The Double Nature of Miyazaki's Howl's Moving Castle

In his book *The Novel and the Cinema,* Geoffrey Wagner sets up three broad types of adaptation: transportation, "in which a novel is given directly on the screen with a minimum of apparent interference" (222); commentary, "where an original is taken and either purposely or inadvertently altered in some respect ... when there has been a different intention on the part of the film maker" (224); and analogy, "which must represent a fairly considerable departure for the sake of making another work of art" (226). Hayao Miyazaki's version of Jones's novel quickly develops into something in between the latter two categories, the main reason for which would seem to be the director's different intention. Osmond suggests that "Miyazaki was first attracted to Jones's book by the images of the castle and the aged heroine" (31), but the film's departures from the novel point to Miyazaki's "different intention." The director's first major change, i.e. omitting the metafictional elements of Jones's novel, also removes its subversive dimension, reversing Colin Manlove's observation that Miyazaki's *Howl* is concerned not with "ontological" but with "moral" questions. Such questions are not absent from the novel, but they are made more obvious in the film. Julie Sanders writes in her study of adaptation and appropriation that "a political or ethical commitment shapes a writer's, director's, or performer's decision to re-interpret a source text" (2). The Japanese director's pacifist concerns, an element not present in the original novel, are evident throughout the movie, underlining Osmond's statement that "[w]hen it comes to adaptation, Miyazaki takes what he wants and invents the rest" (28).

Yet his adaptive strategies prove less successful in the case of *Howl*. The problem here is not a lack of fidelity, a problematic issue in itself. What proves detrimental to the film is that its separate parts — the elements taken from Jones and the added war plot — often fail to come together to form a new whole. As has been discussed in the previous section, the plot strands concerned with the war seem to be but echoes of *Princess Mononoke* and *Porco Rosso*, lacking the depth of the earlier films. Osmond comments: "Increasingly [Miyazaki's] newer films revisit themes and imagery from his simpler pictures, though the storytelling is more elliptical, relying on knowledge of these past films and on stretches of faith in things happening because they should" (31). Likewise, as the earlier themes are simplified, the metafictional element is removed and Jones's characters reduced in their complexity. The novel's appeal finally lies less in its plot points than in its characters and relationships — e.g. Sophie's down-to-earth stubbornness and nagging, Howl's rock-star vanity and smug charm, and their constant squabbling, which hides a growing affection — as well as its humor and its witty, self-aware undermining of the conventions of its genre. Both of these are lost, by and large, to the addition of the war plot and the comparable sentimentality with which Miyazaki depicts his characters, especially Sophie.

The incomplete joining of the two sources is illustrated aptly in a scene that is faithfully and accurately adapted from the novel. After Sophie has cleaned the castle, including Howl's mess of a bathroom, rearranging his mysterious powders and creams (that turn out to be cosmetics and thus rather more mundane than the outlandish and gruesome tinctures Sophie imagines them to be), the vain wizard accidentally uses the wrong coloring to tint his hair, making it ginger. In the comically grotesque scene, Howl throws a tantrum and finally begins to ooze thick green slime, which even threatens to extinguish Calcifer. In spite of the sequence's proximity to the novel, it does not make much sense in the context of the film; Jones's Howl basks in his own vanity and superficiality, changing his looks in order to increase his appeal to the opposite sex, so his childish reaction fits the character with whom we are already familiar. When film Howl has the same reaction, his behavior does not suit the man who regularly returns from aerial battles bloodied and disheveled and whose womanizing is seldom mentioned, however well-groomed he may appear otherwise.

It is in those scenes that free themselves of the two plots and are purely about the world and characters that Miyazaki's film comes into its own, such as when Sophie and the Witch of the Waste struggle up the stairs to the king's palace, Sophie dragging a plump, lazy dog with her as the Witch appears to collapse into herself, shrinking to half her original size; or when Sophie takes out the washing to dry in the open air, aided by the hopping scarecrow; or when the moving castle itself appears as a living being in animation. These scenes find a visual humor that recalls the verbal wit and lightness of Jones's novel without necessarily reproducing any specific details of the book, a lightness becoming increasingly rare as the war plot takes center stage. In such individual moments and images, Miyazaki's animation manages to free itself from the demands of the two plots—and flies.

Notes

1. I do not wish to go into a long critical discussion on the distinction between fantasy and science fiction, as the borders between the genres are fluid and the purpose of this article lies elsewhere. I use the terms here as discussed in the *Encyclopaedia Britannica*, which states that "[s]cience fiction can be seen as a form of fantasy, but the terms are not interchangeable, as science fiction usually is set in the future and is based on some aspect of science or technology, while fantasy is set in an imaginary world and features the magic of mythical beings."

2. Arguably this has also been helped by his being championed in America by the director John Lasseter of Pixar Studios.

3. In this article I will be using the English titles of Miyazaki's films rather than the original Japanese titles.

4. The *Internet Movie Database* notes that pigs are one of the director's trademarks.

5. Miyazaki's frames of reference are not exclusively European, however; *Princess Mononoke* is set in Japan at the dawn of the Iron Age, and *Spirited Away* not only begins in contemporary Japan but is also grounded in Japanese folklore and Shinto beliefs. Cf. Boyd and Nishimura 2004.

6. There are exceptions, perhaps most markedly *Princess Mononoke* with its viscerally violent battle sequences, similarly brutal to (although shorter than) those in Peter Jackson's adaptation of *Lord of the Rings*. On the subject of Miyazaki's adult and child audiences, cf. Prunes 2003.

7. Donne's poem begins as follows:

> Go and catch a falling star,
> Get with child a mandrake root,
> Tell me where all past years are,
> Or who cleft the Devil's foot.

> Teach me to hear the mermaids singing,
> Or to keep off envy's stinging,
>   And find
>   What wind
> Serves to advance an honest mind [qtd. in Jones 127].

8. The film stands at the end of a series of translations (and thus interpretations), from English to Japanese, from novel to film, and in the case of the dubbed version from Japanese back into English. Arguably, Miyazaki's *Howl's Moving Castle* could be seen as an instance of intercultural performance (cf. Pavis 1996); however, it is not my aim here to focus on the intercultural aspects of the film.

9. While Lettie plays a minor part in the film, Sophie's other sister, Martha, does not appear; the only reference to her is that in the film, Howl is reported to have eaten the heart of a girl named Martha. This veiled reference to the book does not play out in the film, however.

10. Cf. Osmond 30.

11. On the subject of Miyazaki's use and representation of the fantastic, also cf. Prunes (2003: 47/48).

12. The harrowing bombings of cities and their visual representation in *Howl's Moving Castle* recall another anime produced by Miyazaki's Studio Ghibli, namely *Grave of the Fireflies* (1988), which is set during and after the firebombing of Kobe during World War II.

13. According to the literal translation from Japanese into English that is available on the region 1 DVD in addition to the closed captions, the throwaway reference to the cause of the war is only given in the English dub, not in the original Japanese.

Works Cited

Boyd, James W., and Tetsuya Nishimura. "Shinto Perspectives in Miyazaki's Anime Film *Spirited Away.*" *The Journal of Religion and Film* 8.2 (2004). <http://www.unomaha. edu/jrf/V018N02/boydShinto.htm>. Accessed March 2006.

"Fantasy." Encyclopaedia Britannica. 2006. Encyclopaedia Britannica Online. <http:// search.eb.com/eb/article-9125578>. Accessed April 25, 2006.

Jones, Diana Wynne. *Howl's Moving Castle.* London: HarperCollins, 2005.

Kraemer, Christine Hoff. "Between the Worlds: Liminality and Self-Sacrifice in *Princess Mononoke.*" *The Journal of Religion and Film* 8.1 (2004). < http://www.unomaha.edu /jrf/V018N01/BetweenWorlds.htm> Accessed March 2006.

Manlove, Colin. *The Fantasy Literature of England.* Basingstoke: Macmillan Press, 1999.

McCloud, Scott. *Understanding Comics: The Invisible Art.* New York: HarperPerennial, 1994.

McFarlane, Brian. *Novel To Film: An Introduction to the Theory of Adaptation.* Clarendon Press: Oxford, 1996.

Mendlesohn, Farah. *Diana Wynne Jones: Children's Literature and the Fantastic Tradition.* London: Routledge, 2005.

Nikolajeva, Maria. "Heterotopia as a Reflection of Postmodern Consciousness in the Works of Diana Wynne Jones." In *Diana Wynne Jones: An Exciting and Exacting Wisdom.* Edited by Teya Rosenberg et al. New York: Peter Lang, 2002.

Osmond, Andrew. "Castles in the Sky." *Sight & Sound*, October (2005). 28–31.

Pavis, Patrice, ed. *The Intercultural Performance Reader.* London: Routledge, 1996.

Prunes, Mariano. "Having It Both Ways: Making Children's Films an Adult Matter in Miyazaki's *My Neighbor Totoro.*" *Asian Cinema*, Spring-Summer 2003: 45–55.

Sanders, Julie. *Adaptation and Appropriation.* London: Routledge, 2005.

Wagner, Geoffrey. *The Novel and the Cinema*. Rutherford, NJ: Fairleigh Dickinson University Press, 1975.

Wells, Paul. "'Thou art translated': Analyzing animated adaptation." In *Adaptations: From Text to Screen, Screen to Text*. Edited by Deborah Cartmell and Imelda Whelehan. London: Routledge, 2000.

Whelehan, Imelda. "Adaptations: The contemporary dilemmas." In *Adaptations: From Text to Screen, Screen to Text*. Edited by Deborah Cartmell and Imelda Whelehan. London: Routledge, 2000.

From Book to Film: The Implications of the Transformation of The Polar Express

ERIC STERLING

Although Chris Van Allsburg's Caldecott Award-winning fantasy book, *The Polar Express*, (1985) has justifiably captured the hearts and imaginations of many children and adults, the 2004 film version perhaps captivates audiences even more because of its universal appeal — a characteristic that the book, to some extent, lacks. The film possesses a greater universal appeal than the book because it is more multicultural and diverse in regard to race and class, it is more genuine because it presents the young narrator's (the Hero Boy's) initial and natural skepticism, and it provides the other children on the Polar Express and his sister (Sarah) with significant roles that they lack in the book.

In the book, only one of Van Allsburg's illustrations contains an African American, a young boy in a crowd who speaks no words and never interacts with the narrator (the young speaker) or anyone else. In the film version, the young African American girl (called the Hero Girl in the credits) immediately befriends the narrator (called the Hero Boy in the credits) and comes to his aid; for instance, sensing that the Hero Boy is nervous about being on the Polar Express, she smiles at him and encourages him to feel comfortable on the train. Furthermore, she defends him after he employs the emergency break to stop the train, telling the conductor that the Hero Boy simply wanted to enable another boy to board the locomotive. The Hero Girl even guides the train temporarily, replacing the conductor. The film, unlike the book, includes children of various socioeconomic backgrounds. The narrator, judging by his large house, comes from a wealthy family. Yet he stops the train for a poor boy (Billy) so that he, too, can see Santa Claus. The bespectacled, know-it-all boy (called the Know-It-All Boy in the credits) in the film seems annoyed that before going to the North Pole, the train makes one last stop: upset, he remarks, "We're headed for the other side of the tracks"—indicating that the locomotive is traveling to a poor neighborhood. The train then stops for Billy, who is wearing old, flimsy pajamas and standing by a small house. Billy is poor, judging by his house, his pajamas, and the Know-It-All Boy's comment.

Furthermore, in his song, a duet with the Hero Girl, Billy (the Lonely Boy) laments that he has never received Christmas presents: "I guess that Santa's busy because he's never come around," and gifts that are red and green are "things I've heard about but never really seen." The music, a significant effect in the film that the book obviously cannot include, greatly enhances the movie, creating a poignant and moving scene that generates empathy for Billy from the audience. Screenwriter William Broyles Jr. says that the song is essential to the film because "it was really the one time in which you saw what the Lonely Boy felt" (Chumo 65). Peter N. Chumo adds that "[b]ecause the Lonely Boy comes from the wrong side of the tracks, so to speak, and has never experienced genuine Christmas cheer, he is so withdrawn that only in the heightened realism of a song could he express himself fully" (65–66). Through the medium of song and music, Billy conveys his thoughts to the Hero Boy and the Hero Girl, yet he does not feel comfortable doing so in speech. The song is also effective because it allows the film to do something that the book does not — show how poor children feel about Christmas. Billy's lament about the disappointment of impoverished children — a frustration that surfaces throughout the world every Christmas— becomes more poignant and heartbreaking because it is sung beautifully to music and because it contrasts with the optimism and happiness present in the Hero Girl's contribution to the duet. The sadness deriving from the realization that countless poor children do not receive Christmas presents because they live in poverty is missing from the book yet prevalent in the film. Chumo observes, "Unafraid to look at the sadder side of the holiday, the screenplay raises the sense of despair a child can feel when he is not included in the festivities" (66). When the Hero Boy stops the Polar Express train for Billy, it serves as an invitation for him to finally participate in Christmas cheer and an invitation to filmgoers to consider how the poor experience Christmas.

Billy is hesitant to board the train, but does so after the Hero Boy stops the locomotive for him by using the emergency brake — indicating that Billy is indeed welcome to join the children of higher social classes. The stopping of the train, which is on a very tight schedule, represents a clear and personal invitation to the poor boy. The altruistic African American girl (the Hero Girl) also helps the poor boy by saving him hot chocolate and risking her life, by walking from one train car to another while the locomotive travels at full speed, to give it to him. Thus, both the Hero Boy and the Hero Girl ensure that Billy feels welcome and invite a blurring of the social classes.

The inclusion of racial and socioeconomic diversity in the film is quite significant. The book concerns one boy, a white male child from a prosperous family, who wants to believe in Santa Claus. For no apparent reason, Santa selects this rich white male child to receive the first gift of Christmas. The book, therefore, lacks universal appeal and could suggest to some people that Santa Claus cares mostly about white male children from wealthy backgrounds. However, the inclusion in the film of a prominent African American female character (who boards the train before the white protagonist and welcomes him) and a boy from a poor family indicates that Santa Claus and Christmas are for everyone; children of all races, both genders, and all social classes are welcome on the train and must believe in Santa Claus. Santa will meet them all in the North Pole, and they will receive gifts. The book lacks this diversity, focusing only on the white male narrator. And it is apparent in the film that the Hero Boy has earned the first gift of Christmas because he has risked life and limb to retrieve the ticket for the African American girl (the Hero Girl) and has allowed the poor boy to board the train, befriending both children. Although one could argue that it should be taken for granted in the book that minorities and people of all social classes are welcome to meet with Santa, the book does not invite this interpretation, as the film clearly does. Such racial and social diversity is, perhaps, key to the film version's critical, aesthetic, and financial success. People watching a movie might want to see characters who resemble themselves in some manner. Thus, the film version of *The Polar Express*, more so than the book, implies that Santa Claus and the excitement of Christmas belong to all children and that Santa loves them all.

But although Santa might love all children, the film suggests that not all children love — or believe in — Santa. The movie employs humor and mysticism to manifest the Hero Boy's skepticism — doubts that unquestionably deviate from the boy's faith revealed in the book. Before the train journey, the Hero Boy encounters an old photograph of a previous Christmas in which he visited a department store Santa who clearly, judging by the thick black glasses, was not the actual man. The boy frowns when he looks at the photograph, wondering, perhaps, how Santa could look so different from his conception of the man. Chumo notes that "in establishing his initial agnosticism, [Screenwriters Richard] Broyles, Jr. and [Robert] Zemeckis created a clever, wordless, visual exposition that succinctly and humorously shows how doubt has been growing in the Boy's mind over several Christmases" (65). The photograph disappoints the boy and brings him to the brink of disbelief, yet it is this closeness to disbelief that makes him an appropriate candidate for a ride on the Polar Express. It is noteworthy that he, and no one else in the neighborhood, hears the train. Chumo adds that "the experience of a department store Santa is something that many people, especially adults, can look back on with a certain fondness. Broyles noted that, even though he and his collaborators were making the movie for children, adults may appreciate it even more because they have already 'passed through [this stage] and have a nostalgia for it'" (65). The screenwriters also employ humorous newspaper clippings that increase the Hero Boy's previously-held doubts about Santa's existence. One headline covers a Santa walkout at a department store, "Santas on Strike!" The idea of mercenary Santas who place salaries and economic interests above children contradicts the Hero Boy's conception of the holiday. Troubled by doubts, the boy hears the sound of the train and walks outside to meet his fate.

In the book, the narrator boards the train when the conductor asks him to do so. When the conductor informs him that the train is going to the North Pole, the boy says, "I took his outstretched hand and he pulled me aboard." The book implies, therefore, that, despite what his friend has told him, the boy already believes in Santa; he never hesitates or doubts whether to board the train. The journey merely validates his previously-held belief. In contrast, Hero Boy of the film initially declines to board the Polar Express. The conductor peers intently into the boy's eyes in an effort to convince him to board, yet the boy backs away, declining to enter the train. The conductor gives up on the Hero Boy and starts the train, at which time the boy changes his mind and hastily boards. When the boy makes the right decision, even the snowman waves his congratulations. The Hero Boy's hesitation in the film manifests natural skepticism; he is not sure if he truly believes in Santa Claus. The Polar Express stops for all children at one point in their lives, and this is a pivotal moment for the Hero Boy, who is tottering between belief and doubt in Santa's existence. The train does not merely represent a journey to the North Pole — it represents belief in Santa and youthful idealism. The boy's initial refusal in the film to board the train and thus to believe in Santa Claus represents a marked and significant departure from the book. His skepticism makes the journey more meaningful and essential. In the film, the Hero Boy needs to board the Polar Express in order to believe in Santa Claus and to find special meaning in this and future Christmases. As the conductor remarks to him, "One thing about trains: it doesn't matter where they're going. What matters is deciding to get on." Without the journey to meet Santa and to obtain the sleigh bell, he will not believe in Santa. He will never again hear the jingle of the sleigh bell. However, in the book, the boy immediately boards the train because he already believes in Santa Claus; his journey on the Polar Express, therefore, is not as meaningful as in the film because although he will enjoy his experience at the North Pole, he lacks skepticism and has less to learn. The film, thus, is more complex and genuine than the book because it portrays to audiences the same natural and inevitable skepticism they have experienced at some point in their lives. The film is also more meaningful than the book because in the latter, the boy does not need to board the train in order to believe in Santa, but in the film, the Hero Boy does need to journey on the train to have faith in Santa.

Readers of *The Polar Express* do not discern the boy's skepticism toward Santa Claus because Van Allsburg does not include it in the book; but if he did, it would be difficult to portray this doubt because the boy hardly talks to anyone (just two words to the conductor and the request for the bell from Santa). In the film, however, the Hero Boy encounters a character absent from the book — the hobo-ghost who rides the train on Christmas Eve. The astute man discerns the protagonist's doubts and questions him. Chumo says that the hobo "functions as an alter ego who verbalizes the Boy's feelings of doubt" (67). The hobo asks the Hero Boy: "And what exactly is your persuasion? When it comes to the Big Man?" When the boy declines to answer the question directly, stating simply that he heard the Polar Express was going to the North Pole and that he will see Santa Claus in person, the hobo continues:

> Don't you believe them? ... You don't want to be bamboozled ... led down the garden path ... duped ... conned ... have the wool pulled over your eyes ... hoodwinked ... taken for a ride ... railroaded ... so to speak. It ain't enough if everybody else in the entire world believes it. No sir! You want to scope them peepers of your own. Seeing is believing, am I right? [first ellipsis is mine].

The insightful hobo verbalizes for the audience the confusion and doubts in the mind of the Hero Boy — the questions that incite the protagonist to leave the safety of his home for a ride on the Polar Express. The Hero Boy does not want to be "railroaded" into believing, suggests the hobo, but it is the railroad train that ultimately will put to rest his doubts for a long time. The train ride is more than a mere trip — it is a boy's epic quest for truth about a matter that has troubled him for years.

The movie, unlike the book, also contains some questions that all children inevitably have about Santa in regard to time and space, queries that raise doubts in their minds. In a poignant scene, the Hero Boy listens guiltily as his sister informs her parents that he told her that it is impossible for Santa to provide presents to all children in the world in only one night: the sleigh must travel at the speed of light in order to go around the world and must be as big as an ocean liner in order to hold so many presents. The Hero Boy laments to himself that it is "the end of the magic." Here in the film the boy refers to the loss of belief in Santa that he and his sister might experience. He feels guilty, for he has contributed to his sister's skepticism and doubt about Santa. Thus, when he reluctantly boards the train and requests a sleigh bell from Santa, he does so not only for himself, but also for his sister; he wants to believe in Santa and to present empirical evidence to her so that she will as well. Consequently, the film provides a motivation for the Hero Boy's decision to ride the train and obtain a sleigh bell that is lacking in the book — guilt because he has contributed to the disillusionment of his little sister regarding Christmas.

The sister, Sarah, plays a larger role in the movie than in the book. In fact, the book seems to displace the Hero Boy and other characters. The Hero Boy is present in only one-third (five out of fifteen) of the book illustrations, and he interacts only briefly with the other children (when he loses the sleigh bell). Van Allsburg focuses his attention on the journey itself — on the train, the wolves, the elves, and the North Pole. Perhaps the author is most concerned with the entire train experience rather than with the Hero Boy's individual journey. When Van Allsburg initially created the story, the focal point was the train; he remarks:

> When I began thinking about what became *The Polar Express*, I had a single image in mind: a young man sees a train standing still in front of his house one night. The boy and I took a few different trips on that train, but we did not, in a figurative sense, go anywhere. Then I headed north, and I got the feeling that this time I'd picked the right direction, because the train kept rolling all the way to the North Pole. At that point the story seemed literally to present itself. Who lives at the North Pole? Undoubtedly a ceremony of some kind, a ceremony requiring a child, delivered by a train and would have to be named the Polar Express [Ruello 170].

The rest of the book then derives from Van Allsburg's focus on the train in front of the house.

The film, in contrast, concerns itself with the way in which the Hero Boy's experience is shaped by the friends he makes during the journey. The Hero Girl, Billy, the conductor, and even the Know-it-All Boy — and not just Santa Claus — make a lasting impression on him. For instance, the Hero Boy observes the Hero Girl acting so benevolently and unselfishly that she, to some extent, inspires him to ask for a sleigh bell to show his sister. The "action is a product of character — it is not just thrown in to fill space or connect key episodes from the book. More specifically, action emanates from the way the children bond with each other" (Chumo 65). It would be difficult for Van Allsburg to create such a bond, given the constraints of a children's book as opposed to a one hundred minute movie. Van Allsburg says that in his children's books he seizes "the opportunity to create a small world between two pieces of cardboard, where time exists yet stands still" (Ingram 306). He creates beautiful images in the book that seem real and three dimensional: Laura Ingram notes that "Van Allsburg's growing sophistication in the manipulation of texture is apparent here as well: the fur of the wolves seems to bristle, Santa's whip looks as if it is about to snap off the page at any moment, and, in the last panel, picturing the bell, the metal looks cold and shiny in contrast to the velvety leather thong attached to the bell and the deep rich tones of the wood table on which it rests" (312). Although Ingram makes valuable observations about the texture in Van Allsburg's drawings, it is important to note that the focal points (wolves, whip, bell) of the drawings she mentions are not human beings, again indicating the displacement of the human in the book.

In their screenplay, Broyles and Zemeckis are not constrained by cardboard and thus employ, for various effects, music, sound (such as when the elves speak in a New York accent or when the boy trudges and slides through the snow in front of his house), and Performance Capture. In Performance Capture,

> human actors perform their roles wearing motion capture suits covered with markers of light-reflective material, sensors that, in essence, capture every nuance of movement. The action is digitally recorded and fed into a computer, where all the images are enhanced with CGI to create the characters and their environments. The technique gives the filmmaker the freedom to manipulate the imagery in the editing stage, to create the film in virtually an infinite number of ways. It is a process somewhere between realism and animation, a perfect method for creating the world of *The Polar Express*, which, in its wide-eyed sense of wonder at a child's vision of Christmas, is meant to exist between real life and a dream world [Chumo 64].

Performance Capture naturally emphasizes human beings, which is significant because human values are at the heart of the film. The possibilities in the film seem limitless and permit the screenwriters to explore the Hero Boy's adventures as he encounters new friends and meets Santa.

Because the book seems to focus more on the setting and the journey than on the human beings, the conflict emanates from the setting, particularly that of the North Pole. The book presents the story in a matter-of-fact way, with little emotion, tension, or suspense until the train arrives at the North Pole. Van Allsburg's illustrations are dark, suggesting that the North Pole is not necessarily a pleasant and safe environment; in fact, Michelle H. Martin calls parts of the story, no doubt the North Pole, "eerie" (142). Joseph Stanton concurs, saying that with

> the restrainedly demonic nature of Van Allsburg's North Pole with its bizarrely vast snow-covered urban appearance, and the quietly nightmarish hugeness of the crowd of identically dressed elves turned out to hear Santa's speech ... we find the surrealist edge of danger subtly implicit. It might even be said that there is something about the visualization of Santa's speech to his army of elves that is reminiscent of the famous filmed sequences of Hitler addressing his storm troopers. Although Santa is treated as an unambiguously benign being in the context of the book, there is an unsettling quality to the North Pole scene that adds an aesthetically interesting element of disorientation to the miraculous presence of the godlike Santa figure [174–175].

Although Stanton probably goes a bit overboard with his comparison between Santa and Hitler, he is correct, nonetheless, that the setting in Van Allsburg's book seems dark and foreboding.

But in the film, unlike in the book, the conflict arises from the Hero Boy's encounter with new friends and their efforts to meet Santa. In the movie, there is conflict because the Lonely Boy desperately hopes to receive a Christmas present and because of the tense and suspenseful situation that occurs at the North Pole. Billy, the Hero Boy, and the Hero Girl become separated from the rest of the passengers and thus must travel the precarious journey back to Santa, ending up, ironically, in Santa's huge, red sack of toys. The venture is fraught with danger. The Lonely Boy, in fact, almost slips off the tracks (the fall would presumably lead to his death) as he hurries to keep pace with the Hero Boy and the Hero Girl attempting to rejoin the other children. The danger originates from the Lonely Boy's fear that he will not receive a new Christmas present — because he doubts Santa. Nonetheless, because the Hero Boy is virtuous and the Hero Girl possesses excellent leadership skills, they eventually find their way back to the other children. They are individuals with clearly defined characteristics; these traits are punched onto their tickets, which is why the tickets are non-transferable. The Hero Boy's decision to comfort and befriend the Lonely Boy, even though it almost costs him an opportunity to meet Santa, reveals to Mr. Claus, who, like God, is omniscient, that the Hero Boy deserves the first gift of Christmas; another reason the Hero Boy has earned the first gift is because he has learned to trust his imagination and to believe in Santa. Earlier in the film the Hero Boy acknowledges to the hobo that "seeing is believing," that he must see Santa to believe in him, but that turns out to be incorrect. The Hero Boy changes his mind about requiring empirical evidence after listening to the conductor, who advises him that "sometimes the most real things in the world are the things we can't see." After arriving at the North Pole, the Hero Boy initially wants to see Santa but cannot lay eyes on him. He then hears the sleigh bell that has fallen from the reindeer, closes his eyes, and says to himself, "I believe." Then — and only then — does he see Santa in the reflection of the bell. Thus, the Hero Boy does not see Santa and then believe; rather it is his faith that allows him to see Santa.

Both the book and the film use the boy's adventures to explore the relationship between the imagination and reality, between belief and doubt. It is fantasy, of course, for a large locomotive to travel through a suburban neighborhood and stop in front of someone's house, with that person alone being able to hear it. The presence of the hobo in the film — drinking, warming himself by a fire, and even skiing on top of a moving train — is the stuff of fantasy, as are the parachuting elves and clocks that incessantly show the time as five minutes to midnight. But as with Van Allsburg's other books, these supposed illusions are, perhaps, real. Ingram says that the author's "fable, reminiscent of William Blake's *Songs of Innocence*, reaffirms Van Allsburg's contention that the fantastic *is* possible for those who believe" (311). Peter F. Neumeyer adds that in Van Allsburg's books

> [i]magination is "real," that the world in the mind, including the child's world of fantasy, is actual, true, even tangible. That may be a difficult concept for a child, but one of the most remarkable aspects of Van Allsburg's work is precisely this desire to translate a metaphysical concept into verbal and pictorial shape so that it may be comprehended — at some level — by a child [2].

The book's first illustration, that of the boy's bed, shows that he is still a young child with a vivid imagination. He keeps a Boston Bull hand puppet on his bedpost; Neumeyer says that "the dog is imaginary rather than real, and this coincides with the topic of the book — the relationship of imagination to 'reality'— though, of course, the very point of the book is that imagination *is also* reality" (5). Although the narrator of the book says that he "lay quietly in my bed" and, according to some readers, might be dreaming the story of *The Polar Express*, he awakes on Christmas morning to find the sleigh bell and a letter from Santa. The note, like the bell, is tangible, empirical, and incontrovertible evidence of the existence of both Santa and the Polar Express. Thus, the Hero Boy can successfully link the imagination and reality for himself and his sister through the sleigh bell. It is a triumph of the power of the imagination and the human spirit.

The film suggests that Christmas is not about presents, but rather about friendship, altruism, and the belief in Santa and one's imagination. In the film, the Hero Girl, during the Polar Express journey, teaches the Hero Boy about friendship and caring for others. She befriends him and teaches him to befriend Billy. As Santa says to Billy, upon learning that he has made new friends, " Lucky lad, there's no greater gift than friendship." It is not just the experience but also the people whom the Hero Boy will never forget that helps shape the idealistic and imaginative person he becomes. The Hero Boy becomes the adult who, unlike his sister, still hears the bell.

Works Cited

Chumo, Peter N. II. "Riding the Polar Express with William Broyles, Jr." In *Creative Screenwriting* 11 (2004): 64–68.

Ingram, Laura. "Chris Van Allsburg." In *Dictionary of Literary Biography: American Writers for Children Since 1960: Poets, Illustrators, and Nonfiction Authors*. Edited by Glenn E. Estes. Vol. 61. Detroit: Gale Research, 1987.

Martin, Michelle H. "Van Allsburg, Chris." *The Oxford Encyclopedia of Children's Literature*. Vol. 4. Edited by Jack Zipes. Oxford: Oxford University Press, 2006.

Neumeyer, Peter F. "How Picture Books Mean: The Case of Chris Van Allsburg." In *Children's Literature Association Quarterly* 15 (1990): 2–8.

The Polar Express. Screenplay by Robert Zemeckis and William Broyles, Jr. Directed by Robert Zemeckis. Warner Bros., 2004.

Ruello, Catherine. "Chris Van Allsburg Interview." In *Something About the Author.* Edited by Anne Commire. Detroit: Gale Research, 1989.

Stanton, Joseph. "The Dreaming Picture Books of Chris Van Allsburg." In *Children's Literature* 24 (1996): 161–179.

Van Allsburg, Chris. *The Polar Express.* Illustrated by Chris Van Allsburg. Boston: Houghton Mifflin, 1985. All quotations from the book are from this edition.

From Peter Pan *to* Finding Neverland: *A Visual Biomythography of James M. Barrie*

Sarah E. Maier

On December 27, 1904, James M. Barrie's play *Peter Pan* opened at London's Duke of York's Theatre.[1] Already a well-established playwright, Barrie offered a new genre of theatrical experience to audience members and critics alike, one that combined reality and fantasy, whimsy and psychological insight, rivalry and revenge. A never aging child — part boy, part Pan[2]— flew on to the stage that night as the "dream-child" (quoted in Green 70) of Barrie, his dual masterpiece and gift, the forgotten product of his interaction with the five Llewelyn Davies boys (George, John, Peter, Michael, Nicholas), the children of Arthur and Sylvia Llewelyn Davies, to whom Barrie dedicated the published play (1928) "in memory of what we have been to each other" (75). In "To the Five: A Dedication," Barrie acknowledges to the boys that he "made Peter by rubbing the five of you violently together, as savages with two sticks produce a flame. That is all he is, the spark I got from you" while also including "the uncomfortable admission that I have no recollection of writing the play"; indeed, he claims to remember only that he "stole back and sewed some of the gory fragments together with a pen-nib. That is what must have happened, but I cannot remember doing it" (76).

While this humility before his subject(s) seems simple devotion, it can equally be seen as an innuendo of the palimpsestic nature of the play. With the declaration on the program that the author was the youngest actress, Miss Ela Q. May, and gossip which pointed to the depressed stage painter as an alternate author of the text, Barrie deliberately foregrounds the artifice of the theater while at the same time encouraging his viewer (later reader) to consider the multiple possibilities of any dramatic creation. R. D. S. Jack, in *The Road to Neverland* (1991), argues further that Barrie was consciously creating a new "myth which stresses rather than hides its nature as artifice"

(286). *Peter Pan* exists in and between children and adults and between fantasy and reality, a fiction concerned with "the conflict between the freedom to create a literary child and its factual non-existence" (Jack 163).

In his essay, "Literary Biomythography" (2005), Michael Benton argues that

> Since literary biographies have a special concern for the life of the imagination, mythologizing plays a bigger role in this sub-genre than with other subjects. In fact, saintliness, idolatry and celebrity appear so frequently in literary biography that "biomythography" is a more apposite term since it recognizes the role of these aspects of myth-making. It encompasses the necessary invention of self and identity by the writer, and the virtual representation of the subject by the biographer [207].

Barrie's life story has become biomythography on two levels; first, critics have engaged in a psychological deconstruction of the author which diverts attention from his texts. Within his own lifetime, Barrie "managed to create the positive image of a modest, eccentric individual whose final years were spent in melancholic brooding." However in literary studies, it seems that his "critical fall from grace has gone hand in hand with a much harsher viewing of his nature" (Jack 7). In either case, whether true or false, such assumptions are far removed from the question of validity in his art. The mythology of *Peter Pan* also haunts its creator, identifying him as the man who was Peter Pan rather than as the author who wrote the play.

The boundaries and distinctions between Barrie's "actual life" and "posthumous life" have been dissolved in the time following his death. This is borne out in *Finding Neverland*. Rather than a simplistic linear biography, the man and the myth are blurred, and the "characters" who accompanied Barrie in life juxtaposed with the characters of his masterpiece where, through fantasy sequences clashing with reality, the Llewelyn Davies boys are Lost, Sylvia becomes his Wendy, Madame du Maurier embodies the femininity of Hook, Mary Barrie illustrates the pixiness of Tinker Bell, and of course, Barrie brings to life his own boyish Peter Pan(s).

In his *Notes on the Acting of A Fairy Play* (1904), Barrie asks for the indulgence as well as understanding from the actors when he asks them to see that, even in the Never Never Land of his play, "the cumulative effect of naturalness is the one thing to aim at. In a fairy play you may have many things to do that are not possible in real life, but you conceive yourself in a world in which they are occurrences, and act accordingly" (Barrie quoted in Jack 166). Further, in his opening stage directions to *Peter Pan*, all "the characters, whether grown-ups or babes, must wear a child's outlook on life as their only important adornment" (Barrie 88). In the recent adaptation of Allan Knee's play, *The Man Who Was Peter Pan* (1999),[3] into David Magee's screenplay for *Finding Neverland* (2004), the audience is asked to join Barrie, now Magee, and suspend disbelief as primary and secondary worlds come together in a tertiary nexus of Pannish play to create a visual bio-mythography of Barrie as the man who wrote — or was— Peter Pan. This creates a *ménage* with the original play, the characters that peopled his life and the imagination of this introspective genius.

Peter Pan, as the original narrative, begins this line of narratives with a complex structure which takes dramatic license with the audience that

> resembles poetic and artistic license insofar as the spectator is aware of conventions sufficiently to know they are invoked, but responds in something other than the customary way to the artist/instigator's invitation to actively suspend disbelief while depending explicitly upon the awareness of how an event is framed by narrative then altered by a disparate frame [Davis 59].

Barrie's text invokes such license to investigate two levels of the "real": the primary world of the Nursery children and the secondary or fantastic world that is Never Never Land. The primary world of the Nursery children is clearly based on late Victorian–Edwardian society. As such, the roles of the characters, before contact with the secondary world order, bear the conventions of that society. They are clearly gendered in a manner which supports generationally-inherited, conventional discourse.

In *Bodies That Matter* (1993), Judith Butler proposes that the performance of gender, via bodies that matter, are "clearly defined by a certain power of creation and rationality," so that to know the "significance of something is to know how and why it matters, where 'to matter' means at once 'to materialize' and 'to mean'" (32). In the case of Barrie's characters, their gender performances are strongly constructed by late Victorian and Edwardian social codes, mores and conventions. How those various bodies come to materialize, mean, or matter is contingent on the origination, transformation, and potentiality of the body to interpret and perform within and without cultural constraints and expectations; therefore, the body's intelligibility is not a given but is produced. The production of this intelligible body is the site of each character's performativity and the seat of his/her available power in the discourse of the text. Such discourse pervades *Peter Pan* and the subsequent *Finding Neverland*; specifically, how the characters are engendered controls the ultimate outcome of the text.

In *Peter Pan*, Wendy wishes to emulate her mother, Mrs. Darling, while her brother, John, assumes his patriarchal role:

> WENDY: I am happy to acquaint you, Mr. Darling, you are now a father.
> JOHN: Boy or girl?
> WENDY: (*presenting herself*) Girl.
> JOHN: Tuts.
> WENDY: You horrid [90].

Although John declares that they are only "doing an act" (90), Wendy has been reminded of the secondary status ascribed to her — she does present her "self" — based solely on her gender as she performs it. Clearly, she imitates the role of her mother, Mrs. Darling, who is relegated to domestic duties, and further infantilized through egocentricity and gender jealousy by her husband who, "knows exactly the right moment to treat a woman as a beloved child" (93). Enacting his role as head of the household, Mr. Darling demands the children take their medicine; when they do not and he is unable to swallow the stuff in an act of machismo, he retaliates against the dog nurse, Nana, to assert "Am I master in this house or is she?" (96). Purely a realist — equating children to costs — Mr. Darling refuses to see the romance of the shadow which Mrs. Darling has caught and pragmatically says, "There is money in this, my love. I shall take it to the British Museum to-morrow and have it priced" (93). The role models whom the children emulate are harshly drawn by Barrie from society. Nevertheless, via dramatic example of the "play" within the play, Barrie suggests that the *status quo* is in need of questioning, and the audience begins to realize that there may be a place for woman in such discourse. Nana must, it is said, "probably be played by a boy, if one clever enough can be found" (88), and it is Mrs. Darling who first sees the shadow and Peter Pan.

The theatrical or literary audience encounters, in *Peter Pan*, the complex performances of gender by several characters, including Wendy, Hook, Smee, Tinker Bell, and Peter Pan, and the entry of Peter Pan and his talk of the secondary world of Never Never Land immediately calls into question the stability of gender conventions as expressed in the nursery. First, the fantastical appearance of a flying boy accompanied by a ball of light announces to the audience that the impossible is now apparent, and second, when Wendy's wounded pride leads her to declare that she is of "no use," Peter instantly crows that "one girl is worth more than twenty boys" (99). This is of course the hyperbolic opposite of the value previously given to a girl by her own primary world society.

The progression of the children into Never Never Land leads to this complexity of gender performances. While Wendy works to reestablish her femininity, "wearing romantic woodland garments, sewn by herself" (127) and acting the mother to all of the Lost Boys, John is reminded of the change to conventions of gender in Never Never Land:

JOHN: Build a house?
   CURLY: For the Wendy.
   JOHN: (*feeling that there must be some mistake here*) For Wendy? Why, she is only a girl.
   CURLY: That is why we are her servants.
   PETER: Yes, and you also [114].

Why is Wendy so revered? Unlike John, she possesses a significant ability unknown among the Lost Boys and Peter Pan; she has the responsibility of storytelling and the power to create. Through words, she creates a tale to sustain the fiction of their "family," as well as outlining for them a fantasy world outside of Never Never Land. She is aware of her power, one she is unused to, and finds herself "melting over the beauty of her present performance" (131).

Never Never Land's secondary world femininity is ambiguously constructed, which leads to a variety of possibilities outside of conventional norms. Barrie uses a creature of fantasy to make one of his most salient points on how the primary world constructs the feminine. The Mermaid, a "lovely girl" with an "excess of scales," a "bewitching ... blue-eyed" creature with "long tresses," sits lazily observing her own "effects in a transparent shell." She is the object of the Lost Boys—and Wendy's—desire; collectively, they wish to capture her, but are warned that mermaids "are such cruel creatures ... that they try to pull boys and girls like you into the water and drown them" (118). While Barrie's portrait of the mermaid is the enchanting stuff of faërie, it may also be his cynical warning to those primary world men who desire to capture an idealized woman in marriage, and to young girls who wish to emulate or attain a false hagiography. Ultimately, the Mermaid attempts to drown Wendy. By way of contrast, Tiger Lily, also sexualized in early drafts, demonstrates the stoicism of a young woman who is valued as the "daughter of a chief and must die as a chief's daughter," unlike in the primary world where lineage is patriarchal. She stands with "her face ... impassive" (119) before the pirates to confront her destiny in a righteous manner.

While in the primary world emotional and social progression demands adherence to a specific gender and demands "the assumption of fictions as truths" (Jack 184), there is an ironic assumption that secondary worlds are simplistic. In an early draft of the play, Barrie theorizes the possibility of a much less strict understanding of gender when Pan comments that "Nature is also excellently set forth with a biformed body ... for no natural being seems to be simple, but as it were participating and compounded of two" (quoted in Jack 184). Later excised, this idea is problematized in the character of Smee and fully embodied in the performance of Captain Hook. Smee is "always ready for a chat" and is constantly "looking for the bright side" (109). Smee also performs domestic duties in Hook's cabin. While "engrossed in his labours at the sewing-machine" (139) Smee is identified by Hook as "Pathetic Smee, the Nonconformist pirate, a happy smile upon his face because he thinks they fear him! How can I break it to him that they think him lovable?" Hook, however, embodies his own contrasts. He is on the one hand a "dark and fearful man" who is the "villainous looking" and "cadaverous and blackavised ... with an iron hook instead of a right hand" (108), while on the other, he possesses "elegance of his diction, the distinction of his demeanour" that is courtly, courageous, and "dandiacal" (108) with "a touch of the feminine as [there is] in all the greatest pirates" (122). Saved from complete foppishness by his Etonian language and education, the dandy of the Jolly Roger ultimately commits suicide, unable to live with his ongoing battle with the youthfulness of his reverse image, Pan, who imitates Hook with such precision that "even the author has a dizzy feeling that at times he was really Hook" (120).

Peter Pan, the central character who moves with ease from the primary to secondary worlds of Barrie's text, is often argued to be the author's maimed psyche or the masquerade of his dead brother, David, who lives on as the eternal boy, a mixture of sadness and play, but for whom nothing holds great import. Peter Pan quickly "forgets" with whom he plays and why just as easily as he issues "silent orders" (115) to the Lost Boys; he explains the one cardinal rule of Never Never Land to Wendy:

> PETER: You mustn't touch me.
> WENDY: Why?
> PETER: No one must ever touch me.
> WENDY: Why?
> PETER: I don't know [98].

Never having known a mother, Peter Pan is incapable of genuine affection, but enjoys his interaction with the various characters in his attempts to live up to their expectations of him as leader, adversary, rescuer, and patriarch, multiple roles which allow him to be the most powerful being in Never Never Land. He embodies the biformed body Barrie envisioned, because in order to progress into manhood — which he vehemently opposes— he would have to equate his nature with masculinity (the trappings of which he abhors) or with the highly regarded, "too clever" (101) femininity already represented by "the Wendy." Rather than assume a role in society, Peter Pan claims he "ran away to Kensington Gardens and lived a long time among the fairies" (99) of whom he speaks with callous disregard, but who represent fitting companions for him. He is defined by his relations with others; in and of himself, Peter Pan is reduced to confusion by "facts, the only things that puzzle him" (129) because he exists in the world of ambiguous, asexual play, quick to fly from any responsibility which might cause him to be a man. When confronted by Hook with "Pan, who and what art thou," Pan can respond only with his true self-conception: "I'm youth, I'm joy" (145).

It is the topsy-turviness of gender in *Peter Pan* that allows for further complexity to be investigated in the film *Finding Neverland*. Fantastic elements in the two worlds of the play allow for the ability to see the world through child-like eyes, much as Barrie might have experienced his com-

peting worlds of publishing, marriage, responsibility, and play. The assig-
nation of performances relates to a third level of fantasy in the film: the real
or artistic realm of Barrie's imagination which significantly includes the idea
of harlequinade and pantomime as fantasy. Harlequinade, a form of theatrical entertainment begun in the Italian *commedia dell'arte,* was introduced into England in the early eighteenth century by John Rich, the
manager of a theater in London. Over time, these entertainments became
pantomimes, which featured fairy tales and humorous sequences; however,
they originally also included the Harlequin, who was a character of "child-
like ignorance, wit, and grace" (Mulgan 224). In *Finding Neverland,* it is safe
to say that Barrie acts the Harlequin, unable to articulate the expectations
of late-Victorian or Edwardian society, but able to enter the imaginative
realm of the child as expressed in the film's dialogue: he "wander[s] between
two worlds in [a] Janus-like split between progress and nostalgia"
(Knoepflmacher 497).

When Barrie was asked by Paramount Studios for ideas to adapt his
play to the screen, he responded with "Twenty-thousand words of the most
carefully re-written scenario, with all the sub-titles, and a mass of fresh
visual detail which to anyone but a film producer and his attendant experts
must surely have seemed like a gift from heaven" (Jack 189). Clearly, he saw
the possibility for the visual to capture what words could not portray. While
not an adaptation following Barrie's ideas, *Finding Neverland* perhaps main-
tains the integrity of his ideas. It begins with unconventional flashes to a
third level of the fantastic that give us some insight into Barrie's depressive
thoughts at the September 24, 1903, opening night of his play, *Little Mary,*
at Wyndham's Theatre when he sees a torrential rain build up and drench
the audience in the theater. He declares his own play to be "pig's pizzle" and
"shite" to an unsuspecting usher as he paces in the hallway with only occasional glimpses through the curtain (sc.1), but such flashes of fantasy later
turn into a full demonstration of the author's imagination when he meets
the Llewelyn Davies boys in Kensington Park. While Barrie sits writing in
his journal, he has with him a first indicator of his unconventional nature:
he has a ball for his dog attached to the end of a fishing pole for easy retrieval.
Michael, the youngest Llewelyn Davies boy in the film, is in prison under
his bench, having been captured by Prince George, the eldest boy. Barrie's
immense Newfoundland dog — real, now made fictional, later dually so as
Nana in *Peter Pan* — attracts the attention of the young, cynical, grief-
stricken Peter Llewelyn Davies (played by Freddie Highmore) who declares
Porthos "just a dog" (sc. 2). Barrie expresses his dismay and proclaims "just"
to be a "soul-crushing word." He tells Peter that "with those eyes, my bonny
lad, I'm afraid you'd never see it," and he encourages the boys to employ
"just a wee bit of imagination" in order to see Porthos in an elaborate pan-

tomime as a dancing bear surrounded by sad-faced clowns who are distressed because Peter refuses to believe in the imaginative realm.

The film then proceeds with a conventional narrative but it is told in an unconventional manner to match the man and the family who are the subject of this biographical picture; his time with the Llewelyn Davies boys increases, and just as their familiarity becomes easy, their imaginative worlds are easily interchangeable, one unto the other. Dinner table play with a spoon — much to the horror of Barrie's wife, Mary (Radha Mitchell), who sees the acquaintance of Sylvia Llewelyn Davies (Kate Winslet) and her mother, Madame du Maurier (Dame Julie Christie), as an opportunity to advance socially — leads to lengthy days spent with Sylvia and her boys, their play weaving between the fictional real and the imaginatively real. A child's game of cowboys and Indians (sc. 3) is intermingled with the flying of a kite (sc. 4) which later inspires him to create Tinker Bell. This growth of imagination in the boys occurs under the encouraging but stable influence of Sylvia who, like Wendy, controls the active critical moments in and out of fantasy worlds which allows Barrie's imagination to run rampant, leading to the ideas for "the play."

His intention to create a world to save the boys from their grief and to allow himself further into their lives demonstrates the real-life Barrie's sense of nostalgia at his own lost childhood; however, it is in narrative parallels between the fictionalized characters of Barrie's own life and those of his imaginative creation, *Peter Pan*, that the film captures the fluidity of Barrie's own child-like imagination and gender in contrast to the prescribed assumptions of social expectations. Even an early critic, writing in 1902 for *The Times* on another of Barrie's plays, recognized that Barrie's work was important not merely for what was apparent: "For the claim of a genuine Barrie, while it is undeniable, is at the same time not very easily explicable. In the ultimate analysis we believe that the pleasure of a genuine Barrie will be found not so much in what the work — either novel or play — says as in what it implies" (quoted in Jack 15). *Finding Neverland* implies, on Barrie's behalf, that his mind's eye was neither malevolent nor pedophilic[4]; rather, it was continuous and overwhelming, the desire to theorize the nature of art and artifice, and to demonstrate that art does not answer to the restraints of social conformity.

Finding Neverland imaginatively re-envisions the transmutation of the characters in Barrie's life at the time that he drafted his odd play; as a result, there are singular (Mr. Darling), dual (Mrs. Darling and Hook) and triple (Wendy, Peter) realms of existence for the characters. The most obvious example of these transformations is motherly Sylvia Llewelyn Davies, who both adopts *per se* and loves the child-like Barrie, taking on the roles of both the idealized Mrs. Darling and the universally desired Wendy, while still representing historical person. Always, like Wendy, "the one of the family, for there is one in every family, who can be trusted to know or not to know" (Barrie 96), Sylvia, as portrayed by the film, looks after all her boys in spite of her increasingly invalid state. A widow in the play when she meets Barrie, she is unwell but in denial about her ailments — both society that sets the parameters for acceptable behavior for a young woman without a husband and the cancer which threatens her body.

> BARRIE: They can see it. You can't go on just pretending.
> SYLVIA: Pretending? You brought pretending into this family, James. You showed us we can change things by simply believing them to be different.
> BARRIE: A lot of things, Sylvia, not everything.
> SYLVIA: But the things that matter. We've pretended for some time that you're a part of this family, haven't we? You've come to mean so much to us all that now it doesn't matter if it's true. And even if it isn't true, even if that can never be, I need to go on pretending until the end ... with you.
> BARRIE: Are you sure there's nothing else I can do for you?
> SYLVIA: No ... well, I have always wanted to go to Never Land. You did promise to tell me about it you know [sc. 9].

On two fronts, Barrie and Sylvia are reminded of these intrusions of reality into their world of extraordinary play: first by Barrie's friend and fellow cricketer Sir Arthur Conan Doyle (Ian Hart), who confronts the multifarious rumors and innuendos which surround Barrie's relationship with Sylvia and her boys, rumors which Barrie dismisses, then by Madame du Maurier who admonishes him, "Have you no idea how much your friendship has already cost my daughter, or are you really that selfish?" (sc.8).

Indeed, Barrie is that selfish, and his confrontation with du Maurier is one of those excellent moments in which the film shows us his child-like reaction to the discipline of one who sees the world through adult eyes. As the boys are scolded — along with Sylvia and Barrie — for being too long at play in the park, Madame du Maurier transforms and transgenders into a manifestation of Captain James Hook, her umbrella becoming a hook, the sleeves on her dress transforming into elongated pirate lace, and her bodice multiplying military buttons (sc. 4). Barrie, in all drafts of the play, intended that Hook should "embody the most extreme horror possible to the childish imagination" (Jack 167); in *Finding Neverland*, du Maurier's horrific words imply that discipline is needed, otherwise the family, specifically the boys, will be Lost, thus solidifying the parallels to Barrie's characters. Michael speaks to the boys' and Barrie's fear when he says, "Is he in trouble? Because I've been alone with grandmother and I know what it is like" (sc. 8).

This portrait of Hook as a kind of master reintroduces into the *Peter Pan* scenario an element that Barrie intended in an early draft of the play, one in which Hook plays a schoolmaster, surrounded by clowns. The ability of film to evoke this wordless transformation from matriarch to master evokes a similar reaction from the audience who are reminded that the real and the imaginative often clash at their boundaries and that the intention of Hook in *Peter Pan* is to be a dark, ever present counterfoil — not a parodic fop — to the ease and forgetfulness of Peter himself. In the second case, their play at a family life is constantly crashing up against the reality of Sylvia's progressive illness, one that hastens the production of the theatrical play and in some ways, implies an ending for Sylvia herself. In Barrie's own life, his mother complex was clear; consequently, his own first masquerade as his dead brother to awaken a will to live in his mother haunts the narrative through the portrayals of both mothers in *Finding Neverland*.

Both women, invalid and matriarch, are treated with respect by Barrie in life and in the screenplay of *Finding Neverland*; however, the portrayal of Barrie's wife, Mary, is just as complex a combination of sympathy and spite as we see in the portrait of Tinker Bell in *Peter Pan*. Originally created as "Tippy" then "Tinker Bell" (Jack 169), the fairy minx appears to be an amalgam of mate and mischievous flirt. *Finding Neverland* transforms her into a jealous, lonely woman who disapproves of Wendy's guiding, maternal, yet desirable influence; she is transformed into the suffering silence of Barrie's wife. Barrie's asexual life with Mary is clearly demarcated in the film by the separate doors they enter every night, with darkness greeting Mary and the glow of Never Never Land waiting behind her husband's door (sc.4). Unlike previous film adaptations, such as Spielberg's *Hook*, which androgynize Tinker Bell as a miniature Pan, or the more recent *Peter Pan* (2004), which silences her into a mean-spirited flirt who is more apparently sexual, *Finding Neverland* portrays Tinker Bell as disdainful toward Wendy's maternal nature; Tinker Bell–Mary is unable to understand the widow Sylvia's hold over her husband since she does not offer money or status. The chronology of the film significantly changes the tenor of Barrie's relationship with Sylvia Llewelyn Davies; in reality, her husband Arthur was alive until 1909 and participated, at various levels, in Barrie's friendship. It is important, however, for *Finding Neverland*, that he is no longer present; first, it allows for a seemingly more passionate Barrie who may see Sylvia in a romantic rather than purely platonic light, an idea which would not be clear if he were still present, and second, it allows for Barrie's wife to perform the role of Tinker Bell to Sylvia's Wendy.

In *Finding Neverland*, Mary's occasional outbursts against the absurdity of their situation, particularly when she recounts the "disastrous" of the dinner party (sc.3), remind the audience — and Barrie — of Tinker Bell's demanding nature, a quality perhaps best seen in Mary's defiance when she confronts Barrie over the status of their marriage after he catches her, unlike in life, with Gilbert Cannon:

MARY: How dare you? This isn't one of your plays.
   BARRIE: I know that Mary. It's quite serious, but I'm not ready for this conversation wherever it may lead [sc. 7].

Not only is Barrie unready to face the confrontations, just as Pan evades Tinker Bell with, "You know, Tink, you can't be my fairy because I am a gentleman and you are a lady" (Barrie 100), but he is also unable to perform his role as gentleman; he is indifferent to the social implications of his wife's adulterous sexuality.

   It is the portrait of Peter Pan constructed in *Finding Neverland* wherein the most levels of performance and fantasy converge, particularly at the opening night of *Peter Pan*:

PETER: It's about our summer together, isn't it?
   BARRIE: It is....
   PETER: It's magical. Thank you.
   BARRIE: No, thank you. Thank you, Peter.
   WOMAN: This is Peter Pan. How wonderful!
   MAN: Peter Pan? Why, you must be quite a little adventurer!
   SECOND WOMAN: Why look — he has no shadow!
   PETER: But I'm not Peter Pan.... He is [sc. 9].

Throughout the reading or viewing of the play *Peter Pan*, there is a lingering suspicion that Barrie is representing himself, at both his best and his worst; here, the two potential Pans find the truth of it in a set piece that might be described as Barrie, in the guise of Pan, speaking to his other childlike self, in the guise of Peter, the child. Two other instances in the play make this conflation of the two Peters possible: the inability for the child Peter Llewelyn Davies's play at the cottage to transport the family — Sylvia in particular — away from reality to a healthy, wonder-filled fantasy world (sc. 7), and the second, the staging of the play *Peter Pan* at the Llewelyn Davies's house for the now deathly ill Sylvia (sc. 10–11). In the first scenario, Peter attempts to use "just a bit of silliness really"— with emphasis on "just" reminding us of how his eyes have changed since the opening scenes—to show his mother an imaginative world beyond the present difficulties; when it fails, the desperation and frustration of Peter leads him to destroy his playhouse and his manuscript. Such emphasis on the distress of the child's and artist's inability to express himself adequately in the face of sorrow reminds us of the limitations of fantasy, and that "a writer's literary fantasies are unfavorably contrasted [at times] with reality represented by a living child" (Geduld 55). Sylvia's cough constantly reminds the family of her mortality, much like Hook's ticking crocodile in *Peter Pan*. The second scene is, perhaps, the most important to the film, and where the most risk is taken in an attempt to find a structure capable of transmitting the various myths of the real/Real using fantasy sequences. Barrie, the exemplar of Peter Pan, has the inability to perform the socially constructed role of gentleman; rather, he is a gentleman whose gift to his dying muse, Sylvia, and to the children surrounding her is the blending of life with the hope provided by his creative nature. This moment in *Finding Neverland*, when Barrie is returned to silence while Peter Pan and his art speak for him, Peter Pan is exemplified by both genders—female actress playing the male Peter in the presence of both Peters—literally breaks through the fourth wall of theatrical and filmic experience. At the moment when Pan asks, "Do you believe?" (sc. 10) so that Tinker Bell will be reinvigorated against death, and as Sylvia watches with the foreboding shadow of her own mortality palpable in the room, Forster lifts the wall of the Llewelyn Davies's house to give us first a theatrical vision of Never Never Land, then to reveal Sylvia and Barrie's immediate belief in the world that awaits her; her dress transforms from invalid robes to those of a princess of the faërie realm when she walks out into Never Never Land, still peopled by Hook, Smee, fairies and mermaids, pirates and pixies, to suspend her disbelief and her own mortality. This challenging moment asks the audience, just as it did in the original play, to enter the fantasy and a realm of possibility to exist other-wise, here further splicing primary, secondary and now tertiary worlds. Barrie, as creator and created, understands the nature of art and of artifice, as well as the importance of youth sacrificed and youth maintained.

It is possible that *Finding Neverland* makes clear what Barrie could not make understood of himself: his life co-existed with his art. The successful melding of Barrie's life through these genres—fiction, film, myth and biography—creates a visual biomythography that empowers an understanding of Barrie befitting his genius because in "Peter Pan, Barrie achieved the rarest alchemy of all, the one that no writer can plan or predict: he invented a myth" (Lane 100) of himself as the man who was Peter Pan.

Notes

1. My discussion of Barrie's work and the film, *Finding Neverland*, is based on the 1928 definitive text of the play. The published novel of 1911 will be referred to by its correct title, *Peter and Wendy*.

2. I wish to thank Alain Chouinard for his insight on the Greek god's relation to the naming of Peter Pan.

3. I would like to thank Allan Knee for his gracious offer of the of his play for consideration here.

4. The Llewelyn Davies boys, each when asked concerning this point of retroactive investigation, deny any wrongdoing on Barrie's behalf (see Birkin).

Works Cited

Barrie, J. M. *Peter Pan in Peter Pan and Other Plays*. Edited by P. Hollindale. Toronto: OUP, 1995.

Beerbohm, M. "The Child Barrie." *Saturday Review,* January 7, 1905: 13–14.

Benton, M. "Literary Biomythography." *Auto/Biography* 13 (2005): 206–226.

Birkin, A. *J. M. Barrie & the Lost Boys*. New York: Potter, 1979.

Butler, J. *Bodies that Matter: On the Discursive Limits of "Sex."* New York: Routledge, 1993.

Davis, T. "'Do You Believe in Fairies?': The Hiss of Dramatic License." *Theatre Journal*. 57.1 (March 2005): 57–81.

Finding Neverland. Screenplay by David Magee. Directed by Marc Forster.

Geduld, Harry M. *James Barrie*. NY: Twayne, 1971.

Green, R. L. *Fifty Years of Peter Pan*. London: Bodley Head, 1960.

Hume, K. *Fantasy and Mimesis*. London: Methuen, 1984.

Jack, R. D. S. *The Road to Neverland: A Reassessment of J M Barrie's Dramatic Art*. Aberdeen: Aberdeen University Press, 1991.

Knee, A. "The Man Who Was Peter Pan." Ts. received from author, 1999.

Knoepflmacher, U. C. "The Balancing of Child and Adult: An Approach to Victorian Fantasies for Children." *Nineteenth-Century Fiction* 37.4 (1983): 497–530.

Lane, Anthony. "Lost Boys: Why J. M. Barrie Created *Peter Pan*." *The New Yorker*. 80.36 (2004): 98–103.

Mulgan, J. *Concise Oxford Dictionary of English Literature*. Oxford: Clarendon Press, 1939.

From Witch to Wicked:
A Mutable and
Transformational Sign

JESSICA ZEBRINE GRAY

The cackling, ugly hag with green skin and pointed hat flies on a broomstick through the night air. This stereotypical Halloween witch is built from folklore, superstitions, and cultural iconography, some dating back to the Renaissance when the image was used to encourage the persecution and oppression of women. Most often it is reviled and cast aside as inaccurate. But could this image be reclaimed and used to challenge stereotypes? The musical *Wicked* questions traditional oppressive binaries, breaking down the definite distinction between good and evil. This essay explores the witch image in European folklore, L. Frank Baum's original book *The Wonderful Wizard of Oz*, the iconic film, Gregory Maguire's novel *Wicked*, and finally the highly successful musical to show how this sign has changed and transformed to reflect society's views of good and evil.

According to Saussure, in his development of semiotics, signs are "unchangeable" in that each one is "the product of historical forces" (72). Yet, the same sign is always mutable (75). Derrida took this theory further, exploring how any sign can be traced through its genealogy, finding the moments of change and rupture which allow us "to transform concepts, to displace them, to turn them against their presuppositions, to reinscribe them in other chains, and little by little to modify the terrain of our work and thereby produce new configurations" (24). Many forces built the image of the "Wicked Witch," which has changed significantly throughout its history. The sign developed in Renaissance Europe, but transformed into the American "Wicked Witch of the West" through a chain of literary, theatrical, and film moments that reflect the social pressures of their time. While aspects of the sign hearken back to early images of witches, the sign continues to shift in content and meaning.

The Witch in Folklore

Images contributing to the sign of the Wicked Witch abound throughout European folklore, though a few are especially significant to the development of the witches in Oz. Witches are most commonly defined as women who practice magic, attempting to change the natural world through supernatural means. Early Christian teachings by St. Augustine (354–430) did not distinguish between good or evil magic, as all magic was thought to rely on a "contract between a human being and a demon" and therefore was considered evil (Behringer 4). However, these demons or devils were associated with powerless pagan gods, and the witches were pitied, not persecuted (4). With rapid expansion in the 12th century, the Christian church sought to maintain discipline and order by radically punishing heresy of all forms. By the 13th and 14th centuries, fears of witchcraft grew more prevalent and the reactions more violent. Heinrich Kramer and James Sprenger developed the image of malevolent witches in their treatise *The Malleus Maleficarum* (published c1486), which specifically outlined how to identify, try, torture, and execute those practicing harmful magic, leading to oppression and persecution that lasted centuries.

Scholars have sought to identify social causes for the persecution, as many of the witches were socially stigmatized, elderly, and disliked for other reasons. Some claim that economics played a big factor, especially since prosecution included a seizure of assets. Violence against the witch was often vengeance for assumed covert violence on the part of the witch (Stewart 168). In folklore a witch is typically pictured as "old, wrinkled, bent, crippled and reclusive.... They may mutter to themselves or display other signs of abnormal or antisocial behavior" (Widdowson 202). This historical image of social alienation became a significant part of the characterization of the Wicked Witch as the sign developed.

While women were more commonly labeled "witches," men also practiced harmful magic as "wizards" or "sorcerers." The defining characteristic of magic represented in this period, as opposed to earlier fantasy representations, is the pact with the Devil, which is represented for men through scholarship. This connection is made as early as the 12th century, where male sorcerers became associated with the image of the mechanical, disembodied head functioning as an oracle, a tradition that may have developed from earlier uses of severed human heads in the practice of divination (LaGrandeur 409). But while the male sorcerer demonstrates his own intellectual power and skill through his magical practice, the female witch demonstrates her bodily weakness through submission (Bailey 127). Kramer and Sprenger suggest that women are inclined to approach magic physically while men are more intellectual in their practice. They indicate that female submission is shown through the witch's willingness to allow her familiar, usually an animal, to touch or suck blood from her body. The witch also uses her skills to command her demonic familiar rather than enact change herself (126). *The Malleus Maleficarum* of women is particularly antifeminist, outlining specifically the reasons women are more susceptible to "evil superstitions" than men, more capable of "carnal abominations," and defective in intelligence, leaving them more open to demonic influence (43–45). This polarity of male and female imagery, especially in relation to the mind-body dichotomy and the magical tools, also became significant in the development of the Wicked Witch sign.

One recurring characteristic of witches frequently cited in their trials and interrogations is their ability to fly, either on a broomstick or by some other means. Seen as utterly unnatural, the ability to fly allows the witch to create harm over a greater distance, thus inspiring great fear among the superstitious. While many scholars argue that the witches' confessions of flight were merely brought about through torture, some of the witches seemed convinced of their journeys. According to Michael Harner, the early European image of witches flying on brooms may actually have its basis in the use of a hallucinogenic "flying ointment," which made the witch think she had traveled on a broomstick. The straddling the broom was "undoubtedly more than a symbolic Freudian act, serving as an applicator for the atropine-containing plant to the sensitive vaginal membranes" (131). Whether the phallic shape was practical or symbolic, the image came to signify a woman's use of male power, the phallus, to transcend the limitations of the physical and, thus, female realm. The vertical has more to do with heavenly concerns, while the horizontal relates to the physical plane (Northrup 30). To fly above the earth brings the female witch into male domain. It is little wonder that in traditional folklore she needed a male demon or phallic broomstick to accomplish this feat.

As for traditional witches' garb, in early woodcut images of witches, the women are pictured wearing little or no clothing during their rites, while images of witches being tried and executed show them wearing clothing similar to other women, simple peasant dresses of neutral colors and various headgear. The association of specific clothing signifiers developed well after the actual witch craze as the images passed into folklore and fairy tales. According to folklorist John Widdowson, "The physical appearance of witch-figures is typically frightening and is often almost a caricature of all the most unpleasant human characteristics. Extreme ugliness, bodily deformity of all kinds, birthmarks, warts…. They often dress in dark, dirty, ragged clothes" (202). Many superstitions evolved around the color black, which has long been associated with death. Harmful magic is often called "black magic," and the Devil was referred to as the "Black Man" (Pickering

34). The representation of the witch wearing dark clothing reinforced an association with evil and destruction.

The conical hat with a wide brim is a more complicated symbol without a clear, definable lineage. Many modern interpretations of the hat relate it to the tendency to see the witch as unfashionable. According to Jung, a deeper meaning of the conical shape is androgyny, "a dual symbol: from one point of view it is penetrating in shape, and therefore active and masculine in significance; and from the other, it is shaped like a receptacle which is feminine in meaning" (Cirlot 151). Thus, the hat could represent a cross between masculine and feminine, much like the broom. These clothing images, based more on fantasy and imagination than on "real" witches, quickly became key identifiers of the Wicked Witch sign.

Once identified, witches were persecuted in a variety of ways, but the most significant for the development of the Oz witches was the "swimming test," a trial by which a woman would be bound hand and foot and thrown into the water. "Those who stay afloat are considered to be witches and are burned; those who, on the contrary, go under are declared innocent of all witchcraft and are set free again" (Behringer 56). Of course, many of those proven "innocent" by their failure to float drowned. The choice of water as method may have been related to folkloric beliefs that a witch could not be baptized by water due to her demonic associations. Thus, refusal of baptism was clear cause for an accusation of witchcraft (204). Water itself is usually seen as a symbol of life and birth, though full immersion in water "signifies a return to the preformal state, with a sense of death and annihilation on the one hand, but of rebirth and regeneration on the other" (Cirlot 365). These connotations of life and death and good and evil are intimately connected to the chain of signifiers leading to the Wicked Witch.

Folklore in American Fiction —
The Wonderful Wizard of Oz

When L. Frank Baum created his fantasyland of Oz, he sought to explore the concepts of good and evil. Deriving his beliefs from the study of theosophy, an esoteric spiritual philosophy associated with the occult, Baum embraced a "vision of a cosmos in which physical and spiritual reality were part of one great whole, filled with beings seen and unseen and governed by those same laws" (Rogers 51). His theosophical beliefs allowed for magic as a supernatural possibility that, nevertheless, obeyed natural laws in which nothing is inherently good or evil. This tension of natural vs. supernatural permeates all of his fantasy work.

Baum's Oz is controlled by witches, but he employs a slightly different definition of witchcraft and magic than did the Early Modern age. Accord-ing to Katherine Rogers, "Baum got his concept of good witches (which upsets fundamentalists to this day) from [his theosophist mother-in-law] Matilda Gage. He agreed with her that magic was simply a form of knowl-edge and that witches (and sorcerers) were people with extraordinary knowl-edge, who could use it for good or ill, depending on their character" (79). Gage was heavily involved in the women's suffrage movement, and although nationwide suffrage was not granted until 1920, the changing view of women had already influenced Baum at the time *Oz* was published in 1900. Prior to the successes of the women's movement in the twentieth century, only men could be leaders, and women were considered little more than property, but in *Oz*, these traditional roles are nearly reversed. All of the male characters in Baum's books are either not human or are significantly flawed. "Baum's male figures provide protection for the children on their journeys, but the real authority belongs to the female characters" (Riley 154). The Wizard is not a very sympathetic character, as he is shown to be merely a "talking head," reminiscent of the disembodied heads of Renaissance sorcery. Dorothy dismantles his disguise, revealing that he is instead "a very good man," but "a very bad Wizard," whose magical powers are merely illusions (157). Only the women have the power to change their surroundings. Thus, Baum criticizes the traditional gender roles so ingrained at the turn of the 20th century.

In contrast to his challenge of gender stereotypes, Baum's treatment of the good-evil binary is quite conventional. Very soon after arriving in Oz, Dorothy meets the Witch of the North, who explains she is a "good witch" (15). When Dorothy protests that she heard all witches are "wicked," the Witch of the North explains that before Dorothy arrived there had been four witches who ruled in Oz, two good and two "wicked" (16). Wicked-ness in this sense could also be defined as "selfishness." As Gardner and Nye point out, "The theme of selflessness as the cardinal principle of love runs through all the *Oz* books, forming the thread that binds them together.... Those who use power for selfish ends, are Bad, and are punished in propor-tion to their crime" (Gardner and Nye 11). Throughout this story, the good witches are selfless in their efforts to help Dorothy, while the wicked witches act out of selfish motivation. Dorothy alternates between the four witches, as she accidentally kills the Witch of the East, is sent on her journey by the Witch of the North, is sent by the Wizard to kill the Witch of the West, and finally finds her way home with the help of Glinda, the Witch of the South.

However, the separation of "good" witches from "wicked" witches blurs the positive portrayal of women in the books, and the witches' geographi-cal associations suggest a negative view of women. The directions East and West create a horizontal, feminine realm, while the North and South are more traditionally related to the masculine. The good witches of the North and South are associated with the ideals of male desire. The Witch of the North is an old woman, but is pleasant and kind-looking, and Glinda, the Good Witch of the South, is described as "both beautiful and young to their eyes. Her hair was a rich red in color and fell in flowing ringlets over her shoulders" (206). These ideal images of goodness reflect the traditional dichotomy of women in the male imagination — mother figures and sexualized beauties. In contrast, the wicked witches of the East and West are associated with the negative feminine attributes. While the Wicked Witch of the West is the primary antagonist of the story, she appears in only two chapters. Baum describes her as having "but one eye, yet that was as powerful as a telescope" (114). W.W. Denslow, the illustrator of the original book, shows the wicked witch as an old woman wearing a pointed hat with brim and an eye-patch and contorting her face and body. This recalls the Renaissance assumptions of old age and ugliness in witches.

This Wicked Witch uses objects to manipulate the world, a silver whistle to command wolves and bees and a golden cap to command the winged monkeys. These animals have no physical relationship with her, so they could not be considered a complete sign of the witch's familiar, but her association with animals continues the chain of signifiers loosely. Unlike the witches of old, she relies on tools rather than on a demonic familiar for power, though there is nary a broomstick in sight. None of the witches transcend the horizontal to fly through the air in the book. Only the Wizard in his hot air balloon and the male flying monkeys defy gravity. The witch's selfish pursuit of Dorothy's silver shoes, which are also presented as magical tools, leads to her demise when Dorothy throws a bucket of water on her and she melts, a new element Baum added to witch folklore (Rogers 265). Instead of floating on the water as many accused witches did in the trials of Early Modern Europe, this witch literally disintegrates as punishment for her crimes.

The Wicked Witch as Icon — The 1939 Film

The 1939 screen version of The Wizard of Oz strongly reinforces the binary between good and bad witches in Oz and reifies the stereotypical image. MGM scriptwriter Noel Langley made several choices that influenced the roles of the witches in the film, amalgamating the two good witches into one and expanding the role of the Wicked Witch of the West. Rather than four witches, the movie shows three, complicating the horizontal and vertical imagery so strong in the original book.

Upon her arrival, Glinda immediately asks Dorothy, "Are you a good witch — or a bad witch?" (Langley 53), though Baum's original uses the term "wicked," not "bad." The film implies the two terms are synonymous. The imagery associated with each witch's physical appearance signifies their nature as much as or more than their names or actions. First, Dorothy announces, "I'm not a witch at all — witches are old and ugly ... I've never heard of a beautiful witch before!" (Langley 54). Glinda assures her that witches can be beautiful, as she is one. This character, played by Billie Burke, personifies the stereotype of femininity: pink and glittery with a crown of stars and a magic wand. In contrast to the light and bright good witch, the Wicked Witch, played by Margaret Hamilton, appears all in black with the stereotypical pointed hat and broom. However, in this film, her physical appearance stands out even more than previous witches, for she has bright green skin.

The image of a green-skinned witch first appeared in the 1939 film, although no official MGM sources choose to take credit for the invention. The film was shot in Technicolor, a major advancement in motion pictures that allowed for colors that appeared bright and true. Langley takes credit for changing the silver shoes in Baum's novel into Dorothy's ruby slippers in order to maximize the impact of color (Hearn 15), but no one specifically knows who decided the witch's skin should be green. Most likely, credit should be given to Jack Dawn, the makeup designer for the film. Hamilton remembers numerous makeup tests trying to solve the problem of contrast between black clothing and white skin. "Black next to your skin seemed to give rise to a thin line of white on the edge of the black, which did not look like edging but rather like a separation. But with *Oz* the problem was solved — perhaps that was why they chose green makeup for my face, neck and hands" (Harmetz xvii). Green makeup in 1939 was highly toxic, being made of copper, and makeup artist Jack Young said, "Every night when I was taking off the Witch's makeup, I would make sure that her face was thoroughly clean. Spotlessly clean. Because you don't take chances with green" (272). Parts of the makeup seeped into the skin, however, and her skin actually took on a green tinge (Scarfone 44). She also sustained serious injury when the makeup caught fire during a mistake in special effects (Harmetz 272).

So why choose such a dangerous color for the witch unless the image of green skin has some sort of significant connotation or historical precedent? Although I've found no references to a green-skinned witch pre-1939, the color green is associated with demons and devils. In medieval morality plays, green was a sign of the devil, and generations of theatre practitioners considered it unlucky to wear green on stage (Pickering 121). Goblins, aliens, and other nonhumans are also often pictured green with lizard-like features. Some pagan goddesses have green skin, and the image of a wild Green Woman paralleled Green Man images in art.

However, the strongest link between witchcraft and green skin comes through the use of flying ointment. Michael Harner quotes some direct accounts from 1681 in which those tried and convicted of witchcraft describe the ointment as "greenish in color" (130). An account by the physician of Pope Julius III in 1545, in describing the assets of a couple seized for witchcraft, claims that, "Among other things found in the hermitage of the said witches was a jar half-filled with a certain green unguent" (135). These ointments were made of green herbs, and if the witches applied them all over their bodies, they themselves would take on a greenish hue. Perhaps this had some influence on the image of the green-skinned witch. Ultimately, the reason makeup artist Jack Dawn chose to use green makeup may never be known, but since 1939 images of green witches have pervaded American folklore and popular culture.

The Wizard is also presented with a green face, though only in his disguise as a disembodied head, an observation made by film critic David Bellin in an effort to reveal the "correspondences between the apparently benign technological force represented by the Wizard and the irremediably malevolent one represented by the Witch" (Bellin 61). Like Baum's original novel and the Renaissance folklore before, the Wizard's head in the film signifies masculine intellectual power, the same power that is later disrupted when the Wizard is shown to be a fraud. The witch herself is associated with other earlier images of masculine sorcery, represented by the open spell books and complicated incantations in her laboratory. The images that were previously associated only with male magic had been layered onto the sign of the witch.

In the film, the images of both good and wicked witches are further complicated from Baum's original when Glinda and the Wicked Witch of the West are allowed to transcend the horizontal in flight. Langley takes credit for inventing Glinda's bubble method of transportation, which moves vertically. In contrast, most shots of the wicked witch's flight show her horizontal on her broom, bringing the masculine phallic image into the feminine dimension. The methods of transport also reinforce the dichotomy between good and evil. Paul Nathanson compares the imagery of the two witches to sacred images of angels and demons. "The Good Witch takes off and lands gently in a silvery bubble accompanied by the tinkle of a glockenspiel; the Wicked Witch takes off and lands violently in a ball of flame and smoke accompanied by claps of thunder" (226). Glinda, as an angelic figure, is more associated with the sky and clouds, while the Wicked Witch is associated with demonic flames and storms.

When the film was released, the Wicked Witch made an immediate impact. In conjunction with the political climate in 1939, the Wicked Witch is often compared to Hitler with "her squadrons of winged monkeys [that] resemble the squadrons of dive-bombers sent by Hitler to Spain during its Civil War" (261–2). At this time in history, clear delineations between "us" and "them" seemed essential to survival. The Wicked Witch thus becomes a symbol of fear itself. In discussing the folkloric image of the witch, John Widdowson claims, "Indeed to some extent witches embody human fears, and the concepts we have of them emphasize their frightening and unpleasant characteristics" (200). The image of the Wicked Witch in this film was so frightening to children that many of her scenes were deleted. Ultimately, the Wicked Witch is only on screen for twelve minutes. Yet, Hamilton says "she's constantly there because she's constantly a threat all the time. So that you're much more aware of her than I think anybody realizes" (Harmetz 296). Indeed, the Wicked Witch of the West quickly becomes the stuff of children's nightmares, while the Good Witch, who appears on screen for less than seven minutes, resembles a fairy godmother. This binary of good and evil is reinforced through these images as children and adults watch the movie again and again.

A New Perspective of the Witch — Wicked, *the Novel*

Gregory Maguire remembers the Wicked Witch from childhood: "Remember the scene where Dorothy sees Auntie Em in the crystal ball and she turns into the Wicked Witch of the West, as the witch's face fills the screen. That is what it was like for me to have this idea. I was looking in the crystal ball, going, 'Who can I write about?' and the witch's face just got bigger and bigger, scarier and scarier and more and more right" (Erstein). But Maguire chose to explore the image in a new way. He became fascinated with the political situation in the early 1990s and particularly the vilification of Saddam Hussein by the British press, which generated many questions: "Was it possible for someone to change his moral stripe? To be born blameless and become evil? Or does one have kind of a kernel of evil inside, like cells that are predisposed to be cancerous?" (Cote 20). Maguire was free to base his characters on Baum's novel as it was now in the public domain. He quickly discovered "however shrill the wicked witch is in the film, in the (first) book we never read a single bad thing she's ever done" (Moore). In Baum's novel, the only witch with a personal name is Glinda, the Good Witch of the South, but Maguire personalizes the "Wicked Witch" by naming her Elphaba (as an homage to L. Frank Baum), giving her opportunity for full character development. He follows her from birth to death, radically questioning the stereotypical image.

Maguire's Oz is much more complex than Baum's original, full of religious and political conflict, in keeping with Baum's "cynical tone, which surfaces now and again in the book, combined with the fact that Oz as it exists in *The Wizard* is a more frightening, more disturbing, and less hospitable place ... may partially explain why Baum's sunlit world has been the inspiration for a number of dark visions" (Riley 58). This quotation refers to *The Wiz* and *Zardoz*, two earlier dark Oz adaptations, but the same holds true for *Wicked*. Elphaba is born to a religious zealot father and promiscuous mother, reinforcing the image of female sexuality as a cause of witchcraft. Her mother was seduced by a stranger with a bottle of green elixir, suggesting the green flying ointment of folklore. As a baby, Elphaba is described as "green as sin. Not an ugly color ... just not a human color" (24). He also explains that the child "would not allow itself to be lowered into a pail of water" (30). Thus from the very outset of the novel, Maguire's witch has green skin (a trait from the movie, not the book) and an unnatural intolerance of water. Her difference from other people is based strictly on these physical traits.

Although Maguire does explore the nature of wickedness in his novel, he creates no clear binary between good and evil. While her social-climbing roommate Glinda studies sorcery, Elphaba prefers to investigate the natural sciences with the goat Dr. Dillamond. Initially, the goat might seem to suggest the classical devil or the witches' familiar, but *Wicked* reverses this association, describing Dr. Dillamond as kind and wise. His death urges Elphaba to fight for animal rights, selflessly striving to right the wrongs that society perpetrates against the animal kingdom. She is not presented as an evil character in the classic Oz sense of "selfish=bad." After many personal losses, she becomes a sort of recluse, accepting the label "witch" and exercising magical powers for the first time through the examination of a magical book called the *Grimmerie* (266). Like male magicians of old, her power derives from scholarship and the use of tools rather than from her physical body; she has the innate ability to read the words that others cannot. Through this book, she endows a broom with the power of flight, resurrecting yet another image from folklore and the film. Her adversary, the Wizard, enters the novel late and reveals that his search for the *Grimmerie* brought him to Oz (352). This implies that the *Grimmerie* is actually a magical tool from the human world. Elphaba's painful aversion to water climaxes when Dorothy tries to save her from fire. Dorothy chooses to bring the Wizard the green elixir bottle as proof of her death, and his recognition of it reveals that the Wizard himself is Elphaba's biological father. There is a suggestion that her peculiarities come from being born of both worlds, a liminal child born betwixt-and-between fantasy and reality. Maguire's novel succeeds in complicating the traditional image of the Wicked Witch.

Defying Expectations —
Wicked, *the Musical*

All of these signs come together in the musical *Wicked*, which challenges the distinction between good and evil, exploring this moral ambiguity by playing off the audience's expectations. In the early San Francisco tryouts, the composer Stephen Schwartz and playwright collaborator Winnie Holzman discovered quickly that "people brought the movie in with them," says Schwartz. "But that meant we could not do anything that contradicted the movie" (Erstein). To explore the themes that most interested them, they eliminated many subplots from Maguire's novel, focusing primarily on the relationship between Elphaba and Glinda.

According to Saussure, all language must be linear, a predecessor to Derrida's sign chains. While visual signifiers "can offer simultaneous groupings in several dimensions, auditory signifiers have at their command only the dimension of time. Their elements are presented in succession; they form a chain" (70). The very first word the audience hears in the musical is "good" and the last word is "wicked," thus the musical takes us on a journey from goodness to wickedness and everywhere in between. Although the show is titled *Wicked*, the actual word "wicked" is only mentioned 51 times in the libretto, while the word "good" is found 92 times. This exploration of goodness is not nearly as prevalent in Maguire's novel, just as the binary of good and evil was not as strong in Baum's novel as it was in the film. The visual enactment of theater and film require stronger tensions and less internal conflict.

Each character in *Wicked* makes choices based on positive motivations, though some of their choices could be defined as selfish. At first, the traditional roles of Glinda and Elphaba seem to be reversed, as Glinda, the popular girl, selfishly treats Elphaba poorly because of the color of her skin. However, through the remainder of the play, each witch experiences moments of ambiguity stronger than any of their earlier incarnations. Glinda offers a sympathetic assessment of Elphaba in the very first song. While the chorus celebrates the death of the Wicked Witch, Glinda sings of the loneliness of the lives of the wicked. While no one else mourns the death of the "Wicked Witch," Glinda attempts to see her rival as a full person.

The image of Elphaba as the Wicked Witch of the West is steadily built through the first act of the play. We discover she is "female" and "wicked" in the opening song, though there is no definition at this time of what it means to be "wicked." Unlike the 1939 film, "wicked" is not automatically equated with "bad." This leads into the flashback sequence of her birth, where we learn Elphaba is the product of adultery and a bottle of green elixir, recalling the novel *Wicked* and the flying ointment. Her gender and sexual nature recall the early descriptions of witchcraft from Kramer and Sprenger. But then we immediately shift to the witch as we have known her in the twentieth century, when at birth she emerges green.

Elphaba's supernatural abilities appear early in the play, and at this point, all the fundamental layers of her "witchiness" have been revealed. Elphaba previously expressed negative feelings about her "weird quirk" but now muses that her powers may aid her in meeting the Wizard. Her song contains much dramatic irony for the audience which already knows the conclusion of the story. First, she idolizes the Wizard, anticipating a positive relationship with him and even imagining the Wizard "degreenifying" her so that she will be more widely accepted. Then she imagines that someday there will be a celebration throughout Oz in her honor, for which she would be so happy she could "melt" (144). Though the character sings with a strong sense of hope, her words prepare the audience for tragedy.

Other features that serve to build Elphaba into a stereotypical witch are completely superficial but immediately recognizable by the audience. Costume designer Susan Hilferty emphasizes the contrast between Glinda and Elphaba, beginning with their school clothes. She says, "By using blue and white as the school colors, I was able to have Elphaba all in blue, and Glinda all in white. The goal was to make the two women be the most outstanding thing in every world they entered" (Barbour 18). All of the other students wore some combination of blue and white. Although Hilferty never dresses Elphaba entirely in black, she uses a combination of dark colors to create the illusion of black. "I see her as connected to things that are inside the earth. So the patterns and textures I wove into her dress include fossils, stalactites, or striations that you see when you crack a stone apart. I mixed different colors into her skirt, so everything is literally twisted" (Cote 120). This image is of terrestrial darkness contrasts with Glinda's sparkling lightness, who Hilferty connects to "the sky, sun, and stars.... She symbolizes lightness, air, bubbles" (120). The costumes overall work to reinforce the images of goodness and wickedness, clearly the strongest visual binaries in the show.

Elphaba then acquires her magical hat, book, and broom. As a joke Glinda gives Elphaba an unfashionable, pointed black hat with a wide brim (150). However, when Elphaba takes the gift as a true act of generosity, Glinda is forced to see her in a different way, and the two become friends, defying all previous expectations. When Elphaba complains to the Wizard of the inequities to which Dr. Dillamond is subjected (though in the play, he is fired, not murdered). After the Wizard reveals that he is actually against animal rights, she steals the *Grimmerie* from him to prevent him from using it for harm (159). In retribution, the Wizard dehumanizes her by taking away her personal name and declaring her a "Wicked Witch." She adds the final sign to her witch image when she enchants a broom, making her escape through flight. The finale of Act I shows Elphaba rising vertically in center stage, as all the layers of symbolism come together in the sign of the Wicked Witch. Yet the image, combined with the lyrics of Schwartz's "Defying Gravity," creates a complicated alteration of the traditional stereotype. As Schwartz explains, "I wanted a series of simple notes that sounded like strength, coming into your own, feeling the power come up from below, from your feet and spreading up through your body.... I wanted the music to be powerful and empowering and thrilling" (Cote 80). Even though her costumes suggest the subterranean, Elphaba arises, both lyrically and physically, from the earth, transforming her femininity into her power. When she sings of having undergone a change and no longer obeying others' dictates, her reasonable defiance challenges the audience's expectations of the image. She adds that she must now follow her instincts. Female intuition has long been opposed to male reason, and the realm of the vertical belonged to the men. She may be "flying solo," but she claims the freedom to make her own decisions, ungrounded by the prejudices and choices of others.

While Maguire's novel minimizes society's reaction to Elphaba, the musical actually reinforces the Renaissance image of witch persecution. The second act shows how Oz reacts to the fully-formed witch, the villagers spreading rumors about Elphaba, suggesting that she has a soul so dirty as to be soluble in water, but this characterization is presented as rumor only. In fact, in an earlier scene, Elphaba sings a song while standing in the rain, defying all previous notions of the Wicked Witch's relation to water. The belief that water will melt her is presented as a delusion of the villagers. While Elphaba attempts several acts of selflessness, each is twisted negatively by public reaction. In the song "No Good Deed," Elphaba questions her own motivations. She then declares her frustration at her inability to help those around her, as "No good deed goes unpunished" (171). She takes the claim others have made about her, that she is "wicked through and through" (171). However, she still does not pursue harmful actions even after this declaration. Instead, she gives Glinda the book and asks her to take on the philanthropic mission. Glinda and the audience then watch Elphaba in silhouette as she appears to melt when a bucket of water is thrown on her, this despite expectations to the contrary.

Glinda and the Wizard act as foils for Elphaba, though none of the three are wholly good or evil. Glinda is presented as a contradiction in the second act. Due to her cooperation, the Wizard has declared her "Glinda the Good" and given her some political power. In her song "Thank Goodness," she expresses moments of regret for the separation between Elphaba and herself, describing the "cost" of "getting your dreams" (165). She takes her inheritance from Elphaba seriously, a significant alteration from her role at the beginning of the play. The Wizard is also presented as a complicated character in his song "Wonderful," as he explains that he was "carried away" by the adoration of the Ozians who needed a figure in whom to place their belief. He even directly refers to "moral ambiguities" as uncomfortable for people, so it is easier to ignore their existence. When Glinda brings him the green bottle after Elphaba's apparent death, he is devastated by the awareness that he has "liquidated" (176) his daughter. While both Glinda and the Wizard are self-aggrandizing and hurtful to others, they each experience remorse and are ambiguous in their motivations.

In *Wicked, The Musical*, the audience is denied its expectation of clear binaries, but they are not as disturbed by moral ambiguities as the Wizard suggests they might be. The play has been enormously popular. Producer Mark Platt claims, "Audiences laugh and applaud and cheer its sets, music, and costumes. But, at the end of the day, they leave the theater feeling different from when they walked in" (Cote 180). Audiences of all ages respond because the play transforms the well known story and problematizes stereotypical images of witches, thus reinventing and reinvigorating the much beloved subject matter.

Works Cited

Bailey, Michael D. "The Feminization of Magic and the Emerging Idea of the Female Witch in the Late Middle Ages." *Essays in Medieval Studies* 19 (2002): 120–134.

Barbour, David, and David Johnson. "Hocus Pocus." *Entertainment Design*, February 2004: 16–25.

Baum, L. Frank. "The Wonderful Wizard of Oz." In *The Wonderful Land of Oz*. New York: Book-of-the-Month Club, 1998.

Behringer, Wolfgang. *Witches and Witch-Hunts: A Global History*. Cambridge: Polity Press, 2004.

Bellin, Joshua David. *Framing Monsters: Fantasy Film and Social Alienation*. Carbondale: Southern Illinois University Press, 2005.

Bornstein, Lisa. "A 'Wicked' Good Time." *Rocky Mountain News*, September 14, 2005, 8D.

Cirlot, J.E. *A Dictionary of Symbols*. Jack Sage, trans. New York: Philosophical Library, 1971.

Cote, David. *Wicked: The Grimmerie*. New York: Hyperion, 2005.

Derrida, Jacques. "Positions." Translated by Alan Bass. Chicago: University of Chicago Press, 1981.

Erstein, Hap. "Somewhere, Before the Rainbow." Review of *Wicked*, directed by Joe Mantello. Broward Center for the Performing Arts, Fort Lauderdale. *The Palm Beach Post*, February 5 2006, 10J.

Essman, Scott. "Return to Oz." *Makeup Artist Magazine*, December-January 1998–1999: 22–35.

Fricke, John. "Supplimentary Material: Feature Commentary." *The Wizard of Oz: Disc One*. DVD. Turner Entertainment, 2005.

Gardner, Martin, and Russel Nye. *The Wizard of Oz and Who He Was*. East Lansing: Michigan State University Press, 1957.

Harmetz, Aljean. *The Making of the Wizard of Oz.* New York: Alfred A. Knopf, 1978.

Harner, Michael J. *Hallucinogens and Shamanism.* New York: Oxford University Press, 1973.

Kramer, Heinrich, and James Sprenger. *The Malleus Maleficarum.* Montague Summers, trans. New York: Dover Publications, 1971.

LaGrandeur, Kevin. "The Talking Brass Head." *English Studies* 5 (1999): 408–422.

Langley, Noel, Florence Ryerson, and Edgar Allan Woolf. *The Wizard of Oz: The Screenplay.* 1939. Michael Patrick Hearn, ed. New York: Dell, 1989.

Maguire, Gregory. *Wicked: The Life and Times of the Wicked Witch of the West.* New York: Harper Collins, 1995.

_____. *Wicked: The Life and Times of the Wicked Witch of the West.* New York: Harper Collins, 1995.

Moore, John. "She's melting, melting ... into a real person: Actress relishes her 'Wicked' role as an 'Oz' witch wronged by society." *The Denver Post,* September 19, 2005, F01.

Nathanson, Paul. *Over the Rainbow: The Wizard of Oz as a Secular Myth of America.* Albany: State University of New York Press, 1991.

Northrup, Lesley. *Ritualizing Women.* Cleveland: Pilgrim's Press, 1997.

Pickering, David. *Cassell Dictionary of Superstitions.* London: Cassell, 1995.

Riley, Michael O. *Oz and Beyond: The Fantasy World of L. Frank Baum.* Lawrence, KS: University Press of Kansas, 1997.

Rogers, Katherine M. *L. Frank Baum: Creator of Oz.* New York: St. Martin's Press, 2002.

Saussure, Ferdinand de. *Course in General Linguistics.* Charles Bally and Albert Sechehaye, eds. Translated by Wade Baskin. New York: McGraw-Hill, 1966.

Scarfone, Jay, and William Stillman. *The Wizardry of Oz.* Milwaukee: Applause Theatre & Cinema Books, 2004.

Stewart, Pamela J., and Andrew Strathern. *Witchcraft, Sorcery, Rumors, and Gossip.* Cambridge: Cambridge University Press, 2004.

Swartz, Mark Evan. *Oz Before the Rainbow.* Baltimore: Johns Hopkins University Press, 2000.

"Wicked: The Road to Broadway" *Broadway: The American Musical, Disc Three.* DVD. PBS Home Video, 2004

Widdowson, John. "The Witch as a Frightening and Threatening Figure." In *The Witch Figure.* Venetia Newall, ed. London: Routledge, 1973.

From Private Practice to Public Coven(ant): Alice Hoffman's Practical Magic and Its Hollywood Transformation

KATHY DAVIS PATTERSON

> Why, we might well ask ourselves, should any woman today see any point in call-
> ing herself a witch when she knows full well that the witch of mythology was a
> misogynistic invention and that the brutal process of witch-labeling led, in Europe,
> to three centuries of gynocide? Who does this new witch think she is [Rountree
> 211]?

These compelling questions direct Kathryn Rountree's investigation
into the motives of women who openly identify themselves as witches in
contemporary Western societies. Her essay, titled "The New Witch of the
West: Feminists Reclaim the Crone," addresses the tendency of these women
to conflate traditional patriarchal images of the witch and the goddess into
a single, empowering female identity. According to Rountree, both images
represent "independent female power which [is] designated off-limits for
'normal' women," and "by self-identifying as 'witch' and as 'goddess,' the
women ... symbolically lay claim" to that power, thereby envisioning "themselves as autonomous, as having the right to choose and direct their own
lives" (212). The witch in history and popular culture is undeniably a potent
symbol, and to publicly claim the label of "witch" is a move fraught with
political implications for both women and the societies in which they live.
The word itself is a stereotype that carries much negative patriarchal bag-
gage. Serious risks are involved in efforts to re-define it, and Rountree
acknowledges that "If ... women claim publicly to be 'witches' but fail to
re-invent the witch for the dominant culture, they may turn out to be unwit-
ting participants in a potentially sado-masochistic perpetuation of the most
misogynistic fantasy the world has known" (226).

Contemporary fiction and film are two important media venues
through which attempts have been made to "re-invent the witch." Popular
films like *The Craft* and television shows like *Bewitched, Charmed,* and *Sab-
rina, the Teenage Witch* contribute, for better or worse, to our culture's

evolving understanding of what it means to be a witch. It is with these ideas in mind that I approach this analysis of Alice Hoffman's *Practical Magic*. As a fan of both the book and the film, I find myself intrigued by the changes the filmmakers have made to Hoffman's original plot, themes, and characterizations—especially as they relate to magic and the figure of the witch.

The world, as Alice Hoffman portrays it in *Practical Magic,* is an inherently magical place, where folklore and superstitions permeate and influence reality. It is a place where lilacs can explode into bloom overnight, out of season, and exert a hypnotic pull. It is a place where "a halo around the moon" truly is a "sign of disruption" (68) and where the newfound love between a man and a woman can so fill the air with sweet yellow light that it makes a young boy "[run] home and [beg] his mother for lemon pound cake, heated, and spread with honey" (165). The central characters in this world are the Owens women — sisters Sally and Gillian and the aunts who raise them, Bridget and Frances; Sally's daughters, Antonia and Kylie; and the ancestor of them all, Maria Owens. Maria begins the legacy of the Owens women who, over the course of more than two hundred years, "have been blamed for everything that has gone wrong in town" (3). When Maria first arrives, she is young, lovely, unmarried, dressed all in black, and carrying a baby daughter. She is also wealthy, with enough funds to hire twelve carpenters to build a large house and enough self-assurance to advise them during the construction process. "If Maria Owens chose to speak to you, she looked you straight in the eye, even if you were her elder or better. She was known to do as she pleased, without stopping to deliberate what the consequences might be" (144). For these and other reasons, the townspeople are both intrigued by and suspicious of Maria Owens, who is clearly not a normal woman according to their standards. Though they never openly label her a witch, they "make the sign of the fox, raising pinky and forefinger in the air ... to unravel a spell" when her back is turned (146). Her reputation for strangeness and supernatural dealings is solidified when a farmer wings a crow in his cornfield and Maria shows up the next day with her arm in a sling. Her injuries have a perfectly natural explanation — she hurt herself knocking relentlessly on her lover's door — but the townspeople have drawn their own conclusions and will continue to do so regarding her female descendants.

The filmmakers' incarnation of Maria departs from the book in some crucial ways. First, as the film opens, the aunts are narrating, telling the story of Maria Owens to their nieces. Maria is immediately and clearly labeled a witch and has been condemned to death as such, and other women have played a key role in condemning her. As a "heartbreaker" whose "lovers had wives on the hanging committee," she inspires jealousy through her beauty and her active, unabashed sexuality, which is itself a common stereotype of witch behavior. Her magic is publicly displayed when the rope around her neck breaks and she lands on her feet after leaping from the platform. She lifts her head and glares defiantly at her accusers who scatter in fear. There is pride in her demeanor and pride in the voices of the aunts as they inform the girls that "she was a witch, the first in our family. And you, my darlings, are the most recent in a long and distinguished line." Young Sally and Gillian are told that Maria was feared "because she had a gift, a power that has been passed on to you children. She had the gift of magic." The narration creates a powerful sense of family legacy — one intended to affirm the girls' identity and origins. The aunts are directly involved in teaching Sally and Gillian spells when they are young, and later they teach Kylie and Antonia. They possess a witches' Book of Shadows, filled with all the spells and wisdom that have come down through family generations. While Hoffman describes them as "so old it's impossible to tell their age," with "white hair" and "crooked" spines, the film depicts them as vibrant, middle-aged women with flamboyant clothing and even more extravagant personalities. Stockard Channing and Dianne Wiest endow their characters with a wicked sense of humor and a boldness that gleefully defies convention, making the aunts a much more vivid and persistent influence on their nieces' lives. Instead of possessing "small, scratchy voices that could scare snails out of the garden but couldn't get Sally off the couch," these women can shout with laughter as they dance while drinking "midnight margaritas." Though older, unmarried, ostracized, and actively practicing witchcraft, they are a far cry from the stereotypical image of the crone as ugly, spiteful, and ultimately victimized.

Sisters Sally and Gillian are the focus of both the book and the film, and in both formats, their childhoods are less than pleasant. In Hoffman's novel, when the orphaned Sally and Gillian come to live with the aunts, none of the children will play with them. They are never invited to parties, and other children cross their fingers in gestures of protection whenever the girls draw near. Unusual yet harmless events acquire darker significance if they are connected with an Owens girl. When Sally makes herself a tuna fish sandwich for lunch and the aunts' black cats follow her into her sixth grade classroom, her horrified classmates begin "whispering witchery" (10). In nursery school, three-year-old Gillian is mercilessly persecuted by the other children, who "[pull] her hair and [call] her the witch-girl" (263). The film condenses this childhood hostility into a rhyme — "Witch! Witch! You're a bitch!" — that is chanted by the neighborhood children, who also throw stones. As Sally and Gillian grow older, they respond in different ways to the persecution they experience. Sally withdraws, refuses to assert herself, and pretends to be less than what she is in a vain effort to avoid being noticed. In both the book and the film, she immerses herself in the minutiae of domestic chores—cooking, cleaning, taking full responsibility for running the household, and desperately desiring to be like everyone else (17). When she finally meets and marries Michael, her life acquires a sense of the normalcy she has always craved. People start waving to her instead of crossing the street when they see her. Children in town covet invitations to her daughters' parties, and life is perfect ... until Michael's untimely death. Sally slips away from the rest of the world and does not talk for an entire year, while the aunts take responsibility for raising her daughters. When she finally begins to regain hope and goes out, she quickly discovers that the old Owens rumors and suspicions have resurfaced and that her daughters have become targets for a new generation of young tormentors from the town. In the book, Sally's response to this chain of events is to flee the house on Magnolia Street. She moves her girls south into New York State, to Long Island, where she purchases a house of her own, because "what she want[s] for her girls [is] something the aunts could never provide. She want[s] a town where no one point[s] when her daughters [walk] down the street" (48). Sally gets a job as an assistant to the vice principal at the local high school and succeeds in establishing a normal life. She is well-respected in the community, and she "is always the first parent listed on the snow chain, since it's best to have someone responsible in charge" (61). Her family legacy has a way of following her though. Before Gillian arrives on her doorstep with some shocking news, Sally reads signs of impending disaster in the moon. When she discovers that Kylie can see "the man under the lilacs" in their backyard, she is forced to confront the fact that "all ... [she] wanted for her, a good and ordinary life, has gone up in smoke. Kylie is anything but ordinary" (137). Indeed, both Kylie and Antonia are teenagers, growing up and away from their mother — a fact that throws Sally into an identity crisis. For years, she has

> been preoccupied with Antonia and Kylie, with fevers and cramps, with new shoes to buy every six months and making sure everyone gets well-balanced meals and at least eight hours of sleep every night. Without such thoughts, she's not certain she will continue to exist. Without them, what exactly is she left with? [182].

Sally's efforts to escape her past, to deny herself any kind of passion, to be perceived and treated by others as a "normal" woman, leave her bereft of a solid independent sense of self.

In the film, Sally makes a radically different choice about where she and her daughters will live following Michael's death: she takes them to live with the aunts. Her decision to return home rather than run away has important ramifications not just for her character, but for her daughters as well. By remaining in the town where her ancestry is known, where she was persecuted in the past and continues to be denigrated in the present, she is forced to cope with being labeled a witch by the townspeople. In this world, she is never trusted enough to be placed at the top of the phone tree until Gillian uses a little magic to alter the list. Still, she strives to live as normal a life as possible and is determined to open a botanical shop she and Michael had planned together. All of the merchandise her shop has been created from her own special recipes, so essentially she is using her craft-related skills and knowledge of herb lore to make an independent living—a detail that suggests some defiance on her part, as it is directly tied to her family heritage as a witch. It also means that Hollywood's incarnation of Sally is much less reliant on her role as mother, which in the novel is the sole purpose of her existence.

By choosing to stay in her hometown, Sally also exposes her daughters to the prejudices that have been passed down through generations. Other children torment them, and when Kylie responds in anger and threatens a boy, Sally pulls her aside and corrects her: "We do not cast, and we do not toy with people's lives. Do you understand? This is not a game." Resentful of the aunts' magical interference in her own love life, she has vowed that neither she nor her children will ever cast spells or practice magic. By simultaneously acknowledging the power of magic and refusing to use it, Sally endeavors to teach her daughters restraint. She also bows to societal pressures which dictate that such power is—and should be—beyond the scope of normal women.

Gillian is her sister's antithesis. As a teenager, she blossoms into such a raving beauty that, in Hoffman's words, "boys looked at her and got so dizzy they had to be rushed to the emergency room for a hit of oxygen or a pint of new blood" (25). She is a classic seductress, adept at breaking hearts. Her intense, reckless sexuality and her capacity to create trouble quickly become legendary until she elopes at age eighteen in search of "a real life ... where nobody has ever heard of the Owenses" (30), but her refusal to commit to any single man or place leads her into a nomadic existence and, eventually, into the arms of Jimmy Hawkins—an abusive drug dealer who gets her into more trouble than she can handle on her own. Tormented by the labels others have given her over the years, she ends up "believ[ing] she [is] worthy of the awful treatment she [gets]" (263). When she moves in with Sally and a good man, named Ben Frye, begins to court her, she resists his advances for a long time, convinced she is undeserving of his attention. However, as she becomes attached to Sally's daughter, Kylie, she begins to re-connect with her family and slowly acquire self-esteem. This, in turn, gives her the freedom to pursue a relationship based on real love.

Gillian's counterpart in film is also a nomadic seductress who finds herself in trouble and ultimately moves back home. Differences in the fate of her character are linked to the character of Jimmy Hawkins, who becomes

Jimmy Angelov in the film. The Hawkins of Hoffman's novel is a drug dealer whose merchandise results in the death of several young college students. When he dies, Gillian takes his corpse to Sally's house in New York, where they bury him in the back yard under the lilacs. His vengeful spirit begins to assert its presence by haunting the house, creating hostility between Sally and Gillian, who ultimately call the aunts for assistance. When the aunts arrive, they work with Sally, Gillian, Kylie, and Antonia to brew a concoction that will dissolve the body, thereby freeing Jimmy's spirit and ending the haunting. The entire sequence of events is strictly a family affair — one that reunites the Owens women and strengthens their bonds as they work together to solve a problem and maintain a secret. The success of this family endeavor allows them to come to terms with their respective pasts and begin to push toward a healing future. Sally and Gillian, in particular, find the courage to be themselves and to fall in love with the genuinely good men who have entered their lives.

In the film, Jimmy Angelov, an immigrant from Bulgaria, is portrayed as a kind of "cowboy-vampire" who preys on women and who has left at least one girl dead by the side of the road, the design of his ring "branded" into her skin. Gillian and Sally are complicit in his death as they accidentally lace his tequila with an overdose of belladonna. They are also guilty of wielding dangerous magic in an attempt to resurrect him. Ultimately, they bury his body in the back yard under the roses. His vengeful spirit influences the plants and animals around his grave, just as Jimmy Hawkins' spirit does in the book, but it also manifests in physical form to confront investigator Gary Hallett and to possess Gillian. The aunts assert that a coven of women will be needed to drive his spirit out of Gillian's body, and Sally activates the phone tree, contacting local women who have ostracized her and asking them for help. As she dials the first number, she can be heard saying "You know the stuff everyone whispers about me ... the hexes, the spells? Well, here's the thing, um ... I'm a witch!" For the first time, Sally claims the label of witch for herself and acknowledges the magical aspect of her identity. It is a pivotal moment, and one of the female employees at her botanical shop is thrilled to announce that "Sally just came out!" — a point that is described by another female employee as "a fabulous affirmation." Instead of being driven away by her pronouncement, the other women find themselves drawn to the Owens house. Curiosity overwhelms jealousy, ignorance, and suspicion as they finally get to come inside and experience a taste of the Owens' power for themselves. When they first arrive and enter the kitchen, one of them observes that "There's a little witch in all of us." It is a simple statement, yet it carries several interesting layers of meaning. By finally accepting the witch label and applying it to themselves, these women take a word they have used against the Owens women in the past and turn it from a weapon into an affirmation, from a tool of segregation into a signal of communion. When they participate in the witchcraft ritual of exorcism, they are effectively embracing and internalizing that which they have previously condemned as other. The power of witchcraft is no longer perceived as exclusive to the Owens women. In effect, the witch has been normalized. When they form a circle and clasp each other's hands, flesh to flesh, their united power creates an explosion of light that exorcises Jimmy's ghost, which then falls to the floor as ashes. One woman utters a very loaded phrase: "Come on, ladies. Let's clean house!" (female exorcists and clean houses seem to be inextricably linked) and together the women sweep Jimmy's remains out into the yard. Getting rid of Jimmy has become a communal effort, an affirmation of the power that all women can wield when they work together.

The scene is both exhilarating and troubling at the same time. While Gillian has been freed from Jimmy's influence — his violence, his utter lack of compassion, his need for control (all hallmarks of the dark side of the patriarchal male) — viewers are left with a stereotypical domestic image of women cleaning house — hardly the stuff of a serious revolution. In later scenes, Gillian is left to watch as Sally runs to embrace Gary Hallett, since her own love interest, Ben Frye, never makes an appearance.

My initial analysis of the novel and the film concerns their respective endings. Hoffman concludes with Gillian married to Ben Frye and Sally running down a path toward the waiting arms of Gary Hallett. The film incorporates the latter scene and then flashes forward to a Halloween sequence. All six of the Owens women appear silhouetted against the night sky. Wearing stereotypical witch costumes of black dresses and conical hats, they clasp hands and leap from the roof of their house. Umbrellas held aloft, they float to the ground before a cheering crowd of neighbors, who then move to embrace them. The camera lingers on their feet as they touch the ground, mimicking a strategy used in the opening scenes when Maria leaps from the scaffold. When Maria displays her true nature, she is feared and rejected. Now that the witch has been normalized through her acknowledged presence in all women, the Owens women are admired and accepted when they display their true nature. Sally narrates the closing passages of the film and poses the question: "Was it our joined hands that finally lifted Maria's curse? I'd like to think so." In the strictest sense, Maria's curse promises death to any man who dares to love an Owens woman, but I would argue that it goes deeper, that a key aspect of her curse involves the persecution and isolation she suffers as a witch. When the women of the community go to the Owens house to help instead of condemn, when they are willing to hold hands instead of throw stones, their prejudice begins to evaporate and the ostracism of the Owens women ends.

Clearly, the filmmakers' version of *Practical Magic* diverges from Alice Hoffman's original storyline in some significant ways. In the novel, while the term "witch" is certainly used in connection with the Owens women, it is never an identity that they claim for themselves. On the contrary, it is always a label applied by outsiders, and as such, it carries with it all the weight of fear and superstition that has resulted in the centuries-old persecution of women. Sally never comes out regarding her heritage in any public way, and there is never any communal validation of the Owens women and their behavior, or indeed of witches or witchcraft in general. Hoffman creates a cast of female characters who are outcasts and places them in situations that compel them to confront and either overcome or accept their outcast status, all within the scope of a family context.

As a film, *Practical Magic* establishes an early and blatantly didactic emphasis on witches and witchcraft that, on the surface, appears designed to correct misapprehensions and challenge existing stereotypes. Witches do exist, they do practice a valid belief system and possess important knowledge and abilities. They are in your community, but they are not a threat; they are good people who are undeservedly persecuted by people who fail to understand them. Those who persecute individuals whom they have labeled witches are at best ill-informed and at worst bigots with a violent streak and an agenda of their own. When Gary Hallett questions the townspeople about the Owens women, he becomes privy to a host of false rumors about the Devil and baby placentas that are only corrected after he gets to know Sally better and learns that "there is no Devil in the Craft," that she is "not into that stuff." Magic is a very real power that is not to be trifled with or taken lightly, and women who practice magic together are capable of remarkable accomplishments. Perhaps not surprisingly, these accomplishments are linked with the defeat and exorcism of a ruthless, domineering patriarchal force—a defeat that allows the witch to be mainstreamed and more broadly accepted as an emblem of the power that lies "in every woman."

Each of these lessons is clearly intended to cast the witch in a positive light—to make what Witchvox reviewer Peg Aloi has termed "a feel-good movie about Witches"—and yet, the damaging stereotypes persist. Both Maria and Gillian are sexually brazen women whose appetites do not exclude married men—witches in the classic seductress mode whose beauty and independence evokes the jealous recriminations of other women. Special effects exaggerate the supernatural impact of witches' power and trivialize it at the same time, allowing them to both raise the dead and cause a spoon to stir a cup of tea without any manual effort. The coven sequence reduces a powerful gathering into a group of women with brooms who are exceptionally good at cleaning house, and the film's tagline—"There's a little witch in every woman"—attempts to normalize the witch as a figure with whom all women have an innate connection.

Presumably, making the witch more common is a move calculated to promote acceptance—but at what cost? At what point does normalization slip into neutralization? Does the witch lose her value as a transgressive symbol of female empowerment when she is embraced and is no longer capable of inspiring fear? The warm, fuzzy ending of *Practical Magic* certainly suggests that this is so. Then again, the witches of *Practical Magic* are not real witches situated in the real world. The film's fantasy presentation of witches and witchcraft promotes a fantasy acceptance that fails to translate into the everyday life experiences of practicing witches and those who are labeled witches in contemporary Western society. Ultimately, perhaps the most subversive message in the film lurks in a seemingly innocuous fact: berated or beloved, cursed or blessed, "in" or "out," the Owens women all manage to land on their feet.

Works Cited

Aloi, Peg. "*Practical Magic*: Curses and Hauntings and Love Spells, Oh My!" *Witchvox*. http://www.witchvox.com/media/practical_magic.html. Accessed October 15, 2004.
Diehl, Kathleen. "Rosemary by the Garden Gate." *ToxicUniverse.com*. <http://www.tox-icuniverse.com/review.php?rid=10002456>. Accessed October 15, 2004.
Hoffman, Alice. *Practical Magic*. New York: Berkley, 2003.
Practical Magic. Directed by Griffin Dunne. Warner Bros., 1998.
Rountree, Kathryn. "The New Witch of the West: Feminists Reclaim the Crone." *Journal of Popular Culture* 30.4 (1997): 211–229.

About the Contributors

Janet Brennan Croft is head of Access Services at the University of Oklahoma libraries. She is the author of *War and the Works of J.R.R. Tolkien* (Greenwood Press, 2004), which won the Mythopoeic Award in Inklings Scholarship in 2005, and the editor of *Tolkien on Film: Essays on Peter Jackson's The Lord of the Rings* (Mythopoeic Press, 2004). She has annotated *The Traveling Rug* by Dorothy L. Sayers (Mythopoeic Press, 2005) and is currently editing *Tolkien and Shakespeare: Influences, Echoes, Revisions* (McFarland, 2007). She is the editor of *Mythlore: A Journal of J.R.R. Tolkien, C.S. Lewis, Charles Williams, and Mythopoeic Literature*. Ms. Croft is also the author of *Legal Solutions in Electronic Reserves and the Electronic Delivery of Interlibrary Loan* (Haworth, 2004) and has written on library issues for a number of journals.

Jessica Zebrine Gray is completing her Ph.D. at Louisiana State University where she is writing her dissertation about the historical representation of gender and witchcraft on stage. She teaches introductory theater courses and is also the director of religious education at the Unitarian Church of Baton Rouge.

James Keller is professor and chair of the English and Theatre Department at Eastern Kentucky University. His monographs include *Princes, Soldiers, and Rogues: The Politic Malcontent of Renaissance Drama* (Peter Lang), *Anne Rice and Sexual Politics* (McFarland), *Queer (Un)Friendly Film and Literature* (McFarland), and *Food, Film, and Culture: A Genre Study* (McFarland). Keller and Stratyner have collaborated on two previous collections: *Almost Shakespeare: Reinventing His Work for Film and Television* (McFarland) and *The New Queer Aesthetic on Television: Essays on Recent Programming* (McFarland). Keller has written over forty academic articles on a variety of subjects including early modern literature, film, African American literature, and cultural studies.

Matt Kimmich is a lecturer for modern English literature at the University of Berne, Switzerland. In 2005, he completed a Ph.D. dissertation on family romance in the works of Salman Rushdie, which is currently being prepared for publication. His research interests are postcolonial and transnational fiction, the elegy in the twentieth century, adaptations of fictional works, and pop culture, popular genres, and postmodernism.

Donald Levin is associate professor of English and director of the master of arts in English program at Marygrove College in Detroit. He has published and presented his research on composition, industrial films, all three versions of *Inva-*

sion of the Body Snatchers, and *8 Mile*, among other films. The author of *In Praise of Old Photographs* (2005), a book of poetry, and editor of the forthcoming poetry anthology *From the Garden of the Gods*, he is widely published as a poet and fiction writer.

Sarah E. Maier is associate professor of English and comparative literature at the University of New Brunswick (Canada). Author of *Dionysian Dominatrices: Nineteenth-Century Female Decadents/ce*, editor of Thomas Hardy's *Tess of the D'Urbervilles* for Broadview Press, Professor Maier has also published recent articles on a variety of subjects: female *Bildungsroman*, "Symbolist Salomes and the Dance of Dionysus," Wollstonecraft, and J. K. Rowling. Her current research projects are on the subjects of *Millennial Madnesses: Cultural Paradigms at the Fin(s) de Siècle(s)*, fictional representations of serial killers, and Marie Corelli. She is also the only literature professor to be the recipient of the Dr. Allan P. Stuart Award for Excellence in Teaching (English and comparative literature) and has just been appointed university teaching scholar.

Sharon D. McCoy received her Ph.D. in English from Emory University in 2003 with a focus on the complex interplay between literature and popular culture in nineteenth- and twentieth-century America. She currently serves as an adjunct instructor at the University of Georgia and Piedmont College and is working on a book-length study of blackface minstrelsy and Mark Twain.

Gwendolyn A. Morgan, professor of British literature and languages at Montana State University, specializes in Anglo-Saxon and medieval literature and contemporary popular culture. She has produced four books, most recently *The Invention of False Medieval Authority as a Literary Device in Popular Fiction* (Edwin Mellen, 2006), and edits the annual *Year's Work in Medievalism* for the International Society for the Study of Medievalism of which she is currently vice president.

Elizabeth Parsons lectures in literary studies at Deakin University, Melbourne, Australia. She is an interdisciplinary scholar whose research encompasses children's literature and film, poetry analysis, theater semiotics, and gender studies.

Kathy Davis Patterson is associate professor of English at the Kent State University, Tuscarawas Campus. The bulk of her research deals with issues of gender, race, and body politics in Gothic literature and film, with special emphasis on vampires and, more recently, on witches. She is also a member of the Association of Science Fiction and Fantasy Artists (ASFA) with a growing list of art publications. To date, her art has appeared on T-shirts, posters, event programs, mugs, CDs, and small press journal covers. Some of her works have also been reproduced as limited edition prints.

June Pulliam is instructor of English and women's and gender studies at Louisiana State University, and is currently completing a Ph.D. in adolescent literature. She has published books and articles on the horror genre and edits the quarterly e-zine *Necropsy: The Review of Horror Fiction.*

Robin Anne Reid is professor of literature and languages at Texas A&M University–Commerce where she teaches advanced writing (creative and technical), critical theory (multicultural, feminist, gender,) and Tolkien. She has a master's degree in creative writing, and her doctoral work is focused on ethnicity and gender in feminist narratives. She has published poetry and is currently working on a vampire novel. Her scholarly work has moved from feminist analysis of science fiction to film and queer studies on *The Lord of the Rings* and *LOTR* fan fiction.**Eric Sterling** earned his Ph.D. in English from Indiana University. He is professor of English at Auburn University, Montgomery, where he has won the Distinguished Research Professor Award and the Distinguished Teaching Professor Award. He has published two books—*The Movement Towards Subversion: The English History Play from Skelton to Shakespeare* and *Life in the Ghettos During the Holocaust.* He has also published essays on modern literature and film.

Megan Stoner is currently a junior English major studying at Mississippi University for Women. "The Lion, the Witch, and the War Scenes: How *Narnia* Went from Allegory to Action Flick" is her first academic paper to be published. In 2004, her paper entitled "Ravished with Sight: The Problem of Sight and Perception in *Doctor Faustus*" was one of ten winners in the National Society of High School Scholar's Annual Academic Paper Competition. She has also had poems published in MUW's literary magazine, *The Dilettanti,* including a second-place prize for poetry in 2005. Her main areas of interest are medieval literature and the cultural connection between films and literature, and she plans to one day be an English professor.

Leslie Stratyner is professor of medieval literature at Mississippi University for Women. She has collaborated with Keller on two previous volumes: *Almost Shakespeare: Reinventing His Work for Film and Television* and *The New Queer Aesthetic on Television: Essays on Recent Programming.* Stratyner has published articles on medieval literature and the oral tradition. Her other research interests include film, gender studies, medievalism, and popular culture.

Paul Tankard is lecturer in English at the world's southernmost university, the University of Otago, Dunedin, New Zealand. His scholarly and teaching interests include Johnson and Boswell, C.S. Lewis and the Inklings, paratextuality and the English essay. He is preparing an edition of the journalism of James Boswell.

Index